Hell's Revenge

Memoir of a Pirate Queen

Krystal N. Craiker

DEDICATION

This book is for every pirate-spirited woman, those who reject boxes and conformity, who fight for their right to live authentically, who fearlessly sail toward their own destiny.

May the winds of your life propel you to happiness.

A NOTE ON NAMES

Angélica prefers the Spanish pronunciation of her name, but few people use it. When her name is written with the accent, it is pronounced the Spanish way. When it is written without the accent, it is pronounced the English way. The differentiation is important for relationships and characterizations.

Quetzalli: keht-ZAHL-ee

Thierry: Tee-ae-ree

Thérèse: Tae-rehz

Chapter 1

JULY 1693, THE CARIBBEAN SEA

It is both one of life's mercies and one of her cruelties that we never comprehend the importance of a moment until long after it becomes a memory. If I had known my first time how holding a sword would shape my life, would I have done things differently? Would I have stopped to savor the moment? Probably not. I was only nineteen years old, and I thought I was invincible.

Isn't that the way of life? It's nothing more than a combination of mercies and cruelties, cruelties and mercies. We never understand the value of what we have until it is ripped from our hands like a pup forced from a bitch's teat too soon.

I wasn't thinking about any of this when I had my first sword-fighting lesson. Instead, I was thinking that fighting in a bodice was going to be a hindrance. I was thinking that it was a hot day on the sea, with no breeze to make the fiery sun less brutal. And I was certainly thinking that Henry Martin was the most handsome man I had ever seen in my life.

Perhaps I should have been offended that it fell to Henry to teach me to fight, but father had decided I needed to be able to defend myself. The high seas are a dangerous place, and the ports more so. I had spent my life on ships, but now that I was older, I couldn't hide in a small nook if we were boarded by pirates or the French. I had also laid out a persuasive argument to my father on why I should not have to stay locked in my room on board whenever he wanted to visit port without me. My father loved a persuasive argument—he had taught me the art of rhetoric himself.

Father was not an advanced enough swordsman to teach me, so he asked the captain to select a teacher. The ones who liked me opposed it due to my sex, and so did the ones who believed I was bad luck to have on board. Stupid men. And, finally, there were the men who leered at me, the ones my father nor the captain trusted.

That left young Henry Martin.

I had noticed the handsome lieutenant before, of course. He was difficult not to notice. He couldn't have been much older than me, but I was not sure of his age. I did know that he was quite young to be a lieutenant, although it wasn't unheard of. Most of these sailors had been on ships since they were boys.

I adjusted my corset and hiked up my skirts so I could move without encumberment, then I ascended the ladder to the main deck. My father was transcribing notes on a new bird species he had discovered in Jamaica last month, but he assured me he would stop by to supervise my training. No matter. I didn't think I wanted him there to begin with.

A tanned hand extended to help me onto the deck, and I nearly rebuffed it. After all, I had been climbing ship ladders since I could walk. But when I glanced up into the ocean-blue eyes of Lieutenant Martin, my hand reached up of its own accord. He had a firm grip that sent shivers down my spine. Once on the deck, he held my hand for a few seconds longer than was proper. I stared down at the wooden floor to mask my blush.

When I looked up, Henry was tying his shoulder-length blond locks back with a bit of leather. He grinned at me, and I smiled shyly back. I am not usually shy, but Henry's deep gaze and dazzling smile left me feeling uneasy.

"Ready to fight?" His voice was a smooth baritone that spread through my body like melted butter.

I shook myself. "Thank you for agreeing to teach me. I hope I prove to be a quick study."

"I'm certain you will." He flashed me a dimpled grin and handed me a lightweight, short sword.

I grabbed the hilt and flourished it through the air.

"Careful now," Henry said with a chuckle.

"Sorry."

He smiled again. "Now, this is a smallsword. It's lighter than a cutlass or a saber. And it's meant more for thrusting than slicing. The edge of the blade isn't as sharp as other swords." He tapped the blade to demonstrate. "That's why we're using this for practice."

"I imagined it would be bigger. Heavier."

He shrugged. "You won't see many sailors using a broadsword or the like. We don't fight on big open fields." He stepped back a foot and sized me up, causing me to flush. "Let's work on your stance."

He guided me through the proper way to stand for fencing, with my left foot forward and my knees slightly bent. Then he taught me a few basic defensive maneuvers, his own sword coming slowly toward me until I mastered each. Beads of sweat dripped from my forehead and neck. I wiped my arms across my brow as I blocked another slash of his sword.

"Excellent! You have good reflexes."

He winked at me, which caused me to stumble, and his sword passed effortlessly through my failed defense. This man would be my downfall.

He laughed. "Ah! She *does* drop her guard."

It wouldn't happen again, I vowed to myself, his flirtatious nature be damned. I blocked his next several moves with ease, even as he sped up his attacks.

After several long minutes, he stepped back and put his hands up in front of him. "Let's work on attacks. We'll focus on cutting and slicing attacks, although you would normally thrust with this sword. Pay attention to my feet when I slash."

I watched his feet move deftly as he attacked an invisible enemy. Perhaps I studied other parts of his body, too, but it was only so I could learn. His broad shoulders shouldn't have been able to move as quickly as they did. His muscular arms should have been slower, less gracile.

He caught me staring and cleared his throat. A touch of red tinged his cheeks. "You try. Attack me."

I did, and he parried each slash with ease. No matter how he guided me through the steps, I couldn't make it past his sword. Within moments, I was panting and covered in sweat. I stamped my foot in frustration, then immediately straightened to a more ladylike pose.

Henry's voice was gentle. "It's all right, Miss Spencer. No one expects you to be an expert on your first day."

No one except me, I thought. I took a deep breath.

"Pretend to attack the mast there," he said. "I want to watch you."

My eyes darted up to meet his, and I raised a brow. He winced and rubbed the back of his neck.

"To see what you're struggling with," he stammered. "To help you."

"Very well."

I attacked the foremast, feeling quite foolish and quite certain the other sailors at work were watching and laughing at me. But the foremast couldn't defend itself, and I sliced it several times, though the dull blade did nothing to the thick wooden post.

"Your movements are too rigid."

I stopped and turned to face my teacher. "Too rigid? What do you mean?"

"Make smaller motions. Use your hips to turn more than your whole body."

It was a stupid instruction. I jutted my hip in an exaggerated back and forth. "Like this?"

Henry gaped. "I... uh... that's... perhaps... " He shook himself. I smirked. "Smaller movements, more subtle. In an attack, you won't have a full range of motion, especially if you have more than one assailant. Use your body wisely."

I nodded, taking in his suggestions. It made sense, and I supposed he was the expert. I turned toward him, ready to attack. I was conscious of my attacks this time, avoiding large steps and turns. While he blocked most of my slashes, I did manage to get several past him.

Soon, he attacked, and I was forced to mix evasion with my thrusts. The sun beat down on us without mercy, and the only sound I heard was the clash of steel on steel. The rest of the world slipped away, and I lost myself to the fight.

I held my own well until the young lieutenant knocked my blade from my hand. His sword rested under my chin, and I held my hands up. "I yield."

He backed away with a bow. "Good fight, Miss." He sheathed his sword. "Shall we take a water break?"

I nodded, suddenly aware of how thirsty I was. We were near Jamaica, and the Caribbean sun was ruthless. I followed him across the deck where a waterskin and his naval jacket lay in a pile. He handed me the skin, and I took a long drink, savoring the cool liquid as it trailed down my parched throat.

"Thank you," I said as I handed him the skin.

"You're welcome." He sat on the deck and took a drink then spread out his jacket and gestured for me to sit next to him. He was certainly a gentleman.

Though my body ached to collapse without ceremony, I lowered myself gently to the ground and managed to sit like a lady. He passed me the waterskin once more.

"You're a natural," he said. I snorted. "No, truly. You picked up the basics quite well."

"You're very kind, Lieutenant."

He smiled. "Call me Henry. I can't be that much older than you."

"How old are you?"

"Two and twenty."

I straightened. "I'll be twenty in just a few months' time." I instantly regretted how young that statement made me sound, as if I were playing at being grown up. I changed the subject. "You're young for a lieutenant."

Henry shrugged and ran a hand through his blond hair. Much of it had escaped the leather band and fell in thick locks around his face. He had just a hint of stubble on his chiseled jawline, and I had the overwhelming urge to touch it. Instead, I folded my hands in my lap.

"I've been on ships since I was twelve. I was a boy seaman until I was fifteen when I was promoted to midshipman. After six years on ships, the captain of my last assignment bought my commission so I could become an officer. I joined the Juliet when my old captain decided to go home for a few months."

"And where is home for you?" I asked.

He gestured out at the sea. "Here. But I was born in Liverpool. Haven't spent any great length of time on land since I set out to sea."

"I understand. My father has an estate near Manchester. But I've been at sea for as long as I can remember."

"What of your mother, if I may ask?"

I gave him a small smile. "Of course. I don't remember her. My father fell in love with a woman on the Spanish Main. Half Spanish, half native. He was studying the fowl and staying at a mission when he met her. She died before my second birthday, and my father returned to the sea with me in tow."

"I'm sorry," he said.

"Don't be. The sea is all I've ever known."

We sat in easy silence for a while, passing the water back and forth until it was gone. I stole several glances at Henry, and he caught me more than once. I hoped he was also stealing glances at me.

"Angelica!" My father's voice rang across the deck.

I stood and dusted off my skirts. "Yes, Father?"

"You still have translations to complete. Are you finished with your lesson with Lieutenant Martin?"

Henry leapt to his feet behind me. "She is, sir. She did very well."

"Good. Perhaps you can have another lesson in the next few days."

"I'd be happy to, sir." Henry gave me a slight bow. "It was an honor, Miss Spencer."

"Angelica," I said. "Call me Angelica."

Henry nodded and smiled, and I could feel my father's inquisitive stare at my back. I turned slowly to face him, and his left eyebrow was cocked ever so slightly. I arched mine back. "Translations, Father?"

My father stifled a laugh. "Yes. I want you to translate a paper from French into Italian before dinner."

"Yes, Father. Good afternoon, Lieuten—Henry."

I stared at the pages of French in front of me, trying to read it for the third or fourth time. I had been speaking French since I could talk, and I learned Italian and Spanish not long after. It wasn't that I couldn't read this paper on the flora of Sierra Leone—it was that there were far more interesting things to think about.

I couldn't get Henry Martin off my mind.

Usually, the men who joined the ships as boys were garish and crude. But not Henry. He was a proper gentleman, despite having been raised at sea. I wondered who his parents were, who had raised him so well for the first dozen years of his life. He spoke the King's English and addressed me as a lady.

He was patient in teaching me, as patient as my father giving me lessons on natural history and philosophy. And though I tried not to think of it, he was incredibly handsome. Strong and tall. The way he smiled at me. . .

"Angélica! Are you finished with that translation yet?" My father's voice jolted me out of my daydream. He spoke in Spanish. I preferred my name pronounced as my mother intended; my father knew this, and usually addressed me as such when we were alone.

I looked down at the parchment and realized I had translated exactly one sentence. I hung my head. "No, Father. I am quite distracted. I am sorry."

My father stood behind me and peered over my shoulder. "I take it you have more interesting things to think about than the grasses of the Africa coast? Perhaps a certain young lieutenant?"

I blushed, though Father's voice was teasing, not cruel.

"No matter. You can finish it tomorrow. Did you enjoy the sword work?"

I grinned in spite of myself. "I did! Henry said I had natural skill."

"I don't doubt it. Your mother picked it up quickly, as well, though I was not much of a teacher." He bent down to kiss the top of my head. "Do not address him as Henry to the other men on board. He's young, and he needs their respect. Keep that between you and him during your lessons."

"Yes, Father."

He sent me off to the galley to get dinner before retiring for the evening. Most of the crew had already eaten, but the cook had saved me half a chicken. I loved the days following a port call because it meant we didn't have to eat endless amounts of fish and turtle. Tin plate in hand, I bade Cook thanks and ran into Henry at the foot of the stairs.

"Good evening, Miss—Angelica." He smiled.

"Good evening, Henry."

The corridors on ships are not spacious, and I found myself barely a hand's width away from his torso. My head only reached to his shoulder. His shirt was unlaced, and I could see the muscular lines of his collarbones. He smelled of salt and sweat and a slight spice. My head grew heavy, and my body felt strange. I had seen handsome men my whole life, but no one had affected me like this.

"Cook made chicken?"

I nodded. What was wrong with me? "Ye-yes."

I backed onto the second step to gain some distance and clear my head. I was now at eye-level with Henry. His eyes were the color of the sea at sunrise.

"What were you translating this afternoon?"

I blinked. What *had* I been translating? "Uh. A paper from a French naturalist on grasses in Africa."

"Hm. And you speak French and Italian?"

"Yes, and Spanish, German, and some Dutch." And my mother's native tongue, but most people thought that was odd. I never mentioned it, nor did my father.

His blue eyes widened. "Impressive."

I blushed and looked at the floor.

"I have picked up a few phrases here and there in Spanish," Henry continued. "I certainly can't read it."

"I could teach you!" The words came out far too earnest, too high-pitched. I steadied my voice. "In exchange for the sword lessons. I wouldn't mind."

"I'd like that." He smiled at me again. I didn't reply, and we stood in silence for what felt like several long moments. "Well. I should get the chicken before it's gone. Have a good night, Angelica."

"Ahn-hel-ica," I replied. In that moment, I wanted nothing more than to hear my name as it was intended fall from his small, pink lips. "Your first Spanish lesson."

"Ahn-hel-ica," he repeated slowly. "Angélica."

I grinned and curtsied before turning up the stairs. I heard him repeating my Spanish name to himself as he walked to the galley.

Once alone in my bunk, I undressed then ate my meal, replaying our exchange in my mind. My heart had not stopped racing since I ran into him. I didn't know then that I was falling in love. All I knew was that I wanted to spend every day looking at Henry Martin and hearing him say my name.

Chapter 2

AUGUST 1693

M y infatuation with Henry did not subside over the next few weeks. Indeed, it only got worse the more time we spent together. The good news was that I was focused when we fought and progressing well at my swordsmanship. Henry had upgraded me to a proper saber once he was certain I would not accidentally maim him.

We were fighting hard on the forecastle, the clink of our swords carrying on the breeze. My hair was falling loose from my braid, and sweat dripped into my eyes. I parried a low slash from Henry's sword and jumped onto a wooden crate, gaining the high ground.

"Good, Angélica!"

I grinned and feigned distraction, knowing he would look for the moment I dropped my guard to launch his next advance. It worked, and I beat him to the attack, knocking his sword from his hand and placing my sword under his dimpled chin.

He shook his head and laughed. "Fine! I yield!"

"Huzzah!" I lowered my sword.

He held a hand out to help me step off the crate. Instead, I leapt onto the deck with both feet, landing with relative grace. Henry laughed again.

I loved that sound.

"Well done. Shall we take a rest?"

"Too tired to continue fighting me?" I asked, but I couldn't hide my shortness of breath. We had fought longer than normal today. He shook his head at me and took a long swig of water. Usually, he offered me the first drink, unless he was pretending to be offended.

He winked when he handed me the waterskin. "What will we be learning today, señorita?"

"You'll be writing dictation."

He groaned but without real irritation. "Again?"

"Just a bit. Perhaps then we can spar more?" I loved our Spanish lessons, but I loved swordplay more.

He shook his head. "I have a shift on the pumps this evening. I need to save my energy."

I crinkled my nose. Henry hated doing his time on the pumps, but the captain insisted every man must take his turn. It was the most loathed job on any ship, repetitive and backbreaking, but a necessary evil.

I gathered the parchment, quill, and inkwell I had brought up from my bunk and sat on a crate. Henry sat opposite me on the deck, using another crate as a table. I dictated simple sentences describing the deck and the sea then corrected his spelling.

I liked watching him think. He would furrow his brow and chew on his lip. That always led me to wonder what his lips would feel like against mine, which then led to odd sensations in my core. The next few weeks continued in much the same way. My father kept me busy with my studies when I wasn't fencing with Henry or teaching him Spanish. My feelings for Henry grew every day, and I was confused by the urges I was experiencing.

One beautiful day, when the sea breeze was warm and gentle, I sat upon the main deck with my sketchbook. I was supposed to be copying some of my father's sketches of birds from Mauritius. But then I saw Henry repairing the mast with some other sailors. He had shed his shirt and had climbed up the rigging a few feet. I watched the taut muscles of his back and shoulders work as he hammered nails in place. I was suddenly very hot and full of feelings I had never experienced. Longing and emptiness and desire.

I wanted to capture that image of Henry forever. I flipped to a clean page in my sketchbook and began sketching him. I had spent so much time studying his face that I could draw it from memory. But I was fascinated by the sinews and divots of his back, the curvature of his arms. I sketched him on the rigging until he went on to his next task, somewhere below deck.

Then I began to draw his face from memory. Lord knew I had studied it enough over the last two months. I struggled to get his brow line right and was so focused on the task at hand that I didn't notice him sneak up behind me.

"Oh, now. I'm far more handsome than that."

I jumped and slammed my sketchbook closed. My cheeks grew hot. How did I let myself get caught drawing him? My tongue felt thick; I couldn't think of anything to say.

"Sorry, sorry. I didn't mean to frighten you." He knelt down beside me. "And I'm teasing you. You were too kind to my attributes in that drawing."

I stared straight ahead, too embarrassed to make eye contact. Henry placed a hand over mine. "Angélica, please. I'm honored that you were drawing me."

"Yes, well. You were an easier subject to draw than the dodo bird." I still wouldn't look at him. He squeezed my hand.

"May I see it again?"

I sighed. There was no reason to tell him no. And I was a rather good artist, so I had no reason to hide it. "Fine."

I flipped to the page where his charcoal visage gazed out at me. I only hoped he would not insist on flipping to the previous page. He took the book from me and traced the outline of his face with his finger. He didn't say anything for a long time.

I cleared my throat. "I, um, had trouble getting your brow just right."

"It's amazing, Angélica. I didn't know you could draw." I loved the way he said my name. "You're talented."

"A naturalist has to be. My father taught me to draw as soon as I could hold a charcoal pencil."

He smiled. "Modesty doesn't become you. You're a fascinating woman. Brilliant and full of surprises."

Heat rose into my neck. "Thank you, Henry."

"Thank you for drawing me so well. I go weeks without seeing my reflection sometimes. It's nice to see myself through your eyes." He closed my sketchbook and handed it back to me. "I'd like to see more of your drawings sometime. And perhaps you could draw one of yourself for me."

He hopped to his feet, leaving me alone on the deck, speechless. Once I regained my composure, I hurried down to my bunk and found my hand mirror to study my own face for my next drawing.

"Land ho!" the rigging climber called. Antigua was in our sights. I leapt up from my spot on the forecastle where I was reading and clamored down to the lower deck. We hadn't docked in nearly two weeks, as the Juliet was tracking a Spanish galleon that had parted ways from its fleet. Though we were allied with Spain against King Louis XIV, one must keep their true enemies close. But politics did not interest me. I was dying to visit the dressmaker and the bookstore. And perhaps get a new pair of boots.

I knocked on the door opposite mine. "Father! We're nearly to port!"

Father opened the door to his bunk. "Land in sight?"

"Yes! Can I get a new pair of boots?"

He ran a hand through his hair. "Angelica, I think you are to stay on board for this stop."

"What? Father, that is hardly fair! I have stayed on the ship for the last two port calls! You promised I could visit the bookshop and get a new dress!"

"Angélique, control your outburst," he said, switching to French. He always preferred to reprimand me in another language so the crew wouldn't eavesdrop, and he knew I hated the way my name sounded in French.

"I will not! I haven't been on land in over a month," I replied in Spanish. I certainly wasn't going to make this argument easy on him. He always struggled to keep up when I switched between languages quickly. I continued in Italian. "There is no good reason to leave me on the ship!"

He paused, translating. "You should watch your tone with me," he warned. "I have business to attend to, and I cannot take you along."

"Business? In a brothel? You'd rather spend time with a whore than let me go ashore!"

He tensed and raised his hand before lowering it. He had never once struck me, but he had come close. I knew exactly what to say to anger him.

"Lower your voice." His own voice was tight, spoken through clenched teeth. "I am a grown man, and I cannot always escort you around town."

"Then don't escort me. You wanted me to learn to defend myself, and I have! I know my way around."

He shook his head. "Angélica, you may be doing well with a sword. But Antigua is full of privateers and drunken sailors. And they are all far more skilled than you. Many of them even carry pistols. It's not safe for a young woman to be walking around by herself, nor is it proper."

"Why even bother to make me learn how to fight?"

He pinched the bridge of his nose. "Oh, Angélica. If I return in time, I shall take you to get a new dress. But we are only in port for one day. You can get off when we stop in Puerto Rico next week."

"What of the bookshop? There's not one in San Juan. And my boots have a hole in them. And I would like a proper meal at an inn."

"I'm finished arguing with you. If I get back in time, we can go to one place. Otherwise, you'll have to wait."

I was shaking in anger. "Father—"

He held up his hand. "That's enough now. Go finish your studies."

"But—"

"Go."

He closed himself in his bunk. I stamped my foot and let out a string of unladylike curses in every language I knew. He wouldn't open the door to reprimand me; once he was finished arguing, he went silent. Angry tears streamed down my face.

I hadn't touched land in weeks. I was nearly twenty—by English law, I had been of a marriageable age for almost eight years. But he still insisted on treating me like a child.

Henry came down the ladder in the midst of my colorful outburst. "Angélica? What's wrong?"

I wiped my eyes. "My father has decided that visiting a brothel is more important than letting me go ashore, even though I haven't gone into port in a month."

He gave me an understanding look. "I'm sorry."

"You've been teaching me to fight. Could I defend myself?"

"You could, but," he said, "Antigua is a wild place. Privateers and drunken sailors. If they have a mind to get their hands on a beautiful young woman walking alone, they will."

"Not you, too." He called me beautiful, but I was too angry to muse on that just then. I opened the door to my bunk and slammed it. I sat on my bed and opened my small porthole window, staring at the thin line of land I could see in the distance. Was I cursed to be under my father's thumb my whole life? If I wanted to remain at sea as a woman, it seemed that I was. It wasn't fair.

Sometime later, I heard a knock next door and muffled voices. It was probably the first mate telling my father we were nearing port or the cabin boy notifying him that dinner was ready. The sun was setting in shades of fiery yellows and oranges.

Then there was a knock on my door. "I'm not hungry!" I called. It was a lie. My stomach growled, but I refused to leave my room. If he wanted me to stay on the ship tomorrow, I would not leave my room.

"I'm not offering you dinner, Angelica," my father said. "I may have found a solution to your. . . situation."

I rolled my eyes but got up and opened the door. My father was standing with Henry. Henry smiled a mischievous smile at me. I arched my brow. "Yes?"

"Lieutenant Martin has informed me that he has leave tomorrow. He offered to escort you around town with his free time. While this would be most improper in England, there is no one to gossip about ruination here. I trust him to protect you, so if you will allow it—"

"Yes!" A grin spread across my face. "Thank you, Father."

"Thank Lieutenant Martin, not me."

"Thank you." I curtsied.

My father looked at me with a stern glare. "You will be back before sundown. You will obey any instructions the Lieutenant gives you. And you will act like the well-bred young woman I raised you to be."

"Yes, Father. Of course."

He nodded and headed to the stairway that led to the lower decks. Henry stood in front of me, grinning like a fool.

"Thank you, Henry."

"It is the least I could do. I couldn't stand to see you so upset." He paused, his brow furrowed as he seemed to weigh his next words. "I know you said you weren't hungry, but the stew Cook has made smells wonderful."

I nodded. He bid me a good evening, unsaid sentiments making the air heavy. When he climbed back to the main deck, I shut my door behind me and headed to the galley and let out a laugh.

I was going to Antigua with Henry as my escort. Henry, who thought I was beautiful.

Chapter 3

The cacophony of sailors' voices and dogs barking washed over me as we docked in Antigua. The sailors on the Juliet hollered across the decks as they eased into port and lowered the gangway. Returning to port after weeks at sea always carried a heavy sense of anticipation, but the thought of spending the day with Henry away from the ship had me thoroughly exhilarated.

"I expect you to behave with the utmost propriety." My father's voice jolted me out of my thoughts. "There are certain... behaviors... that good, god-fearing maidens should not partake in."

"I know, Father. You don't have to worry. Henry is an honorable man."

"But he's still a young man. And it's not him I'm worried about, Angelica. I know you have spent most of your life away from society and its expectations, but... "

I waved my hand. "Father, I will be fine."

Captain Bates walked up and clapped my father on the back. "Shall we, George? We've only got a few hours to get the most out of our—"

Father cleared his throat, and scarlet bloomed on his cheeks. "Business. Out of our business. Yes, Captain, let's away. Take care, Angelica." He narrowed his eyes in a silent, parental lecture. "I expect you back before sunset."

"Have fun with your business." I punctuated the word and smiled sweetly. Father shook his head then headed to the gangway with the captain. I waited on the poop deck, out of the way of the rambunctious sailors, for Henry. I adjusted my frilly fontage on top of my head, which was in disagreement with the breeze, then dusted off my bodice and straightened the pleats of my green, silk overskirt.

"You look lovely."

I glanced up at the sound of Henry's voice and grinned. Usually I wore fewer skirts and a simple bodice on board the ship but dressed more appropriately whenever we made landfall. Today, I had decided on one of my finest frock.

Henry was extra handsome, as well. His long, blue navy coat was crisp and clean over his white breeches. He had combed his hair and wore it loose. I had an overwhelming urge to run my hands through it.

He offered his arm. "Shall we?"

I clasped my hands around his taut arms. "We shall."

Henry escorted me down the steps and off the gangway. I was glad I had him for support. It always took me a few moments to get my land legs again.

"Where are we off to?"

"The dressmaker."

"Now, that is a place I don't know in this town. Lead the way."

We walked together down the cobblestone road, avoiding carriages carrying noble-men's wives and puddles of what one always hoped was just water. I loved port towns. Though some may find it uncivilized compared to the grand European cities, there was an air about them that always filled me with delight. Perhaps it was the brightly painted buildings or the myriad of faces from around the world. Perhaps it was the prostitutes that walked about or the cheerful sailors spending their hard-earned coin. The crash of broken rum bottles, the smell of fishmongers and bakers, the taste of salt on the air. Everything was so alive.

We sidestepped a suspiciously yellow puddle outside a tavern and crossed the street. "This town smells like the bilge," Henry said, wrinkling his nose in disgust.

I shrugged. "Then you should be used to it."

"I suppose." He pointed at a small storefront. "I'm taking you there after the dressmak-er. The baker makes the best sweets. Antigua is known for their sugar cane, you know."

"At quite a cost." I glanced uncomfortably at men in chains, their dark eyes cast downward. It wasn't proper to express such opinions, but I could not resist. The sight of slaves unsettled me, made my stomach wrench. But like every European woman before me, I looked away.

Henry nodded, his mouth in a thin line. "Quite. The plantation owners here are especially cruel."

We walked in silence for a while, and I mused on all the things I was powerless to do. The list was long. I did not like feeling powerless.

As we crossed the road, I stumbled and Henry steadied me. His gaze flickered down to my face. When our eyes met, my breath hitched. His gaze was intense, fiery. But then he loosened his grip on my arm, and we returned to our leisurely stroll.

I smiled. Usually, I walked the towns with my father. But today, I felt independent. Even though Henry was my escort, I was, for the first time, without my parent telling me what to do or where to go. And I had a handsome man on my arm. I saw more than one woman eyeing him with jealousy, which filled me with delight.

We reached the dressmaker, a plump woman named Mrs. Morris who took immediate interest in making sure Henry was comfortable. She placed him on a stool at the front of the shop with a cup of water and bread. Then she hurried me to the back to undress.

She procured several beautiful court dresses and helped me into each. When I had it narrowed down to two—a blue embroidered beauty and one with red ruffles along the front of the bodice—I decided to ask Henry what he thought. Mrs. Morris insisted on adding a large pillow to the bustle and tightening my stays until I could barely breathe.

"You're not a tall girl, and you've too many curves," she muttered. "The bodice needs to give you a vertical silhouette."

I came out in the blue dress, panting from the hot back room and the bodice. "I want your opinion. I can't decide between this one and another one," I said, panting.

"Are you all right?" His voice was filled with concern.

"Just the bodice in this heat. I'll be fine."

He shook his head then gave me a once over. He smiled. "You look lovely."

I spun around so he could see the dress from each side and so I could hide my grin. "Now, hold that image. I will try on the other one."

I fanned myself as Mrs. Morris tied me into the red dress. This one was lower on my chest and showed just a hint of my shoulders. I didn't often wear ruffles, as they weren't practical on the ship. But this dress was gorgeous; it reminded me of dancing flames.

"Oh, my," Henry said when I came out. He stood, his eyes raking over my body. "Red suits you, Angélica."

Heat rose to my cheeks, and I turned slowly to show him the rest of the dress. When I turned back to face him, he had a strange look. "What's wrong?"

"It's nothing."

"Henry."

"I don't like the bustle."

How odd. Morris had assured me that men liked bustles. The bigger, the better. "Really?"

He nodded. "Really. It distracts from. . . you. And your dress doesn't need to be so tight, either."

"Well, I'm hardly blessed with a vertical silhouette."

"I don't see the problem with that."

I cocked my head. "I thought men preferred the straight lines—"

Henry laughed. "Just because some ponce on a throne in France prefers it doesn't mean most of us do." He ran a hand through his hair. "I'll never understand why women insist on changing themselves. You don't need any help from fabric and string to make you more beautiful."

I felt a flutter in my stomach. "You think I'm beautiful."

"Very much so."

I looked down at the ground, unsure what to say. Words and propriety hung between us like cobwebs in the hold. After several moments, I said, "The red dress, then? But no bum roll."

"I do like the red the best. Do you?"

I did, mostly because I liked his response to it. I gave a quick nod. "I'll be done presently."

"He's a nice young man," the dressmaker said as she helped me dress "Are you betrothed?"

"Oh, no. The lieutenant is just my escort around town for the day. My father was otherwise occupied."

"He is much more than your escort, my dear. It's obvious that he fancies you. And you him." She smoothed down my skirts. "There now. Anything else?"

"A petticoat and a plain, black skirt, please."

Henry insisted on carrying my packages. He took me to the bakery he had pointed out earlier and bought me a plump bread, sweet with cream and raisins. Sweets were rareties when one lived on a ship, so I savored every lush bite. We ate our treats as we walked to the bookshop two streets over.

"You have a bit of cream on your face," I said to Henry. I pointed, but he missed it when he tried to wipe his lip. "Here, let me." I reached up to wipe the cream from above his lip. My finger hesitated as I touched him, realizing too late how intimate a gesture this was. My heart pounded in my chest. Henry's breath hitched.

I removed my hand. I had a blob of sweet cream on my finger, and I couldn't very well wipe it on my dress, so I stuck it in my mouth and sucked off the mess. It was a shame to let something that delicious go to waste, anyhow.

Henry closed his eyes. "I think you are trying to kill me, slowly, torturously."

"What do you mean?"

He looked around us. This was not a busy street, what with the bookstore and the parchment shop being the only businesses of note. Only a handful of people were walking, and no one was paying us any mind.

"Angélica, I would very much like to kiss you if you'd allow it."

My eyes widened. I blinked in shock. And I realized I had never wanted anything more. The rest of the world slipped away, and I could hear my heart pounding in my ears. "I would allow it."

He shifted the packages under his arm and took a step closer. Then he leaned down. I raised my head to meet his. His lips brushed mine. They were soft. A jolt of lightning flashed through my body. Our lips lingered together for a few moments. It felt like forever and not at all enough time, and I ached when he pulled away.

He smiled at me, a sweet, close-lipped smile that lit up his whole face. I didn't know what to do; I returned his smile with a demure smirk of my own. Then I stood on my toes to kiss him again, harder this time.

We never made it to the bookstore or the cobbler.

After our second kiss, Henry pulled away, breathless. "We can't. . . people could see. . . "

"Let them see." Propriety be damned. How could something so wonderful be wrong?

"And if your father decides to visit this street?"

"Damn." I looked around. Across the road was a small alley that led behind a chandler shop. "Come with me."

I took his hand and led him down the alley. The area behind the shop was abandoned, save for a few wooden crates and broken clay bottles. Henry studied me with a look of impressed bewilderment. "What?" I asked.

He laughed. "Your name means 'like an angel,' correct?"

"Yes." I was confused.

"You're no angel, Angélica," he said with a smirk.

I batted my eyelashes. "I'm not?"

"No. I think I'll call you Hell. It's more fitting."

I laughed. "That is probably a more accurate moniker." I stepped forward and wrapped my arms around his neck to pull his face down to mine. He stopped talking after that.

We spent the rest of the afternoon kissing and talking, talking and kissing. He told me he wanted to captain his own ship. I told him how I wanted to follow in my father's footsteps as a naturalist, though being a woman worked against me. I learned his mother was a whore in Liverpool, and he didn't even know his father's name. We talked about everything and nothing until the sun was high in the sky above us.

My father had not returned to the ship yet when we returned. Henry walked to my bunk, carrying my packages from the dressmaker. I set them on my small desk by the door. He peered over my shoulder into the room.

"Nice bunk."

I shrugged. "It's not much."

"At least you have a proper bed. And you don't have to share a room with the boatswain. He snores."

I laughed. "That is fortunate. Thank you for today, Henry."

Henry glanced around the corridor to make sure we were alone before brushing a quick kiss on my lips. "Any time, Hell."

He turned and headed up the ladder, whistling an upbeat shanty. I watched him climb up to the top deck with a sigh. Then I plopped down on my bed to reminisce about our day`.

My father knocked on the door an hour later. "Come in!"

"Angelica, did you have a nice day?"

I couldn't help the grin that spread over my face. "Yes, Father."

"Good. You got a new dress then? Any new books?"

My grin faltered. How could I explain that we never made it to the bookstore? "No. They had nothing of interest to me."

My father raised a quizzical eyebrow. It was a terrible lie. Books always interested me. "I see. And the cobbler?"

"The dressmaker took so long, and then we ate and went to the bookstore. We didn't have time to go to the cobbler."

"Ah. Very well, then. I will buy you some when we dock in Havana. We will be calling on a colleague of mine while we're there, too."

"Thank you, Father."

"I'll see you at dinner in a half-hour, yes?"

I nodded, and he left me alone. I had never lied to my Father before. I didn't like it, but he would never approve of me spending an afternoon kissing Henry in an alley.

And I desperately wanted a chance to do that again.

Chapter 4

I did not see Henry the next day, much to my chagrin. He was working down below with the boatswain after the ship had restocked in Antigua. My father kept me busy with my studies, too; he wanted me to brush up on my knowledge of the mammals on the Spanish Main before we met with his friend in San Juan, Puerto Rico. But the day after, I had another lesson with Henry.

I was certain I would never experience anything more difficult than keeping our secret on the ship when all I wanted to do was throw myself into his arms and kiss him.

"Move your feet, Hell. Staying in one place makes it far too easy for your opponent."

"Sorry. I'm distracted today."

"I've noticed." He stepped closer and made me parry a thrust. He lowered his voice. "Any particular reason you're distracted?"

I rolled my eyes and lunged to the side to avoid his sword. "Oh, nothing important," I said. "Had an interesting day in port ere-yesterday. That's all."

"I wouldn't know a thing about that." He feigned left, but I caught his next attack. "But now that you mention it, I had an interesting day, too."

I spun around to attack from behind him. "I see. What made it interesting?"

He darted right and turned to face me. "A pretty girl."

I blushed, dropping my guard. It gave him the perfect opportunity to get past my defense. The tip of his sword rested on my bosom, just above the top of my corset. "Not fair," I said. "I hardly think a pirate would be complimenting me during a battle."

He poked me slightly harder, enough to pinch but not leave a mark. My breath hitched. That was a feeling I had never experienced, and I didn't know what to make of it. "Then that pirate has terrible taste." He winked. "Do you yield?"

"I yield."

He pulled his sword away. "Good. Time for Spanish lessons."

"And water."

"Yes, and water." He handed me his waterskin, and I took a long drink. Though there was a nice breeze today, I felt hotter than normal. "Save some for me now, Hell."

I handed him the water and wiped my face with the back of my hand. "Sorry."

"I have a list of phrases I would like to learn in Spanish, if that's acceptable."

"Of course." I sat on the top of the steps that led from the forecastle to the main deck. Henry sat next to me, so close that his arm brushed against mine. We were bordering on improper. But I made no effort to move. Henry unfolded a piece of paper and read the first sentence to me.

"You are very beautiful."

My eyes widened. "Thank you."

"I want to know how to say it in Spanish."

I chuckled. "All right. Are you saying it to a man or a woman?"

"Hell! You know very well who I'm saying it to."

"Fine!" I threw up my hands in mock surrender. I translated slowly. "Eres bellísima."

"Eres. . . what?"

I repeated it. It took him a few tries before he said it correctly. He also had me teach him the phrases: I like your smile, you are intelligent, and I enjoyed kissing you. It took everything in me not to push him down on the deck and kiss him till neither of us could breathe.

He repeated his new phrases back to me until I didn't need to correct his pronunciation. "I have one more," he said. He glanced down at his paper, his cheeks red. He took a deep breath then looked into my eyes.

"I think I am falling in love with you."

I gasped. "Henry. . . "

He wagged his finger at me and smirked, his usual confidence returning. "In Spanish, please."

I shook my head with a smile. "Creo. . . que. . . me estoy. . . enamorando. . . de ti."

"Creo que. . . "

"Me estoy. . . "

"Me estoy," he repeated.

"Enamorando," I said, slowly. He stumbled over that one. "De ti."

"De ti. Creo que me estoy enamo. . . enamo. . . "

"Enamorando."

"Enamorando. Creo que me estoy enamorando de ti."

"Good!"

He licked his lips and glanced around the deck. No one was paying us any mind. He laid his hand over mine. "Angélica Spencer, creo que me estoy enamorando de ti."

My eyes welled with tears. "Oh, Henry. Me, too."

We sat on the steps for a long time, not saying anything. There were two hundred and fifty men aboard this ship, including my father. Getting a few moments alone would be next to impossible. But there shouldn't be many people near the galley at this time of day.

"I think I'll see if Cook has any apples," I said. I stood and marched down the stairs. I glanced back, hoping he understood to follow me. He nodded at me but made no effort to move. Smart man. It would look less obvious if we weren't going somewhere together.

I made my way down to the kitchen. Cook loved me and was glad to hand me two apples. I headed back to the stairs that led to the upper decks. Henry was waiting for me. "Come here," he said in a low voice. He walked behind the staircase. If someone came looking for us, we would not be well hidden. But it would do for now.

He pushed me against the wooden planks of the wall. I dropped the apples. His lips crashed onto mine. I ran my hands up his muscular back, desperate for more contact. This was not a gentle kiss, nor did I want it to be.

When he pulled away, it was too soon, but we couldn't risk being seen. He pressed his forehead against mine. "I don't think I'm falling in love with you. I already have," he whispered.

A voice from just above pulled us out of our moment. Henry planted one last quick kiss on my lips. "Have a good evening, Hell. Until next time."

Chapter 5

We were to be docked in San Juan for three days. My father and I visited a friend and colleague of his, the French naturalist Jean-Pierre Renaud. Jean-Pierre had recently returned to his home in San Juan from studying monkeys on the Spanish Main. Like most naturalists, Jean-Pierre came from an old, wealthy family. After spending most of his adult life in the New World, he had finally moved his wife and two children to Havana five years before. I had not seen the Renauds since they lived in France six years ago.

Father and I were shown into the parlor of the Renaud estate. I always enjoyed visiting the homes of naturalists, as their homes were filled with articulated skeletons, plant specimens, and scientific sketches. I studied the skeleton of a massive fish that appeared to have teeth from the Portuguese colony of Brazil when Renaud entered the room.

"George Spencer! Quelle surprise! It has been far too long."

"Bonjour, Jean-Pierre. It is good to see you. I hope you do not mind that we are stopping in unannounced."

"Not in the slightest," Renaud said. "I have the workers preparing a fine lunch for us. Marie and the children will join us then."

"Excellent. You remember my daughter."

"Ah, yes. Angélique. My, how she has grown! She is a lovely girl, George."

I plastered a smile on my face. I hated the way my name sounded in French. And I was annoyed that he did not address me directly. I gave a reluctant curtsy. "Bonjour, Monsieur Renaud."

He nodded at me with a smile. "George, I can fetch Marie and to keep your daughter company."

I tried not to roll my eyes. But my father brought me both as his daughter and his apprentice. "Oh, that's quite all right. We came to compare research with you. Angelica is always interested in your latest discoveries."

Renaud looked dubious, but he gestured toward two chairs for us to sit. Father asked the common courtesies about his family and their health, then asked Renaud about the research trip he had just returned from a few months' prior. Renaud talked at length about the monkeys he had seen in the jungles. He had documented several species with tails that could grasp branches and other objects. We, too, had seen some of these on our trips, but Renaud's research was far more in depth.

"How are they able to grip if they are covered in fur? Would they not slip?" I asked.

"Good question, my dear," Renaud said, but he looked at my father when he responded. Men. "There appear to be two types of monkeys with grasping tails. Some can fully grasp as well as we can grasp with our hands. These have a pad of skin that is not covered in fur on their tails. The ones who can only partially grasp do not have this skin patch."

"Fascinating." My father and I said it at the same time; Father smiled.

"Jean-Pierre, could we see your sketches?" he asked.

"But of course! I will return in a moment."

He excused himself. Father looked at me. "What do you think?"

"Other than the fact that he ignores my presence? He's interesting."

Father's eyes were warm and understanding. "The world belongs to men, and academia especially. I know it is easy to forget on the ship because that is what you have always known. It does no good to debate whether that is right or wrong. But do not fault him for what the world tells him is acceptable."

I nodded. I thought it might do good to debate whether it is right or wrong. But Father only enjoyed debating about plants and animals. So, I said nothing.

Renaud returned with a leather-bound book full of monkey sketches. My father handed me the book, and he stood behind me as we flipped through it. We pointed out various anatomical features. The structure of the tails was fascinating and far different from those documented by naturalists in Africa.

My father sat back down and began talking to Renaud about a book published by another colleague last year. I continued to flip through the sketchbook when I noticed something.

"Their noses. . . they are all flat. So very different from the African and Asian monkeys."

Renaud raised his brows in surprise. "Yes! You are correct. I had noticed that."

"Astute observation." Father beamed at me.

"I wonder what the purpose of that is."

Renaud scoffed. "Purpose? What a ridiculous idea! That is just the way the Creator made them."

I opened my mouth to speak when a manservant entered the parlor. "Pardon me," he said in a thick Carib accent. "Lunch is served."

The Renaud's lavish dining room opened onto a large garden full of vibrant tropical plants. The servants stood against the back wall. Marie Renaud greeted me with a kiss on each cheek, then introduced her children to me. Or rather, she re-introduced us. Manon had been only a wee girl when I saw her last. René was my age. We had played together years ago as children. He had grown into an attractive young man, with his father's blue eyes and raven hair.

We ate roasted pork with rice and sweet plantains. I always enjoyed the food in Puerto Rico, with its smoky peppers and herbaceous coriander. The meal was pleasant enough until Jean-Pierre asked my father about his romantic endeavors.

Father coughed on his wine. "Not many opportunities for love on the high seas, my friend. Besides, that chapter of my life died when Angelica's mother did."

"Ah, yes. The Indian woman. What was her name again?"

"She was Nahuatl and Spanish. Her name was Yaretzi." My voice dripped with acid at his dismissal of my mother. Father gave me a warning look.

"Yes, of course," Jean-Pierre said with a wave of his hand. "George, I can introduce you to some wonderful widows here in San Juan. You could buy a home and have someone to watch after Angelique while you're at sea. Prepare her for society and marriage."

Heat flooded my face. I opened my mouth to speak, but my father beat me to it. "Angélica is quite happy living her life at sea. She's learning the sciences well, as I'm sure you noticed."

Jean-Pierre made a noncommittal noise and focused on his food, giving Marie a chance to speak for the first time since we sat down at the table. "Angélique, you must be nearly twenty, yes?"

"In two weeks' time," I replied.

"And what of your future? Have you been betrothed?"

It was my turn to sputter on my wine. "No."

"I see. Nor has René." She gave a pointed glance at her son. "You are nearly—how do the English say?—on the shelf! It is important to marry before you get too old. And a good marriage to a wealthy man is equally important."

I raised an eyebrow at my father. If he was so set on me remaining polite, he needed to save me from this conversation. I'd be damned if I left this meal betrothed to Renaud's son. Men learn how to behave from their fathers, after all. I tuned out as my father changed the conversation. I thought of Henry, my sweet, beautiful Henry. Where had he learned to be so kind? He never treated me less for being born a woman; it's not as if I could help that fact anyway. And he did not ignore my intelligence—he loved me for it.

I thought of all the women I saw on our journeys, the women with whom I was not allowed to associate, the prostitutes and wenches and lightskirts. Other than the time Father hired a madam to prepare me for my monthly courses, as I'd run off every attempt at a nursemaid and governess. The whore had offered me other knowledge for later in my life. Father would have been angry had he known. Women like her always seemed far happier than the married women with whale-boned stays as restrictive as their husbands. Perhaps loose woman simply meant happy and free.

We made it through the meal without any further interrogations into our personal lives. By the time we left, Father was just as glad to leave as I was.

"It was like talking to my old matron aunt," Father said as we walked down the road into town. I laughed. Father had often described his aunt with equal parts disdain and amusement.

"The monkeys were interesting," I said.

"Indeed." We walked in silence for several minutes, each lost deep in thought. I was thinking about the monkeys' noses. Father, apparently, was not. "Angélica, I will not be alive forever. At some point, we must discuss your future." He spoke in Spanish, the way he always did when he was serious. I wondered if perhaps it was his way of connecting to my mother, to bring her here for these sober conversations.

I grabbed his arm and leaned my head against his shoulder. "There will be plenty of time for that conversation at a later time, Father."

"You're right. Come. Let's go visit the cobbler. I believe I promised you a new pair of boots."

"Wait here, Angelica. There is something I must buy."

"What is it?"

"That is not your concern," Father said. "Wait here."

He disappeared into the pawn shop. We had spent the afternoon shopping. I had bought a fine pair of leather boots and several new books to enjoy. I also bought a Spanish primer for Henry to practice reading. I couldn't wait to give it to him.

We were on the row of shops facing the harbor. The sun was setting, and Father and I were headed back to the ship for the night. The road was noisy with drunken sailors spending their pay at taverns and brothels. Ladies of the night stood in clusters every few feet, looking for their next mark.

A large group of soldiers walked up from the pier, hollering and singing. I heard a few familiar voices and squinted. Indeed, they were sailors from the Juliet. Henry was supposed to be on land leave tonight, and I wondered if he was among them. The group split, half heading to the East and the other half toward where I stood.

"Cheers, 'andsome," one of the women said, gesturing at one of the soldiers. "Looking to have a good night?"

"Perhaps," said a voice I knew well. Henry stepped forward from the group. No wonder he had been singled out. He was striking in his black breeches and shirt, and he was by far the most handsome of the group. He held a bottle of rum in his hand.

My heart lurched. Surely, he would not go to her. We had stolen several moments in the last few days. He said he loved me. I thought about calling out his name, but I feared he would reject me.

Instead, I watched as he threw his arm around the woman and let her lead him inside the brothel.

A lump grew in my throat, but I refused to break down. I could run after him, but it was too late. He had already decided to spend the night with her. I bit my lip to keep from crying. Father was too cheerful when he came out of the pawn shop; when he asked what was wrong I lied, saying I was just tired.

That night, I cried myself to sleep.

Chapter 6

If I had had my way, I would not have left my bunk for several days. My father dragged me out to a meal at his favorite inn the next day. But I was sullen, and he was confused. He didn't pry, to his credit.

I spent as much time as possible in my room, reading my new books and working on translations of naturalist essays. I didn't want to think about Henry; it was impossible to not, but I tried my hardest. Every time I remembered him throwing an arm around that slattern, I felt sick to my stomach. Henry was mine!

Wasn't he?

I curled up on my bed and wiped my eyes. Madame Renaud's words hung in my head about marriage. I wondered if my father would ever allow me to marry Henry. I wondered if Henry would even want to. And then I wondered if I even wanted to marry.

Marriage sounded like a curse. Forced to settle down, to have children, to keep house instead of sailing the ocean blue. My father was right, too; once he died, what would I have? Women owned no property, had no rights in England. Perhaps I could become a harlot, too. I would make my own money and be free to do as I pleased. But that would require giving up my studies, and it would also require something I didn't know how to do yet—sex.

A knock on the door interrupted my thoughts. Father was there to remind me that I had a lesson with Henry. Now that we were back at sea, my daily routines would begin again.

Damn.

I took my time climbing to the top deck. Henry could wait on me all day for all I cared. And I couldn't have walked fast if I had tried. My legs were heavy-laden with dread. I hadn't seen him since that night.

"Good afternoon, Hell!" Henry grinned at me. He was so handsome that it hurt. I blinked. "I haven't seen you since before San Juan. Did you have a nice port call?"

I shrugged.

He gave me an odd look and stepped closer. "I missed you," he said in a low voice. Of course, he was pretending that he didn't betray my heart. It was a lie of omission, but I knew the truth. Anger surged through my veins.

"Is that so?"

He stepped back, his eyes wide with surprise. "Hell, what's wrong?"

"Nothing. Let's begin, shall we?"

"Angélica, if I've done something to—"

"Where is my sword?"

He cocked his head for a moment but decided against pressing the matter. Good. I didn't feel like talking. He grabbed the two swords and handed me one of them. I gave him no time to prepare before I launched my first strike.

"Oh, now!" He barely dodged my attack. I went straight into my next lunge, putting him on the defensive.

I poured my anger into the fight, giving him no chance to get a single slash or thrust in. I kept my feet moving quickly, tiring us both out. Soon, I lost myself to the fight. I lunged and twirled and darted around the deck. I was certainly not being as careful as I should have been in a fake fight.

Henry tried to talk to me more than once, but I used those as opportunities for a better attack. He was good with a sword, but he had taught me himself. And hurt and fury made excellent fodder for fighting.

I sliced his arm. Not deep, but enough to rip his sleeve and make a thin line of red leak through.

"Fuck! I yield!" He blocked my next slash. "Angélica, I said I yield!"

I pulled my sword away. For the first time since our fight began, I was aware of how heavy my breathing had become. Sweat dripped down into my eyes.

"What in God's name is wrong with you? You cut me!"

I said nothing. Henry dropped onto a crate and poured water from his waterskin over his slice then held a hand over it to stop the bleeding. I stood, panting. After a few moments, he held out the waterskin to me. I took it with a reluctant grab.

"Angélica," he said, his voice low and desperate. "Please tell me what I have done to upset you so terribly. I can't fix it if I don't know."

"You can't fix it," I said under my breath.

"What?"

"I said you can't fix it!" My voice was nearly a yell. Several sailors turned and looked at us with interest. I lowered my voice to a harsh whisper. "I saw you in San Juan with that-that strumpet!"

He sighed, shoulders heaving, and nodded. "Oh."

"Oh? You tell me you love me all week and that's what you have to say?"

"Angélica, come sit by me so we can discuss this without an audience."

I didn't want to discuss it. I wanted him to fall at my knees in apology, to beg my forgiveness. I wanted to both kiss him and slap him. A sick feeling fell over me. Was this the end?

"Please, Hell."

I sighed. I kicked over a crate to sit near him. The others on board would think we were just having our Spanish lesson.

"Angélica, I'm sorry that you had to see that. And I'm so very sorry that I hurt you."

"But you aren't sorry that you did it?"

He ran a hand through his hair. It had fallen loose during our heated fight. "I'm. . . not sure. How do I explain this?" He paused. "I'm a sailor. I've been visiting brothels since I was fifteen. And being around you all the time. . . I have desires. Desires for you that I can't act on. Kissing you and not being able to. . . It was too much to bear. I went with the intent of releasing frustrations."

I felt the same way, but without the luxury of visiting a brothel. I understood the mechanics from a strictly scientific point-of-view. Confusing as they may be, I knew what these urges were, this emptiness deep inside me. "You went with the intent?"

He sighed. "I couldn't follow through. Instead, I talked about you."

My face lit up. "Truly?" He nodded. "I'm sorry the woman did not profit." It was a lie; I wasn't sorry.

"I still paid her for her time." Henry waved a hand. "I love you, Hell. But this life we have on the ship, it can't be like that all the time. You're the daughter of a wealthy gentryman. I'm the bastard son of a whore. I have no money, no property."

My eyes welled with tears. "Are you saying we should end this? Whatever this is? Because I don't want to, Henry. As bad as it hurt seeing you with that harlot, never kissing you again would hurt so much worse."

"I don't know," he said, running a hand through his blond locks. "I don't want to, either. Your father would never allow it if he knew."

"He likes you." But I knew Henry was correct. I cursed our society's expectations of women and low-borns. "He doesn't have to know."

Henry gave a sardonic laugh. "Hell. . .

"I can," I waved my hand, "do that. With you. I want to."

His eyes widened. "Angélica, you're a maiden. At least, I presume. The consequences. . . Your father, if he found out. . . "

"Well, it's not his choice, is it? I've been legally able to marry since age twelve, according to the crown. I'm certainly old enough to. And I feel the same way about you, Henry."

He looked deep into my eyes. "You really aren't an angel, you know that?" He smiled. "You shouldn't make this decision lightly, my love."

"If we are star-crossed because of the situation of our births, situations we have no control over, then shouldn't we at least control what part of our destinies we can? Don't we at least deserve happiness while we can have it?"

He touched my hand, sending shivers through my body. "I'd like to think so. But please, Angélica, think on it some more."

"All right." I smiled at him. I knew what I would decide. The only problem would be finding privacy aboard this ship. "How's your arm?"

He glanced down. "It stopped bleeding."

"You need to pour rum on it to stave off infection."

"I know. I'm dreading it."

I stood. "Come. I'll clean it up."

He followed me down to the kitchen. Cook wasn't there, so I rummaged around until I found a bottle of clear rum and a cloth. I poured the liquor over the fabric, then ripped his shirt more so I had better access to the wound.

He sucked in a sharp breath through his teeth as I cleaned the gash.

"I'm sorry," I said in a whisper. "Almost done."

I ran my finger over the cut to ensure it had clotted. His breath hitched. "Sorry," I said again.

"That doesn't hurt." He pressed his forehead against mine. "I love you, Hell. And I hope you can forgive me for hurting you."

I smiled. "As long as you can forgive me for slicing you open."

"I'm glad you did because we can do this."

His lips crashed onto mine. I lost myself to him, to his taste and his touch. He ran his hand over my shoulders and down my arms and up my back as his tongue stroked and teased. I pressed my body against his and squeezed his upper arms.

The good and bad thing about ships is that they creak. We jumped apart as we heard someone come down the stairs. I stifled a giggle, and Henry grinned.

"Keep that clean," I said as Cook walked into the galley. He was a large man with a red face. He wasn't friendly to most of the sailors, but for some reason he liked me. I think I reminded him of his daughter back in Wales.

"Good morrow, Angelica! Lieutenant."

Henry nodded at him.

"Hello, Cook," I said. "I sliced Henry open during our swordplay lesson. I was just cleaning him up."

"No problem at all. I have something for you." He reached into a barrel and pulled out a mango. "Should be proper ripe now."

"Thank you, Cook!" He beamed at me.

"Where's mine?" Henry said, teasing. Cook narrowed his eyes at him. Henry held up his hands in mock surrender. "It was a joke."

At the stairs, Henry said, "I can't believe Emrick is so nice to you."

"His name is Emrick?" Six months I had been on the Juliet and had never heard anyone call Cook by his actual name. "Henry, if you'll bring me your shirt, I'll stitch it up. I'm no great seamstress, but I feel bad for ripping it."

Henry responded by pulling his white shirt over his head. I gaped at the well-defined muscles, and he grinned. I couldn't help it. I put my hand on his chest. He breathed in deep and closed his eyes. "Hell. . . "

Reluctantly, I pulled my hand away. "Come get your shirt in an hour."

I ran back to my room. Once inside, I leaned against my door and laughed until tears rolled down my cheeks. I breathed in Henry's scent from his shirt then set to work sewing it. An hour later, he knocked on my door.

I leapt up and flung it open. I was dismayed to see that his shirt had been replaced by another one. He leaned against the doorframe and smiled.

"Here you are." I held out his shirt. He let his hand brush against mine as he took it from me. My hand tingled after he took his hand away. "Oh! I almost forgot." I took the Spanish primer I had bought in San Juan from my desk. "I bought this for you."

"You bought me a gift?" He held the book in his hands like it was one of the crown jewels. "Hell. Thank you."

I smiled and whispered, "Te amo."

Chapter 7

5 NOVEMBER, 1693, THE GULF OF MEXICO

My twentieth birthday dawned clear and bright. Cook served me boiled eggs and the last of the fruit for breakfast. My father surprised me with several gifts. I munched on the bag of hard sweets as I opened a new sketchbook and a book of Italian poetry. He also bought me a new set of charcoals and a gilded inkwell for my quills. The best gift, though, was a necklace that he had bought at the pawnshop in Havana. The chain was braided silver and gold with a teardrop garnet pendant.

"Thank you, Father!" I threw my arms around him.

He laughed a hearty laugh. "Anything for my daughter. Now, we're stuck at sea today, but you are free from all your studies. You can do whatever you'd like."

I thought for a moment. If Henry had been free, I would have asked to fence, just to spend time with him. But he was working on the capstan this morning. "Perhaps a game? Fox and Geese?"

Father smiled. "Sounds wonderful. I'll fetch the board and meet you up on the poop deck. Happy birthday, Angelica."

We spent the morning under the sun, playing strategy games and sketching. It was nice having a new set of charcoals; I had been in need of them for weeks. I loved lazy days at sea more than anything. It was a perfect birthday.

The Juliet had been at sea for over a week. We were a day or three away from Campeche, depending on the winds. We would be in port for at least four days, as the captain met with a council of English and Spanish admirals. I was glad to be headed back to Campeche, as that was as near my birthplace as we usually went.

After a midday meal of birthday sweets, I went to my room to fetch my new book, and I ran into Henry in the corridor.

"I was looking for you," he said. "I don't have long, but I wanted to wish you a happy birthday."

"Thank you." I smiled. Ever since our fight, our interactions had become increasingly fraught with desire. But being at sea for so long meant we barely had a moment to ourselves. The Juliet was no small ship, but it might as well have been a sloop for all the privacy we had.

Henry held out a small package wrapped with brown paper and twine. "For you."

I grinned and snatched the package with excitement. I tore into the paper and opened the small box. Inside lay a small dagger. It was beautiful; the handle was inlaid with mother-of-pearl and etched silver.. And it must have cost him weeks of pay.

"Henry, it's beautiful." I ran my fingers over the hilt, tracing the spiraled pattern. "It's too much."

"Not for you, it's not. I would have bought you a cutlass, but. . . well, I'm just a sailor."

I shouldn't have accepted it. Honest sailors made a pittance, of course, and he could pawn it in Campeche—perhaps even for a profit. But the dagger was exquisite, and it was from Henry. I met his deep, blue eyes. "I love it. Thank you."

He smiled. "I'll teach you how to fight with the dagger. It does well in a pinch, and you can keep it on your person at all times. And you can fight with the dagger in one hand and a sword in the other."

I couldn't help it; privacy be damned. I grabbed him by the shirt and kissed him fiercely. His lips parted, inviting me in. I let out an embarrassing whimper. He pressed a hand against the small of my back, pulling me closer to him. I felt something hard between us.

"Oh!"

Henry pulled away. "I'm sorry, Hell."

"No, no. It's fine. It just surprised me is all." My eyes trailed down to his pants. I licked my lips in spite of myself. "This is killing me, Henry."

He sighed. "Me, too."

"I'm sure we could find a quiet nook to—"

"No." He shook his head. "I'm not going to let your first time be in a dirty corner. It shouldn't be rushed, and we shouldn't be worried about being caught." He leaned down to kiss the top of my head and ran a finger across my cheek. "Soon, Hell. It will be worth the wait."

"Very well." I pressed my cheek against his touch. "Thank you for the dagger, Henry. I love you."

"Happy birthday, my love."

We landed in Campeche two days later. I spent the first day in port with Father, eating too much food and visiting the library at the mission. On the way back to the ship, he asked if I would mind staying on the ship the following day if I couldn't get Henry to escort me. I was quick to oblige. With any luck, Henry and I would finally have some hours to ourselves. The thought filled me with both excitement and nervousness.

In my room, I jotted a quick note on a small piece of parchment and carried it around with me that evening. I finally saw Henry at sundown when he re-embarked and slipped him the paper with a smile.

The next morning, I paced my tiny room. My father had said he would not return until dinner. He gave me a few tasks to complete with my studies but otherwise didn't seem concerned with what I did for the day. Good. I still didn't know whether Henry was even on board; I hadn't seen him at breakfast.

At half-past eleven, someone rapped softly on my door. I flung the door open less than a second later.

Henry.

My heart pounded in my chest. He looked handsome in his brown breeches and tan shirtsleeves. Handsome and nervous. What did he have to be nervous about? As he said, he had been visiting brothels since he was fifteen.

"You came." It was a stupid thing to say.

He nodded. "I waited until as many people were gone as possible. There might be a dozen men left on the ship." He ran a hand through his hair and cleared his throat. "Hell, if anyone sees me leaving your room. . . "

"They won't. Father is gone until sundown, and no one else knocks on my door."

He nodded. We stood staring at each other for a few more moments. Finally, I realized I should let him inside. I opened the door wider and stepped to the side. He ducked his head under the frame as he entered. I closed the door behind him and bolted it.

I forced myself to take steady breaths and stared out the porthole window. "I'm nervous," I said.

"That's to be expected." His voice was low, tender.

"Will it hurt?"

"It might hurt a little. But I promise I will be as gentle as I can." He chuckled nervously. "In San Juan, I asked the whore for advice on how to make it good for you."

I nodded, still turned away from his intense blue eyes. I felt him walk behind me. He placed a strong hand on my shoulder. "Look at me, Hell."

I turned. It wasn't fair how beautiful he was. A new emotion flooded through me—self-consciousness.

"Angélica, are you certain you—?"

"Yes."

He nodded. "You can stop me at any time. Just say the word, and I'll desist."

I smiled to let him know I understood. Then he bent his head and kissed me. Our kisses of late had built in intensity, but this time, he was gentle. I let his lips calm me, let myself get lost in the moment. We had all day. There was no rush. And Henry made it clear that he was going to take his time.

I placed my hand on his jaw to stroke the stubble he had forgotten to shave. He ran his hands over my back, sending tingles through my body, then he pulled his lips away from mine and moved them to kiss my temple. He untied my plait and pushed my hair behind my ears. His soft mouth nuzzled my earlobe, and I let out a small moan.

He placed a line of kisses down my jaw and onto my neck. The intimacy made me weak in the knees, and I grabbed his upper arms for support.

"Henry," I breathed.

A kiss on the top of each breast above my bodice. "Are you well?" he asked in a whisper.

I had never been better in my life. "Yes."

"Shall I continue?"

"Please." The word came out as a half-beg.

He chuckled and nuzzled his head on my chest. The vibrations made me shiver.

He began to unlace my bodice, and my breathing quickened as his hands grazed my breasts through the fabric. My mantua dropped to the floor, leaving me in my stays, petticoats, and chemise. Henry studied me like a specimen he'd never seen before. Then he grinned. "You're beautiful, Hell."

I blushed and looked at the floor. He lifted my chin with two fingers and gazed into my eyes. "Don't be ashamed. You're too perfect to ever be ashamed."

I kissed him, hard, and ran my hands under his shirt like a child unwrapping a parcel. It struck me as hardly fair that he was not at all undressed. He laughed and pulled his shirt over his head. Any sense of shyness I had vanished. I touched and kissed every inch of his toned, golden chest, running my fingers through the smattering of light hair.

He untied my stays and pushed my shift down over my shoulders and breasts. Soon, there was no fabric between the tops of our bodies. I pressed my breasts against his chest, aching for as much contact as possible. He kissed me, the earlier tenderness replaced with urgency as his tongue plundered my mouth. He moved his hips against me. The hard bulge made my core tingle. Frantically, he shoved my shift over my hips until it pooled around my feet.

I was completely and utterly exposed. But Henry whispered to me about my beauty as he ran his hands over my bare skin. Gooseflesh erupted underneath his touch. When his thumbs grazed my hardened nipples, my hips bucked without my control.

Henry perched on the edge of my bed and slid off his boots and stockings. Then he stood again. He took my hand and guided it to the fall of his breeches. My hands shook as I undid the falls. I pulled them over his hips and buttocks, and his penis sprung free.

My eyes widened. I had only ever seen them in anatomical illustrations and never like this. My nerves returned. It was much bigger than I had expected.

"Will it. . . will it fit?"

"Yes. I promise." He held my hands in his and pulled me back toward the bed. He pushed me gently onto my back and then climbed over me.

Could he see my heart beating through my chest?

"I love you," he said breathily.

"I love you, Henry."

He silenced me with another kiss. One hand stroked my hair, and the other fondled my breasts. He alternated between gentle caresses and rough tweaks. My breaths came harder and heavier. I parted my knees on instinct, drawing him closer to me. I longed to be touched lower. I had only ever touched myself this intimately when I washed myself, and I never lingered despite how good it felt. But in that moment, all I wanted was Henry to touch me at the apex of my thighs. I pushed my hips against him to let him know, and he gasped.

He understood. He shifted himself to my side and trailed a hand down my stomach. His fingers coiled in the soft patch of hair until I couldn't stand it anymore. I writhed in an attempt to move his hand lower. He kissed me gently just as he moved a finger to part the flesh between my legs.

"Oh!"

"Are you well?"

"Ye-yes. Please keep going."

He did, and I had never felt anything so wonderful. He stroked a small nub that sent jolts through my body. This part was not in the anatomy books. Nor was the part where he lowered his head and took one of my breasts in his mouth.

He removed his mouth and looked me in the eyes. "You're quite wet."

"Is that good?" I said between pants.

He grinned. "Very. It means you're enjoying yourself." I nodded in agreement. "Angélica, I'm going to do a little more now. Let me know if I hurt you."

He slipped a finger inside of me. I groaned and pushed back against his hand, nudging the sensitive bud against the heel of his hand. It didn't hurt at all. Soon, I felt more as he slipped a second finger inside me, certain I was babbling nonsense as he continued his ministrations. He moved his fingers in and out and used his thumb to rub that small pearl of ecstasy.

It wasn't much longer before my breathing stopped. My back arched, and I was free-falling from the clouds. Magic. We had disappeared into a void of pleasure together. It was too much and yet I never wanted to return to earth.

When I could think again, I asked, "What was that?"

Henry laughed. "That was the best feeling in the world. That is why people enjoy this so much." He kissed my temple. "You came."

"Mm." I could get used to that sensation. My head felt clear. "Henry?"

"Yes, love?"

"Can I... touch you?"

He placed a quick kiss on my lips then took my hand. He showed me how to stroke him. His flesh was both velvet and rock-hard as I moved my hand up and down over the head. I loved the sound of his shallow breaths and the tiny mewls that escaped his lips. His breathing quickened, and he steadied my hand. "Are you ready for the rest, Hell?"

I nodded. Once more, he climbed on top of me. He reached a hand under my buttocks to lift me and positioned himself. Slowly, slowly, he sheathed himself inside of me. I sucked in a breath at the burning stretch of my flesh.

"Does it hurt?"

"A little."

He stopped moving, giving me time to adjust to him. Soon, the discomfort passed. He began a steady rhythm. I allowed myself to get lost in the moment, focusing only on what

I could feel. I felt that free-falling feeling again as he sped up his pace, and I cried out his name.

He stiffened and pulled himself out of me. "Fuck!" he groaned as a wet heat splashed against my upper thigh. He collapsed on top of me. I giggled.

I laid in his arms for awhile. We talked about everything and nothing. I read him some of the love poems from my new book and attempted to translate them into something equally poetic. Though I was somewhat sore, we made love one more time.

Fearing our luck would run out, we dressed. He kissed me once more, a promise, a vow. I looked out into the hallway to make sure no one would see him sneak out.

He winked. "Until next time, Hell."

Chapter 8

The next few months were some of the happiest of my life. If I could go back and bottle that time like sweet Spanish wine, I would without a thought. When one is young—and when life has been kind—one never expects the summers of life to end.

Privacy remained difficult to find on the ship, forcing Henry and I to steal quick moments in dark corners. But every now and again, we would find ourselves with time alone to make love. We often found ourselves on our hands and knees in the carpenter's walk, against the planked walls of the ship, where the waves crashed loudly enough to drown our cries of ecstasy. A few weeks into our affair, Henry showed me something entirely new.

"What are you doing?!" I said as he lowered his head between my legs. I was splayed out on a stack of flour sacks in the hold. He had slid to his knees on the dusty ground

"Trust me, Hell. You'll enjoy it."

And trust Henry, I did. He was right, of course. His tongue replaced the movements normally made by his fingers, bringing me to the crest of my pleasure over and over. And he taught me more ways to please him and myself. How could something so wonderful be wrong?

"Is this a sin?" Henry asked me that day. We were curled up together on the floor of the hold. "I've stolen your virtue."

I laughed. "You've done a bit more than that. Ruination implies I'm useless now. I don't feel useless."

"But doesn't the Bible warn against this? You're no whore who has chosen a life of vice."

"I don't know if I believe all that the Bible has to say."

"Hell! That's blasphemy!"

I shrugged. "Have you read anything by Thomas Hobbes? Or perhaps Spinoza?" Henry shook his head. "John Locke? Charles Blount?"

Henry looked confused. "No. Never heard of them."

"Oh. Well, they are scholars and philosophers. And they've helped develop the move-ment of Deism." I launched into an explanation of Biblical criticism and natural theology. I cited all the facts I could think of to support it. My father and I had spent hours and hours debating these philosophies. I knew the subject like the back of my hand. "You've been all over the world as a sailor. How could all these thousands of people be wrong in their beliefs? They had never heard of Christianity before we began colonizing."

"I have wondered about that before. But the priests have always said it is our duty to spread the word of Christ."

"Perhaps. Or perhaps God created the world and then left us on our own. And if that's the case, does sin even exist?"

Henry was quiet for a few moments. Then he kissed my forehead. "I love your mind."

It was the best compliment he could have paid me. I pushed him back on the floor and had my way with him. Later, I gave him a book by Charles Blount. He was perhaps my favorite of the critics, and I thought it was a good place for him to start.

Our courtship was marked with stolen moments and daydreams about the future. We would buy a small ship and sail the seas, loyal to no one but ourselves. I was naïve enough to believe it.

The next week, the *Juliet* was beached for careening and repairs on a small deserted island in the Bahamas. Careening was dangerous because we had no escape in case of attack. But another naval vessel kept guard a few knots away. We would do the same for them the following week.

Father and I used this time to study the island. He had recently finished his essays on the birds of Hispaniola and was ready for a new project. He continued with birds, and I was to collect as much information as possible on mammals. One fortunate day, Henry was sent to escort me further inland.

We made love near a freshwater pond. Then Henry read a book I had loaned him while I made notes and sketches in my journal. He had breezed through Blount's work and was now reading Spinoza.

"This pantheism makes sense to me," he said. I had trapped a rat in a wire cage and was sketching it. It didn't appear to be any different from the other Caribbean rats.

"Oh?"

"Moreso than Deism." He listed out his reasons. I made a mental note to give him Francis Bacon to read next. I posited a few difficult questions to him, and we discussed it at length. Henry often said he was just a simple sailor, but he was wrong. He was intelligent, though he trusted his intuition far more than reason. He often told me I didn't have to have an answer for everything, though I wasn't so sure.

At dusk each night, Father and I caught bats in our nets. I liked the bats, and I hated killing them. But as a naturalist, there was no other way to study the nocturnal creatures. I documented four unique species in our week on the island. I prepared half the specimens for dissection and the other for taxidermy. It was to be my first lone research project. I hoped to publish, though I would not be able to use my name. The credit would be Father's, but the science was mine.

It was one of the best weeks of my life.

Chapter 9

MARCH 1694

The end of our bliss started with a celebration. Once the Juliet was back in the water, the captain allowed the crew a much-needed party. The sailors popped open a barrel of brandy, and someone brought out a fiddle. The entire crew of 250-odd men gathered on the main deck for dancing and drinking.

Father gave me permission to try the brandy, but it was too sweet for my tastes. I wrinkled my nose, and Henry laughed before handing me a glass flask full of rum. Father nodded.

The dark amber liquid was smoky with just a hint of sweet. It burned my throat as it went down, and I coughed a bit. But the aftertaste was far better than the brandy. I grinned and took another long swig.

"I like it," I said. The men around me laughed their approval.

The sun set, coloring the sky with vibrant shades of orange and pink. The fiddler played jigs and drinking songs, and the sailors danced and sang, getting louder the more they drank. I danced, too, with my skirts in my hand and several winks at Henry. As night fell, the men became rowdier. My head swam, thick with the liquor. And all I wanted was Henry.

My father was deep in drunken discussion with the captain and the quartermaster. The deck was crowded and loud. Henry and I could easily slip away for a few moments. I danced my way over to him and whispered in his ear. "Follow me down to the hold in three minutes."

I slipped through the throngs of intoxicated sailors to the ladder that led below-deck. No one batted an eye at me. Climbing ladders while drunk and at sea was a new challenge that I had not anticipated. I stumbled more than a few times. But I made it to the hold and began to undress.

"Angélica?" Henry's voice was a failed attempt at a whisper. I giggled and dropped my stay to the ground.

"Over here!" I called back.

Henry staggered over to the back corner where the grain sacks were, making a lot of noise on the way. He shushed a crate that he bumped into and apologized to a barrel. I rolled my eyes. "Hurry up, Henry!"

A moment later, he stood in front of me, his eyes studying my body, his mouth in a sloppy grin. His blond hair hung loose around his face, and a new bottle of rum dangled from his left hand. I wore nothing but my chemise.

"Well, hello there," he said. He pulled his shirt over his head, exposing his muscular torso.

I knelt in front of him and unfastened the falls of his breeches. He bucked his hips as I took him deep in my mouth. It didn't take long until he was panting and grabbing my hair to brace himself. Soon, he stepped back and pulled me to my feet. He lifted me under my buttocks. He silenced my surprised shriek with a kiss and pushed me against the wall. I wrapped my legs around his waist.

With the help of all the rum and Henry's intoxicating touch, I easily lost myself to the feeling of making love. It was frantic and sloppy and felt so good. I didn't even care that my back was being pressed against the splintered wood wall. He sped up the pace, and I couldn't stop moaning. He was nearly finished when a shout interrupted us.

"Angelica Helen Spencer!"

We froze. I opened my eyes to see my father and the ship's master standing a few feet away. Even in the dark room lit only by cracks of moonlight, I could see that my father was angrier than he had ever been. His eyes were stone-cold, and his jaw was clenched.

"Put her down right this instant, Lieutenant!" the master said.

Henry dropped me to my feet. I covered my linen-clad breasts with my arms. He knelt and picked up my dress. I turned toward the wall to slip it over my head.

I turned around just in time to see my father's fist land squarely on Henry's jaw.

"No! Father, stop it!" Tears filled my eyes. Henry doubled over in pain. Dark droplets of blood dripped to the floor.

"Quiet, Angelica!" My father stepped closer to Henry. "How dare you! How dare you defile my daughter!"

"I will do the honorable thing and marry her, sir."

Another punch smacked Henry's eye, knocking him to the ground. I screamed and fell to my knees at Henry's side to protect him. Father yanked my arm and pulled me away. He went to hit Henry again, and I stepped in between them. "Stop it! Henry did nothing to me without my consent! It's not his fault!"

I was close enough to see the vein twitching in my father's jaw. "How long?" he asked through his teeth.

My lip quivered. "Five months or so. It was all my idea, Father, I promise."

The master kicked Henry with the toe of his boot. "Get up, boy."

Henry clamored to his feet. His eyes were wide when he looked at me. "I'm sorry."

My father laughed coldly. "Sorry? You were given specific instructions to not do anything untoward with my daughter. And now you've ruined her."

"I love her."

My father spat at him. "You're nothing more than the idiot son of a whore. You're not worthy of loving her."

"A night in the brig for ya," the master said. "Let the capt'n deal with ya tomorrow." He hauled Henry out of the hold by the elbow.

I sobbed. "Father! You can't have him punished! He did nothing wrong! Punish me! It was all my idea!"

"Come with me." His voice was hard, emotionless, and I had no choice.

I followed him to our rooms, pleading with him the entire way, but he said nothing until we reached my bunk.

"You are to stay in your bunk until I fetch you."

"What will happen to Henry?"

He shook his head. "Go. I can't look at you right now."

His words were like a punch to the gut. I hung my head and entered my room, and he slammed the door shut behind me.

I sat on my bed and cried.

Father did not fetch me until nearly midday. He had wordlessly handed me a bowl of gruel for breakfast then slammed the door shut once more. I had sobbed all night, not sleeping a wink. I thought I should never cry again, that all my tears had dried up.

I was wrong.

I was pacing my cramped bunk in anger, the sadness now morphed into body-shaking fury. My father had no right! I was no longer a child, and I could do what I damn well pleased. And I loved Henry more than anything.

Father knocked on my door and simply said, "Come." I followed him up to the main deck, confused about what he could possibly need me up there for. I swallowed. It couldn't be good.

Much of the crew had gathered on the deck, though the men were largely silent. Father pushed past a couple sailors, yanking me along by the hand. In the center of the ship, Henry knelt in front of the mast. He wore no shirt, and his arms were tied round the massive wooden post.

"No!" I screamed and raced toward him. My father grabbed me by the waist and pulled me back. "No! Let him go!"

Henry craned his neck to look at me. His eyes were wide, full of fear and apology. "I'll be fine, Hell."

"Shut up, boy!" the first lieutenant said. "You are guilty of disregarding a direct order of propriety from your captain. The punishment is thirteen lashes."

"Thirteen?!" I struggled against my father's hold, screaming and sobbing. "He did nothing wrong! Punish me instead! Let him go!"

"Silence, Angelica." My father's voice was sharp but quiet in my ear. "You are causing a scene."

"Of course I'm causing a scene! You cannot let them do this, Father! Please, I beg you! This is cruel. Cruel and unwarranted."

The first lash slapped against his skin and echoed across the deck. Other sailors winced at the sound of impact, and I screamed for them to stop again.

Smack. Smack. Smack.

Henry didn't cry out until the fourth one. He was strong, so much stronger and braver than me. I fell to my knees in tears.

His head drooped at the sixth lash. Blood streamed down his back. But he fought against the impact of the whip, trying to stay as upright as the ropes would allow.

Smack. Eleven. I could see tears rolling down his cheeks.

Smack. Twelve. He could no longer take the pain. He slumped forward, hitting his head against the mast. I felt sick.

Smack. Thirteen.

As soon as the first lieutenant stepped away, I rushed to Henry's side before my father could catch me. Henry had taught me how to be fast in our months of swordplay. I knelt beside him and removed the dagger he had given me from my belt. I cut off his ropes. He collapsed into my arms.

"Angélica, get up now!" my father said in Spanish.

I cursed at him in my mother's native tongue. The sailors looked wary, some outright scared. Fools.

I kissed Henry's forehead. Then I tore a strip of fabric off my skirt and gingerly began cleaning the blood from his back. He hissed at the pain. "Sorry, sorry, sorry," I whispered.

"Angélica, you must get up. Now." My father loomed over us. I made the mistake of looking into his face. His eyes shot daggers, and the vein in his jaw twitched feverishly. But I was angry, too.

"You did this to him," I said. It was true. The captain couldn't give a damn who his sailors fucked, direct order or no. But my father was patron of this voyage. The captain had to keep him happy, let him think his sailors were obedient.

"No, Angelica. You did. Your virtue is permanently destroyed."

"Then let me marry Henry! It won't matter then."

Father scoffed. "Let you marry a pauper? No."

"I don't care if he's poor. I love him. And he loves me." Henry nodded in agreement.

"And what do you think life with him would be? He'll either be at sea for months on end while you're making a home, or you'll force him to give up his career as a Navy man. Could you do that to the man you love?"

I opened my mouth to respond, then closed it. My father was right. He was rich and well-respected; that's why he was allowed to bring his daughter onboard every ship. But without him, I was just a woman with no inheritance and no respect.

And I couldn't do that to Henry.

"Get up, Angelica. He needs to see to his wounds."

"Let me help--"

Father silenced me with a glance. I kissed Henry, saying everything I couldn't with my touch. "I love you."

"I love you," he managed to reply, his voice hoarse.

I stood, blinking back more tears. I took one last look at Henry, kneeling on the ground and bleeding before I followed my father back to my bunk.

"Pack your belongings," Father said as I opened my door. "We make landfall tomorrow."

"Where are we going?"

"We will book passage on another ship. We're returning to England. The gossip of your ruination will not follow us across the ocean." He glared at me. "It's time you learned what it means to be a lady in society."

In my wildest dreams, I had not imagined that he would force me to live in England. He loved the sea as much as I did.

I had thought that only Henry was being punished, but I was wrong. My punishment was worse than any I could have imagined.

My father slammed the door to his bunk, and I yelled through it.

"I'll never forgive you for this!"

Chapter 10

MAY 1694

The Spencer Manor stood in the center of the estate, a dull white-faced building with no features of note. The original house had burned down eighty years prior. Due to the mismanagement of money by my ancestors, the resulting rebuild was, at best, modest and, at worst, hideous. Under the grey skies of the Manchester countryside, the house was a prison of mundanity.

I had never spent much time at the Spencer estate, perhaps a collective twelve months in my entire twenty years. Father could never stand to stay here for long, and that wanderlust had passed on to me. But now, the closest bit of sea was thirty miles away, and I didn't know when I would see her again.

"Angélica." My father touched my shoulder. I had been silently gazing out the carriage window since Liverpool. I had spent most of the month-long voyage home refusing to speak to him unless necessary. But the last few days, we had come to a tentative peace. For all my anger, I loved my father. Yet once we docked in Liverpool, the reality of my new life had set in.

"Angélica," he said again, sterner. "You can't ignore me for the rest of your life."

I could try, I thought. He deserved it. Henry was thousands of miles away, lost to me forever. The turquoise waters of the Caribbean were gone. The vibrant greens of the islands were no more, and I was stuck under the dreary skies of the motherland.

The carriage rolled to a stop in front of the manor house and our butler, a grizzled, old man, came through the front door. He had served my family since before I was born, and I couldn't remember his name. When my father climbed out of the carriage, the butler's mouth dropped open.

"Sir George! Could it really be you?" He embraced my father and held him tight. The driver came around and opened my door, but I made no effort to move. My legs felt as if they were made of lead. Leaving the carriage was the final step, the true end to my life at sea. My life with Henry.

"It is good to see you, Harold."

"We did not know you were returning! We would have prepared the house for you."

"I apologize. Our return was rather unexpected. I'm sure the house is fine." Father turned and gestured to me to leave the carriage. I bit my lip to keep from crying and gathered the strength to stand on the estate grounds. Father turned back to the butler. "You remember my daughter, Miss Angelica Spencer."

He said it in the English way, the harshness of the *g* sounding foreign to my ears. I imagined Henry calling me Hell. *That* is who I was.

"Of course! Good day, Miss Spencer. My, you have grown, my dear." He took my hand and kissed it. I forced a smile. "Sir George, your daughter has become a lovely young woman."

I hated him in that moment. I hated both of them. This man had not seen me since I was eleven years old. He didn't know me. Was I nothing more than a pretty face to rest of the world? To Henry, I was so much more. And the old man couldn't even compliment me directly. Here in England, I was the property of my father. He might as well have been complimenting my father's prize horse.

Two more manservants came out to help with our bags and trunks. My father greeted them both by name, though they were nowhere near as old as Harold. I wondered how he remembered the name of his house staff. The Spencer estate essentially ran itself. The steward sent a yearly report to an inn in Havana, and my father collected it when we visited. England and Spain had been in a tentative peace for years, and British naval ships inevitably docked in Havana every few months. When alliances changed, Father sent a letter home with new instructions.

We followed Harold inside where pale memories teased the edges of my mind. The manor had remained unchanged since our last visit. "How long will you be staying this time, Sir?" Harold asked.

"Indefinitely," Father said.

I squeezed my eyes shut to stop the tears that threatened to fall. Indefinitely, then. Father really had no intention of returning to sea.

"Indefinitely?" Harold sounded surprised.

My father had left home to travel the world when he was sixteen. He had returned at twenty when his father died to take over the estate. But once he had it running smoothly, he left again two years later. Shortly after, he landed on the coast of the Spanish Main and fell in love with my mother.

"Yes, I have decided it is time for Angelica to experience life in society. And I've got more than two decades' worth of research to write about now."

The manservants announced that our belongings had been delivered to our rooms. Harold said he would send the maids to put fresh linens on our beds and instruct the cook to prepare us dinner. My father excused himself to change into fresh clothes and unpack.

I climbed the stairs to go to my bedroom. At the top of the stairs, I froze and looked around. I couldn't remember where my room was. A tear escaped my eyes and rolled down my cheek. No. I wiped my face. I would not break down here.

"Down the corridor to your left. Last door on the right," a warm voice said from behind me. I jumped in surprise, and the warm voice chuckled. "Sorry, Miss Spencer."

I turned to see a handsome, dark-skinned man not much older than me on the stairs. I hadn't even heard him come up. This house was much less creaky than a ship. "Thank you."

"Of course, Miss Spencer. You probably don't remember me."

I studied his face, and recognition dawned on me. "Charles?"

He grinned. "Yes, madam. 'Tis a long time since we met."

"Indeed it has." Charles and I had played together as children the few times I had visited home. His mother had worked for my grandfather. When my father took over the estate, he had freed the slaves and added them to his payroll. Charles was the son of one of the maids, a woman named Charlotte. He had grown from a scrawny boy into a man in the six years that I had been gone. "It is nice to see a friendly face. How is your mother?"

His face fell. "She passed last winter, madam. Consumption."

"Oh, dear. My condolences, Charles."

He nodded. "My thanks, Miss Spencer. She was able to meet my daughter before she died, so my soul knows peace."

"Your daughter? You're married." Life had not frozen here the way it had in my memory. My heart ached at the realization that I belonged even less than I had thought.

"Aye, Miss. Two years now. She works in the kitchen."

"Felicitations."

He bowed and flashed me another smile. I made my way to the last room on the right and opened the door. Sighing, I opened the curtains and pushed open the large windows that overlooked the garden. The sunlight illuminated dancing clouds of dust.

I studied my bedroom.

It could have belonged to anyone. Nothing hung on the walls. Nothing sat atop the dresser. A doll that I could only vaguely remember sat on the bed. In the corner of the room, next to the mahogany wardrobe, sat a basket with puppets and wooden animals.

It was a nice room. A large room. But the walls were closing in on me. Though I was used to tiny bunks on ships, this room felt so much smaller. My life felt so much smaller. I was trapped by my sex in a dismal English manor, while the man I loved was halfway across the world.

My breath came in short, painful pants, like someone had twisted a knife in my chest. I unlaced my bodice, desperate to get some air. Then I collapsed onto the window seat, no longer able to stand. I couldn't hold the tears back any longer. I hugged my knees to my chest and sobbed.

I cried for several minutes until I was interrupted by a knock on the door. I wiped my face with my palms. "Come in," I called in a shaky voice.

A maid opened the door and curtsied. She was young and petite, with a kind, round face. "Beggin' your pardon, Miss Spencer. Mister Harold sent me to change your linens."

I nodded. "Thank you."

She gave me a smile but was kind enough not to mention my crying. She sat about stripping the four-poster bed of its blankets. A large cloud of dust puffed up, making us both cough. "I don't know the last time this was changed," she said apologetically. "We dust the furniture regularly, though."

"It's fine," I assured her.

She chatted about nothing of import as she put the fresh bedclothes on. I appreciated her for her kindness. Sitting here in silence would have been uncomfortable for both of us. When she was done, she looked around the room. Her eyes landed on my trunk and bags.

"Would you like me to help you unpack now or later, Miss Spencer?"

Oh. I had servants now. I had been raised to be self-sufficient out of necessity. Unpacking my belongings whenever I was on a new ship had become sort of a ritual for me. "I'd like to do it myself, if you don't mind."

"If you're certain, miss." She bit her lip. "But if'n Mister Harold asks, will you tell him I offered?"

"Of course."

"Can I get you anything else, Miss?"

I shook my head. "No, thank you. What was your name?"

"Molly."

"Thank you, Molly."

She curtsied again and left the room as I looked at my belongings. Unpacking would make this feel more final, but it would also make this room feel less foreign. And a task was just what I needed. I stood and set to work, putting up clothes and books and various trinkets I had collected from around the world.

I unwrapped the dagger Henry had given me for my birthday and turned it over and over in my hands. I felt like a piece of my soul was missing without him. I wished we had run away when we had the chance—before we had been discovered. He wouldn't want me to sit here in misery. He loved me for many reasons, and my fiery personality was one of them.

No more tears, I decided. The situation was less than ideal. But I was a naturalist, an adventurer. I could adapt. I could survive.

I could thrive.

I refused to accept my sentence as a silent woman of English society. If I was stuck here, I would make the best of it. I would make my father realize that he had made a terrible mistake in marooning me here in this dreadful place. Henry's words echoed in my mind. "You're no angel."

I was Hell. I was a tempest that had made landfall. No one would steer my life but me.

I tucked my dagger into my skirts, a tangible reminder that I would not lie down and take my fate and made my way downstairs to dinner.

Chapter 11

1 JUNE 1693

"Stop brooding, Angelica."

"No." I continued to stare out the carriage window at the grey Manchester skies. There wasn't much to look at—just miles of grass and sheep as far as the eye could see—but it was better than the alternative of conversing with Father.

"You've sat at home for weeks. This will be good for you. You can make some friends."

"It's not my home."

Father sighed. "Like it or not, you are the daughter of a baronet. A member of English society. It's time to start rubbing shoulders with people in your own class."

I rolled my eyes, but he couldn't see. It was ridiculous that I couldn't even select my own friends. "Why? So you can marry me off like some brood cow to an acceptable man?"

"I would never force you into an arrangement you don't want to be in."

I barked out humorless laugh. "But you'll take me out of one I do want to be in."

He didn't want to fight, so he fell silent. I wished I was back at the manor, alone in my room with my books. I had made great strides in perfecting my Dutch and was starting to teach myself Portuguese. I had made extensive notes on my dissections of the bats though the memories accompanying them were painful. I had also found a sword in the attic and had taken to practicing by myself in the barn.

Yes, there were many more productive things to do rather than rub shoulders with ladies of society.

"We're nearly here," my father said after a quarter of an hour. "The Campbell estate and Smallclair Manor."

I turned to look out the other window. There was nothing small about this manor. A stately country home at least thrice the size of our manor stood out in the distance. It was lovely, though ostentatious, and clearly told of the success of the peers who made their home here. I wrinkled my nose.

Edmund Campbell, the Right Honorable Lord Smallclair had once been landed gentry like my father. Whereas my father had inherited a peerless title, Smallclair had amassed a fortune exceeding even some of the dukes. He was a devout Protestant, and King William had granted him a barony for his monetary support during the revolution. How fortunate that he still deigned to associate with gentry like us.

"Now, Angelica. Please behave. Act like a lady of your station ought."

"Don't embarrass you. Understood."

Father pinched the bridge of his nose, as the carriage rolled to a stop. "Make friends. Make the most of your time here."

The driver opened the carriage door, and my father climbed out before offering me his hand. A footman bowed and led us inside through the vast wooden doors into a marble-floored hall. A tall man with streaks of grey through his dark hair came down the vast staircase.

"George Spencer! It has been a good many years, my old friend!"

"Edmund! Or should I say Smallclair! How wonderful to see you." Father clasped his hand on Lord Smallclair's arm in greeting. "It's been too long."

"That's on you, you grand adventurer. You've gotten old in the last two decades."

"I don't have nearly the salt and pepper in my hair that you do."

Lord Smallclair laughed, then looked at me. "Your daughter?"

"Yes. This is Angelica."

I lowered myself into a curtsy. "Lord Smallclair."

"A pleasure to meet you, young Miss Spencer." He took my hand and kissed it. "You are close in age to my daughter, Evelyn. She entertains some of the other local ladies every Monday. They're in the south parlor. My butler will show you the way."

I gave a pleading look at my father, but he ignored it and waved me on. I had never spent much time with girls my age, except the occasional daughter of my father's colleagues. I'd become friendly with my maids, but they weren't my friends.

What does one talk about with girls who have never set foot on a ship?

"Miss Campbell, may I present Miss Angelica Spencer?"

The butler bowed toward a seated young woman. There were three others sitting, but the one by the window was clearly their leader. Her blonde coiffe towered above her head. She had the same bright eyes as her father.

"Fetch her some tea, James," she ordered.

"Right away, Miss Campbell."

The girl studied me intensely. I shifted my weight under my heavy skirts. "So you're the new girl. Angelica—may I call you Angelica?—so lovely to meet you. I'm Evelyn Campbell. Father says you have the most fascinating background."

She said the word fascinating as if it were an insult. I forced a smile. "I suppose."

"Hm. Please, sit."

I turned to find a seat. There was room next to a lovely girl with bright red hair and dainty freckles spattered across her nose. Her smile was kind. I sat next to her on the settee.

"I'm Deirdre Byrne," she said in a thick Irish accent. "Glad to meet you."

"Likewise."

Evelyn cleared her throat to gain our attention. I looked back at her. She pointed to a hook-nosed brunette with a coiffe nearly as tall as Evelyn's. "That's Agnes White of Faireview Court."

Agnes inclined her head but didn't smile. I returned the gesture.

"And Felicity Renshaw of Peppington Hall."

This one had darker blonde hair than Evelyn, and she gave me a small smile. "Pleasure."

"Indeed," I said.

Evelyn leaned forward. "The return of the Spencers has been the subject of much talk among society. I'm so glad to finally see the mysterious sea girl."

I didn't know how to respond to that, so I didn't. My skirts rustled as I shifted in discomfort. Unfortunately, I had never translated essays or studied treatises on the social behaviors of highborn ladies.

"Are you enjoying England?" Deirdre asked.

"No," I said honestly.

Evelyn let out a shrill chuckle, which was echoed by Felicity and Agnes. "How funny you are!"

"I can imagine it would be quite difficult to come home after a life at sea," Deirdre said. I looked into her green eyes and found only empathy.

"Well, we must get you settled in properly," Evelyn said. "I'll give you the name of my mantua maker. She can make you a less dated wardrobe."

I glanced down at the red gown with ruffles that Henry had loved. It had only been bought a few months ago, and I didn't quite see what was wrong with it. "Thank you?"

"She's quite talented. She'll be able to tell you which colors will tone down your dark skin."

My skin? I looked at my golden hands. I wasn't dark by Caribbean standards, and the lack of sunlight had already begun to fade my tan. I appeared European, though I wasn't as pale as Evelyn or Deirdre.

"I think your dress is lovely." I liked Deirdre.

"Deirdre is just glad that she is no longer the most exotic girl around." The way Evelyn said exotic was not a compliment. I couldn't help but think she'd look a lot less pretty with a broken nose.

But she changed the subject to some gossip about an adulteress wife among the gentry. She talked with Agnes and Felicity, all but ignoring Deirdre and me. They gossiped about any and everyone. From adultery, to money issues, to the particularly heinous crime of being out of fashion, no one was safe from their judgment. They also talked about the desirable young men their fathers were beginning to court on their behalf.

Relief and exhaustion flooded me when Father retrieved me three hours later. Who knew socialization was so draining? Deirdre asked if she could call upon me that week to hear about life as a naturalist's daughter, and I quickly agreed. Another emotion had bubbled during the afternoon: envy. As much as I disliked Evelyn and the others, I envied their camaraderie and easy company with each other. Perhaps friendship was not as undesirable or unnecessary as I had believed after twenty years alone.

Chapter 12

Deirdre did call on me later that week, and we became fast friends. Somehow, I was invited back to Evelyn's, and soon it became routine. On Mondays, Deirdre and I sat quietly as we listened to the other three gossiping. On Thursdays, Deirdre and I spent the day complaining about the other girls and talking about their insipid expectations.

"I hate wearing my hair up," she told me one day. "It makes my head ache. I hardly understand how wearing a plait could be suggestive."

"If our heads ache, we can't talk about anything improper, don't you know? Tighten the pair of bodies, pile pounds of hair on our heads, layer on the dresses in the middle of summer, and we'll be quiet."

"Evelyn is never quiet."

I laughed. "But she says nothing of import."

We bonded over homesickness. She missed Ireland deeply. Her great-grandfather had married an Irishwoman, and she preferred that side of her family. But her father was the next male heir to an old estate here, and she had moved when she was thirteen. The family had declared their loyalty to William and Mary, though privately, they still practiced Catholicism. She taught me several Irish songs and jigs on our days together.

We also bonded over our lack of desire to marry a wealthy man with an estate. My heart still ached for Henry, though I didn't mention him to anyone. It hurt too much. Deirdre said she had no interest in any of the men she had met. She was perfectly content to die an old maid; her brother would inherit the estate and take care of her.

As for the rest of my days, I fell into a routine of studying, exploring the flora and fauna around the manor, and practicing with a sword in the barn. In the dark of night, I remembered the touch of his hands, his lips, his tongue. I kept myself occupied, but there were moments I couldn't assuage my loneliness. My very soul had been rent in two without Henry.

Father also forced me to continue to rub shoulders with the gentry and nobility of the area. In early July, the Campbells held a large garden party. There were to be games for the men and lots of sitting for the women. My father made me go, telling me it would be good to meet the other young, unwed people in the area.

Evelyn was on her best behavior, as the man she wished to marry was there. Laurence Davy was a handsome man with thick arms, broad shoulders, and an ego to match. He was among Manchester's most eligible bachelors, second son to a viscount, and the Campbell family had been talking in earnest to his grandfather, the head of the Davy estate. The young men spent all their energy trying to impress us. It was hot, and I was bored. Several of the men had tried to speak to me, but I wasn't feeling particularly talkative.

I sat between Deirdre and Evelyn as the men decided to practice their swordsmanship in the most absurd mating ritual I had ever witnessed. The other ladies clapped their hands and cheered them on as they took turns with clumsy footwork and sloppy thrusts.

"They're terrible."

"What?" Deirdre asked. I hadn't realized I had spoken.

"They're not any good. Their form is all wrong. Their footwork is a mess. In a real fight, they'd be dead in moments."

Evelyn scoffed. "And I suppose you could do better then, Sea Girl?"

"I could."

Laurence disarmed his opponent, a man who Agnes couldn't stop fawning over. The young Lord Davy came over for a sip of water. "Could what?"

Evelyn batted her lashes at him. "Angelica here thinks she could best you at a sword-fight."

Everyone laughed. Heat flared up my neck, this time not from the sun. I jumped up and grabbed one of the dull swords the men had thrown carelessly on the ground.

"What are you doing, girl?" Laurence asked.

"Proving it. Surely you aren't scared of losing to a girl." I glanced over at Evelyn, who had me fixed in a stony glare.

"Scared of hurting you, perhaps."

I tossed him another sword. He fumbled it, unprepared. "Don't be."

All eyes were on him. If he refused, he'd be seen as a coward, and his ego was too fragile. He cleared his throat. "Very well."

We bowed to each other. Laurence was hesitant, which made me attack first. He managed to block my first thrust, but barely. He tripped as I walked around him, and I had the tip of my blade to his throat in seconds.

He held his hands up, and I moved my sword. No one said anything. Laurence chuckled, embarrassed.

"I was going easy on you," he said loudly.

"Then, perhaps, you'd like to try again more seriously?"

He studied me. I raised my chin and met his gaze.

"Perhaps."

We began again. He tried harder, but my feet moved too fast. He could block well enough, but he couldn't get a thrust past me. He panted, and sweat rolled down his face in buckets. I was barely winded.

I knocked the sword out of his right hand when he used his left to wipe his eyes.

"I yield!"

I grinned. Deirdre and several of the other men applauded me. Felicity did, too, until Evelyn smacked her shoulder. I curtsied and stared Evelyn down.

Servants brought around canapés and mead. I sat next to Deirdre and talked with her about learning to fight on the *Juliet*, but I left out the extent of my relationship with Henry.

"Well, what can you expect?" I overheard Evelyn say a few minutes later. "Her mother was an actual barbarian. Supposedly her father married the Indian, but I wouldn't be surprised if she were illegitimate."

"Excuse me." I stood, drawing attention to myself. Evelyn smirked at me. I had nothing to say to her and walked away toward the house.

It was cooler in the house and mostly empty. Perfect. I wandered the corridors, thinking of ways to get back at that horrid bitch. How I wished I had had some scathing retort. Some way to bring her down in front of all her subjects, for that's what they were. People like Evelyn didn't have friends.

I found my way to the library and pulled a book off the shelf at random then settled myself onto the settee. It was a book of French poetry. I flipped through the book, skimming love poems here and there. They all reminded me of Henry.

"There you are."

I glanced up to see Laurence in the doorway.

"Here I am." I looked back at the book, hoping he would see my disinterest. But men like Laurence never do. He took a seat next to me. I sighed.

"What are you reading?"

I held the book up so he could see the title but didn't answer.

"Oh. My French isn't very good, much to the chagrin of my childhood tutors."

"Ah."

"Where'd you learn to fight like that?"

"On my last ship from one of the lieutenants." Setting the book in my lap, I resigned myself to the unwanted conversation. At least Laurence was nice to look at.

"Where was the ship?"

"The Caribbean."

He smiled at me. "Are all the women in the Caribbean as beautiful as you?"

I opened my mouth to tell him to leave me alone, then closed it. What was it Evelyn had said to humiliate me? A barbarian. Very well. If that's what she wanted to think, who was I to sully her beliefs? I had my own beliefs about Laurence and was curious if I was correct.

I leaned closer and placed a hand on his thigh. "I'm not sure, but there are few men aboard ships as handsome as you." It was a lie, but Laurence's pride was the way to his heart.

"You are bold," he said with a gleam in his eye.

"Not too bold, I hope?"

He shook his head. "I like bold women."

I wet my lips and succeeded in drawing his gaze to my mouth. I moved my hand further up his leg, and he leaned his head down to mine. My chin tilted up in acquiescence before his rough lips crashed onto mine.

His kiss was sloppy and devoid of all emotion except lust, but it awoken something in me. I deepened the kiss, and soon Laurence's hands were all over me. His mouth moved to my neck, and I took the opportunity to whisper in his ear.

"Lock the door."

Chapter 13

My fire had returned.

Whenever Evelyn talked about how wonderful a gentleman Laurence was, I smirked. I met him at his townhouse several times for a quick tumble, using the guise of visiting the dressmaker or the bookshop or meeting a friend for tea. Charles, my old friend, always drove the carriage, and he was discreet. Father was too busy to worry about a chaperone. He thought I was safe here.

Deirdre still came to my home—or me to hers—every week. Our friendship was mostly tea and small talk, though I often found myself thinking of her and her hair like the Caribbean sunset.

We attended society events, where I managed to slip into abandoned rooms or shadowed corners of gardens with various friends of Laurence's. At home, I corresponded with a female naturalist on the Continent, a Mrs. Merian, who encouraged me to publish under my name when I felt ready. Slowly, Henry became a wistful, sweet memory, though part of my heart believed that one day we would meet again.

Smallclair Manor hosted a ball to usher in autumn. As much as I despised Evelyn and her cronies, I loved dancing and music. The weather turned cooler, and the feasts grew heartier with the harvest. For the first time since arriving in England, I felt happy.

Deirdre and I chatted as we drank sweet ratafia between songs. I quickly picked up the steps to the dances I didn't know. Everyone was cheerful, from guests to servants, and I spent the evening eating too many meat pies.

Laurence caught my eye during a song, and we managed to sneak away for a quick jaunt in the library before anyone missed us. The ballroom and every parlor were packed wall-to-wall with guests.

I laced my stay as he pulled his breeches up. He grinned at me. "That was fun."

"Indeed. How's my hair?" I asked. I peered at my faint reflection in the window and tucked away the only loose strand I saw.

"Perfect. Innocent." He came closer and tried to kiss me. I turned away quickly, not one to linger. His face fell.

"Good."

"I've enjoyed our. . . visits." His voice was hesitant.

I arched an eyebrow. "Are they ending?"

It would be unfortunate to lose the convenience, and Laurence wasn't a terrible lover. But there were other men.

He shrugged. "What are your thoughts on marriage?"

My eyes widened. Shit. This was not where I expected the conversation to go—ever. I chose my words carefully. "I suppose. . . if I were to marry. . . I would like it to be to someone I loved, but I am far from that point."

"Of course." He tensed, and I knew he understood the rejection. He recovered quickly and threw his shoulders back with a lecherous grin. "I wanted to make sure you didn't think I was misleading you. You're not marriage material, what with your *proclivities*."

Ah, yes. The proclivities that had him screaming my name on regular occasions. "Perhaps that's so. But I'd rather die alone than grow old in a dull marriage with someone vapid and vain."

I flashed him my brightest smile and then left the library to return to the ball. I grabbed another glass of ratafia and found Deirdre's red hair in the crowd. She smiled at me. "There you are!"

"I needed some air. It's so crowded!"

Laurence avoided looking my way for the rest of the night. I wasn't sure what had prompted his question about marriage, but I was unphased and would ignore any future requests from him. Instead, I accepted dances from several men I did not yet know, certain one or two could help pass my time in England.

I soon found out what was on Laurence's mind. Toward the end of the night, Lord Smallclair made a speech. Evelyn stood next to him, her flushed face beaming. Her father thanked everyone for coming and gave his wishes for a happy holiday.

"I have an announcement to make. I am pleased to finally tell you that my eldest daughter has accepted an offer of marriage from Lord Davy's son, Laurence. The banns will be read this Sunday."

Everyone burst into applause. Laurence stepped forward from the crowd and took Evelyn's hand. Her eyes were alight, knowing that plenty of the young men and women in the crowd were envious of her.

"What a perfectly bland match," Deirdre whispered. I giggled.

The musicians struck up another lively tune, and the dancing recommenced. I stood against the back wall with my friend until my father came to fetch me with a wide grin on his face.

"I'm getting old, my dear. I should like to return home to bed." His words were slurred from too much punch.

"Of course, Father. Let me just offer my felicitations to Evelyn before we leave."

He nodded and swayed on his feet. "I'll meet you at the carriage."

I bade farewell to Deirdre and promised to come for dinner the following week. Then I made my way through the crowd to Evelyn. Agnes and Felicity were at her elbows, and they were snickering about something.

"Angelica! I hope you enjoyed our little fête."

I smiled. "It was lovely, Evelyn. Thank you so much for having me."

She looked surprised then skeptical at my sincerity. "Of course."

"Father and I are leaving. I wanted to congratulate you on your betrothal to Laurence. You must be so excited."

"Isn't it wonderful?"

"It is! Well, bonne chance, Evelyn. Agnes and Felicity, good evening." I stepped forward and kissed Agnes and Felicity on the cheek in turn. Then I took Evelyn's hand and leaned in for the obligatory kiss among faux friends.

"You're very lucky," I whispered in her ear. "Laurence is a wonderful lover. I've made certain he is skilled enough for your marriage bed."

I pulled away and winked. Evelyn let out a shrill shriek, drawing attention from those nearby. As I walked away, I heard her burst into tears, though no one seemed too bothered.

She could say nothing. Accusing me of impropriety was my word against hers, and it would reflect poorly on her betrothed. I wondered if she would confront Laurence, but I found I didn't really care. I had a skip to my step as I left the ballroom.

Revenge tasted sweeter than ratafia.

Chapter 14

T he fall and winter passed as had the previous months, though the second son of a marquess had taken an interest in me. He had a house in town, and I found that Molly and Charles's silence, as my maid and driver, was easily bought with pin money and sweets. At home, I continued my studies and corresponded frequently with naturalists across England, Scotland, and the Continent.

I was not happy, but I was content.

Father had taken me to Liverpool for my birthday to see the sea. The taste of salt on the air brought me a shimmer of joy. The joy was dimmed by my own foolish disappointment. Part of me had hoped my gift was that the *Juliet* had docked and he was returning me to Henry's arms.

Foolish, foolish girl, I chided myself for weeks after as I cried myself to sleep.

A few weeks after Christmas, I received an unexpected letter. Harold, our butler, brought me the letter while I was translating my report on bats into German because Father wanted to send it to a colleague. With his name on it, of course. Father was away on business, having taken on the role of master of the estate with relative ease, and Deirdre was to arrive shortly.

"A letter, Miss Spencer."

I held out my hand without looking up from the German dictionary. "Thank you, Harold. Will you send Miss Byrne in here when she arrives?"

"Of course."

I set the letter aside until I finished translating the paragraph. When I set my quill down and read the familiar, scribbled handwriting, my heart stopped. It couldn't be.

I turned it over and saw a nondescript seal. Carefully, I pulled apart the wax. My hands shook as I opened the parchment. I gasped as I read the first line.

Dear Hell,

I hope this letter reaches you. Getting letters across the ocean is a tricky business. It's the middle of September, and I'm sitting in a tavern in Kingston. I've ended my tenure on the Juliet *and now sail on board the HMS* Scepter. *I couldn't stay on the* Juliet. *Everywhere I looked, I was reminded of you.*

I often wish we had runaway together like we had dreamed. But your father was right. I had nothing to offer you. Love doesn't build a house or put food on the table. You have a chance for a real life, a good life, Hell. I pray that you find someone who loves you as much as I did but can give you a future.

You've changed me to my soul. I spend my earnings on new books now. I always loved reading, as you know. But now I cannot get enough. I miss you. I miss discussing books and philosophy with you. In all my days, I doubt if I'll ever meet another person as brilliant as you.

It's good you got away when you did. We've seen an uptick in piracy. The destruction of Port Royal last summer seems to have caused them to find new harbors for their villainy.

We're headed north soon for Halifax. Battles between our forces and the French are increasing. I'm scared, Hell. I'm not ready to die. And I'd never tell anyone but you this, but my loyalty waivers. What does a conflict between kings have to do with me and my brothers-at-arms?

There's a good chance I won't survive Nova Scotia. And if I do, I'd be off to my next location. Thought it pains me to write this, I want you to move on. Remember me with fondness, if you'd like. But leave me as a memory. I thank the Creator every day for the opportunity that our crossing paths afforded me.

I'll love you until my dying breath.

All my love,

Henry

My tears blurred the ink, forcing me to set the letter down to preserve this bit of Henry. I buried my face in my hands and let the sobs overtake me. It wasn't fair. We should have run when we had the chance. And now, Henry was off to a likely death. A brutal, bloody death.

"Angelica!"

Deirdre's soft, concerned voice was in my ear, and her arms were around my shoulders. I hadn't even heard her come in. Though I knew I should compose myself, I could only cry harder. She spoke to me gently, offering words of comfort. But there was nothing that would quell this drowning abyss inside me.

I don't know how long I wept in Deirdre's embrace. Slowly, the sobs turned to sniffles. My body and eyes ached, and I wanted nothing more than to crawl into bed and sleep for a month.

Deirdre knelt in front of me and took my hands in hers. "My friend, what has you so distraught?"

I told her. I told her everything. It hurt saying it out loud, but I could no longer keep the burden inside me. I felt lighter, somehow, after telling Deirdre. And she should have scoffed at me for my actions, for bedding a man so below my station before marriage. But she didn't.

"I'm sorry, Angelica. It isn't fair at all."

I sniffed. "No. And he could die. He could die at sea, and I'd never know. He could already be dead for all I know."

We didn't speak much more that afternoon, but Deirdre's quiet presence afforded me a sense of peace. We sat together on the settee in the library. I took out Henry's dagger from where I hid it in my skirts and stroked the handle, thinking of the day he gave it to me. It was hard to believe I'd had it over a year. I had turned one and twenty more than three months ago.

My friendship with Deirdre changed after that day. It was nothing tangible, nothing I could quite pinpoint, but we became more comfortable in each other's presence. Without her companionship, I doubt I could have honored Henry's wish, but slowly, I began to move on.

Chapter 15

My heart began to mend itself. I grieved him still, though I had found some semblance of contentment. But some days, the grief attacked me like a thief in a dark alley, catching me unaware and rendering me breathless.

I grieved, too, the sea. I had convinced Father to take me to Liverpool to usher in spring, just to taste the salt in the air and hear the crash of the waves. I had returned yesterday, and Father had stayed on another day for business, though he was close-lipped about its nature.

"Miss Byrne is here to see you, Miss Spencer," Harold said, jolting me from my latest project. I was writing up research on a species of trees Father and I had studied a few years ago along the coast of South America.

I looked at Harold and blinked. I wasn't expecting Deirdre until next week. "Oh."

"She seems quite distressed, madam."

"Send her in, please."

I straightened the parchment on the small desk and stoppered the inkwell, then stood and stretched while I waited for Harold to show Deirdre to the study. What had happened that had her coming to my home unannounced? She normally sent a note ahead with a servant.

Her freckled face was red and splotchy, and her summer-green eyes were swollen from crying. Despite that, I still thought she was one of the most beautiful things I'd ever laid eyes on. I held my arms out to her, and she crossed the room into my embrace.

"Deirdre, darling. What has happened?"

She hugged me tight, sniffling into my shoulder. "I don't even know where to begin."

I led her to the settee and sat next to her, taking her hands in mine. She hung her head, staring into her lap, and I waited for her to speak. Tears fell onto her blue brocade skirts. Deirdre was always so cheerful; my heart ached to see her distraught.

"Father called us into the parlor after breakfast. Just my brother, mother, and me." She paused and took a deep breath. "It seems that he has made a large share of bad investments and taken out loans to ease the financial burden. But the creditors are demanding payment."

"Oh, dear. How bad is it?"

She looked up at me, eyes glistening with tears. "We could lose everything. The lands, the manor."

"No."

"Aye. He's holding them at bay by giving them the house in London and some of our tenant lands, but there's still a considerable amount of debt." She sniffed. "They've given him half a year to pay off the balance, with pay due every month. He's let go all but the most essential of our staff."

How dreadful. Those people were now without a way to put food on their own tables. Some had lived at the Byrne residence and were now without a home. "Oh, Deirdre. I'm so sorry, my dear friend."

"That's not all." Her voice hitched, and the tears began to run down her face like raindrops on a window in a summer storm. I fought the urge to wipe them away. "My brother will likely inherit naught but our name. And me. . . Father wants to marry me off while I still have something of a dowry."

A strange twist in my gut made me grab my stomach. It felt like jealousy, but I couldn't think on that now. Deirdre had no interest in men, no interest in being a wife or a mother. To her, it was a fate worse than death.

"Must you?"

She looked away. "He's given me an ultimatum. Marriage or a nunnery. I have the spring and summer to decide. And. . ."

"What is it?"

She shook her head. "He thinks my marriage prospects will be better back home."

Back home. Ireland. Either way, I was losing my only friend in a few months. My own eyes burned as I blinked back the wetness. I couldn't bear life in Manchester without her. But I forced a small, reassuring smile.

"Well, we'll have to make it a wonderful half-year."

She tried to return my smile, only to break down in sobs. She leaned her head on my shoulder as she cried. I rubbed small circles on her back. "There now. I'm here."

What else could I say? I couldn't tell her it would all be fine. It wouldn't. And I wouldn't insult her by offering empty words and hollow promises.

"Angelica?"

I looked up to find my father standing in the doorway, back from his business in Liverpool. Deirdre raised her head, wiped her eyes, and stood to give him an awkward curtsy.

"Hello, Father."

His eyes were filled with concern. "Hello, my dearest. Deirdre, it is good to see you. Is everything all right?"

She tried to respond, but she hiccupped instead.

"May I tell him?" I whispered. She nodded. "Very good. Father, could I speak with you in the other room?"

"Of course. Deirdre, won't you stay for dinner?"

She nodded. "Thank you, Mister Spencer."

I led Father out of the study and into the parlor, where I told him what had befallen the Byrne family. He shook his head when he found out what Deirdre's father had done.

"Irresponsible. Byrne wasn't trained on running an estate because he didn't know he stood to inherit. He should have hired someone to manage the books for him."

"I agree. And poor Deirdre."

"Indeed." He patted my shoulder. "You're a good friend to her."

"I'm only trying to show her the same caliber of friendship as she has shown me."

Father smiled. "Why don't you ask if she'd like to stay the night? It's getting late. I can send Charles over with a message for her father."

"I will. Thank you, Father." I leaned up and kissed his cheek.

Deirdre was glad to stay the night. Her tears had begun to give way to anger at her father, and I couldn't blame her. At least we could offer her a small solace. My own father kept the dinner conversation light, regaling Deirdre with tales of our adventures, the most exciting of which had occurred before I was born.

Margaret and Molly prepared the room opposite mine for Deirdre, and I loaned her a spare nightgown and dressing gown. I was reading in my window seat when she knocked on my door.

"Come in."

The door creaked open. "I hope I'm not intruding."

"Not at all." I smiled at her and moved over to make room for her. Her long, red hair hung loosely over her shoulders. I couldn't help but reach out and touch the soft waves. "I've never seen your hair down."

"Oh, it's a mess, isn't it?"

"No, it's lovely."

She blushed and looked away. My heart thudded in my chest, and I didn't completely know why.

"What would you do, Angelica?" she asked in her thick Irish brogue. "Marry some man and bear a brood of children or swear off earthly comforts and devote your life to God?"

I sighed. "I'd make a terrible nun."

"You really would."

We laughed for a few minutes. I understood not wanting to marry, to be subservient to some man. I did not want to have children, either. All I wanted was to return to the sea and study the animals and plants I had not yet seen. But if Henry had showed up that moment and asked for my hand in marriage, I would have said yes in a heartbeat. Deirdre's revulsion to marriage was different, and I didn't quite understand.

"Deirdre?"

"Hm?"

"Why are you so opposed to marriage? If you found a nice, gentle man, it mightn't be terrible."

She wrung her hands and chewed her small pink lips. "I. . . I can't stand the thought of lying with a man."

"It's not so bad. In fact, it can be quite nice."

Her head snapped to mine, eyes wide. "I forgot you've done. . . that. With the sailor. Henry, yes?"

"Yes." Among others, though I kept that to myself.

"Have you heard from him?"

I shook my head. From what reports Father had heard, the battles in Nova Scotia weren't going well for our soldiers. Those who weren't claimed by fighting often fell victim to the frigid climate. I feared him dead.

"I'm sorry."

"It's all right." I smiled at her. "But you shouldn't fear lying with a man. It doesn't have to be unpleasant."

"It's not that. Well, it is that." She blew air out of her lips. "Never mind."

"Deirdre, you can tell me anything. You didn't judge me about bedding a man before marriage."

She shook her head. "No, I can't. It's not right."

I furrowed my brow, confused. "What's not?"

She shifted in the window seat to look out at the bright moon. The stars glittered in the night sky like millions of jewels. The reflecting moonlight made her eyes shine like green glass.

"I don't like men in that way."

I blinked. "In what way?"

"Like you do."

"Oh." I thought. Perhaps the nunnery would be the better option for her then. "Well, that's all right. If you don't experience attraction like that, then a convent—"

"No. I do, though. That's the problem."

"Do what?"

"Experience attraction, as you put it."

"But—"

"But not to men."

"I don't. . . .oh!" I had heard of such things, of course. I had grown up amongst sailors, and we often docked near dens of vice. More commonly, it was men lying with men. Buggery was rampant on ships when ports of call were few and far between. That was what the priests warned about. But I had never personally known someone with such proclivities, at least to my knowledge.

Deirdre wouldn't look at me, and I studied her profile in the dim candlelight of my bedroom. Suddenly, everything began to make sense. The way her beauty enraptured me. The twinge of jealousy when she mentioned marriage. How I thought I couldn't survive without her.

"Do you hate me?" Her voice was small.

I placed my hand over hers, and she turned toward me with her eyes like a rainforest, deep and vibrant. "No, Deirdre."

We gazed into each other's eyes for what felt like an eternity but could have been seconds. Then she leaned closer to me. She paused a finger's breadth from my lips, waiting for permission. I licked my own lips and closed the gap.

Kissing Deirdre was unlike kissing anyone else. Her skin was soft, not stubbled. Her lips were small but plump, not dry or cracked from the sun. She smelled of flowers and honey, her perfume tickling my nose.

The kiss didn't last long, although I could have stayed like that for hours. She giggled, and it was a sweet melody. I blushed and batted my eyes.

"I've wanted to do that since the moment I met you," Deirdre said.

It was my turn to giggle. "I'd like to do it again soon."

She kissed me again, this time with more tenacity. She swiped her tongue against mine. I ran my hand through her silky hair, pulling her closer. She tasted sweet, like the sherry we'd had after dinner.

When we parted, I was panting. Deirdre stood and kissed my hand. "Goodnight, Angelica. Sweet dreams."

Father wasn't at breakfast when I came downstairs the following morning. Neither was Deirdre, which gave me time to compose myself. I had lain in bed for hours, giddy from our kiss, my hands reaching under my nightrail to relieve the tension. I thought of it over and over in my mind until the memory was ingrained in my soul. No matter what happened, nothing could take that moment from me.

Harold entered the dining room with a pitcher of water to fill my cup. "Good morning, Miss Spencer."

"Good morning, Harold."

"You're beaming, which is unusual at this hour."

I blushed. It was true I wasn't pleasant in the mornings. "I slept well. And it's a beautiful autumn day."

"Indeed it is."

"Where's Father?"

Harold adjusted the place setting across from mine until he deemed it perfect. "Sir George ate early and left to take care of some business. He'll return before lunch."

Father and all his mysterious business of late. I hoped something wasn't wrong, particularly something like the Byrne family was experiencing. Although, I knew Father wouldn't be so reckless.

Deirdre came down for breakfast in yesterday's dress. Molly must have done her hair for her this morning, as it was up in a style I often wore. She gave me a small smile and her pale cheeks tinged with pink.

We didn't speak much through the meal, but we exchanged several smiling glances. It was thrilling, having a secret to share with Deirdre. I knew she, too, was happy about what had transpired under the moonlight last night.

After breakfast, we took a walk around the grounds. We strolled arm-in-arm. The few trees that dotted the estate were turning shades of gold and red.

"Have you only been with Henry?" Deirdre asked.

There was no use in lying, not after last night. "No."

"I thought as much."

"Does it bother you?"

"No."

The crisp breeze grazed my face and ruffled our skirts, covering my skin in gooseflesh. "Let's turn out of this wind." We began to walk back toward the manor. "I see some of the local men at balls or other events, but it's hard to get away from watchful eyes."

"I can imagine. My brother is always romping about with the maids. Mother has caught him a few times."

I laughed. I could imagine that. Where Deirdre was timid and shy, Seamus was boisterous and full of confidence.

"I had a short-lived affair with Laurence."

Deirdre stopped and turned to face me, unhooking our arms. "Laurence Davy?"

"Yes."

"But he's such a—"

"An arse. He is. But it meant nothing. He approached me after we fenced. I thought it would be a good way to get back at Evelyn."

She doubled over in laughter. "Oh, how I wish Evelyn knew! I'd love to see her face."

"She does." I told her what I had said to Evelyn at last year's Christmas ball. "I will cherish her appalled shriek until my dying breath."

She shook her head. "I envy your confidence."

"My arrogance, you mean?" I bumped her shoulder with mine. I knew I was more than a little prideful. Modesty did not become me.

But Deirdre saw it differently. "You don't care what anyone thinks. It's refreshing. I've spent my life among people like Evelyn. Even my father—we're only in this mess because he felt he needed to belong amongst his peers. But you—you're unapologetically yourself."

I bowed my head. "Thank you, Deirdre."

We walked back to the manor and settled into the study. Deirdre found a book of plays by the Bard, and I returned to my notes from the day before. It was a comfortable silence, one I could grow used to.

Father returned before lunch, as Harold had said. He had a grin as he settled into his favorite armchair. "I have good news. At least, I think it's good."

I turned to face him. Deirdre set her book down. "What is it, Father?"

"I have just been to Deirdre's home and spoken with her father. I offered to allow you to stay here for a while under my care. He is under a great deal of stress, and this should ease some financial strain until he can figure things out. If you're willing, of course, Deirdre."

We looked at each other. Her face was alight, and I knew mine must be the same. "I would like that very much, sir. Thank you."

"Stay as long as you like. I'll send Charles over to fetch your things this afternoon. My home is yours."

Chapter 16

D eirdre and I settled into a pleasant routine of stolen morning kisses, afternoon walks, and leisurely evenings reading. I read essays by philosophers and scientists and continued to correspond with the naturalist Maria Sybilla Merian. I liked her more with each letter. She had moved to a religious community that believed in total equality of the sexes.

Father began to take Deirdre and me to salons to listen to other scientists and philosophers, and some even allowed me to speak.

Deirdre, on the other hand, spent her time reading the Bible, looking for some wisdom or guidance about the path her life must take.

"Perhaps those aren't my only options," she mused one morning over breakfast. It was just the two of us; Father had ventured into town for some purpose he wouldn't disclose.

"Oh? What are you thinking, my dear?"

Deirdre wrung her hands and glanced at me from the corner of her eyes.

"What, Deirdre?"

"I've heard tell of unwed maidens living together and earning an honest wage through work."

For a moment, I thought she meant prostitution, such was my experience in the New World. But Deirdre would not consider that honest, and there was the slight issue of her general disgust with the male form. I waited for her to continue and slurped my porridge. She wrinkled her nose at my lack of manners but said nothing. How unusual for her not to chide me, I thought. A welcome change, but unusual.

She sighed. "Perhaps we could ask our fathers to buy us a cottage or use our dowries, or rather, your dowry and whatever pittance is left of mine. We could be seamstresses or something."

I laughed. "Seamstresses? No, thank you. I can mend a tear badly, and that is it." My cheeks flushed as I remembered the time Henry had removed his shirtsleeves in the passageway outside my cabin after I had sliced his arm.

"Well, it doesn't need to be sewing. We could bake or raise chickens and sell the eggs. Do the washing."

"What a horrid, dull life that would be!" I crinkled my nose. "Singularly unfulfilling."

Deirdre looked crestfallen. "Well, what is it you plan to do with your life?"

"I've told you. I plan to return to sea to continue my studies. Father will get tired of life in England, eventually."

"And what of me?"

Attempting to delay my response, I raised my cup of water to my lips. All I saw in my future was sea and sun and sand. Interesting creatures and fascinating flora. And there, behind the jungle thicket of my dreams, was the tiny bud of hope that my true love had survived and we would meet again. Without Henry, I had never considered another person in the next chapters of my life.

"You could come with me," I finally said.

"I hate the sea. It smells. Ships are terribly uncomfortable and foul."

"You get used to it. Think of all the wonderful places there are to explore! And there is nothing like the feeling of sailing upon the open water. All you've seen is the channel between England and Ireland, which is rather dreary."

"I don't want to explore places."

My mouth gaped like a fish. How could someone not wish to explore? The world was so vast. There were so many corners yet unturned. I would be filled with regret if I died without an honest attempt to discover as much as I could.

Instead of saying so, I reached to pat her hand and changed the subject. "Well, it's not as if we have to decide today. Shall we take a stroll?"

"Very well." She smiled.

The day turned around, and we had returned to our normal, affectionate selves by the time Father returned from town that afternoon. The sun was high in the sky, and whatever was happening in the kitchen downstairs smelled delicious. Deirdre had gone upstairs to rest and pray her rosary while I sat in the study, transcribing one of my old journals onto fresh parchment with a legible hand.

"Angelica, I've returned."

I turned and grinned at Father. He removed his hat and dusted off his greying hair. "Welcome home. How was town?"

Father waved a hand. "The usual. Crowded with a stink. What are you working on?"

"Notes from Cuba. Attempting to put them all in one language in some way that makes sense."

"You did acquire my terrible note-taking habits," he said with a grin. "We're having a guest for dinner, Angelica."

I had turned back to squinting at my notes and asked with only mild curiosity, "Who?"

"A young man I've been corresponding with of late. He's a passing interest in the insects of central England."

"Ah." I didn't particularly care about the insects of central England, but I did care about the ferns of the Spanish Main. "What do you think I meant by 'las hojas: vertes and SRD?"

"SRD?" Father cocked his head. "Serrated?"

"Oh yes! Green serrated leaves. In three different languages." I laughed and scribbled it down on the fresh parchment.

"He's the youngest son of a baron. Cambridge educated."

"Who?"

He sighed, exasperated. "Our dinner guest."

"Of course. Insect man."

"Angélica! Would you please pay attention?"

When I turned around, Father was pinching the bridge of his nose. It was my turn to sigh. I set down my quill and folded my arms. "I'm listening."

"As I was saying, he has studied the insects near Birmingham as a hobby for some years. He has a breadth of knowledge about the sciences in general. I think you'll like him."

Something hung in the air, unsaid. I narrowed my eyes and studied my father's face, trying to determine what he wasn't disclosing. "I see. And you've invited him here?"

"Yes, he was in town for a few days."

We stared at each other, each waiting for the other to speak. What was I to say to this? Suspecting this was more than a fellow nature enthusiast come to discuss beetles, I waited for Father to continue.

He patted his leg, one of his nervous tics. "Yes, well. Since we have a guest coming, a peer at that, this will be a formal dinner. If you could have Molly. . ." He flapped a hand around his face and above his head. "No loose plaits and the like. Deirdre, too."

I gritted my teeth to keep from letting out a sound of annoyance. "Very well. I shall set my work aside, as it will take some time to dress to your liking."

"Thank you, my dearest daughter." He smiled, and his voice was both tender and sardonic.

Coiffed, powdered, and tied into lovely but unnecessary layers of fabric, Deirdre and I descended the stairs to await our guest in the drawing room hours later. Deirdre reached up to adjust my lace fontage and gave me a coquettish smile. "You look lovely," she whispered.

"We both do." I winked at her and resisted the urge to plant a soft kiss on her painted lips.

Minutes later, Harold announced the arrival of Father's acquaintance. "May I present Mr. Rupert Stanley, son of the Lord Green."

We stood on ceremony, and Deirdre and I gave a small curtsy. Father made our introductions, and I studied the man. He was young, perhaps three or four years older than myself. He had the body of a spoiled noble, with weak arms and the chest of a sapling rather than a strong oak. His hair was hidden under a wig and hat.

"How do you do, Miss Spencer?" He bowed low to kiss my hand, his gaze lingering on his way back to standing. He grinned as though he liked what he saw. Well, of course he would. He was a man with eyes. I, on the other hand, was less than impressed.

"Charmed to meet you, Mr. Stanley," I replied in my best impersonation of a woman who was indeed charmed.

Dinner was not an altogether unpleasant affair. Mr. Stanley did seem quite interested in our studies and discoveries. He flashed several tentative smiles at me and complimented my insights, though his tone was patronizing as he did.

"Sir George," he said after dinner as we took our cordial in the drawing room. "You have raised a fascinating and lovely daughter."

I rolled my eyes and held my glass up to the servant for more drink. I might as well have been invisible.

Father smiled. "Thank you, sir. She is my pride and joy. Though I cannot take credit for her loveliness. She received that from her mother, God rest her soul."

Briefly, I wondered what sort of courting customs my mother's people had. It had to be better than this stilted awkwardness. After all, she was allowed to marry an Englishman of her choice. I nodded politely as their conversation continued, speaking when spoken to, as was my place.

Father dismissed us shortly thereafter. Mr. Stanley rose when Deirdre and I did. He bade Deirdre farewell and kissed my hand once again. "Until we meet again, madam."

I smiled, as it was more polite than saying there was no chance in all of Heaven or Hell.

"Perhaps I can call upon you soon? Or write to you?"

"Perhaps. Goodnight, Mr. Stanley. It was a pleasure."

"The pleasure was all mine."

Of course it was. Upstairs, Deirdre and I fell into a fit of laughter. Father's attempt at matchmaking was both obvious and absurd. Deirdre kissed me goodnight and went to say her prayers, as our coiffing had interrupted her afternoon Hail Marys.

My curiosity got the better of me, and I tiptoed downstairs. The drawing room was empty, but I heard voices in the study. The door was open, blessedly. I stood on the side of the door frame, listening, careful not to let my shadow catch in the firelight from the room beyond.

"She's a bright girl, Spencer. And lovely. She would be the talk of Birmingham society."

Father chuckled. "She is both of those things. Sharp-witted, though I should warn you that she is also sharp-tongued at times."

"Which only adds to her charm, sir."

Mr. Stanley's voice had begun to grate on me. I'd prefer Laurence Davy over this man.

"She is knowledgeable of society's rules and traditions, as well. She knows all the proper forms of address and protocol for various events. You can ask Lord Smallclair, if you'd like. She behaved with the utmost propriety at his Christmas ball."

I put my hand over my mouth to stifle a giggle. If fucking Laurence and whispering what I did to the Earl's daughter was the utmost propriety, then I was indeed proper.

"And her dowry is secure?"

Rage bubbled inside me. I stared down the length of my dress and found that I was not, in fact, a brood mare.

"Yes, the number I wrote to you. It's all in order."

"And her virtue is still intact?"

There was a pause, and I imagined Father covering up a sputter with a drink from his glass. "Yes, of course," he lied.

"Good, good. Then I should like to call upon her soon and begin courting her."

The rage overtook me then. Before Father could respond, I barged into the room, seeing red that did not come from the fire.

"Angelica!" Father exclaimed.

"He lies!" I shouted.

"Angelica! Be quiet!"

Stanley stood and looked back and forth between my father and me. "Spencer, what is the meaning of this?"

A stricken expression bloomed on Father's face. "Er, she is hesitant to marry is all—"

"Well, that's true enough. But he lies about the former. My virtue is not intact. Not in the slightest."

Stanley gaped. "Sir? Did you know this?"

Father opened his mouth, but I cut him off. "He did. Caught me himself in the hold of a ship with a lieutenant. But only after we'd been doing the same for months, right under his nose."

"Angelica! Desist!" Father's face was purple. "This is most improper!"

I scoffed. I was just getting started. "He warned you of my sharp tongue, did he? Well, I fucked that lieutenant for five months before Father dragged me away to this god-forsaken country, hoping to cover up the scandal by the ocean."

"I should go. Sir, your daughter is most contumacious! You must get her under control if you wish to marry her off to anyone. Perhaps an elderly widowed gentry would take her in her ruined state."

He fled the room.

Father and I stood in a standoff, as if we were about to duel. I wondered if I should bow before I continued my tirade, but in my pause, Father took the offensive.

"Foolish, tempestuous child! Do you know what you have done?"

I scoffed. "Saved myself from another one of your attempts to control my life? Told the truth to the boring son of a baron?"

He pulled at his hair. "I brought you here to protect your reputation. But now, thanks to your impetuousness, the entirety of the peerage and landed gentry will know that you are ruined!"

His words stung as if he had slapped me. "Ruined? Is that what you think of me?"

"It's what society thinks!"

Tears welled in my eyes, which made me angrier. "To hell with society! I am not ruined. I am not a piece of parchment covered in spilled ink." I wiped my eyes. My next shout came out as half-scream, half-sob. "I am a person with thoughts and feelings and dreams. I'm smarter than half the peerage combined! This is not the life I want. It is not the life I choose."

Father's face had softened during my monologue. "I know you are all of those things. I'm proud of you for all those things, but Angélica, that is not what the world cares about. I won't always be here to protect you. The law would leave you with nothing."

"I'd rather have nothing."

He shook his head. "As a baronet, my position opens doors for you. But when I'm gone, the estate passes to some distant cousin from London. I've never met him. He would even control your dowry. He could marry you off to whomever he chose or cast you out to beg for scraps."

"Take me back to the New World, then. Please, Father. We could take our money and live faraway from all this nonsense." I fell to my knees, not even caring that I begged.

"Don't you see, darling? Even there, without me, you have nothing. You are the property of your nearest male relative by law."

"Chattel."

He put his hands out. "I cannot change the laws of god and men."

"Then don't die." I folded my arms and pouted my lips, feeling like a child who did not want to do her studies.

He smiled. "If only I had that power, my dearest daughter."

I rubbed my arms and shifted my weight. As the rush of fury faded, I was left feeling depleted. Tired.

"I will shelve the matter for now. We shall soon know if Mr. Stanley is inclined to share the events of the evening. Let us allow any possible scandal to fade. Perhaps we can even discuss returning to find a suitable match in the New World, someone who shares your love of science."

I gave him a partial smile. "Where my reputation does not precede me."

"Yes."

Nodding, I lowered my defenses. I knew, in his own way, he was doing what he thought best for me, though I was still angry. "Goodnight, Father."

"Goodnight." He patted my shoulder as I walked past him. When I reached the doorway, I heard him say in a low voice, "I don't think you're a ruined piece of parchment."

Chapter 17

Father kept a close eye on the gossip rags over the next few weeks. It seemed that Mr. Stanley had better things to do than spread the word about my lack of virginity. Things, too, improved with Deirdre. We had no more discussions about our future together, looking no more than a fortnight ahead at any time.

One rare, sunny day, Deirdre and I sat on a tree log in the woods at the edge of my father's land. We were far from prying eyes and enjoyed the freedom to embrace and kiss in the warm sun. It was warm enough that if I closed my eyes, I could imagine that we were somewhere in the Caribbean. If I imagined hard enough, I could pretend the heat from the body next to me was Henry.

"Angelica?" My name in Deirdre's thick brogue pulled me reluctantly from my daydream.

"Hmm?"

"I've been reading the Bible."

I opened my eyes. "That's not unusual for you."

"Well, no." She blushed. "But I've been reading it for guidance on a particular issue, and. . ."

When she showed no sign of continuing, I prodded her with my elbow. "Go on."

"The Bible has laws about men not lying with men as they would with a woman."

I blanched. "So I've heard." And read myself, though I did not say so. Father had me read the damn thing at age twelve to discuss. In Latin and English, of course. Then Spanish when I turned fourteen.

"Well, I've read the Scripture in its entirety since staying with you, and I have found nothing to suggest. . ." She giggled and blushed an even deeper shade of scarlet. "Nothing that says that women shan't lie with women as they would a man."

She had my full attention. I leaned forward eagerly. Our kisses had grown increasingly heated as of late, but I had not pushed her to do more. I wasn't even sure quite what to do myself, but I was more than willing to experiment and test my hypotheses. "Go on."

"Well, it seems to me that. . . if it were something God cared about, He would have put it in his Holy Word."

I couldn't care less about her logic, but I had to tread carefully if I wanted this conversation to have the outcome I so desired. To act interested, I cocked my head, "That seems. . . reasonable. We do not have seed to waste, as men do."

She lit up, her blush fading only slightly. "Do you think?"

"Yes. What are you trying to say, Deirdre?"

She looked down and fidgeted with the pleats in her petticoat. "Just that I think that I want. . ."

I placed two fingers under her chin and raised her head to look at me. She trembled under my touch. "Continue, please," I whispered.

"I want to. . . do that. . . with you."

My lips curled into a small smile. "Do what?"

"L-lie with you."

My own heart thudded, but I forced myself to remain calm. I wanted her to say it explicitly. I wanted to know for certain that she was consenting to this, and I also wanted to hear the forbidden words fall from her smooth, plump, chaste lips.

"How?" I asked. She tried to look away, but I shook my head. "Tell me how you want to lie with me."

"As if. . . as if one would lie with a man." She licked her lips nervously, and heat flooded my core. "Without. . . without clothes."

I captured her lips in a kiss. "Come to me tonight, when the house is quiet."

The day passed too slowly, and the tension between us crackled like the air before a storm. When night fell, I paced my room in a silk dressing gown over my nightrail. If Deirdre were a man, I would have no nervousness, no hesitation. And though I had dreamed often of this, wondered whether her freckles extended beyond the bounds of her clothes, what she sounded like if I touched her the way I liked to touch myself, I was not confident about how to proceed.

Just after the clock struck eleven o'clock, a gentle knock sounded on my door then the knob turned. We had long passed the point of waiting for entry at night. Deirdre entered the room. Her hair flowed in long, waving tresses, framing her in flames. In the candlelit room, her eyes glittered. She worried her lower lip. Wrapped in an emerald dressing gown, she reminded me of the Gaelic stories of fae queens.

She closed the door behind her gently and locked it. We were alone in this wing of the manor, two floors above the servants' quarters and a floor above and a wing away from Father's rooms. No one would hear us were they to wake.

I smiled, trying to ease her nerves and mine. Deirdre smiled back, her head slightly ducked, as she stepped further into the room.

"I don't know how to start," she whispered.

Stepping closer to her to close the distance between us, I said, "When I've lain with men, I've always started with kissing."

I reached for her hands and pulled her toward me. She was taller than me, though not by much. A lock of her hair had fallen in her eyes, and I brushed it away. She shivered.

"Kissing is something I know." She closed her eyes and lowered her lips to mine. Our kiss started slow and tentative, like it had been months ago when this affair began. But knowing what tonight could bring, I could not long resist deepening the kiss and pulling her warm, soft body against mine.

I ran a hand over her shoulder and grazed the outline of her breast, causing her to gasp breathlessly against my mouth. "Is this—?"

"Yes." Her voice was quiet but certain. "Yes."

We continued to kiss as our hands began to explore each other over our nightclothes. When my fingers reached the ties of her nightgown, I paused, but she did not stop me. Within seconds, I had the emerald silk pooling around our feet, leaving her in her thin summer shift and nothing else.

The outline of her ample breasts sent heat pooling in my core. I stepped back to take her in. In the firelight, I could just see the shadows of her taut nipples. I licked my lips and began to work kisses down her neck and chest, over her shift, until I took one fabric-covered nub in my mouth. She moaned and grabbed my shoulders as I teased her with my tongue and teeth. When I pulled away, she sighed. I grinned at the wet spot on the cotton.

"Perhaps we should. . . continue to disrobe?" she said. Her confidence was building, and it sent jolts of fire through my veins. Deirdre, normally so reserved, so proper, so self-deprecating, was stepping into her own. Unfortunately, her authentic self did not fit with society's laws.

I nodded and removed my own gown, which left us both in our shifts. My hands trembled as I began to lift mine over my head. Gooseflesh covered my arms and legs, despite the fire roaring in the corner.

When I looked up, Deirdre still wore her shift. She gaped at me.

"What is it?" I asked, suddenly self-conscious.

"Sometimes, when we kiss. . . or when I've imagined this"—she gestured wildly—"the strangest thing happens. I feel a wetness betwixt my thighs. I often thought I had started my courses at first. But now, seeing you as God made you, I feel the most wetness I've felt. Is that strange?" Her face was flushed.

A warmth spread over me, different from the heat of desire. Is that how Henry had felt with my innocent questions the first time? "Not strange at all. Quite normal."

Her eyes lit up. "Really? What does it mean?"

"It means you are excited about this. That I excite you."

She giggled. "You do excite me. You are lovely, Angelica."

"Let me see you, Deirdre. Please." Or I else I would rip that cloth from her body with my bare hands.

"Oh, yes. That. I was distracted."

I laughed and watched as she removed her shift. Her timidness crept in again, and she made to cover herself with her arms. I grabbed her hands. "No. Do not be shy."

She nodded. We stood there, for a time, nude and studying each other's bodies, and it was one of the most intimate experiences of my life. Her freckles extended onto her large, heavy breasts, ending before the pink skin at the tips. Her belly was soft and curved, her hips wide and dusted with the brown freckles that covered her arms and legs. Between her thighs, a thick patch of rust-colored hair covered her most sacred place.

I swallowed hard. "Beautiful."

She ducked her head but grinned. "What do we do now? How do we proceed? I know nothing of any type of joining."

"Well, some of this is new to me, as we have the same anatomy." In my nervousness, I had slipped into naturalist mode. I took a deep breath. "I could show you how I touch myself?"

Deirdre's eyes widened. "You can touch yourself? How?"

"Here. Let me show you."

I turned and climbed onto the large four-poster bed. The coverlet had already been drawn back for sleeping. I plumped the pillows at the head and leaned back against them, bending my knees and spreading my thighs. Deirdre stood at the foot of the bed, watching with curiosity and desire.

My heart thudded like a thousand drums in my ears as I smoothed my hand over my breasts and stomach, over the dark hair. My back arched involuntarily as my finger breached the wet, hot silk. Deirdre moaned, causing a pulse deep inside of me. Slowly, I circled the bud of pleasure, never taking my eyes from Deirdre. I moved in response to her reactions, trying new things to make her gasp and sigh and groan. It didn't take long until I began to reach the summit. The exposition added a new layer to my euphoria. My head fell backward, and I dropped over the edge as completion quaked through me.

"Will you show me?"

I opened my eyes to find Deirdre standing next to me, a hand hovering over my body, waiting for an invitation. "Yes."

I shifted over on the bed to make room for her. When she was comfortable, I took her breasts in my hands and thumbed the stiff peaks, which elicited a shocked squeak. But she nodded when I looked at her inquiringly. Unable to resist the siren call of those breasts any longer, I buried my face between them, running one hand over her round stomach.

"Every pillow I ever encounter from this day will pale in comparison to your body," I whispered as I moved my mouth along the side of her right breast to find her nipple. She writhed as I sucked and nibbled and licked, going from one delicious pink treat to the other.

"I want... Oh, my!"

I smiled as I pulled away from her bosom. "What do you want, Deirdre?"

"T-touch me."

I knelt before her spread legs and looked at the glistening cleft. A wet spot was growing on the blanket beneath her, leaving no doubt in my mind that she wanted this. Whatever regret or shame she might feel tomorrow was not in this room, not in this moment between us.

With one finger, I spread her open. She threw an arm over her face and babbled incoherent exclamations as I began to explore her womanhood. I found how she liked to be rubbed in small circles. Her hips ground against the bed, and her wetness throbbed. I used my free hand to breach her with one finger, then curled it as I continued to care for the pulsing bud.

I felt her clench before her body shook as she found her first climax, but I did not stop my ministrations as it worked its way through her. Only when her eyes opened and her arms fell to her sides, did I stop.

She laughed, a deep, rolling chuckle. "That was incredible."

"If you like that, then you'll love this."

"What?"

I lay on my stomach in front of her and pushed her thighs further apart. She smelled both sweet and earthy. She shivered as my breath grazed her sensitive, wet flesh. When my tongue touched her, she let out a small shout. I looked up the length of her body, waiting for her approval to continue. She pushed my head down in response.

Deirdre tasted like saltwater with a hint of something honey-like, and it was divine. If I never ate another dessert but her, I would not want for anything. I explored different motions with my lips and tongue, paying close attention to her body's response and adjusting to keep her in the throes of pleasure. Then I added two fingers, thrusting them in and out of her. Her hands grasped at the blankets. Her hips lifted from the bed. I did not stop until I tasted her culmination.

I lay beside her as she caught her breath, connecting the freckles on her flushed chest with my finger. She gazed at me dreamily. "I think I saw heaven."

With a giggle, I replied, "I certainly tasted it."

"Let me do you now, Angelica."

I rolled onto my back and turned my head toward her. "You'll find no protest from me."

Deirdre took her time exploring my body as if she were the naturalist in the room, not me. I relaxed under her touch as she traced my body with her hands and planted soft kisses on my collarbone, my breasts, my stomach, my womanly hair.

When she parted the space below with her fingers, I felt a type of arousal I had never experienced. Her touch was soft, gentle, like a light breeze on a summer day. There was no urgency as she discovered the parts of me that made me cry out. She was a quick learner and soon, I felt myself reaching another summit, though this time it was more of a leisurely walk up a hill than scaling a mountain. And then I rolled down it with the same sort of pleasure I'd had as a child rolling down sloping hills. No less satisfying than any other time, but different.

Deirdre yawned as she collapsed on the bed next to me, which made me yawn in response. My lids were heavy as I stared at her, admiring how her red locks fanned around her on the pillows.

"I want to do more." She yawned again.

I chuckled. My eyes struggled to remain open. "We will have other nights."

"I suppose I should return to my room.

"Probably for the best."

I shivered when she pried herself from the bed, her absence leaving me cold. As I watched her dress, it occurred to me that though I had lain with several men and now Deirdre, I had always gone to sleep by myself. The thought made me sad, and it was Henry's face I missed in that moment. Tears burned the corners of my tired eyes. Would I have to marry to share a bed with someone? Mr. Stanley's face appeared unbidden in my mind, and I shuddered. Sleeping with someone seemed so much more intimate than making love. Vulnerable. I could never do that with just anyone.

Deirdre whispered goodnight, leaving me somehow feeling more alone than I'd felt since I left the *HMS Juliet* two years prior.

At first, Deirdre and I experienced a rejuvenated energy in our companionship as we continued to explore our desires with each other. But soon autumn came, and as the leaves changed, so did our relationship. Her date by which she must decide her fate loomed ever closer.

One night, she straddled me on the bed after a vigorous lovemaking session. "Come with me, Angelica."

I groaned. "I've already come three times, Deirdre. I am truly spent."

She swatted playfully. "No, silly! Come with me to the nunnery!"

I sat up, forcing her off me in the process. "It's the convent, then?"

She shrugged. "I cannot marry a man. I do not want that life." She grinned a toothy smile, her face lit up. "But if you came with me, then. . ."

"Do you really believe nuns would allow us to continue this?"

Again, she shrugged. "I don't know. But at least we'd be together."

Acid burned up my throat. Why was I afraid of that statement? I shook my head, hoping to dissuade further discussion of the matter. "I am not Catholic, Deirdre."

"But you could become it! You don't have any loyalty to the Anglicans, do you?"

"Not particularly." I rubbed my face. It was too late at night for this conversation. "Deirdre, I'm not going to become a nun."

"It's not so different from the Church of England, you'll see!"

I looked at her. Her eyes were wide with hope, and I had to be the one to put out that spark. "I don't believe in it."

"In what?"

"All of it. How can you be certain who is correct? If the Calvinists are, then our places in Heaven are already chosen. If the Catholics are, I need to pray the rosary and confess my sins. What of the Anglicans? The Lutherans? What of all those who do not worship your Christ? Your own people who secretly worship the old gods, for instance."

Deirdre's mouth dropped, stricken. "That is blasphemy, Angelica!"

"Says who? Who has the right to determine it? The Pope? The King?"

"Do you. . . do you not believe in Christ?" Her voice was strained, as if she were in physical pain.

"I'm certain a man like him existed once." I scoffed. "We are all of us the bastard children of a God who spilt his seed in a whore and fucked off, never to be seen again."

"You cannot mean that! If you would just read the Scriptures—"

"I have. Every word of them. And I've read the Moslem holy book and some sacred scriptures from the Orient and the Mughal empire. I've read every great English, Italian, and French philosopher."

Deirdre scrambled off the bed and began to put her nightclothes back on. "Those are not the word of God, though!"

"There are those who believe only their book is the true word of God." I shook my head. "We will not agree on this, Deirdre. Please don't try."

She looked at me, her emerald eyes glistening in the candle and fire-lit room. "Tell me the truth, Angelica. Was there any version of a future in which you saw us together? Some boat in the New World even?"

I closed my eyes, picturing my future, full of sun and sea. Freedom. If I saw anyone by my side, it was Henry. But he was certainly dead, as I never heard from him after he went to Halifax.

I hesitated. Deirdre was a friend and a lover, but she was not the other half of my soul. "No, Deirdre. There wasn't."

Chapter 18

AUTUMN 1695

The day Deirdre left dawned grey and dismal. The dark clouds outside my window swelled with rain that would not fall.

Much like my tears.

After the hurt had healed from our fight, we understood where we stood with each other. We had made an agreement to honor our special kind of love until she left. It was love, but it was like the summer: bound by time with a definite end. Her love for her Christ was evergreen, as was my love for Henry. But she had still left a mark upon my soul, a kiss of the sun upon my face. We captured every moment we could together.

I had cried in the black hours of midnight for a week. I cried as Deirdre and I made love one last time the night before, our fingers and lips moving in slow, tender strokes, trying to capture each other in our memory. But I woke this morning numb, on the precipice of a fall into utter despair.

As I sat in the window seat, I ran my fingers over the blade that Henry had given me, the edge sharp against my skin. Since Deirdre had arrived months before, I had stopped wearing it in my skirts every day. How naïve I had been a to think I could choose my own destiny.

Foolish. Childish.

"Angelica?"

I turned away from the window and forced a smile. "Yes, darling?"

"Lace me up?"

I nodded and crossed the room to where Deirdre stood. I took the laces of her stays in each hand and pulled, taking my time to make sure they were tight and even. When I had finished, I ran my fingers over her exposed collarbone that was dotted with freckles, committing each to my memory.

I looked up and saw her green eyes full of tears. She took my hands and squeezed hard. I placed my forehead against hers, breathing in her sweet scent for the last time. When her lips met mine, I poured my soul into our kiss. Deirdre tasted like warmth and home and all that was good in the world. She was never for me.

A knock at the door forced us apart. Molly's voice was muffled as she told us it was time.

"We'll be downstairs in a moment," I called, my voice thick.

"Yes, Miss Spencer."

I wiped Deirdre's tears away with my thumbs. "You'll always be a part of me."

"You were my truest friend, Angelica. I will pray for your happiness every day, until my dying breath."

I had no doubt that she would, though I doubted whether I deserved it after hurting her so badly.

Deirdre's father was in the sitting room with my father and Harold, our butler. Deirdre greeted her father with a kiss on each cheek then turned to mine, curtsied, and thanked him for his hospitality the last year. Father grinned and kissed her cheek.

"The pleasure was mine. Thank you for bringing such joy to my daughter. You'll be missed."

I had to stifle a snort. Father would never understand how much joy was leaving me today. My cheeks were hot with a flash of anger. This wasn't fair. Not to Deirdre, to lock her away in some convent away from her family and friends. Not to me, who only wanted to be happy.

Charles entered the sitting room at that moment. "Miss Byrne's belongings are in the carriage."

"Thank you, Charles," my father said.

I inhaled deeply and rolled my shoulders back, determined not to break. Father and I followed Deirdre and her father outside. Thunder rumbled overhead, and the musty scent of a storm filled the bitter winter air. Deirdre pulled me into a long embrace, kissed my cheek, and climbed into the carriage without a word. I swallowed the tears that threatened to fall.

Father put his arm around my shoulders as we watched the carriage roll down the road away from the manor. I watched until the carriage became a black speck on the horizon, carrying away my only friend. My eyes stung in the frigid air, but I stayed in place until the carriage had disappeared from sight.

"Come with me, Angélica," Father whispered in my mother's native tongue.

For want of anything better to do, I followed him inside to the sitting room. He opened a cabinet and pulled out a bottle of a golden-brown liquid then filled two small glasses. I sat on the settee when he handed me my glass. I sniffed. Rum from the Caribbean.

The memory of the first night I drank rum came rushing back. My last night with Henry. Another day of utter powerlessness.

I cried and drank all morning. After lunch, I drank more, my father a silent companion who refilled my glass when it emptied. By dinner, the rum had worked its magic. The two of us laughed and joked and downed more of the smoky sweet elixir until I fell asleep on the sofa.

Yuletide that year was somber. The house felt empty without Deirdre. Cold. Father tried to be cheerful for me, which I appreciated. But in every room, I could see Deirdre and her bright smile. It was like living with a ghost. The little sleep I managed was restless, and my dreams were of storms at sea, often of Henry or Deirdre falling overboard.

We attended no holiday parties, for which I was grateful. The Campbells had invited us to their annual fête, but the thought of facing Evelyn and Laurence without Deirdre was unbearable. Instead, Father and I spent every evening with chalices of wine and new books. By the new year, our home felt warm again, but my heart was still cold.

Chapter 19

"Ow!"

I glanced up from the essay I was translating to see what my father had exclaimed about. He was dissecting a large hawk he'd hunted the day before to add its bones to his specimen collection.

"What happened?"

"Nicked myself. Nothing major." Father wiped his bloodied finger on his trousers and went back to his dissection on his desk.

I wrinkled my nose. "Is that your blood or the hawk's?"

He shrugged. "Not sure. Both, probably."

"Pour some rum on it."

"It's barely a scratch, Angelica, not a battle wound."

"Why didn't you bleed the damn thing first? The maids hate it when you get blood everywhere."

"It's harder to see the veins."

I rolled my eyes and turned my eyes back to my essay on rodent teeth morphology. Sometimes, Father was little more than a child with his excitement over living things. I came by my interest naturally.

It had been three months since Deirdre left. The days were getting longer and lighter, both in nature and in my heart. She sent a letter when she arrived at the convent to let me know she had arrived. I hadn't written back yet as I hadn't the heart, but I thought I would be ready soon.

Once again, I threw myself into my studies. I had neglected my Dutch during the year Deirdre had been here. I spent two hours a day practicing and found that I had forgotten little. I pored through years of my and Father's journals and began to compile the research in ways that made sense. Learning always healed my heart. The reminder that there was so much left to discover in the world made my problems seem fainter.

I took a walk before dinner, and when I returned, I put on a clean dress and made my way downstairs to the dining room. Father was already seated. Harold pulled out my seat for me.

"Thank you."

He nodded and disappeared to the kitchen.

"I think we'll have an early spring," I said to Father. "I heard many birds chirping, and it wasn't too cold."

"That's pleasant news." He grimaced as he grabbed his chalice of wine.

"What's wrong?"

He shook his head. "Nothing." He laughed when I arched my eyebrow at him. "You look like your mother when you do that."

I gave him a pointed glance. "What's wrong?"

He sighed and held out his hand. "Just that cut from earlier. It's a bit tender."

I took his hand in mine. His right index finger was bright red and swollen. Yellowish pus oozed from the slice made by his small knife. I grazed the red skin near his knuckle, and he sucked air through his teeth with a wince.

"Sorry, Father. It feels like fire."

He nodded. "The pus is a good sign, however."

"Should we send for a physician?"

"It's just a small cut, Angelica. Nothing to worry about. I've got a poultice I can put on it after dinner."

"What's in it?"

"Not a clue. Got it from a shopkeeper in Cuba years ago. Nasty, pungent stuff, but the man's wife swore by it."

His smile and cheerful affect eased my mind. Father was the portrait of health, and it wouldn't be the first time he nicked himself. He could be quite careless when he was lost in thought. We ate our dinner of roast hen and potatoes with merry conversation then enjoyed a game of Nine Man Morris before bed.

When I moved my stone along the line in my final move, Father chuckled. "I'm not sure the last time I won a game to you."

"You taught me well."

"Yes, but you've a mind for strategy in a way I never will." He rose and kissed my forehead. "I'm off to bed, my dear. Sleep well."

"Good night, Father."

That night, I dreamed of freedom. I stood in the bow of a ship, staring off into the horizon. Salty air kissed my skin and tickled my nose. Cold splashes from the turquoise waters landed on my outstretched hands. I woke happier than I'd been in weeks, still tasting the dream-sea on my tongue.

With a spring in my step, I made my way downstairs to the dining room for breakfast. Something meaty filled the air, and freshly baked bread sat in the center of the table. Through the window, the sun shone.

My happiness ended there.

Father entered the room with heavy steps. Dark circles under his eyes stood out from his pallid face like a black omen. He forced a small smile at me.

"Father?" I tried to swallow the worry in my voice. "You look unwell."

He took a seat at the head of the table. "I had a terrible night of sleep is all."

"Your hand?"

I outstretched my own, and he reluctantly placed his swollen hand in mine. His skin burned to the touch. The wound had dried green and yellow pus around the edge. "You need a physician."

"I just need rest, Angélica. That's all."

I placed my other hand on his forehead. "You're feverish, Father. Send Charles to fetch the physician, please."

He shook his head. "I don't need a physician for a minute slice because I'm clumsy. I'll rest today and feel better tomorrow."

"If you don't, I'm sending for the physician."

"Fair enough."

I sent Father back to bed to rest and had Harold bring his meals to his room. I kept vigil by his bedside. When he was awake, I read to him from works by Locke and Voltaire. That night, he sent me to my room, telling me to rest. I barely slept.

At first light, I threw open the door to his room. Though it seemed impossible, he was paler than the day before. His hair was plastered to his head with dried sweat, and every inch of his skin burned hot with fever.

"You were right," he said with a weak smile. "I'm not better."

"I'll send for the physician straight away."

I ran downstairs to find Charles and request a basin of water and rags from the maids. I attempted to cool Father's skin while I waited for the doctor to arrive. Every tick of the clock felt like a slow march to the gallows, but I tried to stay calm for Father's sake. Harold helped me encourage Father to eat and drink some, but he had little appetite. I begged him to eat a few bites; he needed his strength. He worsened by the hour.

The physician was away, but the barber-surgeon arrived three hours later, and I had to bite my tongue to refrain from commenting on his tardiness. Instead, I explained that Father had cut himself while dissecting a hawk two days prior. The man, Rutherford, peered over his hooked nose at Father's finger.

"Infection, as I'm sure you've deduced. We should try to prevent any further spread, and it needs to fester more." He looked at me. "Tell the cook we need a small pot of boiling oil."

"Of course."

There was some debate in the scientific literature about the efficacy of the ancient wound care method set forth by Galen, and sailors had long known that pouring spirits on a wound often worked better than a humours approach. But this was no time for theory. Rutherford had been a barber-surgeon for a long time, and I could do nothing but trust him. I carefully carried the boiling oil up the stairs as quick as possible. Charles and Harold were standing on either side of the bed.

"Thank you, Miss Spencer. You'll want to leave for this."

"No." I had seen far worse onboard ships, and this was my Father.

"She can stay." Father's voice was hoarse.

Rutherford sighed. "Very well. Bite down on this, Sir George." He placed a strap of leather between Father's teeth then glanced at the two servants who flanked the bed. "Hold him."

The old man dipped a piece of linen on a stick in the hot oil then applied it to the wound. The leather bit did little to muffle Father's cries of agony. He writhed against the strong hands holding him down. Tears stung my eyes as I watched, helpless. I rubbed his feet and spoke soothing, stilted words even as the smell of burning flesh stung my nose.

"That should do it," Rutherford said. "The wound should fester nicely now. I'll come back in the morning to see if he's improved."

Chapter 20

Father did not improve overnight. The wound took on a putrid smell, and pus oozed out most of the afternoon. But Father was lucid, and his greatest fear was the need for amputation. He asked me to read to him again, which I did until the candlelight strained my eyes.

I could only get him to drink water at breakfast the next morning. I stayed by his side, leaving only when he used the chamber pot. Rutherford arrived after breakfast and looked down at my father with a furrowed brow.

"The wound has festered well, but I believe your humors are out of balance. It would explain the fever."

He rummaged in his leather satchel and pulled out two glass jars, one small and one large. In the small one, a small spider scurried about. "Helps with fever," he explained. Then he made Father swallow the tiny arachnid with a sip of water.

"I'll need to let you, George," Rutherford said in a quiet voice. "Shall I send your daughter away?"

Father shook his head against the pillow.

"Very well." He took a knife and ripped the fabric of my father's shirt, exposing his bare chest to the cold room. Then he unscrewed the large jar full of blackish-red slivers of slime. One by one, the surgeon placed leeches on my father's abdomen. Father hissed as each of the six parasites latched onto his skin.

Then, we waited.

The first leech fell off within a half-hour, and the rest followed. Rutherford placed his hands on Father's forehead and frowned. "Give it some time to balance out. I'll come back tomorrow. We might need to let some more."

He bent down to whisper something in Father's ear then gazed sadly at me. "Send for me if he takes a turn for the worse."

I fell asleep in the chair by Father's bed before dinner out of sheer exhaustion. I woke to the gentle touch of a warm hand on mine.

"Angélica."

I opened my eyes to find Father staring straight at me, the most lucid he'd been all day. "Feeling better?"

"Somewhat." He struggled to sit up in bed. "I need to tell you something very important."

My heart leapt to my throat. I did not like the sound of that at all. "All right."

"I have money hidden away for you. No one knows about it. Your dowry and then some."

"Father. . ."

"No, you must listen, Angélica. It's a sizeable sum. If I die—" He weakly held up his hand before I could object. "If I die, you must find this money before your cousin comes to take the estate."

My voice was thick. "And do what?"

"Take care of yourself. You're bright. You're the most intelligent person I've ever met, darling. Far smarter than myself."

"No, Father. . ."

"Don't let anyone dim your spirit. And do. . . do what makes you happy, Angélica. I regret how unhappy I made you when we returned to England. Your mother would be disappointed in me."

"Don't, Father. You're the greatest man I've ever known. And you're going to pull through this."

"Of course. Now listen carefully. There is a loose floorboard under this bed."

Father's fever did not break. Rutherford returned the next morning but did not stay long.

"Infection of the blood," he told me in a hushed voice in the corridor. "I could try letting him again, but I am not optimistic about the outcome."

I nodded, biting my lip to remain stoic. "How long?"

"It's hard to say, but he'll be with the Lord before the week is out. All there is to do is keep him comfortable."

"Yes, of course."

"It will get worse, my dear, before the end." He smiled. "But you've got spirit. If only women could train as barber-surgeons, I'd take you as my apprentice."

"Thank you, Mr. Rutherford."

He patted my arm and took his leave. I informed Harold of Father's prognosis before wetting a rag from the washbasin to wipe over his sweat-stained skin.

"Feels nice." He smiled with closed eyes.

I crawled in bed with him, the way I had done as a small child when a storm tossed the ship. He always felt safe, an anchor in the chaos. He leaned his head against my shoulder and fell asleep. For the first time, I let myself cry.

Silent tears fell down my face. Somehow, I had never imagined life without him. Anytime he discussed this future, I ended the conversation. After all, Father was the picture of health. What would my world look like without him? I could not see through the fog. This was no storm that he could get me through safely.

Father took a turn for the worse in the night. His fever spiked, and his skin turned clammy. When he had not expelled any of the liquids I had forced down his throat in over twenty-four hours, I knew the end was near.

He began to have bouts of confusion on the fifth day of his illness, though he still had spells of lucidity.

"Two decades exploring the dangerous barbarian world, and I get taken down by a dead bird in my father's home," he joked in a moment of clarity.

"Quelle chance," I murmured back.

"Oui. Terrible luck, indeed."

In the early hours of the next morning, he cried out in his sleep.

"Yaretzi!"

I closed my eyes to stop the tears. My mother had been dead for nearly twenty years.

"Yaretzi, is that you?"

"Yes," I answered in Nahuatl. "It's me."

"I missed you."

"I missed you, too, George."

A smile crossed his face. "Angélica. . . you'd be so proud, Yaretzi."

He fell asleep, and I broke down into sobs. I cried until the dark room turned grey, the sounds of my father's labored breathing my only companion. I was utterly alone in the world, and I had never been so terrified in my life.

In the first light of dawn, Father drew his last breath.

Chapter 21

MARCH 1696

"I don't know if you can hear me, Father, but I miss you."

I toed the mound of rich earth in the church's graveyard with my boot, the fresh smell of soil lingering with the petrichor of last night's rain. The grey headstone had been placed this morning; I had used some of the money Father had hidden to ensure his grave was marked with dignity. It was the last task that needed to be completed.

I laid my shawl on the grass next to the grave and sat down on top of it. The spring air was crisp, and gooseflesh dotted my arms. I picked up a clump of the soft, dark earth, still moist from the rain, and fingered it absentmindedly. "Your heir arrives at the end of the week. He's eager to leave London behind. But I'll be gone."

Perhaps my distant cousin would have allowed me to stay at Spencer Manor or allowed me to live in a small cottage on land that he now owned. It would have been proper and afforded him a sense of respect among the elite of Manchester. How philanthropic, caring for George Spencer's daughter, already a spinster at age twenty-two. The heir to the estate was young and unwed and could cement himself as a kind, desirable husband. He might even offer his hand to me.

But I did not belong in Manchester. Father's deathbed wish echoed in my ears during the last month of grieving. "Do what makes you happy," he had commanded me. I would honor his wish. That's why Charles waited outside the church in a carriage with my belongings.

"This is goodbye," I said to the silent grave. "I doubt if I'll ever return. Manchester holds nothing for me, now that you're gone." I swallowed against the hard lump in my throat. "I'm returning to the sea. I hope to book passage to the New World to continue our studies."

There were so many things I could say, so many things I wanted him to know. But there was no reason, and I was delaying the inevitable. I had to have faith in what he had taught me. And faith in myself, my fiery spirit, as he often called it. I lingered a moment longer before standing and shaking out my shawl.

I kissed my fingertips and touched the headstone. "Farewell, Father. I love you."

I straightened and wiped the wetness from my eyes before turning away. Charles said nothing, offering me only a smile as I climbed into the carriage. With one parting glance at the churchyard, I nodded at Charles, who urged the horses into a trot. We would be in Liverpool by the evening.

I clasped the garnet pendant that hung from my neck to ground me, remembering when he had given this to me on my eighteenth birthday. It was my last tie to my father. Squeezing my eyes shut against more tears, I hit the ceiling of the carriage with the palm of my hand to tell Charles I was ready to go.

Onward to my destiny, whatever it may be.

The bustle of Liverpool made my heart pound. I had no idea if my plan would work, but all I could do was try. Amidst the excitement was a streak of fear. I had never been alone for any period of time.

The streets were crowded with people and horses. As Charles drove the carriage closer to the docks, I breathed in the salty, fishy air. Already I felt more at home, knowing the sea was nearby. I studied the shops and inns as we rolled past. Charles turned down a street of brothels, and I wondered if one of these was where Henry had been born. I had never asked him, and the thought saddened me.

The carriage stopped in front of an inn just two streets from the docks. I had stayed here last summer with Deirdre and Father before our disagreement. She didn't care much for the smell, calling it fish rot. I had laughed but now realized it was a sign that she and I did not belong together.

"Are you certain you'll be all right?" Charles asked. He was looking at all the fishermen and whalers milling around the street, tattered and sea-worn from years aboard ships.

I touched his arm. "Yes. I can defend myself. I'm not frightened."

"I am."

He smiled at me, hopped off the carriage, and came round to help me. I gathered my skirts and walked inside. It was dinnertime, but this inn was not crowded. A few patrons, mostly families or elderly noblemen, sat at tables eating stew and bread. My mouth watered at the meaty aroma; I had not eaten since early that morning. The innkeeper's wife, a plump woman with streaks of grey in her dull brown hair, was wiping down the bar. She glanced up at me and smiled a toothless grin.

"I remember you," she said. "Where is your father? And that Irish girl?"

"My father has passed, and my friend is no longer with me." I smiled. "I'm afraid it is only me. I'd like a room, please."

"Oh, dearie. How dreadful about your father. He was a good man."

"Indeed."

Her brown eyes were warm with concern, but she did not ask any questions about why I was there. "I've a room with a window overlooking the street. Solid lock on the door."

"That will suffice. Thank you."

"And how long will ye be staying?"

"I—" I paused. I had no clue. If I had no luck here in Liverpool, I would try to fetch a carriage to London. "I'm unsure."

She smiled. "Not a problem at all, Miss. You are welcome as long as you'd like." She leaned forward and whispered, "If money is an issue, you can earn your keep in the kitchen."

"Thank you. It shouldn't be, but I'll keep it in mind."

"Very well." She dusted off her apron. "Should I fetch my son for your belongings?"

"No, my man will bring it upstairs."

I followed her up the creaky stairs to the room. She pulled a key from the full, jingling ring on her belt and unlocked the door. How she knew exactly which key, I had no clue. The room was small but clean, with a single bed and a washbasin on a small dresser.

"Chamber pot's under the bed. I clean 'em after breakfast." She patted my arm. "I'm Mrs. Howell."

"Angelica Spencer."

She handed me the key, and I went downstairs to fetch Charles from the carriage. He carried my trunk upstairs and placed it under the window.

"Write if you need me to return to fetch you," he said.

"I won't."

"I know." He smiled. "I wish you the best."

I placed a small purse in his hands. "It's not much, but it's a start. Buy a cottage with your wife."

He nodded. "Thank you. Take care of yourself."

"I will."

"I know."

With a final parting grin, Charles left. I looked out the window and watched him drive away. Then I turned and stared at my small room. I was alone.

Chapter 22

The captain eyed me up and down and licked his lips. "I'm certain we could find something for you to do onboard."

I wrinkled my nose. "Never mind."

"You'd do well in a brothel."

With a sigh, I shifted my journals of research in my arms and turned away. I ignored the leers of navy men and whalers as I walked down the docks back to the streets of Liverpool. This was the seventh captain I had propositioned for a role as their naturalist, offering a sizeable sum of money. Three had laughed in my face. Two had lectured me about being a young woman alone in the city. And one had told me I'd best give up my dreams and become a tavern wench.

And this one hadn't the decency to hide his lasciviousness.

Perhaps I needed to adjust my monologue and lead with my years of experience onboard ships before I discussed my naturalist training and research. Or perhaps I should try my luck in London.

I sidestepped a puddle of unknown origin and narrowly dodged a horse.

"Oi! Mind yerself!" the rider chastised me.

I straightened and found myself face-to-face with a painted lady. She grinned at me. "Men think they own these streets, eh?"

"Indeed."

She patted my cheek, long, brittle nails grazing my face. "Cheer up, Miss. Whatever's got you down is nothing but a fleeting inconvenience."

Despite my best attempts at stoicism, I had always worn my emotions painted on my face thicker than this woman's rouge. I smiled. "Thank you."

I walked away toward the inn where I was staying, doubting her words. Doubt crept in like a grey storm cloud on a clear day. This was a foolish plan, to think a ship would take me on. The last captain's parting words echoed in my mind. I *would* do well in a brothel. I was attractive and had experience.

I paused and looked back. A hunch-backed man with stringy hair and only two teeth held a coin out to the kind whore. She batted her eyelashes and took his hand to lead him inside.

"Or perhaps not," I said aloud to no one with a shiver.

I would not give up. Not yet. Three more of His Majesty's ships were set to arrive soon. I'd try my luck with those before deciding on my next steps. I could go to London where there were more vessels, perhaps even garnering favor with an admiral. Or I could book passage to the New World and see what work I could find there. My money would go further in the Caribbean. I'd be happier as a tavern wench on a sunny island than a naturalist here in dismal England.

I glanced through the door of a tavern at a table of boisterous navy men. Sailors loved to gossip, especially when the ale was flowing freely. Soon, this pub would be filled with the sailors looking for dinner and a pint. I could overhear some valuable bit of news that might aid me in my quest for a post with a willing captain. And perhaps find myself an attractive companion for the night.

I hurried back to my room at Howell's inn and dressed in something more appealing before returning to the tavern. I took a small table behind a post in the corner for myself and ate the bowl of fish stew the lady of the house brought me, along with a pint of bitter ale. It would do.

As I had expected, the sailors began crowding in, eager for a night off from their duties and glad to be back on land to indulge their vices. I watched the wenches bustle through the hungry sailors, flirting in a way that made each man feel special without inviting any unseemly advances. Biting remarks and eye rolls accompanied winks and endearments. I smirked as I watched young sailor after young sailor fluster in their wooing attempts.

Men were clueless.

As the sun set, the candlelight and hearth warmed the loud tavern with a golden glow. Amid the bragging and singing and clanking of mugs, I felt more at home than I had in years. I had made myself all but invisible in my corner and let the noise wash over me, gleaning bits of conversation here and there.

"The brigands approached us just off the coast of Africa! I thought for certain we'd be meeting our Maker that night!"

All eyes turned toward the booming voice of a scarred face. The speaker looked older than most of the men in the pub, and the conversation quieted in deferential respect.

"Aye," he continued, "Three small ships sailing under the black. I quaked in my boots. There was no chance of outrunning them."

He looked around. "Cap'n said to stand our ground, and I thought he was touched in the mind. We should accept our fate or surrender what goods we had and hope they'd leave us be. But he rallied us."

I leaned forward, intently, enraptured by his storytelling. He closed his eyes and smiled, remembering. "Seeing him fight was a thing of beauty. Poetic even. Whenever we felt weary or ready to surrender, we'd turn to see him fighting off three pirates at once, barely a bead of sweat on his brow."

"I fought with him in Halifax," another sailor said. "Never seen anyone quite so skilled with a blade. Made it look easy."

Several voices agreed. The older sailor went on. "But it's not just the fighting. He is the captain we've all desired in our service."

"Gets his hands dirty, that one," a Scottish accent added.

"Yes, and kind, too. A true gentleman, learned and polite. But that's not to say he doesn't run a tight ship," another man I couldn't see from my vantage point said.

"Greatest captain I've ever sailed under," a grizzled voice attached to an equally grizzled man piped up. "And I've sailed under many."

I was intrigued. If any captain would take me on, this one had to be the most likely.

The original storyteller grunted in agreement. "And young. But he's earned his title. Certainly, we'll see an Admiral Martin in two years' time."

Martin? It couldn't be.

"To young Henry Martin!" the Scotsman shouted, lifting his tankard high in the air. "A truer sailor has never been seen in His Majesty's navy!"

"Huzzah!" shouted the sailors.

I blinked. Captain Henry Martin? It must be a coincidence. A common name. But all the ways the men described him were accurate. Kind and learned. A master with the blade. He always believed captains were not above grunt work. And he was young. Henry would be twenty-five next month.

But he was dead. Or so I thought. He never expected to return from Halifax. Why didn't he write me? Or come find me?

I shook my head. He must have moved on by now. Perhaps he was married and had a wife here in Liverpool or someplace else. It had been years since we were parted.

I had to know.

"'Ello, Miss." I jumped at the sound, having been lost in my thoughts, and looked up into the bright-eyed, round face of a young private.

I smiled. "Good evening. You may call me Miss Spencer."

"Miss Spencer." He nodded and sat across from me, taking my politeness for an invitation. I fought hard not to roll my eyes. "You're all alone here."

"Yes." A thought occurred to me. I puffed out my bosom and leaned forward. "I was intrigued by the story the man was telling. Have you faced pirates, as well?"

He sat up straight and looked straight at my chest. "I have. And lived to tell the tale. I was on board that ship."

"How terrifying. You're so brave."

He blushed. "All in the name of the king, Miss."

"So noble. And what ship are you stationed on?"

"The *Integrity*. 'Tis my first post."

And first return to England, I had no doubt. "How fortunate you are to have survived. Your captain—what was his name?—he sounds like an incredible officer."

"Henry Martin. Youngest captain in the fleet. Earned it when all his superiors fell in Nova Scotia."

"And he's not out celebrating the safe return with his men tonight?"

The novice sailor shook his head. "No, Miss. He prefers to stay in most nights we're docked. Buys a new book and locks himself in his chambers."

It was him.

I let him ramble on a bit, feigning interest. When he broke his monologue, I asked, "Do you have a naturalist onboard your ship?"

"No, ma'am. Had one at the start of the journey and left 'im in Barbados to look at turtles or sumthin."

"I see." I stood and patted his cheek. "It's been lovely speaking with you. I wish you all the luck on your future in the navy."

"You're leaving?"

"Yes. It's late." I smiled. "Perhaps we'll see each other again."

His eyes widened with hope. "We're here for three days!"

I inclined my head and bade him goodnight. Tomorrow, I would find the *HMS Integrity* and its captain.

Chapter 23

I dressed with extra care that morning. I wore the red dress Henry had loved years ago in Antigua; despite Evelyn's comments about its lack of style, I had been unable to part with it. I tied a black ribbon with the garnet pendant from Father around my neck and glanced in my small mirror one last time to ensure my hair was stiffly in place. The dark circles under my eyes were the only part of me that looked less than perfect.

I had barely slept, my thoughts swimming with thoughts of Henry. Why hadn't he told me he was alive? A knot formed in my stomach. This could be a terrible idea. He might laugh in my face like the other captains or send me away, scorned. But if he didn't? What then? Would we resume our relationship? I thought briefly of Deirdre and how I had rejected a future with her. Would I want that with Henry?

Oh, God. What if he had married?

No sense in delaying any longer. I touched my hair one last time, gathered my books, and left my room, locking the door behind me. Henry's dagger bounced against my hip, hidden in my skirts. I had grown used to the feel of the weapon, but I could not anticipate what I would feel when I saw Henry.

The sun was bright overhead, unusual for March in Liverpool. I squinted my eyes as I walked toward the docks. The city was alive this morning, and people milled about with smiles, happy for a bit of sunshine. Seagulls squawked overhead, and sailors whistled as they loaded cargo on and off wagons.

The dockmaster nodded at me, no longer curious about my business here. This was the fourth day I had approached ships, after all.

"Good day," I greeted him with a smile.

"G'day, Miss Spencer."

"Could you direct me toward the *HMS Integrity*?"

He studied me and winked. "Young Captain Martin, eh? He's a handsome lad."

I bit my tongue to keep from replying that I knew that already. "I heard his ship left their naturalist in the New World."

"Good a chance as any, I suppose." He pointed north. "Down yonder, three ships past the Resurrection."

"Thank you."

I ignored the stares and vulgarities from fishermen and whalers as I made my way to the *Integrity*. Two sailors were on post in front of the gangplank. They were deep in discussion about some fellow sailor and did not notice me until I cleared my throat.

One raised an eyebrow. "Good morrow, Miss."

"Good morrow. I've come to request an audience with your captain."

They glanced at each other. "For what purpose?"

"My business is my own."

Each of them looked me up and down, and the one who had spoken—a lieutenant judging by his coat—shrugged. He jerked his head at the other, who walked on board to fetch the captain. The lieutenant and I waited in silence, though his curiosity, and his judgment, was palpable.

I saw him before he saw me. His blond hair was hidden by a fashionable powdered wig, but I would know him anywhere. The way he moved, the angle of his jaw. My heart raced, and for a moment, I considered running away. It would hurt less than the ache in my heart at that moment.

His mouth dropped open when he saw me. "Hell?"

My eyes watered. No one had called me Hell in years, and the sound of his voice hit me like a punch to the gut. He stood only a few feet away, a spectre made flesh, and I damn near ran to him.

"Good morning, Henry." My voice cracked. I should have addressed him as Captain Martin, but I couldn't control my words.

His blue eyes were wide, and his jaw worked up and down, as if he could not decide what to say. I watched the lump on his throat move as he swallowed. "What—what are you doing here?"

I could not tell whether he was glad to see me or not. I swallowed and straightened my posture. "I am in search of a naturalist posting."

He blinked and stared for a moment, before a smile spread over his face. His beautiful, perfect face. He laughed, but not a demeaning, ridiculing laugh. "Come with me, Hell."

He stepped aside, clearing the path onto the ship. The lieutenant offered his hand as I stepped on the gangplank, but I did not take it. I wobbled at my first few steps onboard, but soon the sealegs I was born with returned. Henry knew not to offer me any aid as I regained my balance.

I followed him to the captain's quarters. Several of his men stopped their tasks to watch us with interest and confusion. I supposed the confusion was a good sign—it meant he didn't often bring ladies to his quarters. Henry held the door open for me, and I stepped inside.

It was a large room; indeed, the *Integrity* was a large ship. Sunlight gleamed through the glass, illuminating a heavy oak desk of neatly stacked logbooks. His bed was neatly made next to a bookshelf. To put some distance between us, I ran my fingers over the spines of the books. Philosophy, history, sciences. Even some poetry. I smiled to myself.

"I cannot believe you're here."

I turned to face him. He was leaning against the door, arms folded. Guarded. I said nothing, for what could I say?

"How did you find me?" he asked.

"Sailors gossip worse than highborn ladies. I heard grand tales of your fighting prowess last night and came to see if it was really you."

He nodded and removed his wig from his head and tossed it on the bed. A symbol of informality. Of peace. His blond hair was tied back in a queue, though loose strands frayed around his temples. The familiarity hurt.

"It's really me."

I swallowed. "Yes. It is."

"How are you?" he asked to fill the pregnant pause.

I had no idea. I had thought I was prepared to see him, but I had not anticipated the confusing waves of emotions—nostalgia, sadness, desire.

Anger.

"I'm in good health, if that's what you're asking."

He took two steps closer. "Your father?"

"Dead."

Henry's expression softened. "Oh, Hell. I am sorry."

"Thank you." I cleared my throat and plastered a fake smile on my face. "You are doing well for yourself."

He shrugged. "I suppose."

"How long were you in Nova Scotia?" I asked. My meaning was clear: why didn't you write to me and tell me you were alive?

"Six months."

I closed my eyes. A year and a half since he returned a captain. A year and a half of leaving me in the dark when I was half a day's carriage ride away.

"You, uh, you are looking for a naturalist posting?"

Yes. That's why I was there. I opened my eyes and found he had moved closer to me. He was an arm's length away. "I am."

"You're not. . . married?"

"No. You?"

He shook his head, his blue eyes soft and sad. "No."

He shuffled his feet and behind his mature captain's eyes. I caught a glimpse of the young lieutenant I had known years ago. I closed the distance between us. I could smell his familiar scent, and it filled me with heat. If I reached out a hand, I could touch him.

I raised my chin, challenging. "I've not been celibate, if that's what you want to know."

His lips twitched with mirth. "Neither have I."

Then, I grabbed his coat and kissed him, hard. His strong hands settled on my hips, and he deepened the kiss. His lips were chapped from the dry sea air, and his stubble scratched my chin. He tasted sweet like honey and smokey like whiskey as his tongue urged its way into my mouth. I put my arms around his shoulders and ran a hand through his tied-back hair.

He walked me backward until I felt the edge of the desk on my backside. I hooked my leg around his and pulled him closer. His hands ran up my sides as he pressed his bulge into me. His lips pulled away from mine and kissed his way to my earlobe.

"You still have that dress." His voice was hot and husky in my ear.

I stiffened, and he stepped back, with a puzzled expression.

"What did I do?"

Then I slapped him with a resounding smack. My hand stung, and its imprint was bright red on his cheek. He stretched his jaw and looked at me, eyes wide.

"You bastard! You let me think you were dead!" Heat flooded my cheeks, and tears welled in my eyes.

"I'm sorry, Hell. I did not think you would want to hear from me. I wanted you to move on, to find happiness. You deserve it."

"What gives you the right to decide what you think I want? What you think I deserve? I mourned you, Henry. For months."

"I—" He shook his head. "I thought it was the right thing to do. I was never good enough for you."

"You're the bloody youngest captain in the Royal Navy!" I pushed him away and paced his quarters, the ship rocking gently beneath my feet. "I am sick of people deciding what is good enough for me. Sick of it!"

"Forgive me, Angélica. I implore you. Forgive me and sail with me."

I stopped pacing. "What?"

"I've got a posting. It will be dangerous. The seas are far more treacherous than the last time you sailed. But my ship outguns most pirate vessels. And I know you can defend yourself." He wrung his hands, his sea-blue eyes darting around nervously. "I have no need of a naturalist, but I do need an interpreter. We've many allies against the French who speak different languages."

My heart pounded. It was what I wanted more than anything. My chance at freedom. But Henry.

I scoffed. "And we continue where we left off three years ago?"

He looked at the floor. "If you want. The men would talk, but they're good people. If you don't, the offer still stands. No one is in the cabin where our last naturalist slept."

I chewed my lip. Did I want to continue my affair with Henry? Much had changed in the last two years. I had changed—I was no longer an impetuous girl under her father's thumb. Briefly, I wondered if he would want me once he realized I'd grown.

But his eyes twinkled, and I knew he would. Oh, I had loved Deirdre, but never like this. Henry was the other piece of my soul. He helped shape me. He knew my flaws, yet still believed in me. And he was willing to take a chance on me, even now.

"Say yes, Hell."

"Yes." I grinned. "Yes."

His face lit up like a Caribbean sunrise. "You will?" I nodded. He took my hand and placed it over his heart. "Do you forgive me?"

"Of course, you silly man."

I ran my fingers over the thick fabric of his captain's coat and down his torso, He bent his head down, inquiring, and I lifted mine to meet him. He captured my lips in another kiss. Softer. Steadier.

I unbuttoned his coat and pulled it over his shoulders. His hands moved deftly to unlace my overdress. He smiled against my mouth as he found the dagger tied to the string I hid on my waist. I pulled his cotton shirtsleeves over his head and stepped back to admire his chiseled chest. There were scars there that had not been before. A long scratch on his left side over his ribcage, and a raised round bump near his right shoulder. Despite these, he was still as perfect as I remembered.

From that moment, the undressing happened in a flash. He lifted me and settled me on his desk. He kissed my chin, my collarbone, the space between my breasts, as his hand lowered between my legs. I writhed against him and dug my nails into his strong biceps.

"I want you now," I whispered. "I don't want to wait." Not after I had waited so long.

He did not need to be told twice. With his arms braced on either side of me, he pushed the wet head of his cock against my opening. I wrapped my legs around his waist and pulled him into me. With one swift motion, as if we had never missed a moment, he sheathed himself in my core.

We tried to pace ourselves, tried to savor languid strokes. But the urgency built and within moments, I had fallen into the abyss with him right behind me. He kissed me as he crested, catching my cries with his warm mouth.

After, we lay intertwined on his bed, sticky with sweat. He kissed my brow. "I cannot believe you're here."

I laughed. "I'm not certain how else to prove it to you."

He smiled and closed his eyes. "Stay with me, Hell. I don't want to spend another night away from you."

"But your crew—"

"Doesn't give a damn what I do in my personal time."

"Very well."

He raised our interlocked hands to his mouth and kissed my knuckles. "I'll send someone for your belongings." He yawned. "After a bit of nap."

I shifted and curled around his body. With my head on his chest and his arm around me, I found restful sleep for the first time since Father had died.

Chapter 24

1 APRIL 1696

Three days later, I bade farewell to England. I had dreamt of the moment for years, but I did not expect the lump in my throat as I watched her shores fade into the horizon from the quarterdeck. When I had arrived three years prior, I was certain I could never be happy here, but I had found happiness. Deirdre had been a light in the dark, and I had repaired my relationship with my father. But in all the moments of joy, I had never found contentment.

Henry smiled at me from across the deck. The ship cleared the harbor and picked up speed. Cold spray hit my cheeks, and my skirts whipped in the wind. I turned to face the port side of the ship. The grey waters had passed into a deep blue, with bits of white foam atop the waves.

I was home.

Henry had officially introduced me to the crew that morning. No one grumbled about a woman on board nor mentioned that I was staying in the captain's quarters, at least audibly. Certainly gossip would follow, but it seemed they had the sense to keep it away from their captain.

Far more incredible than their easy acceptance of me was how they responded to Henry and the way he treated them in kind. He spoke softly but firmly, and every crew member gave him their undivided attention. As he walked the deck, he made jovial conversation with his men while they worked. And when we cleared the bay, and the sails went up, Henry pulled one of the ropes attached to the mainstay.

A pod of dolphins swam and jumped alongside the ship. I laughed to myself as they passed. Once such a common occurrence, it had been so long since I had heard the chirps of these happy creatures and watched them play in the water.

Someone cleared their throat behind me. I turned to find the young sailor from the tavern. His eyes darted round, not meeting mine, and his cheeks were red.

"Hello, again," I said kindly.

"Hullo, Miss Spencer."

I waited for him to continue, but he said nothing. "Was there something you needed, sailor?"

"Ye-yes." He swallowed. "I wanted to 'pologize if I was untoward the other night. At the tavern."

Ah. He didn't want word of his attempts to make it back to his captain. "You were not untoward. In fact, you were quite polite."

He met my eyes and smiled. "Truly?"

"Truly. What is your name?"

"Ben Davies, Miss."

"It's a pleasure to meet you, Mr. Davies."

"Likewise, Miss." He nodded, a large grin plastered on his face, and hurried back to his station.

I felt Henry behind me as if my heart were tuned to his. I spun 'round and greeted him. "Captain."

"Miss Spencer." His eyes twinkled, but he did not move to kiss me. As an officer of His Majesty's Navy, he needed to maintain a sense of propriety in public. And I wanted my skills to be my reputation on board this ship, not my relationship with Henry. We were already sharing quarters, after all. On the deck, we decided we would meet the expectations of our professions.

"What did Ben want?"

"To properly introduce himself. We had met in town, and he is the one who told me where to find you."

"He's a good lad. It's only his second voyage."

I nodded. "He thinks highly of you. It seems they all do."

"I think highly of them." He shrugged, his powdered wig shifting off center. "My first captain taught me that to earn true respect, not respect of the title, I must give it first."

"His lessons have served you well."

"More than I could ever describe." He grinned. "Fancy a fight later?"

"Yes!" I laughed. Memories of our lessons rushed back, and it took everything in me not to kiss him there on the deck.

"Good. I'm going to make my rounds below. I'll find you at midday."

I spent most of the morning observing the crew moving about the deck or staring out at the vast, blue expanse. We were headed south to Accra, a port on the west coast of Africa. I had not been there since I was twelve, and I was excited to see how it had changed. Though I would have taken a ship anywhere with Henry, I was pleased we weren't headed north. The climate grew warmer with each passing moment.

Henry stood with his quartermaster, the older man who had sung Henry's praises at the tavern, at the helm, one steady hand on the wheel and the other holding a compass. The captain caught my eye from across the deck and winked. Despite that ridiculous wig that his station dictated he wear, he was beautiful.

I went below deck to acquaint myself with the *HMS Integrity*. The ship was a 70-gun, third-rate ship-of-line, barely eight years old. A fine ship with a crew of two hundred twenty-five sailors. The two gundecks stank of sweat and powder, but the crew worked diligently hauling ropes and polishing the guns. Most of the crew paid me no mind, and those that did greeted me with a nod. The four men working the pump sang a shanty as they heaved the lever up and down, not noticing as I walked past.

It was down below in the hold where the sentiment toward me changed. I blinked as my eyes adjusted to the dark belly of the ship. The boatswain and the second lieutenant were taking inventory of the powder and shots in the magazine, lit only by one glass lamp. They did not see me, but I recognized their voices, as Henry had introduced me to the officers the day before.

"Never seen him smitten over a lass before," the boatswain, a husky-voiced man named Mr. Oakes, said. "Seems they've a history together."

"And claiming she's a naturalist. A woman. Can you imagine?" Lieutenant Wheatley, who had met me on the dock the other day, scoffed. "Another mouth to feed and body to protect while all she does is warm his bed."

"Aye. But Captain Martin's quite keen on the girl, so don't go running yer mouth to everyone. It'll get back to him."

"I know. But you agree?"

"Bad luck to have a female on board, even one so pretty as her."

Wheatley laughed. "She's pretty, but I would say a woman is more of a nuisance on board than bad luck."

I swallowed the lump in my throat; I had become soft in my years in England. They had said nothing I hadn't heard before, but the insinuation that I was nothing more than a whore to warm the captain's bed stung. I wasn't ignorant; I knew what sharing his quarters looked like.

I made my way up the ladder, stepping softly so as not to reveal my presence. As the daughter of a wealthy gentryman, there were little crews could complain about when I was younger. But Father was dead, and I had already established myself with an undesirable reputation. That sort of gossip could quickly get out of hand, making not just my life miserable, but Henry's as well.

"There you are! I've been searching for you."

Henry grinned at me from across the orlop deck. Some of the crew turned and glanced at us, but quickly turned back to their jobs as their captain walked past.

"I was familiarizing myself with the *Integrity*."

"She's a beauty, isn't she?"

"She is."

"I'm taking lunch with Rainsford and Easton in my dining room. Will you join us?"

I nodded. Hugh Rainsford was the first lieutenant, Henry's second-in-command. Arthur Easton was the ship's master, in charge of plotting the course and navigating the ship. I had only met them briefly.

"Excellent." Henry held out his arm to escort me to the stairs that led to the upper decks. The officers' private dining room was in the aft of first gundeck. "And then we'll spar?"

I smiled at the hopefulness in his voice. "I hope I'm not too out-of-practice." Another thought occurred to me. "How's your Spanish?"

"I've kept up my studies and even read their books," he replied in perfect Castilian Spanish.

"Excellent." A thought occurred to me. "Henry, I may be familiar with ships and how they work, but I've never done any sailing work myself. Would you teach me?"

"What sort of work?"

I climbed the ladder ahead of him and waited for him to come up. "All of it. Rigging, cleaning, the pumps. Steering if you'd let me."

Anyone else would laugh at me, but not Henry. Never Henry.

"I can do that. Where is this coming from?"

"I want to earn my keep."

Henry studied me, arms folded across his chest. "Did someone say something to you?"

I could tell him, I knew, and he'd speak to Wheatley and Oakes, but that would do nothing to ingratiate myself to them. I shook my head. "I don't have my father's coattails to hide behind now."

"Fair enough. But you can't climb the rigging in a dress without giving my entire crew a view they'll never forget. And perhaps I'm possessive, but I'd rather not have that happen."

I laughed. "Fine. I will buy trousers when we arrive at port."

"I'd expect nothing less from you." He opened the door to the officers' dining room. First Lieutenant Rainsford and Master Easton were already seated at the table. Ben, who was acting as the captain's servant on this voyage, pulled out the chair at the head of the table, but Henry pulled out my chair opposite him first. Ben blushed and apologized.

"Well, lads, the skies are clear as far as the eye can see," Easton said. "I say we should expect to arrive in Accra in three weeks or so, barring any major setbacks."

"Good. Are we sticking close to the shoreline like before or sailing further out?" Henry asked.

They paused as the cook delivered the meal, and Ben set the table. I savored each bite of the roasted winter vegetables and braised beef, knowing our days with such fresh fare were limited. Soon it would be potatoes, chicken, and turtle.

"I should think if we don't get too close to France, we can move closer in as we approach Africa." Easton chewed thoughtfully.

Henry nodded. "My meeting with the admirals confirmed what we thought. King Louis is nearing bankruptcy. The corsairs are the main threat, not their navy."

Lieutenant Rainsford cut a glance over at me, then back at Henry. "The corsairs will be far more aggressive than before. They won't get coin from the crown, and Louis needs his cut of their loot. They might look for other prizes."

"Miss Spencer can defend herself, if that's what you're implying." Henry took a sip of his wine and met my eyes. "Far better than many of the men below decks. I taught her myself."

"Of course, Captain. I meant no offense—"

"You can address her instead. She is right there."

Easton snorted into his food as Rainsford flustered. "Apologies, Miss Spencer."

I nodded. "I assure you, Lieutenant, that I will not be a burden."

"Of course not." He smiled. "I trust our Captain."

The rest of the meal continued without event. I learned that the *Integrity* was delivering both supplies and orders to the admiral stationed in Accra, off the coast of Africa. There, the ship would receive new orders to the Caribbean or the Indian Ocean. The *HMS Integrity* was fast, and Henry was a clever captain. He could easily face down or outrun pirate and privateer threats without a fleet to support him; therefore, the *Integrity* was used mostly as a reconnaissance ship.

After the meal, Easton and Rainsford excused themselves, and Henry shooed away Ben, who had stood in the corner during the meal.

"Interesting choice for your servant," I said. Captain's servants were usually gentry or nobles training for a future as an officer. Ben was clearly not of high birth.

Henry shrugged. "My last boy, Tim, was injured and wanted to go home. Ben reminds me of myself."

"You were far more confident."

He laughed and pulled me into an embrace. "I was good at pretending. But he's a quick learner and has a good heart."

"That does sound like you." I planted a quick kiss on his lips. "Now, you promised me a fight."

"That I did. Do you need a sword?"

I shook my head. I had taken my family sword off the wall of my father's study when I left Manchester, proper heir be damned. What use did a gentryman from London have for a fine sword in the middle of Manchester? Charles had taken it to the blacksmith for sharpening the day before I departed. "Mine is in the cabin."

"Hell, I want you to wear it at all times. As I said before, the seas are more dangerous than the last time you sailed, what with Captain Every building a pirate haven out of Nassau and the French corsairs. You need to be armed constantly."

I pulled my dagger from where it hid in my skirts, held it out to him, and grinned. "I am."

His expression softened. He placed his hands under my own and studied the dagger he had gifted me with interest.

"You still have it," he said, his voice thick. "I saw it the other day, but I couldn't be sure if it was that one."

"This dagger has been my rock in the storm," I whispered. "It kept me from losing myself. *You* kept me from losing myself."

His lips crashed onto mine. His strong hand stroked down my back and settled on my hips, pulling me closer against him. I placed a hand over his heart as I kissed him back in earnest, never feeling more at home than I did in his arms.

When I pulled away to take a breath, Henry cleared his throat. "I'm glad you're here, Hell."

I straightened my rumpled dress. "I am, as well. Now, are we going to spar or not?"

Henry laughed. "Fetch your sword and meet me on the quarterdeck."

I hurried up to his cabin and found my sword among my belongings before rushing past the quartermaster and up the stairs to the topmost deck.

"G'day, Miss Spencer," the older man called from his place at the helm.

"Good day, Mr. Gresham."

Henry leaned against the mizzenmast and winked when I approached. "That's a fine sword."

"It's been in my family for generations."

"Excellent. Let's see how well you remember."

He slashed at me so fast, I barely noticed him remove his sword from its hilt. But I parried it successfully. My footwork was messy. I hadn't practiced on board a moving ship in too long, but soon I found a rhythm.

I lost myself in the sounds of sword clanking sword amidst our laughter. I squinted against the sunlight that gleamed off our blades as we sparred. Henry was stronger, but I was faster. I had improved with practice, occasionally fencing with Charles in the barn, but I hadn't had an opponent at Henry's skill level.

Neither of us managed to get past each other. Henry panted as he put up his hands. "I yield."

"Huzzah!" I wiped my brow with the back of my hand. "Oh, it's been far too long."

"You've improved." Sweat glistened upon his face, and a familiar heat rushed through me. I licked my lips.

"Impressed?"

"I am. Come, I have water in my cabin."

He held out his arm to me, and I took it. No longer lost in the trance of fighting, I became aware that we had acquired an audience. Two dozen sailors stared at us. Rainsford nodded at me. Mr. Oakes, the boatswain, whispered something to Lieutenant Wheatley, who had a stern look on his face. Ben gaped.

"Have we suddenly run ashore?" Henry yelled. "Back to work!"

Murmurs of "Aye, Captain" filled the deck. Henry rolled his eyes and led me down to the cabin. "Nosy bastards."

I laughed. "At least they don't think I'm a useless maiden."

Henry closed the door and unbuttoned his dark blue coat. Then he closed the gap and pulled at the laces of my bodice.

"Useless maiden is something you'll never be, Hell."

Chapter 25

25 April 1696

"Good, Hell! Now guide her round the port side."

I turned the wheel to the left. The coast of Ghana was just off the bow. We were to anchor in the bay and disembark to the boats. Henry had let me guide the ship into port, sending Mr. Gresham off to help at the capstan.

I liked Gresham. He had taken me under his wing as soon as Henry had asked him to teach me to steer the ship. Of course, Henry had also worked with me, but he could not devote all of his time to my training. Gresham was patient and did not mind that I was a woman, and he told wonderful stories of his adventures at sea. How many were true, I was not certain, but I enjoyed his company. Though not like my own father, who I missed dearly, Gresham's fatherly nature was a balm.

I stretched my neck from side to side. I had worked a shift on the pumps with Henry yesterday, and my shoulders ached from the strain. I'm not sure how much help I had been as we pumped the iron back and forth, but I was getting stronger.

Henry noticed and gave me a reassuring smile. "You know you don't have to work the pumps or the capstan."

"I know. But I want to."

He kissed the top of my head. Sometime in the last three and a half weeks, he had become less concerned with propriety. Between my sword skills and my hard work on the ship, I had begun to earn the respect of most of the crew. Even Mr. Oakes was thawing, though Lieutenant Wheatley spent most of our interactions glaring at me.

"I'll send the officers ahead to the fort with the supplies while I show you to the inn. I'm certain I'll be stuck in meetings all day tomorrow, if not this afternoon."

"That's quite all right," I said. "It's been so long since I've set foot in Africa. I believe I was twelve when Father and I shifted our studies to the Caribbean."

"Oh, I'm not worried about you entertaining yourself," he said. "I'm worried about how bored I'll be."

The coast was getting clearer, and more than a dozen other ships anchored in the pale blue waters of the bay. Dutch merchant ships, first-rate man o' wars, a few slaver ships. Even one lone Spanish Galleon. Accra was a busy trading port, and both the Dutch and the English had forts here.

We dropped anchor next to another royal ship, and the crew began to unload the supplies for the fort. I tied up my clothes and journals in a watertight leather bag, and Henry pulled a small trunk of gold from a hidden cabinet under the cabin's windows. He was delivering salaries from the crown.

Lieutenant Rainsford climbed into the small boat, and Henry lowered the trunk to him. Henry went next, and I could feel his watchful eye on my back as I descended the rope ladder. We had only disembarked once on our journey so far, in Madeira, where we could lay the gangway on the docks. But I had not forgotten how to climb down the hull of a ship, even though my skirts were a hindrance.

Rainsford and Henry rowed us into port, past ships of noisy sailors. I watched the *Integrity* grow smaller as the water grew lighter. Schools of colorful fish swam past our little boat. We reached land with a thud, and Henry helped me out of the boat onto the soft sand.

A bustling market lined the edge of the beach. Exotic spices mingled with the smell of human sweat and fresh meats. Vendors yelled out their prices in a mix of Dutch, English, and other languages I could not identify. Henry guided me through the stalls toward the town, Rainsford trailing behind us with the trunk.

Henry turned just past a large cage of wooden bars reeking of urine. Some two dozen Africans were crammed inside with no room to move, chained together through heavy metal collars around their necks. I met the dark eyes of one man as we rounded a corner, his pain and anger searing through me. I quickly looked away.

"No need for such poor conditions," I said in a low voice. "Utterly humiliating."

Henry glanced down at me. "The slavers are worried they'll run."

"Wouldn't you run?"

He nodded. "I would." He paused. "I didn't say it was right."

"I know."

We walked in silence to an inn near the English fort. It was quieter than the others we passed. Only a few officers and merchant captains sat at the small tables, sipping their drinks and talking in low voices. Henry greeted the landlord behind the bar with a grin.

"Good morrow, Cap'n. Can I get you a pint?"

"Not today, Will. My friend and I will be needing a room for the next two nights."

Will, a small man with a grey beard and a scar over one eye, glanced at me. Whatever he thought, he kept it off his face. "One room?"

"Aye." Henry squeezed my hand. "Just one."

Will led us upstairs to a small room with a window overlooking a line of tropical trees and handed Henry the key. The bed was smaller than the one in the captain's cabin, but it would be fine. Normally Henry would sleep on the ship in port, as his quarters were luxurious, but the prospect of two nights without a crew of over two hundred nosy sailors nearby thrilled us both.

Henry looked at his pocket watch. "I will meet you back here by eight o'clock for dinner, if you'd like."

"Of course. I think I'll explore the town today and collect flora samples in the hills tomorrow."

He smiled. "You have your sword and your dagger on you?"

"Yes."

"Good. I trust Will, if you need anything, or send for me at the fort." He brushed a kiss on my lips. "I'll see you tonight."

I spent the afternoon in town, avoiding the slavers as best I could. Instead, I sampled tropical fruits and spiced meats. I visited a tailor, who fitted me for two more pairs of breeches. I had only purchased one in Portugal and found them preferable to dresses for moving about the ship.

I meandered down a section of the market where vendors were selling live animals. One man showed me a vibrant parrot, just a few weeks past hatching.

"You teach it speak," he told me. "Much loyal."

I was intrigued but shook my head. Two booths down, a woman tried to sell me a baby monkey. The creature was precious, but I knew how troublesome they could be. There was a litter of pups recently weaned, and a cat that the seller swore could catch a dozen rats a day.

I always wanted a pet. Father only liked animals to study them and didn't want the added responsibility of another dependent living thing on a ship. But Father was gone. I wondered how Henry would react to me having a pet. Many navy captains kept a dog for protection and hunting when they were on land.

Henry was waiting for me when I arrived back at Will's tavern at sunset. He was deep in conversation with a Dutch captain, but he excused himself as soon as he saw me. We sat at a small table in the corner, and Will brought out a spicy fish stew. I moaned as I took the first bite.

"That good?" Henry asked with a chuckle.

"It has more flavor than every food in England combined."

He raised his mug of ale and tipped it toward me. "To better food and a better view."

"Huzzah." I clanked my own mug against his. "How were your meetings with the admirals?"

Henry rolled his eyes. "Boring and long. Those men love to hear themselves speak and won't get to the point."

"Have they told you your next assignment?"

He nodded as he took a drink, causing a dribble of dark ale to roll down his chin. I reached over to wipe it away and licked my fingers. He gave me a devilish grin. "Whoever thought to name you Angélica was mad."

I laughed. "Where are we going next, Captain Martin?"

"Caribbean. I will check in with the admiral at St. Martin." He looked pleased. "There was talk of me joining a fleet if I had gone to the Indian Ocean, and I'm not sure what that would have meant for you. It would be war. But the increase in piracy has the Navy in a bind in the New World. They need more heavy-gunned ships for reconnaissance."

"Good. I love St. Martin."

"And I love you." I rolled my eyes at his joke. "What did you do today?"

I told him about my day at the market. "What would you think if I got a pet?"

"What sort of pet?" He furrowed his brow. "Do you mean a tiger cub or a dog?"

"Clearly, I mean an elephant." We laughed. "But something small. Perhaps a parrot or a cat."

"I'm not opposed."

We finished our meal and then went upstairs to take advantage of our time away from the ship. I fell asleep wrapped in his arms, the sounds of the wildlife and drunken sailors in the streets below lulling me to sleep.

I spent the next two days in the lush rolling hills past the town. The second morning, I passed the furthest hut by a mile and settled under a palm tree with my journals and charcoals. Below me, I could see the town and beyond, the sparkling azure bay filled with ships. I spent some time sketching the view before collecting a few samples from the various plants.

Hours passed, and the sun was high overhead. I pulled a piece of bread from my bag and chewed as I recorded notes and sketched. Soon, I had the feeling of being watched. My sword lay next to me, and I put my hand on the hilt as I looked around.

Sitting a foot from me was the largest rat I had ever seen. It wasn't a typical rat. Its face and ears were more elongated, and its cheeks were puffy.

"Well, hello there. Aren't you a pretty thing?"

Instead of running at the sound of my voice, it moved closer. Then it sat on its hind legs, looked me straight in the eye, and squeaked.

I laughed. "Is that so?"

It squeaked back.

"Would you like some of my bread?"

I placed a small chunk of the loaf between us. The rat-like creature stuffed it in its mouth, and its cheeks got puffier. I blinked. I had only seen hamsters stuff their cheeks, but this creature had a tail the length of its body.

"Have another."

The rat took the next piece of bread and stuffed its pouches again before staring at me expectantly. I laughed. "That's enough for now, you little coquette."

The rat began to lick its tiny paws and groom its head, and it was the most darling thing I'd ever seen. I turned to a new page in my journal and began to sketch my new friend. It sat still for me, posing like a noblewoman getting her portrait painted. I finished my sketch and began writing down the behaviors I had observed.

Something furry nudged my elbow. I looked down to see the rat standing on its hind legs and gazing inquisitively at my journal.

"I've written nothing unkind, I promise."

Then it crawled into my lap. Tentatively, I reached my hand down to pet it, worried it would bite me. But it didn't. It pressed its face against my fingers as I stroked its soft, furry head. Its eyes closed, and soon, it curled into a ball and fell asleep.

I scribbled notes as it slept and pet its fur, careful not to wake it. In all my training as a naturalist, I had never had a wild animal approach me so brazenly. Certainly, one had never taken a nap in my lap. I watched in awe as it slept.

The sun was getting higher, and I was to meet Henry so we could take the boat back to the ship before nightfall. I still needed to pick up my trousers from the tailor, as well. I sighed, reluctant to leave my new friend.

"Little darling," I whispered as I prodder her gently—I had deduced that she was a female based on the anatomy—or rather, lack thereof—under her tail. "Time to wake up."

The rat stirred. She stretched her little legs and yawned, and my heart melted. I placed her gently on the ground and gave her another piece of bread. "Goodbye, little one."

I began to walk back to the town, only to hear rustling behind me. I turned around. The rat was following me. I shook my head and kept walking. As I reached the edge of Accra, I looked back once more. She had followed me over a mile.

"What are you doing?"

She stood on her hind legs again and squeaked at me.

"Do you want to come with me?"

It sounded mad, but I swore she understood me. She clawed at my skirt and tried to hoist herself up like a tiny rigging climber.

"Very well then." I leaned down and held out my hand to her. She jumped into my outstretched palm and climbed up my arm. Her claws were sharp but not unduly painful. "Careful now."

She perched herself on my right shoulder and nuzzled her face against mine. Her tail wrapped around my neck, a strange sensation. I laughed and continued my walk into town, the rat riding comfortably on my shoulder.

We garnered a few strange expressions as we made our way to the tailor's shop. I walked inside, and the tailor and his assistant, a local Ashanti man, looked up at me in surprise.

"My dear, you have a rat on your shoulder!" the tailor exclaimed.

"Do I?" I laughed. "This little thing has adopted me, it seems. She spent the afternoon with me and followed me back to town."

The servant nodded. "They can be friendly."

"What is it? It's no normal rat," I asked him.

He shrugged and said a word in his native tongue. "We say they are rats with pouches," he explained.

"Do they often domesticate themselves like this?"

He shook his head. "Rarely. The babies can be. . . how do you say? Trapped?"

"Trapped?"

"And trained to be," he searched for the word, "furry friends."

"Pets," I told him. "Well, I believe she has claimed me as her own."

The tailor shook his head and handed me a bundle of folded cloth. "Here are your trousers, Miss."

"Thank you."

The rat squeaked, and we turned to the door. As we left, I heard the tailor mutter, "What a strange young woman."

We met Henry outside of Will's tavern. He was leaning against the outside wall, his tall figure relaxed and handsome, and smiled when he saw me. Then his smile faded and his mouth dropped open.

"Hell. What is that?"

"A pouched rat."

He stared at me. "A pouched rat."

"Yes. She's adopted me." I explained how she came up to me out in the hills and took a nap on top of me. "Then she followed me over a mile into town. So, I let her ride on my shoulders."

Henry pinched the bridge of his nose. "If you wanted a rat, there are plenty in the hold, I'm sure."

"I didn't *want* a rat. She found me. And she's no ordinary rat."

"Clearly. I suppose this is the pet you discussed?"

I shrugged. The rat shifted and stood on my shoulder, placing her front paws on top of my head to get a better look at Henry.

"You're buying it a cage. I'll not have it chewing my cabin to bits while we sleep."

I grinned. "That's fair."

Henry shook his head and took my leather bag from me. We walked down to the market to the section with all the animals. There, we found a bird cage. It wasn't large, but if the rat curled up, she'd be comfortable enough.

"Have you named it yet?" Henry asked as we walked down the beach. One of the boatswain's mates was waiting with a boat.

I thought, and a long-forgotten memory crept into my mind. The only memory of my mother, and the name she called me in her native tongue.

"Quetzalli," I said. The rat squeaked and nuzzled my face.

"I think she likes it. What does it mean?"

"Precious. Or lovely. Or feather. It doesn't translate well."

Henry laughed and took my arm in his. "I can't wait to see you explain this rat to the crew."

Chapter 26

MAY 1696

Quetzalli settled in comfortably to life aboard a ship, caring not that the crew looked at her with suspicion. She spent much of the days riding on my shoulders or scampering behind me on deck. Henry had given up insisting that she sleep in her cage at night. She made too much noise and instead curled up between our heads. He muttered about her under his breath, but he had also taken to petting her while she sat in his lap at his desk.

Ben liked my rat as well, though he still blushed and refused to make eye contact with me. Even Mr. Gresham had begun to accept her with mostly indifference, which was better than the shudders that greeted us as we made our way through the ship. But I continued to work hard, taking shifts swabbing the deck, mending sails, and greasing the shot to keep it from rusting. I had also begun assisting the ship's surgeon, Gil. I had an exceptional knowledge of anatomy, but Father's death had left me feeling inadequate at healing. Gil welcomed my scientific mind, and I enjoyed learning the practical applications of medicine.

I had just finished climbing into a part of the hold that the carpenter couldn't squeeze into to patch a hole. My trousers were wet, and I was eager to get into dry clothes. Quetzalli climbed up the ladder to the main deck and turned back to look at me expectantly.

"I'm coming, I'm coming."

The air was thick and humid, and the air smelled like rain was on its way. I glanced up at the sky but saw only white fluffy clouds floating along the blue. Of course, that meant nothing. Henry was standing on the forecastle, looking over the bow of the ship with his spyglass. I scooped Quetzalli into my arms and went over to find out what he saw. Dry clothes could wait.

"What's wrong?" I asked.

He handed me the spyglass. I peered through it into the distance. There were no ships and no land. But a black blur loomed in the distance. I handed the monocular back to him.

"A storm?"

Henry nodded, still staring out at the sky. "It's moved fast, and it's so dark."

"And the air feels stale."

"Yes. We're in for a long day." He glanced down at me. "Did you get that hole patched?"

"I did."

"Good. We don't need any leaks heading into this." He tucked the spyglass into its holder on his belt. "I've got to ready the men for a storm."

I watched as he descended the steps to the main deck and signaled to Rainsford and Wheatley. I could tell by Henry's posture and tone that he was worried, and I trusted his instinct. With one last glance over my shoulder at the oncoming clouds, I hurried to the cabin and placed Quetzalli in her cage.

She chittered in protest.

"I know, I know." I handed her a hunk of bread leftover from my breakfast through the bars, and she yanked it from my fingers. "Have a peace offering."

When I emerged from the cabin, the dark clouds had moved closer, now visible without a spyglass. Sailors hurried about amid the shouts of officers. They adjusted the sails and secured items on the deck. Gresham stood at the helm, his brow furrowed at the impending darkness. Master Easton stood next to him, looking down at his compass and back up at the sky.

I rubbed my arms against and stood on Gresham's other side. "What do you think?"

"A nasty one. She's moving fast." His hands gripped the wheel tightly as he glanced at Easton. "No going 'round, either, I'd say."

Easton shook his head. "It's too wide." He leaned forward to get a better look at me. "Might be best to hunker down in the cabin, Miss Spencer."

"It's hardly my first tempest, Master Easton. I've been on ships since I was knee-high."

Gresham patted me on the back. "Leave her be, Arthur. She's more of a sailor than half the crew"

I couldn't fight my smile. "Where's the captain?"

"Down below," Easton said. "Meeting with the carpenter and the boatswain."

I busied myself helping secure the ropes connected to the sails until I heard Henry's voice across the deck. The skies had darkened, and the low rumble of thunder sounded in the distance. Amidst a flash of lightning, I hurried over to the helm where he stood with Mr. Gresham. Easton had disappeared.

"Where do you want me, Captain?" I asked him.

Henry looked at me, his jaw set. "Somewhere safe, though I know you won't listen."

"You're correct."

Gresham snorted, and Henry shot him a stern glance. "Below deck, I'd say. The carpenter and his mates will be busy plugging holes and could use all the help they can get. And we're bound to have injuries, so let Gil know you can assist if he gets overwhelmed."

"Of course."

A loud crack from the skies made me jump. The ship jolted as Gresham had been startled and loosened his grip on the wheel. Henry grabbed the spinning wooden helm to stabilize it. At that moment, the winds increased their frantic sighs, and drops of rain began to fall in a slow but steady pitter-patter.

"It's picked up speed," Henry said, raising his voice against the pounding of the sails against the wind. "Hell, find Ben and have him secure our cabin now. I don't have time."

I nodded and began to turn away, but Henry grabbed my wrist and pulled me into a fierce kiss.

"Stay safe," he muttered in my ear before letting me go.

"You, too."

The ship rocked, and the waves crashed against the hull as the rain beat down faster and faster. By the time I made it below deck, I was drenched. On the first gun deck, sailors secured the guns and passed supplies in a line to safer locations in interior cabins.

My wet shirt and trousers clung to me, and rain dripped from my brow. I saw one of the boatswain's mates.

"Where's the captain's boy?" I yelled over the ruckus of the deck and the increasing thunder.

The ship lurched, nearly knocking us to our feet. The mate grabbed my arm to stabilize us both. "Saw 'im in the aft cabins."

"Thank you." I moved as fast as I could toward the aft of the ship, grabbing onto various beams and ropes. The ship rocked violently, and bodies bumped into bodies. The smell of fear mingled with the rain and sweat.

I found Ben in the officers' dining room, storing crates of supplies underneath the fixed furniture.

"Ben!" A crack from the skies above drowned out my voice. I yelled again. "Ben!"

"Miss Spencer!" He fumbled toward me, grabbing the table for support.

"Captain wants you to secure his cabin right away."

"Aye, Miss."

My stomach churned in time with the ship's swaying as we moved to the ladders. The deck was slick from the rain that poured through the hatches. I waited as Ben climbed up on his hands and knees in case he fell before carefully clambering down to the orlop deck.

My eyes adjusted to the darkness. The lamps had been put out to prevent fires. Gil, the surgeon, was hoisting a man with a broken leg onto a stack of flour sacks. The sailor screamed in agony, an eerie harmony to the storm's melody.

"Need help?" I asked.

Gil looked up with relief in his eyes. "I'll brace him, if you'll set the leg."

He handed me two sticks and strips of cloth before moving to the sailor's head. He slipped a leather strip in the writhing man's mouth. "Bite down hard."

I placed the sticks alongside the warped bone when a massive wave crashed against the starboard side, launching me backward. I landed hard on my back, a searing pain coursed through my body.

"Fuck!" I scrambled back into an upright position and set the sticks back against the sailor. I'd only ever seen this done, and awareness at my lack of knowledge hit me like a strike to the head. I looked at Gil who had his full weight on the sailor's shoulders.

"Wrap them tight round the leg." Though only a few feet away, Gil's voice sounded distant in the roar. I did as he said, step-by-step.

"Now twist. Hard, Miss. Spencer."

I twisted, and though I could not hear the screams between the storm and the leather bit, I could feel them in his body. I grunted with the effort of manipulating the leg until Gil hollered to stop.

"Good. That's enough."

"We've got a leak!" someone screamed.

"Buckets!" came another voice.

Other's echoed, "Buckets!"

The carpenter's head emerged from the hold. "More wood!"

I heaved an empty crate over my head and smashed it to the ground. Pieces shattered, and I scooped them up.

"Here!"

I handed the chunks of wood to the carpenter. Buckets of water sloshed by my head as sailors passed them from one person to the next, up to the higher decks.

I lowered myself into the hold and planted my feet into a knee-high puddle of water. The water smelled fresh and salty, without a single hint of urine. Not a good sign at all. Water was pouring in faster than it could be pumped out.

"There's hole I can't get to," the carpenter yelled in my ear. He thrust some pitch, a hammer, and nails at me. I waded behind him in the rising waters.

The lady's hole at the stern of the ship was covered by water. It was the safest part of the ship unless it was leaking. I swallowed the bile rising in my throat. I would be completely submerged in absolute darkness.

"You'll have to do it by feel."

I nodded. He helped me lower myself into the hatch. Just before I went under, I took a deep breath.

The frigid water stung my skin. I kept my eyes closed; I couldn't see down here anyway. Quickly, I moved my hands along the planks. Water gushed through open spots. One. Two. Three.

I swam upward, the only way I could move. I gasped as my head breached the surface. "There's three, size of my palm!"

"One at a time, lass." He handed me some pitch, and I took another breath.

There was no leverage for hammering underwater, but I did what I could where the pitch wasn't enough.. It took three trips to the surface for air to secure the first. My heart thudded as the water's pressure crushed my chest.

When I finally finished patching each, the carpenter pulled me up by the arms. My clothes were heavy and sopping, and I gave a silent prayer of thanks that I hadn't been caught in skirts.

We swam back, the water in the main part of the hold now at my chest. Sailors helped pull us up to the orlop deck. A line of men still passed buckets at a frenetic pace.

"Lass, we need the pumps to go faster," the carpenter said. "Tell the cap'n."

"Aye." I pushed through the crowd of soldiers and squeezed past the ones on the ladders. A bucket of cold water splashed over my head, and the salt stung my eyes. I blinked and climbed further up, slipping backward every few steps.

The sky was blacker than midnight, and I could barely see through the sheets of rain on the main deck. I grabbed the nearest rope and worked my way toward the quarterdeck to find Henry.

Someone screamed. I looked up and saw a sailor fall from a yard arm just above me. He hit the water with a resounding splash.

"Man overboard!" I hollered, but my voice was drowned out by the crashes and cries of the tempest.

Lightning flashed, illuminating the deck. I saw Henry with Gresham, trying desperately to keep the wheel steady. He was so far away. The pit in my stomach grew as I prepared to cross the main deck.

I leaned forward and back, opposite the rocking ship. The rope burned my hands as I pulled myself along. Without warning, the ship pitched. The deck was nearly vertical. Lightning flashed, and I saw three men slide past me across the slick planks and into the vicious waters of the sea.

"NO!"

I bit my lip and steeled myself as the ship righted itself. Overhead, the skysail on the mainmast was flapping loudly, and men clung to the ropes. The sail had to be stuck. The mast began to bow. I slipped as I stared up and lost my grip on the rope.

"HELL!"

A strong hand wrapped around my wrist. I fell on top of Henry in a pile on the wet planks.

"The pumps!" I shouted. "More men."

Henry grabbed the ankle of the nearest sailor. "To the pumps. Grab anyone you can."

"Aye, Cap'n."

We heaved ourselves to standing, and Henry pulled me to the helm. We stood with Gresham, pouring our entire strength into steering. A loud crack sounded, and it wasn't thunder.

"The mast! Henry! The mast!"

"GET DOWN!" he bellowed. "GET THEM DOWN!"

The orders passed from voice to voice. The riggers began their descent, fighting against the raging gales that threatened to fling them from up high. I watched from the helm, trembling in trepidation.

The ship pitched, and a piercing scream broke through the thunderous storm. A man fell from the rigging, arms and legs flailing in the air. The sky lit up the moment before he hit the deck, as if the storm were gloating about what it had done.

Henry cursed. But no sooner had the words left his mouth when the mast broke at the royal sail, two-thirds up from the deck. It was if the world slowed down, the fall of the mast and half a dozen sailors inching toward the depths. My ears rang at the deafening splash of the mast hitting the ship's side before falling into the sea.

A colossal wave rose from the impact, towering above the ship like Goliath. I grabbed the wheel with both hands between Henry and Gresham and clenched my eyes shut.

My skin burned from the crash of the wave, such was its force. I sputtered and coughed; the salt water burned my throat and nose. But when I opened my eyes, I found the sky lighter. The sun was fighting to break through the clouds.

The winds eased, and the thunder rolled further and further away. The rain, no longer falling in sheets, dropped from pale grey clouds. I let go of the wheel, as did Henry, and Gresham did not struggle to keep it steady. Just past the prow of the ship, I could see a line of blue sky.

A fickle thing, storms. With one final squall, the storm passed us by, having taken all it wanted. The rain stopped, and the clouds drifted behind the ship, leaving wreckage and death in its wake.

Chapter 27

7 MAY 1696

A knock sounded on the door of the cabin, and I groaned. I had been trying to catch up on some sleep. After the storm, we hadn't rested in our attempts to repair what we could and keep the ship afloat. Master Easton had spent hours at his maps with his various navigation instruments, attempting to determine where the storm had blown us and where we could find land to repair the mast and the hull.

"Come in!" Henry called from his desk. He'd spent the last hour writing his report in his captain's log.

I sat up and brushed my dark hair out of my eyes and yawned. I was clothed but in a state of deshabille, and at this point, I didn't care if anyone saw me less than decent. Quetzalli opened one eye from her spot on Henry's pillow then went back to sleep.

"Little devil," I whispered.

Ben entered the cabin, dark circles under his green eyes and a gash through his filthy shirt. "Cap'n. Miss."

I smiled at him, and he looked away quickly. Henry set down his quill and leaned back in his chair. "What is it, Ben?"

"Land's been spot."

"Spotted. Land's been spotted." Henry's voice was gentle as he corrected his young servant.

Ben cleared his throat. "Land's been spotted."

"How far?"

"Two leagues or so, Master Easton said."

"Thank you, Ben."

Ben turned to walk away, but Henry stopped him. "Lad, didn't you have something you wanted to ask Miss Spencer?"

I raised an eyebrow at Henry. He hadn't mentioned anything about this to me. But he didn't glance my way.

Ben stammered and shifted his weight from foot to foot. "Oh, uh. I didn't think. . . what with the storm and the mast. . . that you. . . or she. . ."

"Go ahead, Ben." Henry chuckled. "She won't bite. Will you, Hell?"

I rolled my eyes. "Only when provoked. What is it, Ben?"

"It's, you see. . . well, the captain said. . . and I don't want to be a bother, but. . ." His eyes were on the ground as he stammered.

"Spit it out, boy," Henry said. "And you look at a lady when you're speaking to her."

"Aye, cap'n." Ben took a deep breath and turned to face me. "I dunno how to read, Miss Spencer. And the captain supposed maybe perhaps you could teach me?"

A warm smile crossed my tired face. I liked Ben. He was a good lad, and I understood why Henry had taken to him. Of course Henry would suggest that I teach him how to read. He saw potential for advancement in Ben, but being an officer required literacy.

"I would be honored to teach you, Ben. On one condition."

"Yes'm?" His eyes lit up.

"You must stop acting like a jittery squirrel when you're around me."

"Ye-yes, miss. I can do that. Stop, I mean."

I bit my lip to keep from laughing, and Henry shooed him away. Once Ben left, he came and joined me on the bed, laying with his head in my lap.

"You could have asked me about helping him yourself, you know." I traced my fingertips over the lines of his face, and his eyelids fluttered shut. He was exhausted and hurting for the men he'd lost to the storm, poor thing.

"That feels nice." I felt his body relax into the bed. "Ben's got to learn some confidence."

I thought back to when the boy had approached me in the tavern in Liverpool. "He's got some when there's ale in his hand."

"What?"

I relayed the story to Henry and made him swear not to reveal to Ben that he knew. Henry roared with laughter.

"I heard about that! I can't believe *you're* the lass. All but broke his heart."

"Oh, be serious."

Henry grinned. "'Twas a blow to his ego is all. Not the first, and you won't be his last."

"You need to get the poor boy to a brothel. Let him conquer his fears."

Henry opened his eyes and stared up at me, blue eyes full of mirth. "We tried. He kept drinking more for courage until he passed out drunk and still a virgin."

I giggled. I could picture it clear as day. "Well, you should try again in St. Martin's."

"I've no need to step foot in a brothel." He sat up and brushed his lips against mine. "I've all the entertainment I need right here."

"Your entertainment is tired." I stretched out on the bed, kicking him out of my way. "Fancy a kip?"

"Just a quick one." He moved Quetzalli off his pillow and placed her on the table at our heads. She let out the tiniest yawn before curling back into a ball. "I suppose storms are exhausting for little beasts, too."

The island Easton had selected was small but full of tall, strong trees for replacing the mast. It was pure luck there were no inhabitants, plenty of freshwater, and trees. Henry sent me with Lieutenant Wheatley and the scouts while he oversaw the rest of the crew hauling the *Integrity* aground with ropes.

Quetzalli scampered a few feet in front of me as we traipsed through the thick foliage. I breathed in the mossy scent of the rainforest. Tall, green ferns brushed my arms and face. Amid the sounds of birds, I wondered if we were the first people to set foot here. My eyes were on my rat, and I didn't notice as I ran face first into a branch full of mangoes.

"A mango tree!" I pulled my dagger from my belt, cut one from its tree, and sliced it open. The sticky, sweet flesh had the consistency of a rich, Christmas custard. Quetzalli tugged at my boots when she noticed I had food.

I bent down and offered her my arm. She crawled up and rested on my shoulder, and I handed her a small piece of the yellow fruit.

"Disgusting," Wheatley said with a sneer.

"You don't like mango?" How could anyone not like mango?

"The vermin, eating out of your hand like that."

I shrugged. "Disgusting is relative. Quetzalli spends more time grooming herself than all of the crew combined."

Two of the other sailors laughed, and Wheatley silenced them with a glare. He looked up at the trees, and I followed his gaze.

Breadfruit, papayas, coconuts. They dangled overhead like vast quantities of glittering gold. We'd lost the last bit of fresh food to the ship's flooding.

"Cook'll be pleased," one of the sailors observed.

Wheatley grunted. "Let's hope there's meat on this island, too."

He stomped off. I pulled two more mangoes from the trees and tossed them to the sailors. They grinned, and I put my finger over my lips. We followed Wheatley and continued scouting, quietly enjoying our fresh fruit. We found our way back to the beach two hours later. The *Integrity* was turned on its side with her cargo unloaded. On the white sand of this tiny island, the ship was massive, like a fallen fortress. My eyes scanned the camp for the largest tent and went to find Henry.

"There you are!" He stood outside of his tent, giving orders to some of the crew. When he saw me, he pulled me into his arms and gave me a deep kiss. "You taste of mango."

"Got attacked by a mango tree."

"Mm. It's delicious."

"It's in a very private part of the island. I'll have to show you later."

Wheatley cleared his throat. Henry dropped his arms from my waist and smiled at his second lieutenant.

"John! What news?"

"Uninhabited. Small freshwater pond near the center of the island. Plenty of fruit, and I saw tracks to suggest there is some source of meat here."

"Excellent. Thank you. Go find Rainsford and see where he needs you."

Wheatley nodded and walked away. I stared after him with a frown. "He's an unpleasant fellow, isn't he?"

Henry chuckled. "He's practical. Takes his office very seriously."

"He doesn't like me."

"It's nothing personal, Hell. It's only because you're a woman."

He held open the flap of the tent, and I ducked inside. "How is that not personal?"

My trunk sat in the corner of the tent with Quetzalli's cage on top. She climbed down my back and onto the sand to explore our new, temporary lodgings. Henry came up behind me and kissed the curve where my neck met my shoulder. I shivered.

"Still tired?"

I forgot my frustration at his comment about Wheatley and turned to face him. "No, but the canvas walls are quite thin, and it's broad daylight."

"Hmph." He looked around the tent and found the trunk he needed. He opened it and pulled out a bottle of rum then threw a blanket from the pallet over his shoulder. "Fetch your journals. We'll go find some privacy."

"My journals?"

"Yes. I miss watching you do your work."

"Don't you have captainly duties to attend to?"

He shook his head. "They'll forgive me. I'll let them open some barrels of ale tonight."

I collected my things and called to Quetzalli. She scurried over to me, and I scooped her up, placing her on my shoulder. Henry took my hand and led me out of the tent. We didn't speak much as we made our way to another part of the island. The crew stared, and it was obvious what our objective was, but I didn't care, and neither did Henry. We walked along the edge of the treeline as the island circled round. When Henry felt we were far enough away from the crew, he stopped and threw down the blanket. I set Quetzalli down and handed her a bit of dried bread I had stashed for her. Henry sat down and pulled off his black boots.

I followed suit and stared out at the crystalline blue waters. The waves were gentle on this part of the beach, lapping against the shore and fading back, beckoning shyly. I glanced at Henry. He had a gleam in his eye, and I knew we had the same thought.

We undressed and raced down the hot, satiny sand in naught but our skin. The moment my feet touched the cool waters, rejuvenating joy washed over me. I waded in up to my thighs. Henry was up to his ankles. Quetzalli had tested the waters and immediately ran back up the beach to her snack.

"Hurry up, you sloth!" I said to Henry.

"It's cold!"

"No, it's not!"

"It is if you've got bollocks!"

I laughed. "What happened to the legendary bravery of Captain Martin? Will the hero of Nova Scotia be brought down by his shivering manhood?"

Salt water splashed into my face and up my nose, rendering me blind for a few moments. I coughed. When I looked up, Henry was laughing at me, but he had moved deeper into the water.

"How rude!"

He threw back his head and guffawed! "Your face! You should have seen your face!"

"That's it, Henry Martin!"

I waded deeper and splashed him in return, and he was quick to retaliate. Back and forth we splashed around and dunked each other under the clear waters. Colorful schools of fish rushed past us with urgency to get away from our chaos. Finally, Henry captured me. I tried half-heartedly to wriggle out of his grip, but he was too strong. He held me against his chest, and I laid my wet head against his racing heart.

"I win," he whispered.

"I'm letting you win."

"I'm fine with that."

I wrapped my legs around his waist, and he carried me from the water back to the beach. He laid down with his back on the blanket, and I straddled his hips.

"So beautiful." His fingers explored my arms, my stomach, my breasts. Henry always made me feel like Helen of Troy, when in fact he was the beautiful one. Perfect, with the body of a Greek god and the soul of a saint. I sighed and shifted lower, taking him inside me. His hands gripped my hips, and I knew there would be bruises there later. Marks of honor. I turned my face to the warm sun as I moved against him. As his pants grew faster, and heavier, so did my motions.

He cried out before me, but my own ecstasy followed, a wave crashing over me, undoing me, destroying me. And then it passed. I trembled as Henry pulled me down to meet his lips. He tucked my hair behind my ears and kissed each eyelid. With each touch, he put me back together again.

That afternoon, my journals were all but forgotten. We laughed and drank and swam and made love. Henry practiced his Spanish, and I taught him a few words in Dutch. Henry began teaching me to shoot, although it did not come naturally to me.

He gave his entire crew the night off and opened barrels of rum and whiskey. Fiddlers took turns playing music, and we sang shanties well into the clear, moonlit night. At one point, I found myself in a drinking game with the boatswain, the carpenter's mate, and Rainsford. I won, easily.

The week passed too quickly. Repairing the ship and replacing the mast was hard work, but Henry kept everyone working in short shifts so they'd have plenty of time to rest. Every afternoon, he and I went to our secluded slice of paradise. I recorded notes on the flora while he read with his head in my lap. He patiently guided me on shooting with both a pistol and a rifle. I preferred the sword, and I told him as much. He said I only preferred it because I was better at it. He wasn't wrong.

The entire crew was bright-eyed and ready to sail when the *Integrity* was finally ready to launch again. They heaved her into the water, and she floated. Cries of "huzzah" filled the air, and we set sail to St. Martin's.

Chapter 28

JUNE 1696

St. Martin sat at the Eastern edge of the Caribbean, a glimmering oasis to sailors after a long voyage across the Atlantic. Its prime location had served as a sort of gateway to the New World for buccaneers, privateers, and navies. The English had only had control for six years, thanks to the merger of Dutch and English territories from William and Mary's ascension to the throne in 1689. France wanted it back.

St. Martin was a lovely island. The blues of the water blended together like paint on a canvas. The sand shone ivory in the sunlight. And my favorite part was the symphony of myriad languages mingling in the streets.

We arrived early in the day, dropping anchor in the bay next to a Dutch West India Company ship. I left Quetzalli in the cabin as I didn't figure shopkeepers would be too pleased with her presence and rowed ashore with Henry and Rainsford. I set out to buy new parchment and some books to continue my reading lessons. Word of my lessons with Ben had spread through the ship, and I now taught classes to over fifty sailors. After my purchases, I waited to meet Henry at the fort's tavern. I drank with Easton and Gresham, who were among the first shift to have shore leave, and met a friendly, Irish merchant with the thickest accent I'd ever heard. I thought of Deirdre, locked away in a convent halfway across the world, and my heart twinged. I hoped she had found happiness.

Easton and Gresham disappeared after a few hours, and Henry still had not arrived. My head was foggy with drink, and the tavern was getting busier and louder. I decided to wait for him outside, leaning against the outside wall of the tavern. It was nearly sunset; surely, he'd be along soon. It stank of piss, and flies buzzed around my head. I closed my eyes, hand on the hilt of my sword, while I sobered up. The late evening sun beat mercilessly on my skin.

"Damn it, Henry. Hurry up."

I checked my timepiece. I'd been out here for over half an hour. Soon, the sky would have streaks of purple and red across it. Sailors would fill the streets for gambling and whoring. I wanted to go back and read in our cabin.

Henry arrived a few minutes later, looking absurd in his powdered wig.

"Took you long—" I paused. A vein throbbed in his clenched jaw, and his eyes were stony. "What's wrong?"

He thrust a letter in my hands. I read it. Blinked. Read it again. Was I drunker than I thought? I read it one more time.

"Henry. . ."

"Not here."

He stalked off, and I struggled to keep pace with his long, angry strides.

I lowered my voice. "Henry, this is essentially—"

"I know."

We bypassed a rogue pack of chickens, who squawked angrily at our intrusion. "You can't possibly—"

"Not here."

He took a right at the bottom of the hill toward the bay. The sun had begun to set, bathing the beach full of sailors and boats in a blood-red light. "But Henry—"

He spun around. "I said not here, Angélica!"

It was the closest he'd ever come to yelling at me. I swallowed hard and glared at him. "Fine. But we're discussing it on the ship."

He turned back around and continued walking, muttering something under his breath about stubborn women. A group of our crew huddled near our three boats. They chatted with excitement about their night off, unaware of what awaited them when we set sail. Henry refused help getting back to the ship, and we rowed in silence through the darkening bay.

I thought about what I'd read. Though it wasn't stated as such, Henry had essentially received a letter of marque. The document had been signed by the King and ordered an act of war against an ally. But it made no sense. Henry was no privateer. The *Integrity* belonged to His Majesty's fleet.

We climbed the rope ladders up the side of the hull. Henry didn't so much as smile at his crew. I followed him to our cabin and slammed the door shut. Quetzalli chittered and ran over to greet me. I picked her up and cradled her in my arms as I watched Henry throw off his wig and pace the width of the room.

"Henry, why did they give you this?"

He stopped pacing and stared out the window. The last light was fading into all-encompassing darkness. "Reasons only the king and his advisors are aware of, apparently."

"And the admiralty?"

He shrugged.

"You can't possibly be considering. . ."

"Of course I am, Hell." He shook his head. "I'm loyal to my king. I'm loyal to this navy. I've been given orders, and I have to carry them out."

"But Henry, it makes no sense. Why would the king—our Dutch king!—order you to attack a Dutch ship?"

"I don't know. I'm just a lowly captain. The whys of royal courts don't concern me."

His shoulders dropped, and he pressed his head against the glass. I crossed the room and took his hand in mine. "It does concern you, though. It concerns every crewman on board. We aren't at war with the Dutch."

"Maybe we are. News doesn't exactly travel fast from England."

I considered his words. He was right. "Then how long ago did the king order you to attack this exact ship and know exactly when it would be arriving in the New World?"

He looked at me, eyes wide. "What are you saying?"

"It's suspicious, and I think you know that."

"But I've been given my orders—"

"Then question them! Sinking this ship is murder!"

Quetzalli leapt off my shoulder onto the floor at the sound of my raised voice. I closed my eyes and took a deep breath before continuing, calmer. "Henry, you can't—"

"Angélica, stop. You don't understand. Not everything can be challenged in life, certainly not the admiralty or the crown."

"But if it's wrong—"

"Stop! I have my orders. And that is what I'm going to do."

Chapter 29

19 JUNE 1696

Henry spent the next several days brooding in his cabin. It was unlike him to sequester himself away for hours on end, and his absence was noticed by everyone. Every time we were together, we argued, so I spent most of my time helping Gresham or Gil or teaching the sailors to read. Many members of the crew, including Wheatley and the boatswain, Mr. Oakes, assumed that the captain's shift in demeanor was due to my influence. Anyone could see that our relationship was strained, but this was no lover's quarrel. As of yet, he had not told his officers what their orders were.

"Never shoulda brought her on board," I heard Mr. Oakes say to one of his mates when I came up from the hold after fetching fresh water for Gil's latest patient.

"Bewitched 'im, most like," the mate agreed. "No other explanation."

I bit my tongue. Stupid, superstitious men. They couldn't fathom that something could be wrong that was bigger than a woman in their captain's bed. The suspect glares I received as I passed the sailors filled me with a burning rage. I gave Gil the water and excused myself to the top deck.

"Ship ho!" the barrelman crowed from the raven's nest as I emerged in the bright summer sun.

My stomach turned. It had to be the *Keerpunt*, the Dutch ship we were to sink. I hurried into the cabin. Henry had his head down on his desk. Quetzalli sat by his head, playing with his blond hair.

"Ship sighted, Captain." I kept my voice neutral, standing in the doorway.

He didn't move for a moment, then heaved a sigh and raised his head. "Thank you. I need my officers."

I turned and went to find Easton, Rainsford, and Wheatley. When I returned to the cabin, Henry stood by the window. He had donned his wig and put on his navy coat.

"Should I leave, Henry?"

He shook his head. "I need. . . I have to board the ship. I need your Dutch skills."

"I don't think. . ."

He turned to face me. His eyes were puffy and red. "Please, Hell. Please don't make this harder."

My heart ached. The admiralty, and the crown supposedly, had put a good man in a terrible position. The pain was evident on his face. I nodded. Rainsford and Easton entered then, followed shortly by Wheatley. I moved to a corner, and Quetzalli climbed on my shoulder. All three officers eyed me with suspicion. Though only Wheatley hated me, it was clear they did not think I should be there.

"We've received orders, gentlemen," Henry said. "The ship that was just spotted is likely the Dutch ship *Keerpunt*."

"Too soon to see the colors, Captain," Rainsford said.

Henry nodded. "We need to get closer. The crown has determined that the *Keerpunt* is a threat to British safety in the New World. We are to sink it."

I couldn't see the faces of the officers, but Wheatley shuffled his feet in discomfort. I folded my arms and leaned against the wall.

"Are we preparing for battle then, sir?" Rainsford asked.

"Not exactly."

Easton ran a hand through his graying hair. "If we come in guns at the ready, they'll fight back."

"I know." Henry cleared his throat. "We are to engender goodwill with them, then attack as we sail off. Get shot to the cannons, but don't open the gun ports."

The three men stood still, waiting for Henry to continue.

"Dismissed."

The officers left. Easton shook his head, and Rainsford chewed his lower lip. Neither looked my way, but Wheatley met my eyes. He flexed his hand in discomfort then sighed and exited through the doorway.

Henry loosened his collar. "Angélica, please understand. We would all lose our posts if I do not do this. We could all be hung for treason."

"I know."

"I have over two hundred men I'm responsible for."

"I know, Henry." I set Quetzalli on the floor and crossed the room. I folded my arms around Henry, and he rested his chin on top of my head. "No way to lie about it? Say you never found the *Keerpunt*?"

"No. Word would get back." He squeezed me tighter. "I've considered every possible way out of this. But I can't betray my king."

"Bloody gossiping sailors," I said in an attempt to lighten the mood.

"Aye. Bloody sailors, indeed."

The *Keerpunt* was not a naval vessel.

Nor did it belong to the Dutch West India Company. As the *Integrity* neared the Dutch ship, we learned quickly that this mission was infinitely more complicated. Henry grabbed my hand and gave it a squeeze. This was either a private merchant ship or a passenger ship. I smoothed my skirts for lack of something better to do. The pit that had formed in my stomach earlier was growing into a small boulder.

"Are you certain?" I whispered, careful not to let his crew overhear from where we stood on the main deck.

"Not at all."

He raised his hand in greeting to the people on board the Dutch ship. We were nearly close enough for the gangplank to reach the other vessel. A man, who I presumed was the captain, raised his hand back in greeting.

We were, after all, on the same side.

When we were close enough to speak without screaming, Henry spoke. "Good morrow! I'm Captain Martin, and this is the *HMS Integrity*."

"Good day, Captain." The man who spoke had a thick brown, beard and a friendly smile. His accent was thick. "I am Captain Janssen of the *Keerpunt*."

"Captain Janssen, a pleasure. I'm afraid we've run into an obstacle for our journey, and I was hoping you might help." The lies oozed out of Henry's mouth like butter. If it weren't for the way he wrung his hands behind his back, I'd believe him myself.

"My English is. . ." Janssen gestured with his hands. "Not good."

Henry turned to me. I sighed and plastered on a smile before relaying Henry's message in Dutch.

"We will help if we are able! Please, come aboard!"

"Thank you, Captain." I switched back to English. "He wants us to come aboard."

Henry smiled and signaled to his men to place the gangplank. He walked over first, followed by Lieutenant Rainsford then myself. I studied the small deck. Men stood in clusters. Some were leather-skinned and scarred, clearly seamen. The others looked like guests I might find at an Evelyn Campbell party. A passenger ship, then. Certainly, there were women and children below deck, hidden until they could ensure we were not a threat.

Janssen took my hand and kissed my knuckles. "And you are?"

"Angelica Spencer, sir. The ship's naturalist and the captain's translator."

He chortled, his hand over his broad belly. "A woman! Fancy that. Good on you, my dear. I'm certain you're smarter than all the lads aboard."

My breath hitched. I liked this man.

I nodded and looked at Henry expectantly. He rolled his shoulders back. "Captain Janssen, we've had two barrels of freshwater leak out in their entirety. I fear we don't have enough for our journey back to England."

Rainsford stiffened next to me. I jabbed him with my elbow, then translated. The words were bitter on my tongue.

Janssen nodded. I could see him calculating his supplies in his head. "We are nearly to our destination. We could spare two barrels. Do you need any food?"

I relayed the response to Henry. He pressed his lips together. I knew he had not expected this much kindness. "A-a bag of grain, if you can spare."

The captain smiled and clapped Henry on the back after I translated. "I will give you some chickens, too."

He turned and called to his boatswain, giving him orders in Dutch. I looked at Henry, whose fake smile had faltered. I raised a pleading eyebrow, but he shook his head.

Janssen broke our silent exchange. "My men will bring up the supplies."

"Thank you." I looked around the deck to avoid eye contact and fiddled with my garnet necklace to steady my nerves. The ship was clean and organized. The crew appeared healthy. He ran a good ship. "This is a passenger ship?"

"Yes. We have forty passengers on board, seeking a fresh start in the New World."

The pit in my stomach grew again. I swallowed. "All Dutch?"

The captain shook his head. "Mostly. We have a French family who've fled Louis, and two English families."

"Oh?" My voice cracked high. "Henry, he said he has two English families on board."

"Interesting." Henry shot me a warning glance.

I smiled at Janssen and refrained from asking any further questions. I did not need to know how many women or children were on board. My conscience had guilt enough. Shortly, two of the Dutch crew emerged from below deck with a large barrel.

"Lieutenant, get the men ready to bring the supplies on board." There was a hidden order in Henry's controlled tone.

"Aye, Captain," Rainsford replied in a short voice. He understood the implication and crossed over the gangway.

We watched as the Dutch handed off supplies, given out of nothing but kindness, to our own crew.

"Thank you for your kindness," I told Janssen. "It won't be forgotten."

He kissed my knuckles again. "You will do great things, young lady."

My eyes stung. Henry shook the captain's hand, and I hurried over to the *Integrity*. After Henry crossed, he paused and closed his eyes. Then he motioned to Gresham to start sailing away.

I watched as the *Keerpunt* moved further away. Captain Janssen waved at us, along with several of his men.

"Open the starboard ports and fire immediately. Give them no time to react," Henry said to Rainsford. He walked away toward the quarterdeck.

I hurried after him. "Henry, no."

"Don't, Angélica."

"Henry, there are women! And children! Innocent lives!"

He turned on his heels. "Lower your voice."

"There are English citizens on board." Tears streamed down my cheeks. "A French family who are fleeing Louis' tyrannical rule."

"Damn it, woman!"

Shouts traveled across the water from the *Keerpunt*, two seconds before the guns exploded.

"No!" I screamed and ran toward the side of the ship. "Stop!"

Hands grabbed me around my waist and pulled me back, holding me against him. Thick, black smoke obscured my vision, but it did nothing to stifle the screams. So many screams. My stomach roiled at the smell of gunpowder and burning flesh.

"Let me go!" I fought against his grip. I didn't care if I made a scene. "How could you?!"

Henry let go and rushed into his cabin. I ran forward. Our crew stared at the burning ship, transfixed by the horrors. Another round of cannon fire launched with a bang. It crashed into the side of the Dutch ship. There was no hope. We were nowhere near land. They had no time to prepare an escape. Every person on that ship would burn or drown.

Rainsford's voice hollered from somewhere behind me. "Back to work! Sails up!"

His order jolted the crew out of their haze. No one spoke as they returned to their duties. The screams were fading, though I could still hear echoes in my ears. I watched as the masts of the ship fell, aflame, and broke the surface of the ocean with a crash. A blast exploded from the burning ship, sending angry waves toward us. Their magazine had caught fire, then. I grabbed the nearest rope and braced myself against the swell. Water sprayed my face as we picked up speed.

Someone touched my hand. I looked up to see Mr. Oakes standing next to me. His face was ashen, his shoulders drooped. "Watching won't save 'em, Miss."

I swallowed against the lump in my throat. "I know."

"Come on, lass. The cap'n needs ye, I'm certain of it." He tugged my hand gently. "Look away now."

My legs quaked as I tried to walk. He led me toward the door of the captain's cabin. I barely gave a thought to his unexpected kindness, but it was too much to contemplate. Instead, I placed my hand on the warm, metal doorknob and turned it slowly. The door creaked open, and the smell of sick hit me. Henry knelt on the floor near the bed. He had retched into the chamber pot, and Quetzalli peered over the edge of the bed with concern.

"Henry?" I closed the door and went to sit beside him. He was trembling. "Henry, look at me, darling."

He wiped his mouth and raised his head. My heart ached at the sight of him. His face was splotchy and wet from crying.

"What have I done, Hell?" He closed his eyes, and more tears fell like a rainstorm. "What have I done?"

I had no answer. He had murdered innocent people seeking a new life. But he knew that. Instead, I sat with him in silence as we both replayed the nightmare in our minds.

He was sick once more. I dumped the vile chamber pot out the window into the sea. In the distance, I could see a tower of black smoke. I rubbed my arms against an unexpected chill, then tucked Henry into the bed. The rat curled up on his chest.

"I'll be back soon, love." I kissed his forehead. He stared blankly at the ceiling.

The deck was as quiet as a deck could be. No one whistled or chatted. The only sounds were the splashes of the ship in the water and the wind beating on the sails. I slipped below deck to fetch some fresh water for Henry.

Down in the orlop deck near the water, I heard soft sobs coming from a dark corner. Curious, I grabbed the nearest lamp to investigate.

Lieutenant Wheatley sat with his knees to his chest. His shoulders heaved up and down, and his palms pressed against his eyes.

"Lieutenant?"

He dropped his hands and stared up at me. "I murdered them."

"We all did, Lieutenant."

"No." He shook his head, casting an eerie, moving shadow. "No, Miss Spencer. I—I did. I should have said something."

I drew my brows together. Was this simply shame at not having spoken up to his superior officer? Or something else? "What do you mean?"

"I. . . I heard a rumor in St. Martin." He glanced down and squeezed his hands into fists. "That's all I thought it was until. . . So I didn't. . ."

"Wheatley, what did you hear?"

He took a deep breath. "That the admiral in St. Martin—and some of the others—are Jacobites."

Dizzy. I felt dizzy. I put my hand against the wall to steady myself. "Jacobites?"

"Aye. But I didn't want to speak against them, as they're officers of the crown. But then we got the order from Captain today and. . ."

It made sense. There was no way that King William would order us to attack a small passenger ship full of his own people. But there were so many who wanted James back on the throne. If the Dutch declared war, the anti-Dutch sentiment would rise. King William would be forced to take action, either ensuring a war with his former country or a rebellion in his own.

But to have the details about this voyage. . . this ran far deeper than a few token admirals in St. Martin.

"Wheatley, you must tell the captain." I nudged him with my boot. "Get up. He needs to know." It took some encouragement, but he followed me to the cabin. Henry was still lying in bed when we entered.

"Darling, Lieutenant Wheatley has something to tell you."

Henry sat up abruptly. "Lieutenant. Apologies. I'm not feeling well."

I waved my hand. "Stop with the niceties. Wheatley, tell him what you told me."

"John?" Henry swung his legs off the bed and stood. "What is it?"

"Captain, forgive me for saying this. But I believe that this assignment didn't come from the king. I think—I think we were used."

"What? I got the orders from the admiral myself."

Wheatley nodded and told him how he had overheard rumors that several of the high-ranking officers were Jacobites. Henry stiffened, and his jaw set as he listened.

When the lieutenant finished, Henry said, "Thank you. You're dismissed."

Wheatley looked at me, eyes wide and questioning. I shrugged. He left the cabin, closing the door behind him. Henry went to the window. The smoke from the wreckage was still visible.

"What do you think, Hell?"

I sat on the edge of the desk. "It makes sense."

"Too much sense." He shook his head. "It felt wrong from the beginning. If I had just—"

"Spoken out and been killed for it?"

"At least I'd have died with a clear conscience." He turned to face me. "I made us all commit treason."

"No," I said, straightening, "they made us commit treason. They used you like a pawn in a game of chess."

"Easy to sacrifice should things go wrong."

The pit in my stomach had been replaced by a blaze of rage. "Yes. All two hundred odd of us."

Henry wiped his eyes and thought for a few moments. I watched the emotions flash across his face. Betrayal. Hurt. Anger.

Resolve.

"What are you going to do?" I asked.

"The right thing."

Chapter 30

27 JUNE 1696

I t is one of life's most vicious truths that the moment when the curtains of childhood and innocence are stripped away is also the moment we find ourselves utterly alone in this new and frightening world. If Father had been there to guide me, would I have even listened? What would Father have done if it were him facing this crossroad?

"Father, what should I do?" I asked the wind. But of course, Father did not answer.

Fingering the garnet pendant around my neck, I stared at the blue expanse, squinting my eyes against the sunbeams bouncing off the waves. The salt spray tickled my face as I stood on the ship's bow and breathed in the crisp sea air. The warm wind blew strands of my loose hair, obscuring my view of the turquoise horizon with soft, black tendrils. I had always felt monumental and untouchable when I stared into the sea.

But now I felt small. Naked. Vulnerable. I was no longer the queen of my world. I was an insignificant speck in a universe of cruelty and politics and impossible choices. I looked to the sea for answers, but none came.

The wind had picked up, propelling us closer to our destination.

We had resupplied in St. Martin's yesterday, and Henry had decided to return to report that the *Keerpunt* was sunk to the admiral. He also tried to discover more information about their plot. Now we were headed to the Dutch settlement of Curacao. The official orders were to report on the number of ships in the harbor and how well-gunned they were. Henry was also to find out any information about the state of the fort.

"To see if our Dutch allies need any support," the admirals had told him. "But no need to ask them. The governor won't admit if he needs assistance. A proud fellow, that Dutchman."

But the implication was clear. We were to spy on our allies for some (unseemly) purpose, likely an attack. Henry hadn't made up his mind about what actions we would take, but his stance was decided. The *Integrity* would not commit treason against the crown, even if it meant treason against the admiralty in the New World.

Last night, he had given me a choice. I could stay with him and join in his rebellion. We would never be safe once word reached the rest of the English colonies in the Caribbean. There would be no more fine dinners at cozy inns near the forts. I could not safely continue my career as a naturalist.

Or I could stay in Curacao. I could make a life there among the Dutch and Spanish or find my way to another colony, even an English one. I could settle into a quiet routine away from the sea. I hadn't the means to pursue a naturalist career on private charters, and no one but Henry took me seriously anyway.

Did I want to live safely away from Henry, never tasting adventure? Or did I want to stay by his side at the helm, with unknown dangers ahead of us and behind?

I had spent most of the day here, peering over the bow. This was where I found peace. The crash of the waves was the only thing that drowned out the screams I heard whenever I closed my eyes. I didn't sleep much at all since the *Keerpunt*. Each night, I lay awake in bed next to a restless Henry until we gave up and decided to drink ourselves into dreams. But the sweet rum would wear off, and I'd wake to the sounds of Henry pacing the cabin.

I yawned and Quetzalli nibbled my earlobe. Absentmindedly, I reached my hand up to scratch her coarse fur. In my state of exhaustion, I had nearly forgotten that she sat on my shoulder.

"Are you hungry, little darling?"

She licked my hand.

"Right. Let's get you something to eat."

We made our way across the deck to the cabin. Ben was inside cleaning, but Henry was nowhere to be found.

"Cheers, Miss Spencer."

"Good afternoon, Ben. I've just come to fetch some food for Quetzalli."

"Oh, yes. I moved the scraps from your breakfast over to the dresser." He walked to the other side of the cabin and held up a small piece of bread.

Quetzalli jumped off my shoulder and scurried over to Ben. He picked her up and stroked her little brown face as she ate. Other than Henry and myself, Ben was the only person on board who had warmed to my furry companion.

"Where's the captain?" I asked.

"In the magazine with the lieutenants. Taking stock of our powder himself, he said."

Ben sat Quetzalli on the dresser, and she stuffed bits of fruit in her cheek pouches. The young sailor shuffled his feet, his eyes darting around the room.

I sighed. "What is it, Ben? You must learn to be direct with your words."

"Begging your pardon, Miss. But I'm not certain it's me place to ask."

"Which is why you're asking me and not the captain?" I raised an eyebrow.

"Aye." He fiddled with his shirt. "There's been talk, see. Among the crew."

"Talk?" I narrowed my eyes. The last thing Henry needed was a disgruntled crew and a mutiny. "What sort of talk?"

"That perhaps the Captain has. . . That maybe he isn't quite. . . Well, no one wants to say it outright, but that he is perhaps. . ."

"Are you questioning the captain's sanity?"

"Aye. Well, no. But with the *Keerpunt*, and he's been brooding like." His voice was laced with concern for the man he respected so deeply.

"The captain is not mad," I assured him. "There are. . ." I searched for the words. "Political issues that have arisen, and Captain Martin is searching for the best course of action."

Ben looked up and grinned, appearing more boyish than normal. "He'll choose the right one, I've no doubt."

I nodded. Ben excused himself, and I sat at my desk. Henry's crew had faith in him. I had faith in him. Still, he was playing a dangerous game. The Jacobites would use him and his crew as pawns, and to what end? War with the Dutch? A deposition of the king because he was half-Dutch and grew up in the Netherlands?

Quetzalli climbed into my lap, cheeks filled with food, and curled up for an afternoon nap. I stroked her as I stared blankly at my open journal. The shape of palm leaves didn't seem important anymore. The coloring of parrots seemed insignificant.

I had made my decision.

"I've made my decision," I said as I closed the door to the officers' dining room.

Henry and his officers raised their heads to look at me from where they sat. Besides Lieutenants Rainsford and Wheatley and Master Easton, Henry had included Mr. Gresham, the quartermaster, and Mr. Oakes, the boatswain, in his discussions of rebellion against the admiralty. At my urging, he had also taken Gil, the ship's surgeon, into his inner fold. We needed another rational mind. All pledged their fealty to the king privately before Henry. He trusted them implicitly. Other than Gil and Gresham, I had my doubts.

Henry's sharp eyes studied me from his seat at the head of the table. "Already? This is not the time for rashness, Hell."

He knew what I had decided, perhaps had known all along. I could see it in the concerned brow and hopeful gleam in his eye.

"What do you mean already? I've spent the last twelve hours debating the merits of each choice. My loyalty is to the king."

It wasn't entirely true. I couldn't care less about some ponce on a throne thousands of miles away. My loyalty was to Henry and to the sea. My loyalty was to whoever did not force me to be complicit in mass murder for their own insipid reasons.

I suspected the same was true for many of the men who sat before me.

I held Henry's gaze for several long moments, challenging him silently to speak against me. Finally, he sighed and muttered, "Angelic, my arse."

He gestured to the open seat next to him, and I crossed the room. Gresham rose to pull out my chair, but I waved him off. Henry smirked.

"Miss Spencer is our official interpreter and will be a part of all our proceedings. Any grievance about her position should be addressed now."

I looked at Lieutenant Wheatley. His jaw was set as he stared me down, but he did not speak. Mr. Oakes, however, cleared his throat.

"What is it, Tobias?" Henry's voice was exasperated. Oakes was a suspicious man, and well-loved by the crew.

"I. . . I like the girl meself, but there be talk amongst the crew, cap'n. We've 'ad a run of bad luck since you brought the lass on board. What with the storm and the Dutch ship."

I tensed, prepared to defend myself, but Henry placed a steadying hand on my arm.

"Tobias. You've been at sea most of your life, yes?"

"Aye, Cap'n."

Henry nodded. "And how many storms have you sailed through?"

"Can't count that high, sir."

"And storms like the one a few weeks' past? Where men were lost and the ship took heavy damage?"

"Upwards of a dozen."

"I see." Henry leaned forward. "And you've survived the doldrums before when others starved?"

"Aye."

Oakes shifted in his chair and cast his eyes downward, but Henry continued. "And you've been in battle? Or lost men in other accidents?"

The boatswain grumbled.

"Were there women aboard those ships?"

"No, Cap'n."

Henry sat back and studied the men. "If any of you think that somehow Miss Spencer is responsible for the admiralty's betrayal of the crown, you are fools. This treachery runs deep, years deep, in all likelihood. Miss Spencer works twice as hard as any man onboard, and she's thrice as smart. If you have a problem with that, you may disembark in Curacao and consider yourselves released from duty."

I smiled. At least someone on this ship recognized my worth. No one spoke, although Mr. Gresham smiled at me.

"And I suggest you dispel those rumors among the crew. Any man who believes me so weak-minded that I could be bewitched merely by sharing my bed with a lady has no place on my crew. Understood?"

Murmurs of "aye, Captain" echoed from around the table.

"Good, now back to it. We'll send an emissary with a report from Curacao back to St. Martin. We shall determine what the missive will say once we arrive and meet with the Dutch admiral."

"And then?" Lieutenant Rainsford asked.

Henry shrugged. "We wait."

Wheatley shook his head. "But where do we go? Once word gets out that we've acted against our orders, we won't be able to dock in any English port."

"How will we get our wages?" Oakes asked.

"What about the rest of the men?" Rainsford said. "Are we making this decision for them?"

The captain closed his eyes and pinched his brow. He looked old under his white wig, the weight of the world bearing down on him. "There are no good answers here, my friends. Not yet."

"Perhaps we could return to England." Gil spoke for the first time, his voice quiet. "Gain an audience with His Majesty and tell him."

Supportive murmurs filled the tense air.

"We can't," I said.

Wheatley sneered. "And why not?"

"We don't know how deep this Jacobite conspiracy runs."

"The First Lord Admiral and the Admiral of the Fleet both aided King William in the deposition. Rumor has it they begged him to come claim the throne." The young lieutenant folded his arms as if he had me in checkmate.

"But Captain Martin must first report to the Commodore and Rear Admirals of the Blue. The offices have been in a constant state of disarray for years. If they don't believe us, they'll hang us for treason, and if they do believe us and are sympathetic to the Jacobite cause, they'll accuse us of treason and hang us. If they *do* believe us and our complaint reaches higher Jacobite ears, then the Rear Admirals will swing alongside us."

I smirked at Wheatley, who glared back.

"Miss Spencer is correct," Henry said. "There was an assassination plot on His Majesty just prior to our last docking in England. I don't like our odds."

The men around the table nodded. Henry's lips were set in a firm line.

"I've no plans to be crow food," Mr. Gresham said. "I stand with you, Captain."

Slowly, the rest of the men murmured their assent. Henry cleared his throat and stood. "Very well, men. We shall reconvene tomorrow. I expect a full report of our stock and supplies, and I want this ship so clean it glistens in the sunlight."

He reached the door then turned his head back to meet my eye. I rose and followed him to our cabin. He had me pinned against the door the moment I shut it, his mouth crashing onto mine with pent-up stress.

We never made it to the bed.

Chapter 31

"If what you are saying is true," the Dutch governor of Curacao said, his fingers steepled as he peered at us. "Then we are all of us in danger in the New World."

I shifted on the wooden chair and glanced at Henry before translating. I had to swallow my indignation at what the governor insinuated. Why would we lie?

Henry nodded. "You're correct, my lord. But we are always in danger. Despite the best efforts of gentlemen like you, the New World lacks the civility of our motherlands. We are far from the crowns we are loyal to, which is why the Jacobites have the freedom to act."

I smiled. This is why Henry was such a successful captain. He complimented his superiors while standing firm in his statements. All I wanted to do was tell the governor to get his head out of his arse and listen. Instead, I delivered Henry's response.

The governor leaned back in his chair, his face blank under his powdered wig. Then the lines around his eyes crinkled. "You do not speak with the forked tongue of most lords. Your directness is most refreshing."

I translated, and Henry stiffened at the praise. "I am not a lord, your excellency."

"Thank the heavens that you are not," the governor said. He leaned forward and dipped a quill in the inkwell on his desk. He scribbled something on a piece of parchment and sealed it. "Take this to my purser. Something to make up for the allotments you will miss for your loyalty."

"You are most kind, sir." Henry tucked the letter in his coat and stood, but I remained seated.

"Your excellency," I said. "Your kindness is appreciated. Is there no way you can write to His Majesty so that he might put a swift end to this conspiracy?"

"My dear. The world is not so simple as that."

"Are truth and justice not simple?"

He smiled warmly, and something in his eyes reminded me of Father. "Not when everyone has their own version of truth and justice. If I were to write to the Stadthold-er"—he used King William's Dutch title instead of his royal one— "it would be taken as inciting violence at best or at worst, paranoia. My people here need me, and I cannot risk some ambitious youth taking my spot as governor."

Henry touched my shoulder. Reluctantly, I stood and thanked the governor for his ear and his gift.

We said nothing as we made our way out of the governor's house to the building where his purser kept office. The purser disappeared to fetch the gold, and Henry reached out and squeezed my hand.

"What did you say to him?"

"I asked why he could not write to the king and tell him of the insurrection here."

"My bold Hell." His eyes twinkled in the window-filtered sunlight of the office. "And what did he say?"

I waved a hand. "Politics."

But in my mind, I chewed on his words about truth and justice. I did not understand, not entirely. What Henry and I were doing was right. Loyalty, integrity. These things were rewarded by the heavens and the king, yes? That's what I had been taught. That's what the priests and philosophers agreed upon. What motivation was there for virtue if it meant different things to different people?

The purser returned and counted out the coins on his oak desk. My eyes widened as he counted ever higher. Henry inhaled sharply. I did not know the expense of keeping the *Integrity*, but this seemed substantial. I tried to do calculations in my head, but that was never my strength.

We thanked the Dutchman and exited the office into the blinding tropical sun. It was hot in Curacao with little sea breeze today. My dress plastered to my skin. I pulled my fan from inside my bodice. It, too, was covered in sweat, but I fanned myself anyway.

I squinted in the brightness at Henry. "That was. . ."

"Good fortune." He wiped his brow with the back of his hand. "Barring any major repairs, enough to feed the crew for two or three months. Longer if we cut rations."

"Why? Why would he do it?"

Henry shrugged. "Gratitude? Apologies that he cannot do more?"

"Will not do more, you mean."

He held out his arm to me, and I took it. We walked through the sandy streets. "You know politics is nothing more than a pissing contest," he said.

I pouted my lip. "Foolish men."

"Come now! What of Her Majesty Queen Mary?"

"She's a bloody fool, too. All the intrigue and scandal. Starting wars over who worships God Almighty the best, at what cost? The blood of regular people who just want to live their lives." I gestured with the fan emphatically as I spoke. "Using God to their own personal gain. It is about power and nothing more. How is that fair to the Creator? That is why I'm certain He has fucked off and let us be. I certainly would if I were Him."

Henry stopped as we reached the beach and turned to face me, a smirk on his face.

"What?" I asked.

"Do you even realize that you stopped speaking English?"

"Did I?"

He threw his head back and laughed. "I heard at least three other languages, I believe. And you spoke as if they were all one."

I wrinkled my nose. "Sorry. Old habit with Father."

Henry leaned down to place a gentle kiss on my lips. "It is endearing."

"'Twas a most excellent speech. Shame you didn't understand most of it."

"I have no doubt."

He surveyed the beachfront and pointed when he spotted Ben. "Come, I want Ben to take this to my office. I would prefer the purser not know of this money. I'd rather it not be spent unless we are desperate."

"Do you trust Ben not to speak of it?"

He nodded. "I trust the lad with my life."

"Ahoy, captain! Miss Spencer!" Ben waved. "I didn't expect you back for a time."

"We are not returning to the ship as of yet, Ben. I still have business to attend to." He relayed his instructions, and Ben nodded gravely.

The boy rolled his shoulders back. "I won't let you down, Captain."

"I know you won't. When you've secured it, you are free to go ashore. Report back before breakfast."

Ben's pimpled face lit up. "You are most kind, Captain."

He pushed the small boat into the water and rowed quickly toward the *Integrity*. I called after him. "Feed Quetzalli, would you?"

Ben raised his hand in acknowledgement. Henry chuckled. "He's a good lad."

"What business do we have to attend to?"

Henry had said he would send the missive to his admiral the following day. He planned to report that Curacao harbor was virtually undefended, although it was far from the truth.

"You'll see."

I hiked my skirts up and followed him through the thick white sand. He stopped at a bustling brothel. Music poured through the open doors and windows, accompanied by the off-key singing and boisterous laughter of drunken sailors.

"Henry!" I hissed. "What are you doing?"

He rolled his eyes. "Best damn punch on the island."

"Oh, I'm quite certain that's it." I folded my arms and glared at him.

"You're lovely when you're insecure," he said. I glared harder. "Darling, look around. Why would I want any of these fork-tongued demons when I've the company of the Devil herself?"

I softened my gaze and met his eyes, blue as the cloudless sky above. He smiled, and it was both lust and love. "Fine. But I have no qualms about putting a harlot in her place if they put a hand on you."

"Someone has to defend my honor." He offered his hand, and I allowed him to lead me inside.

Two pints of Kill Devil punch later, I sat on Henry's knee and sang along to the catch that the ballad singer led in rounds. Prostitutes milled around in varying states of undress, charming the raucous sailors and merchants. A lovely dark-haired whore from across the room, with amber skin and eyes to match, winked at me. Her bosom was ample and barely contained by her bodice. Heat rose to my cheeks.

The song ended, and the crowd cheered. The singer stepped off the small stage, and the fiddler stepped forward. I planted a wet kiss on Henry's mouth. He tasted of sweat and sweet tropical fruits from the punch.

"She's pretty," Henry whispered in my ear.

"What? Who?"

"The girl you cannot keep your eyes off over there."

I pulled away. "I don't know what you're talking about!"

"Calm down, Hell. There's nothing wrong with it."

I blushed and cast my eyes down. A wench walked up and offered more punch at that moment. I grabbed the glass from her tray and downed half of it. "Henry, I haven't a clue what you're implying."

"I'm not angry, Hell. In fact, I have coin if you want to try. . ." He gestured toward the staircase.

I glanced back at the whore, unable to stop myself and giving myself away. Memories of Deirdre's soft skin bubbled like sea foam in my rum-addled mind. I considered it until I looked back at Henry. His eyes searched mine intently, a warm half-smile on his flushed face.

"I have no need. I have you."

"But if you ever want to dip your toes in other waters, I wouldn't mind. Things are different inside the brothels."

I swallowed hard. "Henry, I already have."

"Oh. Oh! Oh?"

I took another swig. The pineapple and coconut hid the burn of the rum, and the drink flowed smoothly down my throat. "Aye. Her name was Deirdre. She's a nun now."

My eyes misted. The rum, certainly. I wiped them.

"Did you—" He hiccuped. "Did you love her?"

I squeezed my eyes shut, too drunk to think about such difficult questions. "I did. . . or I wanted to. But. . ."

"But what?"

"She wasn't you. She didn't understand me the way you do."

The patrons cheered, and I glanced up. The singer was returning to the stage. His doublet was improperly buttoned, and his auburn hair was mussed. The surrealism of my situation hit me as the last of that pint washed over me. At some point, I had fully straddled Henry's lap, and my hair hung loose. His bulge pressed against me. What would Deirdre think of my behavior? Or my father?

I chuckled, and once I started, I couldn't stop. Henry fell into a fit of laughter, too, and I wondered if I had spoken out loud. We chortled as if we were mad. And perhaps we were. Henry'd made me a full member of the crew. We had turned rogue. And I had nearly gone upstairs with a bawd in the full light of day.

I kissed Henry unabashed. It wasn't decent or proper, but there were no rules in here, in a brothel at the edge of the world. His hands ran over my body, and the sounds of the room melted away.

Eventually, Henry led me through the crowd toward a back door. Behind the brothel were empty crates and smashed bottles. I considered hazily that it reminded me of our first kiss behind the chandler's shop years before. Then I pushed him against the wall and made quick work of his buttons.

It was sloppy and rushed and the world spun a little as my legs hugged his waist. But his hot breath and sharp bite on my neck kept me grounded, and I lost myself. Better than any rum punch.

When we finished, Henry laced his breeches but kept his officer's coat open over his cotton shirt. I straightened my bodice and fluffed my skirts. He flashed me his best lopsided grin.

"I left a mark," he slurred.

I reached up to my neck. "Henry!"

"Apologies, m'lady." He tried to bow and stumbled.

Another memory bubbled to the surface. Another drunken tryst against a wall. The night we were discovered. The night before Henry was flogged and we were forced apart. I could still feel the scream in my throat as the lash hit his skin. I could still see his crimson blood on the deck.

"Whasswrong? Hell?"

I shook off the memory and smiled to reassure him. "I want to get out of this bloody dress. Let's return to the ship."

If I gripped his arm harder as we staggered toward the beach, it was not because of the drinks.

Chapter 32

We sailed from Curacao three days later. Henry sent the missive and informed the admiralty that the harbor was undefended. We set a course for Trinidad. Spain was our ally, and we could safely dock in Spanish harbors, even if we weren't warmly received. But Trinidad had become home to the Dutch, English, and Courlander settlers, as well.

The *Integrity* dropped anchor a few miles south of the town of Port-of-Spain, and Henry ordered the entire crew to disembark. Everyone gathered on the beach, murmuring among themselves in confusion. I stood behind Henry's right side with Quetzalli on my shoulder as he stood on top of a large barrel. He did not need to say even a word to bring his men to attention.

He cleared his throat. His hand trembled, not visible to anyone but me, but when he spoke, his voice was steady. Strong.

"My brothers. The good Lord himself has blessed me with the finest crew in His Majesty's navy. We have broken bread together. Fought together. Bled together. I respect each and every one of you, and I would sail to hell itself with you!"

The crew cheered. Henry clenched and unclenched a fist a few times before he continued. "I stand before you today with grave news and a choice. A fortnight past, I gave you the orders to sink a Dutch passenger ship, the *Keerpunt*. Those orders came from Admiral Wells in St. Martin, who led me to believe the ship was a danger to the safety of England's colonies. But after, I discovered the truth."

The crowd rustled with heavy whispers. Henry continued, "Admiral Wells, among other members of the admiralty, has betrayed their Royal Majesties. They are supporting a Jacobite rebellion and overthrow of the throne."

Cries of disbelief. From the treeline, the sinister squawks of birds rang out like an omen. I shivered, despite the sun's heat. Quetzalli nuzzled my cheek.

"We are sworn to defend the Crown. I care not for politics, only for my oath. The other officers agree. Therefore, we have acted against the Admiralty by foiling their plans for an attack on the Dutch in Curacao."

Silence, save for the sounds of the jungle and crash of the waves. The faces of the crew that I could see were wide-eyed and thin-lipped as they waited for the captain to continue.

"I will not decide for you if you will act in rebellion against the admiralty. We will be in danger, but I intend to honor my oath to God and King William. I cannot promise safety, only that I will defend you as I can. It may come to shedding English blood by our own swords. But I offer you this choice: you may stay aboard the *Integrity* and swear fealty to the King and Queen before me, or you may leave. You may receive your year's wages and stay in Trinidad, or book passage to elsewhere. I will relieve you of your duty with honor. Please record your intention with Lieutenants Rainsford and Wheatley before sundown."

Henry leapt down from the barrel. I smiled at him, and he nodded. Only his eyes gave away his worry.

"Well done, Captain," Wheatley said.

"Thank you. Did you fetch the things I asked for?"

Wheatley handed him two rifles and a satchel. "Are you certain you will be safe to go alone?"

"I won't be alone. I'll have Miss Spencer."

Wheatley glared at me, and I flashed my most saccharine grin.

"Kindness, Wheatley. No matter what you hear the men say, treat them with kindness. I'll return soon."

"Yes, Captain. Safe hunting."

Henry offered a rifle to me. I took it. I preferred the blade, and if not that, a pistol. But my aim had improved with the rifle, and a chance to be alone with Henry among the trees was worth it. I had even brought my sketchbook. I kissed Quetzalli's little head and handed her to Ben for safekeeping. "The jungle isn't safe for you, little darling."

She chittered and crawled on top of Ben's head. Then I followed Henry to the jungle while the crew decided the fate of the *Integrity*.

"What if we are not left with enough men to sail the ship?" I asked. "What then?"

Henry stepped carefully over the roots of a large tree. We walked several more paces before he answered.

"Then we'll establish ourselves in Port-of-Spain and figure out our next steps."

Insects buzzed around our heads, and the stale smell of moss mingled with the fragrant flowers. I swatted away some species of fly from my face. We didn't speak for a long time, focusing on our violent, verdant environment. An anaconda leered at us from where it lay, curled around a tree branch. The guttural screeching of monkeys, high in the treetops, performed the haunting harmony to the melody of the rainforest's symphony.

I was no stranger to the humid heat of the New World, but the jungle was something else entirely. My eyes stung from the sweat that flooded my eyes. Every sip from my waterskin tasted of the salt from my upper lip. The further into the foliage we ventured, the harder it became to breathe.

Still, it was beautiful. Peaceful. Full of life. There were no politics here, no heartbreaks and no betrayals.

My mind wandered as I traipsed behind Henry. I shifted the rifle to my opposite shoulder and heard the words of the Curacao governor in my head once again. There were many ideals I knew were wrong and many customs I resented. The fact that I could not inherit the Spencer estate, that my fate was always dependent on a man, all the wars kings had started over who was anointed by God, sacrificing innocent lives for it since time in memoriam. Surely, I had believed, everyone else recognized how wrong these things were?

I studied Henry as he hacked through the vines with his sword. His back muscles rippled through his stained shirt. His loyalty lay with the king and queen. The admirals' loyalty lay with another king. I knew beyond a shadow of a doubt that Henry would sacrifice himself for what he deemed right.

Was he right? Did I believe that? As an Englishwoman, I should have felt the same loyalty.

Henry stopped and crouched down to study the floor. I knelt beside him to see what he had spotted. Tracks, similar to Quetzalli's feet, but much larger.

"Tepezcuintle," I whispered. "I know only the Nahuatl word."

"Lappe." He looked at me, a smile spreading across his face. "At least, that is what they are called here."

"Why are you smiling?"

"Because Cook makes a delicious salt-brined lappe."

He hopped to his feet with boyish enthusiasm and held his hand out to me. "The tracks are fresh. Let's go."

In that moment, I knew where my loyalties lay. With Henry and nowhere else. A breath escaped my lungs. My father had taught me never to place my worth on another person.

"Your brilliant mind and fiery spirit are all you need," he had told me, over and over. He'd be disappointed in me, committing treason for the love of a man.

But then, he'd tried to marry me off, knowing I could never be the woman he wanted me to be if I married a gentleman. I'd be trapped in the worst sort of prison—my own caged mind withering from disuse.

I loved Henry. I loved him far more than I loved myself, and I loved him because he let me be who I was born to be. The way Father had wanted to but couldn't because he had been bound by his own loyalty to tradition.

Kings and countries be damned. The only homeland I had ever had was the sea. The only person worth dying for walked ahead of me. Whatever the rest of the world deemed was just and fair, I cared not. A sailor follows true north, always, and the lodestone in my heart pointed straight to Henry.

When we emerged from the jungle with fifty pounds of fresh lappe between us, tents lined the beach and sailors milled around, chatting and drinking. No factions, no bloodshed. I raised an eyebrow at Henry, and he looked equally quizzical.

"Doesn't seem like a mutiny." He kept his voice light, but I could hear the fear underneath.

I squeezed his hand. "I do believe they would be armed with more than flasks of rum if they were to turn on us."

"You're probably correct." He swallowed hard, his Adam's apple bobbing. Then he gave me a wavering smile. "Now or never."

We left the safety of the treeline. The sun was high and bright, and I sighed as a gentle sea breeze cooled my sweat-laden skin. As we approached, sailors raised their flasks or greeted Henry with an "Ahoy, Captain." Henry's fear turned to confusion, as I felt him ease next to me. The other officers were gathered round a table near the largest tent. Rainsford sat on a wooden chair with a stack of parchment in front of him.

"Good hunting, Captain?" Wheatley asked with a grin.

"Aye." He sat down the dead creatures that he carried, and I followed suit. "Everyone seems. . . amiable."

Rainsford leaned back in his chair and placed his feet on the desk. He'd removed his officer's coat, and his auburn hair was not hidden by his usual brown wig. "Everyone is amiable. We have good news."

Ben emerged from the tent with my rat on his shoulder. She leapt the distance and landed squarely on my shoulders with her sharp claws. "Ouch!"

She licked my ear, and Wheatley rolled his eyes.

"How many?" Henry asked. "How many are leaving?"

I held my breath. We needed a large enough crew to sail the *Integrity*. If too many left, we would be stranded in Trinidad.

"Twenty."

I blinked. Henry reached behind him and grabbed my hand.

"What?" Henry and I said in unison.

"Twenty. Not Jacobites, I do not believe," Wheatley answered. "Just honest men eager to return home."

Henry laughed, a loud, joyful melody, and the rest of the officers joined in. I chuckled, relieved. These men were also loyal to Henry. Not in the same way I was, but as their trusted captain, the man who treated each of them as brothers. Warmth blossomed in my chest. I was proud of him.

"Very well. I want to speak with each of them this evening. Tomorrow, we can listen to oaths from the rest of the men." Henry glanced at his cabin boy. "Ben, take this meat to the cook. Tell him I'd like it the way he prepared last year near Jamaica."

"Aye, Captain," Ben replied, and the other officers stood and bowed.

In our tent, I unlaced my bodice and boots. Henry removed his shirt and collapsed on the pallet Ben had prepared.

"Can you believe it, Hell?" He lay back with his hands behind his head. Quetzalli snuggled into a ball on his bare chest.

"Believe what? That you're on our bed with your filthy boots?"

He moved his feet. "Sorry."

I giggled. "I can believe it, Henry. Your men love you."

"They're good men."

"So are you."

I pulled my chemise over my head and slipped off my breeches before dipping a cloth in a basin of water by my trunk. I closed my eyes and moaned at the cool, damp sensation against my grimy, sweaty skin.

"I think we should go for a moonlight swim this—"

Henry placed his hand over mine and took the cloth. I shivered as he ran it over my breasts and down my stomach. He bent his head down and whispered in my ear. "Are you trying to torture me?"

"Torture? Why Captain Martin! Whatever do you mean?" My fingers pulled at his breeches, and he tugged me against his body, hard.

I pressed into him and moved my hips, eliciting a groan from deep in his throat.

"I think I will have to punish you, sailor," he murmured in a husky voice. "You cannot torture your captain."

"Oh no. Well, I deserve it, I suppose."

"Oh, yes, you do."

He spun me around and pushed me down on the pallet before removing his breeches and stockings. Then he was on me, biting my neck. He kept my arms pinned at my sides, leaving me to writhe helplessly as he moved his mouth lower. I panted and squirmed, and he chuckled against my skin.

Just as his mouth began to move past my navel, a flash of sunlight blinded us.

"Captain! I was—oh! Oh God!"

Lieutenant Wheatley froze in the entry of our tent. Henry rolled off the pallet in surprise, which left me utterly exposed to the man I disliked most on the ship. We scrambled to cover ourselves.

"John! Christ, man!" Henry sat up and tried to shield me with his body. "Step outside, Lieutenant!"

"Yes, yes, of course. I am so sorry, Captain, I—" The man's face was red as he backed away slowly.

"Wheatley! Get the fuck out!" I half-screamed.

The flap of the tent closed, and I blinked to adjust to the dimmer light. I stood and rummaged in my trunk for a fresh chemise. "I'm going to kill that fucking bastard."

"It was a mistake," Henry said. "Although I do not appreciate another man getting to see your. . . assets."

"Why do you defend him? He is insufferable!" I stomped my way into a petticoat.

"Keep your voice down." Henry closed the distance between us and took my hands in his. "Wheatley is a good man, Hell. He should not have barged in here like that, but it was a mistake. We've certainly scarred him."

I huffed. "Usually have to pay good coin to see a show like that."

He dressed, and I found a green silk mantua that I slipped on over my shift and petticoat. It was too hot for stays, so I simply attached the top of the dress to a matching stomacher and tied the bottom up into a bustle.

Then I set to work brushing my hair while Henry stepped outside. I listened to their conversation through the tent walls.

"Lieutenant." Henry's voice was gruff.

"Captain, please accept my most humble apologies. I will accept whatever punishment you deem fit with grace."

Bloody sycophant, I thought. I hate the type.

"Oh, get up, Lieutenant. I'm not going to beat you for a mistake."

"Yes, sir. Thank you, sir."

"I trust you have learned to knock, but in order to make it stick. . ." His voice lowered, and I couldn't understand what he said. Damn. I'd force it out of him later.

Henry poked his head inside the tent. "Oh, good, you're dressed. Darling, Lieutenant Wheatley has something he wants to say to you."

I rolled my eyes and folded my arms across my chest. Henry held open the tent flap and Wheatley ducked inside. He wouldn't look at me.

"Miss Spencer."

"Lieutenant."

There was a long pause. Henry clapped the second lieutenant on his shoulder, hard. "Miss Spencer is not on the ground, man."

Wheatley sighed and raised his head. His brown eyes were hard, and heat flushed his cheeks. "My apologies, Miss Spencer, for violating your privacy."

I gave one stiff nod. "Very well then."

Henry smiled and laughed. "Excellent. Now, I have work to do, Hell. But the lieutenant will be stationed just outside the tent. Anything you need, anything at all, ask him, and he will be happy to fetch it for you. Isn't that correct, Lieutenant?"

"Aye, captain." But he did not sound happy.

My eyes widened as understanding dawned on me. I smirked. "That is most kind of you. Would you fetch Quetzalli some fruit from the trees? I saw mangoes and bananas."

"Yes, Miss Spencer." He left the tent with an exasperated sigh. Henry winked at me and followed him out.

I spent the afternoon and evening sending Wheatley on errands. He fetched me water, then rum. I sent him to find limes and then more fruit for myself. I had plenty of ink, but I told him I needed a fresh inkwell. By the time I joined Henry outside for dinner, Wheatley was well and truly tired of me, although he could not speak against me.

That night, Henry drummed his fingers on his chest as we lay in bed.

"What is on your mind, my love?" I turned and propped myself on my elbow, although I could not make out more than his silhouette in the darkness.

"The men that want to leave. They apologized profusely for abandoning the crew."

I took his hand to stop his nervous tapping, lifting it to my lips to kiss his fingertips. "What were their reasons?"

Henry sighed. "Two of them are old, ready for an easier life, and thought they'd take the chance. Five of them have wives and children back home. But the rest. . ."

"What?"

"They were press-ganged into service. Some for petty theft, others for no reason at all. They never wanted to be sailors."

I swallowed. It wasn't as if I didn't know that His Majesty's Navy press-ganged sailors in times of war. And it seemed England was always at war. But I had never spoken to a sailor about it.

"I cannot imagine."

"No. Neither can I."

Henry was trying to make sense of something, trying to come to some sort of epiphany. I could tell; I knew him that well. But then exhaustion washed over me, weighing down my eyelids as if they wore irons. I yawned and kissed Henry's shoulder. Then I reached between us to scratch a sleeping Quetzalli before drifting into dreams.

Chapter 33

A FEW MONTHS LATER

"Ship ahoy!" the rigger climbed from the crow's nest.

Henry turned away from Master Easton, who was giving his latest update on our course and looked up at the mainmast. I was at the wheel while Mr. Gresham visited the bilge to answer nature's call. I followed Henry's gaze.

The sun shone brightly against the blue skies, and only a few white clouds floated by. We sailed at a steady speed, the wind fair and strong. Quetzalli had curled up on top of my hat, which I had purchased in Trinidad—a black, leather, tricorn sailor's hat.

"Can you see their colors?" Henry yelled.

Boatswain Oakes repeated the message as he stood closer to the mainmast. We waited expectantly for the response. The rigging climber was naught but a speck from where I stood.

"'Tis the bloody French!"

Henry threw his head back and laughed a deep, wild laugh I had never heard before. "The sea has blessed us today. Prepare for battle!"

"Prepare for battle!" the officers echoed.

When Henry looked at me, there was a gleam in his eye. My heart thudded, and my palms sweat against the handles of the helm. The ship descended into a frenzy as sailors rushed to ready for engagement. Henry stepped toward me.

"We need the prize," he said. I nodded, and he continued. "We are still at war with the French. I would never have allowed you onboard last spring if we were actively attacking ships, but. . ."

"I know, Henry." I swallowed.

"I trust you. I know you can defend yourself, but I'm giving you the choice. . . you can hide—"

"No." I rolled my shoulders back and raised my chin to appear confident and brave. "I am a member of this crew. I fight."

"This won't be like the *Keerpunt*," he promised. "They would as soon attack us."

"I understand, Henry."

He studied me for a moment before speaking. "Fetch your pistol and powder purse, and secure your rat. Is your blade sharpened?"

"Aye."

"Good. We have a half-hour at this speed, but we will put the sails up as we draw nearer." He grabbed the wheel. "I will sail until Gresham returns. What is taking him so long?"

I shrugged, then hurried into our cabin. Quetzalli climbed down my back onto the floor. She yawned and stretched. My heart ached. What if I did not survive this? What would happen to her?

"Quetzalli, cage." I pointed to her small cage on the desk. She reluctantly made her way to it, but she glanced back before she went in to be certain I had not changed my mind. "Cage, little darling."

My eyes watered, but I blinked them away. I scratched her behind her ears, then closed the small, metal door. Then I hid her in the cabinet under the window where Henry had made small air holes.

With a deep breath, I found my powder purse and checked it. Full and dry with plenty of shot. Good. I fastened it to the belt I wore everywhere these days, since Henry demanded I always be armed. I pulled my cutlass from its sheath and ran my finger over the flat side of the blade. Could I do it? Could I kill a man?

Prizes were the only we could survive now. It was too dangerous to go into English harbors. And as England was still at war with the Sun King in Versailles, attacking French vessels were allowed under the rules of war.

Rules of war. What a ridiculous notion.

I sheathed my sword and tried to ignore the stone in the pit of my stomach. As I prepared to return to the main deck, the sunlight glinted off a bottle on the table by the door. I said a silent prayer of thanks, unstoppered the bottle, and let the smoky amber liquid pour down my throat.

"Now or never," I said aloud to the empty room.

When I emerged onto the main deck again, a feeling of tension and excitement blew on the breeze. And fear, though it was stifled by the energy of the crew. I looked around for Henry and found him on the forecastle with his spyglass.

"Captain," I said as I approached.

He handed me the spyglass. "Tell me what you see."

I peered through the tool at the French ship ahead. "Naval, not privateer."

"Good. And the class?"

I stared at the ship as I ran through my rarely used knowledge of French vessel. Two gun decks with a forecastle, but still sizeable. "Vaisseaux de. . . Troisième Rang?"

"Yes, it appears so. How many guns is that?"

"Oh, my." I pulled the telescope away from my eye and blinked at Henry. "I don't know."

"Less than fifty. What else do you notice?"

We outgunned them then. I returned my gaze to the ship and tried to notice something else, anything else. "Uh. . . it's sailing away from us?"

He chuckled. "Yes, and we'll catch them. But why are they sailing away?"

"Because we have more guns?"

"That's part of it. Look to the hull."

I looked. And looked. I tried to find any sign of damage, anything out of the norm. "I don't know Henry."

"She rides high. She's not weighed down in the water. At all."

"Oh." I handed him the spyglass and thought, chewing my lip and furrowing my brow. "It won't be a big prize. But. . . they also may not have much shot."

He smiled his approval. "Or food or water. They flee quickly, without treasure to defend. There's a good chance the crew is quite desperate."

"Ah." I shivered, though the sun was hot. We were so close, I could see the colors of the flag without a telescope. Henry folded me into his arms.

"Remember everything I taught you, Hell. You're better with a blade than most sailors, but don't be afraid to use your flintlock or anything else at your disposal. And if things turn sour, hide if you can."

I nodded and trembled.

"I need to speak with the lieutenants. Stand near the port side so you won't be in the initial onslaught." He dropped his arms, and nausea washed over me as I lost my anchor. "I love you, Hell. You can do this."

I gripped my cutlass too hard, as I stood out of the way, and my fingers went numb. The minutes passed, feeling both like seconds and hours. I barely noticed what was going on around me, as everyone passed by me in a blur.

"Miss Spencer, are you well?"

Jolted out of my oblivion, I looked up to see young Ben standing before me. He had a short sword in his hand.

I opened my mouth to respond, but nothing came out.

"I was scared my first battle, Miss. I'm still scared. But once it starts, you'll be so focused on staying alive, you won't even notice the fear. And besides,"—he smiled at me—"you're one of the best swordsmen I've ever seen. Er, not that you're a man. . ."

"Thank you, Ben." I took a deep breath and rolled my shoulders back. "But I've never been in true danger before when I've fought."

"To your posts!" Henry called from across the deck.

"Posts!" the officers echoed.

We were nearly upon the French ship. Henry and Rainsford barked orders to open the gun ports and lower the sails. At the wheel, Mister Gresham had a maniacal grin on his face as he steered the *Integrity* alongside the other vessel.

My ears rang and my vision blurred in the cacophany from both ships. The only sound I could make out was the rapid percussion of my heart, and the only sensation I could feel was the smooth metal of my sword's hilt, which had grown hot in my grip.

Someone grabbed my wrist, yanking me from the abyss of my terror. I looked up into Henry's eyes, blue as the sea. His lips crashed onto mine, and the kiss pulled me back to the deck of the *Integrity*, saving me from the frozen void. A blaze rushed through my veins.

Henry pulled away, laughed, and then yelled, "FIRE!"

Our cannons roared like a sea monster. Every voice was drowned, and the ship rocked. I nearly lost my footing, but Ben grabbed hold of my arm until I steadied. The acrid smell of gunpowder singed my nose and burned my throat.

The return fire threw us both backward, and a wave crashed over the side of the ship, drenching me in a cold, salty spray that stung my eyes. The smoke offered no refuge of visibility.

I scrambled to my feet and grabbed hold of the ropes that lined the deck.

"Get us closer, Gresham!" I heard Henry scream.

More cannons. More waves. More smoke. This time, I was prepared. I coughed through the bitter, rotten smell of burnt powder. I could taste the fear and anticipation of my crewmates, sweet and sweaty on my tongue. The French vessel drew ever closer.

Within minutes, we were too close to loose the cannons, or else we'd both enter Davy Jones' locker.

"Gangways!" a voice shouted. I couldn't make out whose.

I swallowed hard, sparing one last fleeting thought of dread. The wooden planks hit the other ship with a resounding thud. Through the smoke, I saw Henry at the head of the fray. He drew his sword, and an inhuman cry escaped his lips. Then he led the charge onto the enemy's deck.

Snarls and shouts echoed around me, and I lost myself in them. My feet moved without any instruction from my mind. I followed the crowd of sailors who pushed and shoved to get aboard the other vessel. I took the plank nearest the aft in three large strides and was immediately greeted by a Frenchman's sabre.

I parried it with ease and sliced his leg as I leapt onto the main deck. He stumbled, and his eyes widened as he realized I was no ordinary seaman.

"La garce!" *You bitch.*

I took advantage of his surprise and kicked him between the legs. He fell to the ground, and I pushed into the heart of the battle.

Ben was right; there was no time to think. I slashed and parried and dodged. I grunted and screamed. My sword arm moved as an extension of myself, adding its own rhythm to the clanking symphony of steel on steel.

Battle was a storm. Swords clashed like thunder. Sweat poured like rain. Sprays of blood were flashes of lightning. It was wild and angry. But in the midst of the tempest, there was something primal and instinctive, a sense of order in the gyre of insanity.

I found myself dueling a Frenchman on the steps to the quarterdeck. His blade slipped past my defenses and pierced through my shirt on my stomach. But the tip of his sword did not break skin. It halted. He had hit exactly on a piece of boning in my stays.

He froze, panic spreading across his face. "Vous êtes sorcière!"

He tripped over his own feet as he tried to ascend the steps backward. He fell, and I rolled my eyes.

"Je suis une femme." Not a witch, just a woman.

I took the rest of the stairs in two strides. The throng was thinner on the quarterdeck. Henry dueled two sailors with a mad grin on his face, while the Frenchmen panted in their attempts to keep up.

But across the deck, someone had Wheatley pinned against the edge. I ran to help. Wheatley's sword lay a foot away from him. He attempted to fight off each stab with only a dagger.

Everyone around me was embroiled in their own fight, and no one had noticed me yet on this deck. With soft steps, I crept behind the enemy swordsman and ran my blade through his back. Blood spurted, covering my face. A scream died on the man's throat as he crumpled to the ground.

Wheatley looked surprised. He grabbed his sword. "Thanks."

I nodded and turned to face the rest of the battle. Henry was now surrounded. I glanced at Wheatley, then together we went to aid our captain. Soon, all I knew was the sunlight glinting on silver, clinking metal ringing in my ears, and blood.

It might have been mere seconds or years before we heard a roaring voice yell for surrender in French. As the fighting slowed, I began to return from my bloodlust. I blinked and wiped my face.

"You know what to do," Henry said to Wheatley.

"Aye, Captain." The lieutenant commanded the enemy in fluent French to make their way to the main mast. Others from our crew followed, their swords or guns pointed at the French, who slowly walked to the center of the main deck.

Henry smiled at me. "Stay with them, Hell. Keep them in line."

I joined my crewmates in surrounding the French sailors while Henry took men to raid the hold and the captain's cabin. The defeated men put up no resistance. As we stood on guard, I saw the weariness in their faces. Not from this battle alone; their eyes did not match the eyes of my own crew, who were exhausted but excited.

This vessel had known hunger and defeat in recent days. Their shoulders slumped, and when they met our eyes, there was no hatred. Only resignation.

Within a half-hour, we had taken the last of the gold, barrels of fine French wine, two barrels of gunpowder, and some wheat flour. Henry was correct—this ship had little left to defend.

Back on the *Integrity*, I followed Henry into our cabin. I glanced in the vanity mirror. My face was stained with blood, as was my shirt. The gravity of what I had just done fell over me, and I thought of the sailors I had felled with a wave of nausea. But I had saved the lives of my crewmates, and without a prize, our own circumstances would soon be as dire as those of the French.

An unexpected smile spread across my face, and Henry came up behind me.

He wrapped his arms around my waist, and I saw the same smile on his own visage. "Euphoric, isn't it?"

"Yes," I agreed. "A thrilling rush. Primal, even."

"You're beautiful, Hell."

I laughed. Beautiful is not how I would have described myself at that moment, covered in blood and sweat, my shirt ripped and eyes tired. "You jest, sir."

"No." He shook his head and kissed my neck. "I've always said that red suits you."

Chapter 34

"**B**ollocks. Shit. Henry!" I was perched in the crow's nest, relieving the watch. Three ships approached in the horizon, off the starboard bow. They moved quickly through the water. My heart thudded as I tried to remember what to do.

"Ships ahoy! Starboard bow!" I yelled. I smacked myself for forgetting such a simple holler. "Idiot."

"How many?" a faint voice down below called. I peered down. Rainsford.

"Three."

"Colors?"

I turned back and looked through the telescope again. "I cannot make them out! But I am not sure they are man-of-wars."

"Come down, Hell! Smith is coming up." It was Henry's voice this time, and I could hear the edge in his voice.

I shoved the telescope into its pouch on my belt. Then I scrambled over the edge of the basket and twined my foot in the rigging until I had gained security. The rigging blew in the breeze, and I moved as quickly as I dared down the ropes. My heart beat as fast as the canvas sails slapped in the wind.

Henry grabbed my hand like a gentleman as I neared the deck. "No colors?"

"Too far to see."

He shook his head. "Three ships cannot be a good sign either way."

"I daresay not," Rainsford agreed.

"Mr. Gresham!" Henry called across the deck. "Hard to port! Turn her 'round."

"Aye, Captain!"

Rainsford and Henry began barking orders to the crew. The rigging climbers scurried up the ropes to release all the sails. We picked up speed as we turned. I wrapped my hand in the ropes to steady myself.

"Do you think it's the Navy?" I asked Henry.

"Perhaps. Or pirates."

Pirates. In all my days at sea, I had never come face to face with a pirate. The New World had long had buccaneers and filibusters who set their sights on merchant ships. Once, any pirate vessel gave naval vessels a wide berth. But the age of the buccaneer was over. Anarchist sea rovers, many of whom now commanded fleets, were on the rise.

I shivered, though the sun beat hot on my face. Henry placed a hand on my shoulder. "It may be a Spanish fleet or Dutch."

But a stone grew in my stomach. The bright blue skies belied the ominous feeling that had fallen over the ship. "Perhaps."

The *Integrity* sailed straight ahead now, opposite the three ships in the distance. Henry called up to Smith to ask for an update, but they were still too far away.

"Bloody hell."

Henry hurried up the steps to the quarterdeck and pulled his own telescope from his belt. I stood next to him, looking for any sort of sign. The distance stretched between us, and it seemed for a time that we faced no threat.

A quarter of an hour passed. Henry spoke to Easton about what course we could chart in this new direction that would bypass English fleets. I kept watch on the ships. They were further than before, as we soared through the water at high speed.

And then they weren't. My breath hitched as I made sure my eyes did not deceive me. But the ships had picked up speed.

"They give chase!" I yelled.

Henry whirled around and put his telescope to his eye. "Fuck." He shouted orders to loose the topgallant sails and increase our velocity.

The salt spray burned as the *Integrity* rushed through the water at breakneck pace. I rushed into the cabin to secure Quetzalli but thought better of it. She could not lie waiting for death if our ship was taken and we all met our watery graves. Instead, I kissed her on the head and hurried back to the main deck to help.

"Pirates!" I heard Smith yell from the crow's nest.

Curses sounded from the mouths of the crew and officers. I wobbled a bit on my feet and tried to steady my stomach. I had never been on a ship that moved so rapidly through the sea. It was as if we tried to part her like Moses to get his people to freedom. To safety.

I glanced back. I could now see the ship's masts with clarity. They were not man-of-wars, not at that speed. And a flotilla of pirate ships? How could we survive?

I offered a silent prayer to any god who would listen, although I doubted they'd answer. Once they could see that we were not a merchant ship, would they depart and leave us be? What booty had we to offer three pirate crews?

"Can you see the emblem?" Henry shouted to Smith over the deafening roar of the sea. There was no response for several heartbeats.

Then, "Every."

Henry stiffened, and even from several feet away, I saw a vein twitch in his neck. He muttered something to Wheatley, who nodded and scrambled below deck. Then he came to me and took my hand in his.

"Captain Every and his crew have a reputation for cruelty. Particularly toward women." His eyes glistened with fear. "Angélica, I cannot guarantee that—"

"Henry. You have far more to worry about than me."

He squeezed my hand that he still held. "Do whatever you must to stay safe, Hell. Loyalty be damned."

I knew in my heart that order did not extend to him. Henry would never sacrifice his loyalty to the crown, and I would never sacrifice my loyalty to him. But I nodded. "Henry, don't be a hero."

He shook his head. "There are no heroes when it comes to pirates."

He kissed my forehead and rushed off. I made my way to the aft of the ship and climbed the stairs to the quarterdeck. The prow of the first ship was so close that I saw the face of the figurehead, a Medieval queen.

The pit in my stomach tossed around like it was in the water during a storm, but my blood pulsed through my veins with something other than fear.

Anticipation.

If I survived—or if I didn't—I could count myself as a real sailor. And though my terror was real, so too was my excitement. But I shook out of my fantasy as a crewman pushed past me, a white cloth in his hands. He began to attach it to the ropes where England's colors flapped angrily in the wind.

My eyes widened, and I scanned the deck for Henry. He stood on the foredeck with Rainsford, deep in conversation as his eyes surveyed his ship. I ran.

"A white flag?!" I exclaimed.

Rainsford glared at me, but Henry took my elbow and guided me away and spoke in a lowered voice. "Hell, there are three ships. We do not stand a chance against three pirate crews, certainly not any sailing under Captain Every."

"But Henry. . ."

"No, I will not argue with you." His voice was more stern than I'd ever heard him speak to me. "If we do not fight, he will likely give most of the men a chance to join him. I will not lead my men into a fight we cannot win."

"And what of you?" The acid in my stomach came out in my tone. "Pirates do not ask captains to join their crews."

He sighed and placed a hand on my shoulder. "This is my job, Hell. My oath."

I yanked myself away from his touch. "If you die, I'll kill you."

A sad smile loosened the lines on his face. It tugged on my heartstrings. He was young, barely a quarter of a century. How had I missed the crevices that deepened on his face, aging him in recent weeks? I softened and placed a gentle kiss on his lips.

"You told me not to be a hero," he murmured against my mouth.

"I meant not to sacrifice yourself, you bloody fool."

Wheatley appeared out of nowhere, as he was wont to do. "Captain, they've gained on us. We've no chance to outrun them."

"Lower the sails. Prepare to be boarded." Henry cleared his throat. "And John, if you are given the opportunity—"

"I'll do what is right in my heart, Henry." He turned on his heel and yelled to the crew, "Prepare to be boarded."

Everything happened in a flash. The bannerman raised the white flag. The *Integrity* slowed in the wind, and soon the first of the ships pulled alongside our port side. The men on the opposite ship paced along their starboard side like a hungry pack of sharks. Another ship pulled on our opposite end. The third gave a wide berth, and I imagined they were to head us off in case we tried to flee again.

And they boarded us, ignoring the planks and jumping straight over. Fearless and feral. They rounded us up around the mizzenmast and went below to secure the others. I stood next to Henry, my littlest finger brushing against his for comfort.

"Disarm yerselves," one of the pirates instructed. Henry gave a slight nod and was the first to toss his sword and dagger to the ground. His men followed suit, and weapons clashed onto the deck floor, deafening against the somber silence of our crew. I tossed my own flintlock and cutlass, feeling humiliated, though I could still feel the cold metal of my dagger inside my stay, hidden betwixt my breasts. The pirates kicked them out of our reach and kept their pistols pointed at us.

Their clothes were tattered, though many wore fancy hats and silk waistcoats open over their stained sailing clothes. Henry shifted, trying to block me with his body.

A man dressed in gold and red finery with a large plume in his hat pushed past the crew. He laughed, a wicked, wild laugh that echoed on the breeze.

"You are a smart lot for Navy men," he said with a sneer. "Yielding without a fight."

He spoke the King's English, I was shocked to discover. And he held himself as if he'd been a gentleman once. I wondered about his history and his reputation as he circled us.

He stopped in front of Henry, barely an arm span away. "You are the captain?"

"I am." Henry's voice did not quaver. He held his head high. "Captain Henry Martin of the *HMS Integrity*."

The pirate smirked. "And I am Captain Every, though I am quite certain you know that."

"Aye. You'll find no quarrel here, Captain Every."

"'Tis a shame," Every said with mock disappointment. "My men and I were hoping for a bit of. . . amusement."

Henry said nothing, but he continued to hold Every's eye.

"You're young," the pirate captain continued. "Yet you do not seem inexperienced. 'Twas fine sailing."

"I am most grateful for the praise of such a fine sailor. Your reputation precedes you."

Every threw back his head and laughed. "I like you, young Captain Martin." But then the smile faded from his sea-worn face. "But alas, I cannot afford attachments in my line of work. Step forward."

Henry took two steps closer, and I gasped. My hand flew to cover my mouth, but Every had heard me.

"What's this? A lass? Perhaps this ship does hold treasure for us, boys!"

Every shoved Henry aside and came so close to me, I could smell his rancid breath. He took my hand forcefully and kissed my knuckles. A wave of nausea flashed over me. "Enchantée. What is your name?"

"Miss Spencer," I choked out.

"And what, pray tell, is a young, beautiful woman doing on board a man-of-war and dressed as a sailor no less?"

I flicked my eyes over at Henry, but he stared straight ahead. I blinked, "I am the captain's interpreter and naturalist."

Every leaned back and studied me from head to toe. I felt naked under his gaze, which turned lecherous as he stared at my bosom. But I did not look away, I did not downcast my eyes in shame.

"Interesting." He clapped his hands. "Come with me, Miss Spencer. You can show me around the captain's cabin. I have a feeling you are most acquainted with it."

I trembled as I began to follow him. This time, when I looked at Henry, he met my eyes. They were wide, pleading, desperate, as if they were reflecting my own emotions back at me. Every told his men not to harm the prisoners until he returned.

Quetzalli ran to me as I opened the door, and I had to stifle a sob. She climbed up the length of my body and perched on my shoulder.

"What in the seven hells is that?" Every exclaimed. He pointed his sword at my rat.

"She is my pet, sir. An African pouched rat. She is most loyal and intelligent."

His eyes narrowed. "Rats have no place as pets."

"She is no bilge rat, Captain. With respect."

He shook his head and took off his leather tricorn. He wore a brown, curled wig underneath. Then he crossed the room and sat at Henry's desk, placing his large, booted feet on the surface.

"Pour me a drink, Miss Spencer."

I rolled my shoulders back and sighed. "What will you have, sir?"

"Wine, if you have it."

I pulled a bottle of Madeira from the cabinet, along with two small glasses. I poured his and set it on the edge of the desk, as close as I dared get to him. Then I poured my own and downed it in one gulp.

"At ease, Miss Spencer. I just want to talk. For now."

I studied him as I backed into a nearby chair. He was older than me, old enough to be my father. But he had been an attractive man once, beneath the sun's and sea's marks. I steeled my courage. "What would you like to talk about?"

He chuckled. "You. You said you are a naturalist?"

"Yes. I was trained by my father, George Martin, from my childhood."

"And you serve as the ship's translator? How many languages do you speak?"

"Eight."

He cocked his head. "Impressive. I do not see how those professions require you to dress like a man."

"Moving about a ship in heavy skirts is most unpractical, Captain Every."

"I can imagine. But it seems to me that a woman of such a position should not need to move about a ship, unless she is a member of the crew."

I inclined my head. "I have spent more of my life at sea than on land. I do not believe anyone should be just a useless body aboard a vessel."

"I agree." He leaned back in the chair. "So you are a sailor?"

"I am."

"And what of your relationship with the captain? Not Henry Martin the naval officer, but Henry Martin the man."

I swallowed. "We are friends and confidants."

"And?" He licked his lips at me, a vulgar motion.

I poured myself more Madeira and took a sip. "We are lovers."

"Ah." He said it as though it was some great revelation.

"Captain Every." I finished my wine before I continued. "I am at your service. I would offer you whatever you care to take of me in exchange for sparing my captain and my crew."

I leaned forward in such a way that my shirt hung low and my meaning was clear.

He raised an eyebrow. "I did not take you for a woman of loose morals, Miss Spencer."

"Morality is relative, sir. Is not sacrifice for others a virtue extolled by the priests and philosophers?" I straightened. I thought of Laurence and Evelyn back in Manchester. "Besides, I've fucked men for far less important reasons."

"I like you, Miss Spencer." He paused. "Tell me of the captain's orders. To where do you sail?"

I swallowed. "We have no orders. We became a pawn in a Jacobite plot headed by the Navy admirals. But Captain Martin is loyal to King William, and so we sail as rogues in the name of the crown."

"Oh, yes, I've heard rumors of a rogue ship in His Majesty's fleet. Although the Jacobite bit is new."

I said nothing. He gestured toward his chalice, and I refilled it.

"Your captain is loyal to the crown, but what of your loyalty?"

I decided honesty was useful in this situation. "The crown has done naught for me. My loyalty is to the sea and my captain."

He sipped his glass, considering me. "So, you all sail as rogues. How do you survive without sailing into English ports?"

"We take prizes and trade it in Spanish ports. They do not give a damn about our loyalties or our betrayal of the admiralty."

"Not commissioned by the Royal Navy. No letters of marque. It seems to me you are true sea rovers."

I chuckled. "I would ask you not to suggest as much to Captain Martin, but yes, it is a fair observation."

"Miss Spencer, you have the makings of a fine pirate." He rose from the desk suddenly. "I have no quarrel with fellow rogues. My crews and I will depart."

I stood as well. My shock must have been written on my face, as he smirked again when he looked at me.

"I am not leaving without payment, Miss Spencer."

There it was. I smoothed my shirt to steady my trembling. I would not give him the satisfaction of force, but I would not enjoy this. "How may I repay your mercy?"

"Relax, Miss Spencer." He plucked the bottle of Madeira wine from my hand. "I'll take the rest of this and a kiss."

I should not trust him, not knowing what I knew about pirates. But I did. It was as if a unifying sense of honor, or rather a sense of dishonor, connected us. He brushed his chapped lips against mine. It was chaste, and unexpected, and bearable.

Then he pulled away. He scratched Quetzalli behind her ears from her perch on my shoulder before leaving the cabin. I followed after him.

"Nothing of value here, boys!" he called to his lads. "We'll catch us a prize on our way back to harbor. Back on the ships!"

His men grumbled but went back to whence they came. Captain Every took my hand and kissed my knuckles. "I was not lying when I said you would make a fine pirate, lass. The *Integrity* is welcome in Nassau. If you ever find yourself in need of assistance, I am never too many days away from Madam Liza's tavern."

With that, he followed his men overboard and waved from his ship. Henry rushed to me and took me in his arms. "Hell, what happened? Did he hurt you? Take your honor?"

I shook my head. I would not tell him I offered in exchange for his safety. "No. We just talked."

His shoulders slumped in relief. "Whatever you said, thank you."

I smiled at him, though it did not reach my eyes. "I'll be in the cabin if you need me, darling."

And with that, I turned on my heel and went to empty the contents of my stomach.

Chapter 35

With no more run-ins from pirates, we settled into a pattern of taking French prize ships and selling what we could in Spanish ports. We gathered timber and freshwater, as well as whatever food we could find, exclusively on unsettled islands. But for my twenty-third birthday, we docked in Havana.

A third of the crew were on shore leave, spending their meager earnings on wine and women. Henry and I had partaken at a tavern the night before, where I'd paid two lovely whores to repay Ben for his kindness with Quetzalli. But this night, we enjoyed the quiet of the ship alone in our cabin.

I wore the red and gold dress that Henry loved so much. We bantered and philosophized over a feast of pork and beef and fine Spanish bread. My mouth watered at the tender, meaty food. I had tired of turtle and fish.

After, Henry stood and extended his hand to me. Quetzalli took our leave as a cue to ascend the table and eat whatever scraps we had left behind.

"You are beautiful, Hell." His breath was hot and wet against my ear, and his strong hands ran up my sides and rested over my breast. Deft fingers unlaced the stomacher from the front of my dress, baring the stay beneath it. He cast the V-shaped stiff fabric aside and slipped the dress over my shoulders until I stood only in my petticoat and undergarments. As his hands worked the laces of my stay, his lips peppered kisses on the tops of my breasts.

I captured his mouth in a kiss as I pulled at his jacket buttons. He shoved out of his officer's coat as I shimmied the petticoat over my hips and stepped out of the pile of fabric in only my shift. Henry's gaze was adoring as he looked at me in the moonlight through the cabin windows.

"What?" I asked. I smiled, confident, empowered.

"How did I become this fortunate? How am I so blessed to have you as my own?"

I stepped closer to him and pulled his white linen shirt over his toned abdomen and broad shoulders. "We are a pair, Henry Martin. We deserve each other."

He shivered as I ran my nails over his chest, down to the trail of hair that led into his breeches. His erection sprung free as I pushed the clothes over his hips, and I softly grazed my nails over his cock. He gasped. "Fuck, Hell."

I bit my lip in feigned innocence. "Is that all right?"

"You minx. Get that damn shift off you before I tear it to shreds."

I laughed and slowly began to pull the shift over my knees, then my thighs, all while keeping my eyes locked on his. "Like this?"

"You'll be the death of me," he said in a throaty voice. He had one hand wrapped around his length as he watched me.

"Oh, we wouldn't want that, would me?" I lifted the bottom of the chemise over my hips and stomach. Then I flashed a lecherous grin before removing it entirely.

Henry pulled me close as soon as the thin fabric hit the floor. He sank his teeth at the spot where my neck met my collarbone. I could feel his member leaking against my stomach. I began to walk him back toward the bed and pushed him down on the mattress. He grunted. I straddled his hips and reached up to my hair to untie my fontage.

"What are you doing?" he breathed.

"Do you trust me?"

He raised his chin, baring his neck in submission. "With my life."

"Good."

I gathered the long strips of lace in one hand and pulled his hands together with the other, then I bound his wrists and pushed his arms above his shoulders. He had done this to me many times, with his belt or a strip of cloth, but I had never returned the favor.

Shifting to where I was no longer on top of him, I ran my fingers over his lips and the strong line of his stubbled jaw until I reached the pulse of his neck. I kept my hand there for a long moment, feeling his heart throbbing erratically. He met my eyes with a heated stare. Passion and trust bore through me like a warm fire until I could feel it deep in my core. I leaned forward and began to kiss my way from his clavicle to the patch of hair on his sternum to the hard lines of his stomach.

He sucked a breath through his teeth as I ran my tongue over his stomach and around the edge of his navel. As I did, I unpinned my hair and let it fall over him, offering a new sensation to his most sensitive parts. He bucked his hips and tried to reach for me, though his hands were still bound.

"No," I said firmly but not maliciously. "Keep still."

"Fuck, that feels incredible."

I giggled as I positioned myself. I braced my hands against his strong, solid thighs and lowered my mouth to the thick, purple head of his cock. Alternating between swirling and sucking, I brought him to the edge and backed away over and over. The sounds he released were filthy, animalistic, and raw. Anytime he tried to move, I pushed him back down and held him against the bed.

Finally, I released him from his blissful agony. His seed spilled with force, and I had to pull away. He panted as I sat up next to him, his arms still tied above his head.

"Untie me, wench."

"Oh, I do not know. I enjoy having you as my prisoner." I teased one of his nipples with my thumb and forefinger.

"You'll enjoy it more if you release me. I'll make certain of it."

"Oh very well." I pressed my body against the length of his and slinked my way up his torso until I could reach his wrists.

The moment he was free, he flipped me over onto my back and loomed over me. He was hardening again already; I could feel it against the patch of hair below my stomach. When he kissed me, it was hard and primal, all teeth and tongue. I bit his lip back, and he pressed himself against me with a groan.

His hand moved between us, and I parted my legs to allow him access to my desperate quim. But he did not touch me. Instead, he ran his finger over every other surface he could reach. He teased and avoided my wet core until I was moaning and mewling and damn near crying in need of release. From only his touch. It was torture. Blissful, rapturous torture.

He gazed into my eyes as he continued to make me suffer. He never looked away. "Please," I begged. "Please, Henry."

He leaned down to growl in my ear. "No."

"Fuck you, you son of a whore."

Henry laughed. "Let's not bring my mother into this most sacred act, yes?"

"Fuck you, you bloody seadog." But as I said it between pants and cries, it sounded far from threatening.

He placed one hand over my neck, and the other moved between my thighs. He hadn't touched me, though I could tell he was so close. All I had to do was raise my hips slightly to end my suffering. But I did not. With his hand on my neck, I was at his mercy, but I trusted him.

"Good lass," he whispered. He squeezed my neck, not enough to stop my breathing, but enough to be pleasurably uncomfortable. Then he finally—finally!—placed a finger in my wet, hot core. His thumb stroked the sensitive nub as his fingers moved in and out of me. I damn near screamed at the sudden release.

"Henry!" It took mere seconds for me to fall over the edge. My muscles clenched around his steady fingers. But still, he did not stop. He worked me as if he were a painter and I his canvas until I was utterly complete. Once, twice, thrice more.

Only then did he remove his hand. I was spent and could have collapsed into a dreamless sleep for a week, but still I wanted more. Needed more. Henry did, too. He thrust his length inside me. The hand on my neck cradled my head as I arched underneath him. I wrapped my legs around his waist and pressed my feet against his muscular buttocks to urge him deeper and deeper inside of me. I wanted him to become a part of me, to become one with me.

He came with a shout and a shudder. I could hear the blood rushing in my ears as I followed. We lay there, breathing heavily for a time. The breeze was cool in the ethereal moonlit cabin. He pulled a fur blanket over both of us when I shivered.

His hand rested on my stomach. "Perhaps one day, when we're safe again, I'll put a baby inside your womb."

I shook my head. "No."

"You don't want to be a mother? Raise a family with me?"

I smiled. "I'm not the mothering type. I keep a stash of herbs and tonics on hand and take them faithfully to bring on my courses."

"Oh." He cocked his head. "But you're so nurturing to Quetzalli."

I laughed. "She's a rat, Henry."

"Fair enough." He kissed my shoulder.

"Does this change how you look at me?" I closed my eyes, bracing myself for his answer.

"No, Angélica. I love you, not some possibility of a future with you that you might not want in the first place. I love you now, in this moment, and in each moment, just how you are."

Hot tears leaked from my eyes. "I am forever your woman, Henry Martin. My heart belongs to you."

"I'm your prisoner, Hell. You've taken my heart captive, and I don't want it back."

Chapter 36

When we left Cuba, I was the happiest I had ever been. Though Henry was captain, I felt as if we were equals. We were a partnership. I had spent my life as a subordinate. Though my father had viewed me as an intellectual equal, I was never his social equal. In fact, other than Henry, every man in my life viewed me as nothing more than frippery, but I was smarter and more skilled than the vast majority of the opposite sex.

Well, perhaps Ben was an exception. He hung on every word I taught him. His reading and writing lessons had progressed quickly. Henry began to give him more responsibility on the ship. Far from English propriety, he did not need a servant so much as a loyal man for delicate tasks. Ben was a smart lad, and if my rat were a judge of character, a good man. Quetzalli loved Ben; he was the only person besides Henry and myself that she allowed to hold her.

It was late afternoon, and we had anchored in the bay of a small, deserted key. We were due for a careen and repair, but Henry did not want to risk it so close to English ports. We were to sail west toward Africa and find a place to clear the barnacles that weighed down our ship. But with so much uncertainty in the Atlantic, we had stopped here to collect lumber and water that we did not have to trade for.

I mopped my brow in the muggy heat of the cabin. Ben was reading aloud from Milton, and I tried my damndest to pay attention. Though I had opted for my lightest petticoat and bodice, the heat was stifling. Quetzalli had found a cool, shaded spot under the dresser, and I envied her.

"Do you think the men will return soon?" I asked. Twenty of the strongest men had been sent ashore to collect the lumber and water and perhaps some fresh meat. I winced. I had interrupted his reading. "Sorry. This bloody heat is miserable. I want to sail and feel a breeze."

"I hope so, Miss Spencer. Captain made it clear he wanted to set sail before sundown."

"I hope so, too. Please, continue."

Ben continued to stumble through the story, though he needed little guidance from me. A commotion on deck jolted us from our activities. Even Quetzalli raised her sleep head in concern.

"They must be back, Miss."

Henry burst into the room, slamming the door behind him. "The English. They've found us."

I stood abruptly. The chair I had been sitting in clambered to the floor. "What do you mean?"

"Three ships, at least. We cannot flee. They've cornered us."

Sheer terror was painted on his sweaty face. "Then we'll fight the bloody Jacobite traitors."

Henry gave me a strange smile. "We shall try."

Bile rose in my throat. We would likely die, but at least I would die alongside Henry. I embraced him and kissed his cheek, stifling my own fear to assuage his own. "No matter what," I whispered in his ear.

"No matter what." His voice was flat, numb. The poor thing. After all, he'd tried to do, all the honor he'd tried to protect, this was his repayment.

"Hell, go help on deck. Ben, stay with me. I need your help here."

Henry kissed my forehead before I ran out of the room. My last calm thought was that fighting a battle in a dress would be a feat, but then anticipation took over my brain.

I helped turn the capstan for the sails while Mr. Gresham turned the *Integrity* at an angle, her prow pointed northwest. A smart move by Henry. We were a smaller target now than revealing our entire port side to the enemy, but our guns could still fire.

The ships loomed ever closer. Three first-rate vessels, sailing angrily toward us. But I had no time for fear. There was too much to do.

I glanced around the deck. No one laughed and whooped as we usually did before battle. No one spoke except what their tasks required. Panic hummed in the thick, still air. Henry had emerged from the cabin and whispered something in Wheatley's ear, who nodded. Henry held something in his left hand, but it was obscured from the angle of his body.

Then Ben emerged from the cabin carrying a trunk. Odd, I thought. But realization dawned on me. My eyes widened, and I leapt across the ropes and crates to reach Henry.

"What are you doing with my trunk?"

Ben stared at me, then looked over at Henry, panicked. Wheatley's face was set in stone. And when Henry turned to face me, his eyes glistened with tears. In his left hand, he held Quetzalli's cage.

A sob caught in my throat. "What are you doing, Henry?"

"Angélica, we will not survive this unless. . . unless we reach the shore. There, we stand a chance. We aren't far from other ports."

"And you're coming, too?"

"I—" he hung his head. He could not lie to me. "I will never forgive myself if—"

"Don't you dare, Henry Martin! Don't you dare say it! I chose my fate. I knew the risks. You'll not choose this for me." Heat rose in my cheeks, but not from the sun. I clenched my fist and my resolve. "I refuse."

"Hell, please. Please." He stepped closer to me.

"No." I beat my fists against his chest. "I will not. I don't want to be without you. Let me fight with you."

Tears streamed down my face as I pleaded and screamed, burning salty on my tongue. Henry folded me in his arms.

"I can fight, Henry. You taught me yourself. Please."

"Oh, my fierce little devil." He placed two fingers under my chin and tilted my head up to him. "My beautiful, brilliant Hell. The English have taken everything from you and me. I don't want them to take you, too."

He kissed me, even though snot and tears covered my face. Fierce and tender at the same time. A kiss of farewell.

When he pulled away, he nodded at Wheatley. Gresham had appeared and took Quetzalli's cage. Ben and my trunk were already gone.

Wheatley grabbed me then. He pinned my arms against my sides as he lifted me. I screamed and thrashed, but he was stronger. "I'm sorry," he said in my ear.

"No, you're bloody not! Let me go!"

He put me over his shoulder, and I beat his back. I tried to kick, but he held my legs still. Then he carried me over the side of the ship, slowly climbing down as I shouted and cried and pleaded. Henry cried as he watched.

"Henry! Please! Don't leave me!"

Lower, lower down the rope ladder. Further, further away from Henry. But he did not sway in his resolve. "I love you, Hell. I have from the moment I met you, and I will love you past death."

Wheatley landed in the longboat with an unsteady wobble. We nearly fell into the water. If we had, I could have swum to the hull and climbed up the side. But Wheatley's grasp on me did not budge. Gresham tossed down the cage, which Ben caught easily.

"Go, Ben. Make haste," Wheatley ordered. His voice broke.

Wheatley sat and forced me onto his lap, where he held me tightly. I cried. I could not move. But I would swim back as soon as we reached the shore.

Quetzalli reached her arms toward me between the cage bars from where she sat next to Ben.

Ben. He liked me. Perhaps. . .

"Ben. Ben, please take me back. Please."

He ducked his head as he rowed faster. "I cannot, Miss Spencer. Captain's orders."

I looked over the edge of the longboat. The water was deep here, too deep for a woman of my height to stand in. It would be dangerous to swim, and we were such a long way from the *Integrity* already. We were only halfway to the shore, and I could steal the longboat, but I was not as strong as the men. It would take a long time for me to row back by myself.

Ben heaved as the labor of rowing three people, a trunk of books, and a rat weighed on him. But to his credit, he did not stop. I shifted in Wheatley's hold to look behind us. I could hear distant shouts from the deck, but the massive vessel obscured anything in the distance. How far were the English, I wondered?

Finally, we hit land and Wheatley finally released me. Determined, I drew my sword and tried to steal the boat once they were on land.

"Miss Spencer, please don't. The captain only wants you safe," Ben begged.

Wheatley drew his own sword, ready to fight me for my own fate.

"I won't hesitate to kill you, Wheatley."

"I know." He moved into a fighting stance and began to circle. I followed suit. "But Miss Spencer. Angelica. I have to get back to fight."

"Take me with you, then."

He shook his head. "I cannot. The crew is already short of your superior skills. I need to get there to help."

By this time, we had circled halfway round. Now he stood by the boat. Damn. If I had been in my right mind, I would have noticed his ruse.

"What's happening?" a voice shouted.

We all turned then. The twenty men Henry had sent ashore had emerged from the treeline, carrying lumber and jugs of water. I glanced around and noticed the other two longboats on the shore.

"The Navy found us," Wheatley called back.

"We have to get back," one of the men shouted. "To fight with our brothers."

"And our captain!"

"Yes, we do!" I agreed. But with the three boats, it would take a long time to get all of us back.

At that moment, a deafening explosion sounded from behind me. "No."

In the distance, smoke and flames billowed from the *Integrity*, marring the picturesque blue bay with a painting straight from hell itself. Distant screams sounded, and I squinted against the late afternoon sun as more explosions sounded. Men jumped overboard, or fell, as it was impossible to tell the difference.

More cannons. The *Integrity* rocked back and forth as she withstood the blasts. And then she went up in flames with a roar that drowned out my own screams.

"Henry!" I rushed toward the water, wailing as I tried to get back to him. "Henry!"

My ears rang. I coughed as the smoke from the inferno reached the beach. But still. . . I had to reach him. I had to get him before he went down with the ship. I had to force him to ignore his bloody honor, his bloody *Integrity*, and come back to me.

"Henry!" It unnerved me that I screamed without noise. Just as my toes touched the edge of the water, arms pulled me back, and I kicked as they hauled me backward. I sputtered and sobbed and choked against the burning black smoke. I could no longer see anything through the dark cloud, save for flames.

"It's too late!" Ben's voice shouted in my ear. My hearing had returned. "Miss Spencer, it's too late!"

We collapsed backward onto the sand. And it jolted me out of my sobs. I looked around. The other men stood in small groups or pairs, clutching each other, crying or screaming. Ben wiped his face with his sleeve, but he could not keep up with the flow of tears.

And Wheatley. . .

Wheatley had sunk to his knees. He stared off to the fire, eyes hollow, tearing at his hair. Something compelled me to go to him. I was not within my body. I felt as though I floated above the beach, surveying the damage from above. I watched myself as I knelt beside him. I reached for his hand and pulled it away from his hair to squeeze it. He squeezed back.

All we could do was watch in horror as the English destroyed everything and everyone we loved.

Chapter 37

I woke the next morning to blinding sunshine. My head ached from tears, and every part of my body was covered in sand. I hadn't moved in hours. I'm not certain how long I stared out at the horizon next to Wheatley, but we had both fallen asleep on the beach. After sundown, some of the other men had the sense to build fires.

Throughout the rest of the evening, a few more of our crew had reached the shore alive. A few bodies washed ashore, too, including Lieutenant Rainsford and Mr. Oakes. But none had been Henry.

I groaned as I forced my muscles to move and sat up. Quetzalli was looking at me intently from her cage, which someone had placed by my head. Ben, I'm certain. On my other side, Wheatley still slept, one arm thrown over his eyes.

Quetzalli bounded happily out of her cage when I unlatched it. I stroked her soft fur absentmindedly as I surveyed my surroundings. Most of the men sat silently with their heads lowered in despair. Some still slept. More bodies had washed ashore overnight, it seemed, and a few sailors dragged their brethren to the shore to the collection of bodies. Henry was nowhere in sight.

I forced myself to my feet and dusted off the sand that had accumulated over my sweaty clothes. My rat climbed to my shoulder as I reached down to grab my hat. Dry sand fell out like a rainstorm.

It was at that point that every emotion hit me at once. The surrealism of waking had passed. I clutched my stomach as grief knifed me in the gut. I couldn't cry; at least tears didn't fall. But my heart ached. And between those feelings was a fire rising from the pit of my soul, burning its way into my face.

The bloody English had cornered us, attacked us. Murdered us. Those of us who hadn't died would likely do so on this tiny island. And they had taken Henry. Loyal, purely good, brave, compassionate Henry. And for what? To cover up a conspiracy to overthrow some Dutch royal with his head up his arse? Fuck the Jacobites, and fuck the king.

I kicked Wheatley's leg. "Get up, Wheatley."

"Wha—?" He opened his eyes, looked around, and began to cry again. "Leave me. Leave me to die. It's what I deserve."

My rage boiled over. "Oh, for Christ's sake. Are we still on that? Yes, we know, we know. If only you'd told Henry about the gossip you'd heard in the tavern, we never would have sunk the *Keerpunt*." I tossed my hands in the air. "That's horseshit. Henry would have chosen this course either way. And either way, the English would have bloody killed us. Stop wallowing. We're stranded, and I have no intention of dying on this godforsaken beach."

"Oh, and you are somehow infallible in this? You've been encouraging Henry to become bolder and bolder. If it weren't for you and your snaked tongue, Henry could have sailed us back to England and revealed the traitors to the King."

"Are you that naïve, you bastard? I only pointed out the obvious—that we were just as likely to meet Jacobites in England, and we'd all be hanged for it." I shook my head. "While you've been off brooding on ships for years, the opposition to the crown has been growing. There was an attempted assassination on his majesty just before you arrived in port. Habeas Corpus had been suspended. We could have been thrown in jail or killed without so much as a chance to say hello. That has nothing to do with my snake tongue."

He jumped to his feet and pointed his fingers at my chest. "You were a distraction to him! Every day, he could look at no one but you, not even the sea. He went to you for counsel before his own officers." He spat at my feet. "If it weren't for you, he might still be alive. Whatever you said was as good as law. And now what? All you care about is getting off the island when the man you said you loved has been dead for mere hours?"

I slapped him, then. "How dare you! How dare you question my love for him? I don't give a damn about you or your bloody Navy or the king and queen! I gave a damn about Henry. That's it."

A vein twitched in Wheatley's jaw, but I continued. "Do you think Henry would let us sit here and moan and cry? Would he let you accept death when you survived? If that's what you learned from him, then you did not know him at all."

"I knew him, you bitch. I knew him, until you came along and—"

"You're jealous." I laughed, a bitter, wet sound. "It all makes sense now. You're jealous of me. Of how much Henry loved me."

Wheatley's red, swollen eyes widened then looked away quickly. I shook my head. "Stay here and die, if you must. Just keep out of my way."

I stalked away toward the bodies on the beach. Too many familiar faces, though swollen and grey with seawater. I wrinkled my nose at the smell as I looked at each of them. Henry was not among them.

I closed my eyes and blinked away tears. I wish I had not been so angry when he'd sent me away. I wish I could have savored his kiss, told him I loved him. "Oh, Henry," I whispered to the breeze. "I'm sorry."

Then I spun around and stared out at the bay. Some of the wreckage was floating, along with some barrels and crates. On the beach, I counted the men. Only thirty-eight of us had survived.

Quetzalli chittered in my ear. I swallowed against the despair and focused on that fire within me. I walked along the treeline and found a passion fruit tree. Using my knife, I cut two from a branch. Quetzalli grasped hers happily and stained my shirt with her eager eating. I forced myself to chew mine. I needed strength.

Some of the men who had ventured for supplies sat near a pile of timber. Ben sat a few feet away, his knees curled to his chest.

"Ben, go collect some food from that tree over there." I pointed. "You need to eat. We all do."

His pale eyes locked with mine, rimmed by dark circles. He looked at me as if I were a specter.

"Ben, my dear." I softened my voice. "Come, get up, lad."

I offered my hand, and he took it. He shook as he rose to his feet. I put a hand on his shoulder. "Everything will be fine. Go get some fruit."

He nodded and ambled away toward the tree line. I studied the group of men who appeared as lost as Ben did.

"Is the water source easy to access?" I asked. A few nodded. "Good. And did you see much game?"

An older sailor, Brooks, stubble tinged with grey, grunted. "Aye. Some of them big rodents and monkeys."

"I saw boar tracks," another offered.

Now I raised my voice so everyone could hear me. "I need five men to go find food. There is plenty on this island to sustain us for now."

Heads turned toward me, but no one moved.

"We do not have the means to bury our dead. Some of you need to weigh them down with whatever you can find. We'll give them a sailor's burial at sunset."

A few of the crew nodded.

"We have lumber we've already collected, and we can get more. We need a shelter in case a storm blows in. Everyone else, scavenge what you can from the water. Set it in a line by the trees so that we can inventory it. Up you get! Let's go!"

My words lit something in them. A purpose. A long time ago, I had sworn that only I would choose my fate. Henry had put me on this island because he knew I could survive. The English would not choose my destiny. I would get off this island, one way or another, or die trying.

The men set to work. They came to me with questions and to report their progress. A carpenter's apprentice had been with the men on the island yesterday. His name was Theodore. I put him in charge of construction. It was a blessing that the group had been ashore with guns for hunting and blades for cutting trees, among other supplies.

I began directing the sailors who brought pieces of the ship from the water. The trunk Henry had sent ashore with me marked the barrier between food and supplies. I opened it.

Inside were my books and journals. I smiled. He knew that I would mourn their loss. Tears stung my eyes, and I wiped them away. Even in the face of death, Henry had been kind and thoughtful. But I had no time to cry.

I rummaged through my belongings and found two other pistols besides my own and a bag of shot and powder. He'd also stored a bottle of rum and a small bag of coin. It wouldn't buy much, but if we got off this island, we could at least get some warm food and ale.

Much of the food that had washed ashore was spoiled or waterlogged. I told two men to clean out and repair the barrels that were ruined so we could put freshwater in them. Down the beach, Wheatley had finally risen and was helping the men prepare bodies for a sea burial. Good.

One strapping sailor carried a familiar trunk from the water.

"My dresses!" I ran down the sand to meet him. "My dresses! Thank God!"

I heard muttering behind me about stupid women. But I threw open the trunk and pulled out a blue petticoat.

"No, you cursed fools." I ripped a small pouch that was sewn into the underside of a petticoat. The gold that fell into my hand was cold and refreshing in my hand. "It's where my money is."

Their eyes lit up and smiles spread across their face. It was a sign of hope that we all needed.

"Now to get off this damn island."

Chapter 38

Over the next several days, we prepared a camp that would sustain us for a time. Once we had a rough shelter and had collected plenty of firewood and kindling, I directed Theodore to design and oversee the building of rafts and longboats. We only had two that could hold three men, each.

I marked the days in the trunk of a tree. I did not know how to get off this island. None of us did. Wheatley and I had made a tentative peace after we nearly came to blows, and we spent hours proposing plans and poking holes in them. We had no maps, only a rough estimate of how far we were from Havana.

My heart ached for Henry. At night, huddled in the corner of our crude shelter, memories would flood me unbidden. I only allowed myself to cry silently. The rest of the crew were mourning, too. Each night, some wailed while other whimpered at the loss of their brethren, of their home. In the daylight, tensions were high, and I broke up more than a few fights.

The morning of the eighth day after we became trapped on the island, I walked along the water line, lost in my grief. The cool water lapped against my bare feet, in sharp contrast to the hot tears that streamed down my face. I could barely breathe. I gasped for air between sobs.

Quetzalli paid me no mind. She ran a few feet ahead of me in the sand, occasionally darting to catch a small wave. Instead, I was utterly alone once again. I had thought, naively, that once I had found Henry again, I would never be alone. Part of me wished I had been aboard the ship, had fallen to my death alongside him.

But I refused to go down that path. I had overcome loss before. And somehow, someway, I would avenge him. This time was different. A child knows that one day her parents will die, and though it had occurred far too soon, there was no question that I could go on. But Henry was so young. Henry was the other half of my soul, and I was broken.

I wiped my eyes and saw someone sitting a few feet ahead. I glanced back. I'd walked a long way from camp, but I was not destined to be alone, it appeared.

Wheatley. Of course. I was going to turn back when Quetzalli scampered forward at top speed and nudged him with her nose.

He looked down at her, then up at me, and gave me a watery smile. "You would think a deserted island would have more opportunities for being alone."

His tone wasn't malevolent or even sardonic. It was almost. . . friendly?

"Forgive me. I did not see you. I can turn back."

"No, stay." He patted the sand next to him. "I owe you an explanation and an apology."

Intrigued, I sat a foot away and stared out at the horizon. Quetzalli climbed on my lap and promptly went to sleep. Wheatley and I sat in silence for a long time before he spoke.

"I was jealous of you," he said after a long time. He sighed like he'd held his breath for days.

I didn't look at him. "I know you and Henry were good friends."

Out of the corner of my eye, I saw him shaking his head. "No. Well, yes, we were but I-I. . ."

"You loved him."

Wheatley hung his head. "Yes. Well, I did once."

I nodded slowly, thinking about what to say. "Did Henry know?"

"Yes. He was kind in his dismissal and never treated me any less."

That was how Henry was. Kind and compassionate. A single rogue tear ran down my cheek.

He continued. "I have not been in love with him for some time. After his rejection, I had a brief affair." He waved his hand. "Now, I love him like a brother. I was protective of him. And the thought of you having what I had once wanted, of knowing him a way I never would. . . I judged you harshly and unfairly."

"I have been rather unfair toward you, too."

Out of the corner of my eye, I saw him smirk. "I'm certain I deserve it. I am sorry for the way I have treated you. It hurt seeing how Henry adored you, the way I wished he had looked at me."

I chuckled. "It wasn't because I'm a woman, then?"

"No. It was because you were Henry's woman." He turned toward me for the first time. "But if there was anyone in the world good enough for him, it was you."

I swallowed against the lump in my throat. "Thank you, Wheatley. Henry respected you and considered you a good friend. I know that doesn't help ease the heartbreak, but. . ."

"It does. And knowing he never revealed my. . . my disgusting secret."

"Disgusting?" I cocked my head. "How so?"

His eyebrows raised in surprise. "I'm a bloody Sodomite."

I laughed out loud then, a most unattractive guffaw. "You know as well as I do how many Sodomites are in the Navy."

"It's different, though. They do it for long stretches away from land, away from brothels. To scratch an itch. But I. . . I've always been. . ."

"Me, too," I interrupted, surprising myself with my admission. "I feel that way about women and men."

His surprise was greater than my own. He quickly raised his dropped jaw. "Well, I've never fancied a woman, but that is interesting."

I couldn't fathom not fancying women with their soft curves and tender lips, but I smiled at him. He grinned back.

"I miss him," I admitted. "I don't know how to go on without him." A sob caught in my throat. To my shock, Wheatley scooted closer and patted my knee.

"He didn't deserve this. None of us did, but especially not Henry."

The tear flowed freely now from both of us. "I want them to pay, Wheatley. I want them to suffer for what they did."

"If we get off this island, I will put a sword through Admiral Wells' heart myself."

If we get off this island. The hopelessness crept back in, but Wheatley changed the subject.

"Tell me about this rat of yours."

Relieved for the distraction from the darkness of my thoughts, I described how she is different from regular rats and how she is the same. I told him the story of how she found me and claimed me in Accra. He then told me about a dog he had as a boy. We shared light stories until someone shouted my name.

"Miss Spencer! Miss Spencer!"

I stood abruptly, and Quetzalli scrambled to get to my shoulder. One of the men we'd assigned as a hunter ran toward us, along with Ben.

"Miss Spencer! Lieutenant!"

"What's the matter?" I yelled back.

They stopped in front of us, doubled over and huffing to catch their breaths. "There's—a—ship."

Wheatley and I looked at each with wide eyes. "A ship?"

Ben caught his breath first. "A small barque on the other side of the island. They've made camp."

"They're Spanish," the crewman said.

"Are they careening?"

He shook his head. "No, the vessel is in the bay. Perhaps they could take us to safety?"

"If they've a full crew, I doubt it," Wheatley said. He scratched his chin and looked to me. "What do you think?"

I thought for a moment, dozens of scenarios playing out in my mind in an instant. Then I gave Wheatley a devilish grin. "I think we're going to steal that ship."

Chapter 39

We broke camp and hid amongst the trees in the jungle, lest we be discovered. This ship was our ticket out of here. A plan was forming in my mind. If my calculations were correct, we were a day's sail to Nassau.

I ordered some of the cleverer men to gather reconnaissance on the camp. They appeared to have had stopped to supply and rest before continuing their voyage to the Spanish main. I found it curious that they did not stop in nearby Cuba instead. They weren't pirates, but perhaps their wares weren't entirely legal.

From what we could deduce, a few men had stayed on the ship, but on the island was a crew of fifty-odd men. Large barrels of wine had been carried off the small barque, and the Spanish crew was cheerful and full of song and laughter. They planned to drink all night.

I gathered with my crew in the thickest part of the jungle. Wheatley sat on my right side and Ben sat to my left, holding Quetzalli.

"I do not think it will take many of us to overtake the barque," I said in a low voice. "We must hurry before the crew gets to us. But let us wait until after midnight when they are well into the drinks."

"How will we get to the ship?" one man asked.

"We have how many longboats now?" I asked Theodore.

"Four."

I nodded. "Twelve of us will row 'round the island and wait."

"They'll hear us," Wheatley said. "They'll hear the paddles against the sides of the boats."

"And here you thought it was ridiculous that I needed my dresses." I grinned. "We'll wrap the oars in cloth."

"Brilliant," Ben said.

"Now, as for the rest of you. Six of you will be ready to take their two longboats as soon as the sails go up. I need the fastest and most discreet among you. Speak with Wheatley if you are up for the task. You will be armed."

Wheatley straightened. "You must be able to reach the ship before we are too far away, or you'll be left behind to make peace with the Spaniards you just stole from."

The men murmured among themselves with excitement.

"Now, everyone else. Load the rafts we've built with our supplies and wait for us in the bay. We'll make a wide berth round the island so they won't think we've just sailed to the opposite side. But it likely won't be long before they discover you're here. Wait in the bay on board the rafts so we can load you up quickly." I paused. "And do not forget my trunks!"

"Any questions?" Wheatley asked.

"What's the plan after we steal the ship, Miss Spencer?"

I glanced at Wheatley. "We're still discussing it. Any other questions, direct them to Ben and he'll relay them to the Lieutenant and me."

I stood from where I crouched in the thicket and beckoned for Wheatley to follow me. "Do we have a plan?" he whispered when we were alone.

"As much as I'd like to head to St. Martin and kill the lot of them, we aren't equipped for that. We are supposed to be dead. They don't know I even exist. We are operating strictly outside of the law."

"We're pirates."

I shrugged. "Once we steal the ship, I think we are."

Wheatley sighed and ran a hand through his hair. "Well, then you can stop calling me Lieutenant."

I laughed. "This part of the plan you may not like, but if you have any other suggestions. . ."

"What is it?"

"We shouldn't be far from Nassau. It should be due north. Captain Every had extended an. . . offer. . . to me."

He raised an eyebrow. "An offer? From the king of the pirates?"

"He said I'd make a good pirate and extended his welcome and aid should I find myself in Nassau. I never told Henry because. . ."

"He'd never have agreed." He paused for a moment, staring up into the canopy as if answers would fall like fruit and leaves. "I don't like it, but I see no other option."

"I want revenge, John." I'd never used his first name before now. "I want to avenge Henry's death and the rest of our crew, too."

"Me, too, Miss Spencer."

I shook my head. "We're about to lead our men to steal a ship. We're past formalities. Call me—" I paused. Angelica didn't feel right, nor did the Spanish Angélica. That part of me died along with Henry. "Call me Hell."

He smiled. "Me, too, Hell."

We spent the afternoon and evening lying in wait among the trees. Monkeys screeched and critters climbed up my legs. I put Quetzalli back in her cage for safety. At nightfall, I sent two men to gather intelligence and report back. The Spanish were celebrating something. They also had whores with them that had emerged from a tent. They'd been in port recently. I hoped that these were not friends of anyone I would meet in Nassau.

By ten o'clock, the Spanish had been drinking for hours. At midnight, Wheatley, Ben, and I, along with nine other of our best fighters, hauled our longboats out to the beach on our side of the ocean. I tore one of my older dresses and chemise into strips that we wrapped around the oars.

I sent up a silent prayer as we pushed the boats into the water. The moon cast an eerie glow over us, reflecting off the water in a hazy, white light. But the skies were clear; a good omen for sailors.

As we began to row out into the bay, Wheatley leaned forward and whispered to me. "It worked!"

"Of course it did. Did you doubt me?"

"Less and less every day."

We were nearly silent as we rowed round the island, stopping at a point where we could see the barque but not the camp. But we could hear them. When the sounds of reverie faded and the stillness of the night began to scream, I nodded at Wheatley. We began to row, the sign to the others to follow suit.

The barque was drastically smaller than the *Integrity* and any fears I had about a crew of thirty-eight sailing it faded. As long as we did not go far, we would be fine. No one saw us as we sailed alongside the hull. No one looked overboard. I could make out the fires and some shadows at the camp. It was much quieter. Hopefully, the Spaniards had fallen into a drunken slumber and our other men would have great luck stealing their longboats.

Wheatley climbed up the side of the hull first and peered over the edge to the main deck. A moment later, he lowered his head. In the starlight, I made out his hand gesture: three men on board.

But where? Clustered together? Spread out across the deck? Could we surprise them before they screamed and gave us away?

My heart pounded as I clenched my dagger in my teeth and prepared to climb. If we failed, we'd all be caught and killed. This was too small an island to coexist with men we'd attempted to rob. I swallowed the acid in my throat and placed my hands on the hull behind Wheatley.

Somehow, he landed without making a noise. He pulled my hand as I reached the top. I had only seconds to take in my surroundings. Two men were drinking near the helm, facing away from us. One was asleep on the steps to the poop deck. I moved from the shadows and drew my sword.

"¡Ah, la gran puta!" they sputtered.

I slit one of the drinking men's throats before he could finish his statement. Wheatley finished off the other. Blood spurted, but there was no noise besides the gentle splashes of the sea and the creaking of the ship as it rocked. The other man still had not awoken, and a crewman pointed at him and, then looked toward me. I shook my head. We could toss him overboard to swim to shore once we began to move. His screaming wasn't a risk once the anchor was up.

The barque only had two masts. I pushed the capstan and raised the sails with two other men. Wheatley and another man hauled up the anchor. Ben helped the rest raise two of the longboats. To my surprise, it was several minutes before we heard shouting from the beach.

The sleeping man woke up, confused and rambling in Spanish. I spoke to him in a low voice and told him we would not kill him as long as he did not put up a fight. His panic subsided, and he sat on the steps to the uppermost deck with his head buried in his hands, mumbling about how he had failed in the most basic task of protecting the ship.

We heard splashing and frantic rowing. I could not spare more than a passing prayer that the men rowing were ours. Instead, I focused on our heading and grasped the helm. The barque was swift and smooth on the water, so different from the bulky *Integrity*.

"Let us up!" I heard someone yell.

Somehow, the six men had caught up to us, leaving the Spaniards stranded on the beach. As soon as we were far enough away that there was no chance of being caught, Wheatley tossed the lone Spanish sailor overboard.

"He got a boat," Ben shouted.

Now all that was left was to fetch the rest of our crew before they were discovered by the Spanish. I sent a silent to prayer to Dionysus or whatever god of wine might be out there that they were too drunk to think straight.

Within minutes, we were back to the bay where the English Navy had murdered our comrades. An intense rage filled me. Somewhere in these depths were my friends. Mr. Gresham, Master Easton, even Gil. And Henry.

"There they are!" Ben alerted us.

"Lower the topgallants!" I yelled.

In the moonlight, the sight of twenty-odd men on rafts looked like spectres sent to lure us below.

"Hurry, hurry, hurry," I muttered under my breath as supplies were hauled up and the men climbed aboard. It was taking too long.

Ben handed me Quetzalli's bronze cage, glinting in the stars. She was squeaking angrily, and I unlatched the door. She jumped onto my shoulder and licked my face. I felt a weight lifted off my shoulders that I didn't even realize was there.

Shouts echoed from the shore as the last of my crew climbed onto the deck. "Raise the topgallants!" Wheatley ordered.

And within minutes, we sailed away. We had arrived as traitors to the Navy and loyalists to the crown. We left this island, fueled by anger, as pirates.

Chapter 40

We were closer to Nassau than I thought. We found maps in the captain's cabin, and Wheatley and I plotted our course. New Providence Island was due north. Though the Bahamas were still an English colony, Every and his fellow pirates had all but taken over. The Navy was no longer welcome there, and we weren't sure how a Spanish barque would be welcomed.

We sailed through the night, and I was at the helm as the sun crept over the starboard side, casting a yellowish glow over the ship. A new dawn. We were safe, for now. We were not destined to die on a deserted island. No one spoke much as the weight of our new destiny settled over us. Some of the men went below to investigate what was in the hold, and it soon became apparent why the Spaniards had been celebrating.

There were a large amount of jewels, silks, and even some gold. I asked among our men who excelled at mathematics, and only one sailor raised his hand. A man called Jameson. He went with Wheatley to tally up the booty and negotiate shares for each man.

The wind was on our side, and we sailed at a brisk speed toward the Bahamas. Nassau was on the northern side of the New Providence Island, so we planned to anchor on the eastern side and walk into the town, leaving most of the crew to guard our ship.

I changed into one of my finer dresses with false pockets as we approached land so that we would not be without coin or have to carry coin purses through a crowd of pirates. It was late afternoon. The breeze was hot through the windows of the cabin. I pinned my hair on top of my head in lieu of my ratted braid to cool my neck.

What would Henry think of me? I'd stolen a ship and killed two men, and now I prepared to consort with a pirate.

But would he have changed his mind about his loyalties after the English murdered over nearly two hundred members of his crew? Would he have avenged my death and theirs?

Tears stung my eyes as fastened my belt around my waist. I did not know the answer. I only hoped that I would not let him down. Henry had tried to do the right thing. Tried and been killed for it. I began to think that the right thing was not so black and white. That, in fact, the right thing had shaky morals, a lightskirt among the angelic host.

The creak of the anchor shook me from my thoughts. I grabbed Quetzalli from where she ate fine Spanish sausage and placed her on my shoulder. If I died at the hands of pirates, at least she could run to freedom.

Wheatley, Ben, Jameson, and I rowed to shore. By my calculation, we needed to walk northwest to reach the town for a few miles. With a compass to guide us, we walked in relative silence for just over an hour before the first signs of buildings.

We smelled Nassau before we reached it, piss and rum and sweat. Though a small village, the noise from the taverns and busy streets reminded me of a summer I had spent in London as a child. Whores were in varying states of undress, some with even their breasts exposed. We sidestepped puddles of vomit and excrement. Quetzalli pressed herself against my neck, and I wished I could do the same to Henry. Instead, I kept my hand on the hilt of my sword.

"What is it we're looking for?" Wheatley asked.

I dodged a man passed out in the middle of the street. He clutched a bottle of a brown spirit in one hand.

"Madam Liza's."

He nodded and stopped to ask a gruff man with a scar across his face for directions. "Good sir, can you point me to Madam Liza's?"

"Oh, has we got a gentleman in our midst? We has!" The man bowed and belched as he straightened back up. "Ma'am Liza's over yonder."

He pointed south, where several more buildings stood. I rolled my eyes. "Helpful."

We continued in that direction. An old man with a hook nose hollered at me. "Eh, lass! I've got a prick fit for a princess for ye."

"Not likely." I continued past them.

He ran ahead of me and reached out his hands as if to grab my breasts when Quetzalli bristled. "Fuck! Izzat a rat?"

"Aye. Touch me again, and I'll have her gnaw that special prick of yours right off."

"Crazy bitch," he mumbled as he staggered away.

Madam Liza's tavern and brothel was at the top of the high street. It was quieter here, as most of the chaos was closer to the beach. Easier for lonely sailors to find a fix for their troubles. The sun was setting, and a warm glow emanated from the open windows, along with a yeasty, sweet smell of fresh bread. My mouth watered.

Inside, the men sat at tables, and they were less raucous as they partook in their drinks. A woman played the pianoforte and sang a soft ballad. The brothel workers were dressed finer and with more propriety than the ones we had seen before.

"Can I help you?" An older woman greeted us, her black hair tinged with grey at the temples. She was beautiful, once, though the trials of her life had etched themselves on her face. She wore a silk mantua in browns and forest greens, and her hair was fixed in a proper fontange.

I smiled and gave a slight curtsy. "I am seeking Captain Every. He told me I might find him here."

"And you are?"

"Miss Spencer. A friend."

She eyed me with suspicion. "You've got a rat on your shoulder."

"She's no bilge rat and better behaved than a cat, I assure you."

Madam Liza shook her head. "Better than a parrot or a monkey. Give me a moment while I ask the Captain if he'll see you."

She walked away, her dress trailing on the dirty floor behind her. Would he see us? Would he remember my name? I had not anticipated that he'd have a guard. I assumed she was the madam, and she was formidable.

But when she returned a few moments later, her stern expression had softened into neutrality. "Come with me."

She led us to the back of the tavern and pushed back a thick velvet curtain in a deep shade of blue. Captain Every sat at a table with several other men I assumed were pirate captains. They were dressed in a mix of leather and delicate fabrics, and the hats that rested on the tables in front of them had large plumes in a rainbow of tropical colors.

Every looked up with a wide smile. "Miss Spencer. What a pleasant surprise! Where is your handsome captain?"

"Dead." I spit the word out. "The English killed him and the vast majority of our crew."

His smile changed from light to sinister. His eyebrows narrowed. His eyebrows narrowed, shifting his smile from lighthearted to sinister. "Bloody bastards and their politics."

"We agree."

He beckoned to woman who stood in the corner. "Get them chairs and some ale. And food."

The pirates shifted and made room for four more chairs. Madam Liza sat a pint of ale and steaming bowl of soup in front of me, along with a large chunk of bread. I devoured it, my body desperate for the taste of leavened wheat.

Every introduced us to the rest of his companions, though I barely acknowledged their names as I tore into my supper. Jameson and Ben ate with equal voraciousness, though Wheatley nibbled and sat stiff in his seat as if at any moment they'd attack us.

I supposed it could have been possible.

As my soup bowl dwindled, Every leaned back in his chair. "You eat as though you've been starved for months."

I shook my head. "Not starved, though we haven't had a decent meal in weeks." I stopped with the spoon halfway to my mouth. Had it been weeks? When were in Cuba? As strange as it seemed, it was less than a fortnight past. "A diet of roasted lappe and fruit alone is not satisfying."

"Do tell of your adventures and how you've come to find me."

I took a long drink of ale, which one of the girls promptly refilled, before launching into our story from the attack, to stealing the ship. Every and the other men leaned forward, enraptured. I had always excelled at telling a good story after life among sailors. Even my compatriots were engrossed.

"You stole a barque?" One of the pirates asked. "In the middle of the night?"

"Yes. The Spaniards thought they were alone on the island. They were more interested in drinking and whoring than in their ship."

The pirates laughed.

"Sounds right," Every agreed. "Now, what brings you to me?"

I shifted. "We are not even supposed to be alive, therefore, we cannot return to any English colonies. And now that we've committed an act of piracy, if the Spanish crew finds their way off the island, we will not long be welcomed in Spanish ports."

"And you seek safe haven?" The captain raised an eyebrow.

I waited a long moment before I answered, gathering my thoughts. "No. I seek a ship. And a crew. In addition to the small crew we have."

Every held his belly as he chortled. Heat flashed in my cheeks. "Taking my advice then?" he asked. "Becoming a pirate?"

"I seek freedom. And revenge."

He stopped laughing. "Freedom, that makes sense. That's a language I understand. But revenge. . . Miss Spencer, buying a ship and a crew will not give you enough power to seek revenge."

"You'd need a fleet," the quietest of the pirates said.

There was no way I could afford a fleet, not with every bit of my gold and every last jewel from the barque.

"And a reason for a crew to join you." Every looked thoughtful. "English Navy ships are not full of prizes."

"English forts are," I countered.

He frowned in contemplation. "You must build a fleet, and for that you will need capital."

I took another drink of my ale. "And how do you propose I gather capital?"

Every leaned forward. "You become a pirate and sail the pirate round."

I took a deep breath and waited for him to continue.

"In the Indian Ocean, there are riches ripe for the taking. The merchant ships are full of spices and gold and silks and jewels. More than you can imagine. You'd be set for life. Or you could buy and steal a fleet."

Another pirate piped up. "You sail down 'round the Cape of Good Hope. Stop off in Madagascar or Ile Saint Marie. Then go a-hunting."

"The Mughal ships are large and heavy-laden. Easy to overtake."

I looked at each of them in turn. Excitement lit up their faces, and nostalgia had glossed over their eyes. "And that's what you've done?"

"Aye," they chorused.

"But you cannot run a pirate vessel as a Navy ship," Every said. "None of us want that life anymore."

I listened as these pirate captains gave me their best advice for piracy. None of them seemed to mind that I was a woman. Perhaps they thought I would fail. But I listened in earnest and learned. Captains were to be democratically elected. Captains only have complete command in battle. The quartermaster and boatswain could be elected, as well. Pirates followed a Code of Ethics that was to be drawn up, agreed upon, and signed before sailing. Captains received two shares of prizes, and rarely more. A good cook and competent surgeon were the most valuable men on board.

"And I recommend trading yer booty for slaves," one of them added. "Massive quantities of gold and jewel draw suspicion in ports."

Wheatley placed a hand on my knee when I stiffened. I bit back what I thought of that advice. I would trade for ships, not humans, but the rest of the advice seemed sound. Then I inquired where I could get a ship, as the barque was not equipped for a voyage to Africa. The waters near the cape could be treacherous.

"I could use a small vessel like you stole for closer sailing. I've a two-masted sloop I'd sell you for the right price," Every said. "Then you'll need to vote on captain and quartermaster, draw up your Code, and recruit."

We stayed at Madam Liza's that night. The men shared a room, but Madam Liza led me to a well-kept room with a large bed and window overlooking the night sky. The candles cast a warm, homey glow, but as the door shut, I felt trapped. A crushing loneliness settled over my soul, and a sob caught in my throat.

I had not slept alone since leaving England. I went from sharing Henry's bed to sleeping under a makeshift shelter with my surviving crewmates. After days of playing the leader, of pretending to be fine, the thought of being alone with my grief for a night threatened to swallow me whole.

Distraction. Comfort. That was what I needed tonight. I closed my eyes and thought of Henry's strong arms around me, but it hurt too much. Perhaps I could share the room with the men. It was a brothel, after all. Propriety was not a concern.

It *was* a brothel. Before I was completely aware of my actions, my hand turned the doorknob and my feet found their way downstairs. Madam Liza was behind the bar, cleaning bowls and glasses. She glanced up and raised her eyebrow.

With a few quiet words and coin exchanged, Liza beckoned to one of her girls. The woman, a tall, Black woman with a thick French accent named Thérèse, took my trembling hand in her dark one and led me back to my room. Her smile was warm, and her skin was cool against the sweltering night.

She stood in front of me and gingerly unpinned my hair until it fell around my shoulders. She smiled and stroked my face, then moved her hands deftly to unlace the stomach from my mantua, pushing the gown over my shoulders. Tears leaked from my eyes as she moved around me and began to unlace my stay.

"I will take care of you now," she whispered, brushing my hair over. "You are safe now."

I didn't have it in me to fight embarrassment at my emotional state. In that moment, all I wanted was to be taken care of. I nodded. She untied my petticoat, which fell to the floor, then lifted my chemise over my head.

She placed a gentle kiss on my lips, then led me to the bed. I leaned back against the plush cushions and watched her undress through my wet eyes. Briefly, I wondered if I would ever lie with another man and decided that I wasn't sure I would want to. Thérèse was beautiful, all dark curves and curly hair, and plump breasts.

She climbed onto the bed with me and began peppering kisses from my brow to my neck. I shivered under her touch as she grazed my skin with her fingertips. She was tender, which was so different from what I usually enjoyed, and yet, it was exactly what I needed.

She kneaded my breasts and murmured compliments against my flesh. I reached for her, pulling her bosom to my mouth. I breathed in her floral perfume, a refreshing, comforting scent after so many months at sea.

Her hand moved over the roundness of my belly to the spot between my thighs. I gasped as she slipped her fingers over my wetness. Soon, I lost myself in her ministrations. She played me like a slow, sweet ballad, moving over every spot that felt good. I came under her skilled touch over and over, and each time, I cried hot tears, losing my burdens to her care.

When her hand stopped playing, her mouth replaced it. My back arched at the deft movements of her tongue. I no longer knew whether I was crying from days of grief and uncertainty or pure joy from the ecstasy of her attentions.

She finally pulled away, and I lay utterly spent. I smiled up at her through sticky lashes. "Shall I do you?"

Thérèse shook her head. "Not tonight. Sleep."

She pulled back the blankets and held me as I fell into a dreamless, restful sleep.

Chapter 41

The next day, Captain Every walked back to the barque with us, along with his quartermaster. I kept my hand near my sword; I did not trust him entirely, but I had no choice but to place my faith in his word. Even amongst pirates, Every had a reputation. He allowed his crew to commit whatever sins and atrocities they saw fit when capturing a vessel. It was a stark contrast to the jolly, clever man who whistled as we walked through New Providence Island.

Every and his quartermaster approved of the barque, and I negotiated an additional sum that would not leave us wanting for supplies, pending my approval of the sloop he wanted to trade. We sailed to the main harbor of Nassau Town, and Wheatley went with me to inspect Every's ship.

The sloop needed work. The ropes were tattered and needed to be replaced. There were more than a few repairs needed on the main deck and the hold. And the bilge smelled far too fresh.

"It needs considerable work," I said as we climbed the ladders back to the main deck. It had potential, and I was certain it was as fast as he said.

Every waved a hand. "New rope and patch that hole on the poop deck, and she'll be good as new."

"There's a slow leak in the bilge. The kitchen is in utter disrepair—first cooking fire would blow the ship to pieces. The pump sticks. A third of the guns are rusted, and. . ."

The pirate sighed and ran a hand threw his beard. "Very well. I'll take half the gold we discussed."

"Half? Your ship may be larger, but mine is nearly freshly christened. The barque alone."

He laughed. "The barque alone? Christ, woman. You are bold."

"But smart."

"No deal."

"The barque and a quarter of the sum we discussed." I folded my arms and stared him down. "I've been on ships as long as you, Captain Every. I am no ignorant woman."

"No, that you are not." He sighed, resigned. "A third."

I smiled. I would have paid more; indeed, I was desperate enough for a ship that wouldn't blow off course with the first African tempest that I would have paid the full sum. I stuck my hand out to shake his. "That is a deal, Captain Every."

He shook my hand and turned it over as if he to kiss my knuckles, but I pulled away. He chuckled. "Madam Liza's in two hours to finalize the deal. I've asked some of the other captains to bring copies of their codes for you to look over."

"You are most kind." A dirty scoundrel, but kind.

Back on the barque, Wheatley and I conferred with our crew. Like Henry had done when we left Curacao, I gave any the option of staying in Nassau and booking passage elsewhere who wanted a more honest life. Wheatley and I spoke of our desire for retribution, and we were met with hollers and huzzahs.

"We need a larger crew, so we will be in port for a few days. But first, as new pirates, we must adopt the principles of democracy. We must vote on the officer positions. Any nominations for captain?"

The men looked around at each other, seemingly perplexed. Wheatley cleared his throat. "I nominate you."

My eyes widened. "Me?"

"Yes. If it weren't for you, we would have let ourselves die on that beach. You rallied us into caring. The entire plan for getting off the island was yours. You already *are* our captain, Miss Spencer."

Murmurs of agreement echoed around the deck. "I second the motion," Ben said with a smile. He held Quetzalli in his arms and scratched her behind her ears. She squeaked her nomination.

"Very well. All in favor of Miss Spencer as our captain, say aye." Wheatley looked around at the men.

Enthusiastic "ayes" rang in my ears.

"All opposed?"

No one spoke. My jaw dropped.

"Do you accept, Hell?" Wheatley asked me.

"I accept."

I grinned as the men clapped and shouted. How far life had taken me, from a naïve child who wanted only to study the sciences, to the captain of a pirate ship.

I led the nominations for quartermaster, which went with equal enthusiasm to Wheatley. Ben became our boatswain to another unanimous vote. His first task was to prepare for transferring ships, while Wheatley and I rowed to shore to secure the sloop from Captain Every.

Our code was a masterpiece. The men heartily agreed to it. The shares would allow them to make far more wealth than they would as Navy sailors. I had drawn it up after reading through the codes of four other crews, taking what I liked and making it my own. My crew knew no better, and I presented it with enthusiasm.

In addition to the usual laws of retribution for theft and dividing the booty, I included a strict policy of capital punishment for rape, even of a whore. We would not become the men who sailed with Every. I also conveniently left off the rules about no women on board, as it seemed hypocritical. Indeed, more women on a ship would likely result in more efficiency.

We began the work of recruiting, with Ben and the other crewmen boasting of our adventures and encouraging a hatred of the Navy. Wheatley and I spent the afternoon at Madam Liza's waiting for interested crew.

Five men came. We needed more than that. Ben reported back that while the lure of Mughal ships and an agenda of anarchic retribution was appealing, most pirates had no desire to sail under the command of a woman. Bloody men and their superstitions and bigotry.

I spent another night with Thérèse, this time taking a less tearful, more active interest. She kept the dark thoughts away, and I slept soundly once again. We made love at dawn before I went to oversee repairs on the as-yet-unchristened sloop.

When she was sated, and I'd had my fill of her exquisite beauty, I sat up and began to dress in trousers and a men's shirt. She watched me from the bed, the morning light glowing on her naked form, making her shine like amber.

"You are the captain," she said in her melded French and African accent. "You can sail a ship like a man."

I winked and replied in French, "I can sail a ship better than a man."

Her eyes lit up. "And you are free to do as you wish?"

I held up my stay and beckoned for her to come tie me in. She rose and ran her hands over my breasts before she did. "I am free to do as I wish. I've never been one to listen to men. And after my father died, leaving me with nothing more than a dowry I would never use, I decided that I would never listen to one again."

Other than Henry, I thought. Although I had tried not to listen to him that day. The fleeting thought of wishing I had died alongside him flitted through my brain. I shook myself and smiled.

"I had a choice, once. I made a similar decision, although it has granted me far less freedom than yours." She braided my hair. "Is it hard sailing a ship?"

"Hard, but like anything, it can be learned."

"Even for women?"

I turned and raised my eyebrow. There was another question hiding behind this obvious one. "What are you asking, Thérèse?"

She darted her eyes around the room and wrung her hands. I placed my hand on her shoulder. "Thérèse?"

"I had the choice between a plantation or a brothel. I have never considered another option."

I smiled.

"I do not know about ships, but I am a hard worker and a quick learner. Labor does not scare me."

"And violence?"

She laughed without mirth. "I'm a whore and a former slave. Violence is an old friend, although it would be nice to be on the other end of it."

"Indeed." I smiled. "Will Madam Liza free you from your duties?"

Thérèse nodded. "Yes. She does not own me."

"You'll need more practical clothes. Can you afford them?"

"I believe so." She barked out a laugh. "I've never liked wearing dresses."

"But you look so fetching in them." I grabbed my hat from the dresser. Quetzalli was asleep underneath it, and I scooped her into my arms. "Come sign the contract this afternoon. Welcome to my crew."

Thérèse was waiting for me when I arrived back at the tavern for luncheon, along with a dozen other ladies. Wheatley looked at me in surprise.

"If I can do it, so can they."

He put his hands up. "I said nothing."

Chapter 42

1 JANUARY 1697

When we sailed from Nassau a fortnight later, we had a crew of fifty-five, including twenty former whores. Madam Liza had turned frosty toward me as I had taken some of her finest girls, but she spoke the language of gold and kept my quarters cleaned and meals hot.

I stood at the helm of the sloop, which we had christened the *Salvation*, with Quetzalli perched on my shoulder as we left the bay. We sailed east into the bright morning sun, and the further we moved from land, the calmer my breathing became. Too long on land had me uneasy. Disjointed. But here, with the gentle rocking waves and the flapping sails, the creaking of wood, I had returned to myself. I had returned to Henry, as close as I could. With both of my hands on the freshly polished wooden wheel, I could almost imagine him behind me. The sea breeze was his breath on my ear. *"Good work, Hell. Keep her steady."*

We picked up speed as we hit open water. I tuned out the bustling noise of my crew and lost myself in the feeling of freedom.

Was this freedom? This was what I had always wanted, was it not? To answer to no man, sail the seas, and venture where I pleased.

Freedom did not provide me the relief I had always expected. It had come at great cost. The loss of Father. The loss of my only friend in Deirdre. The loss of my identity as an Englishwoman.

The loss of Henry.

A strange mix of anger and sadness boiled in my belly. Heat rose to my cheeks that had nothing to do with the bright sun in the distance. He had left me. He had chosen his ship over me, his crew. How had I expected anything less? It's why I loved him, wasn't it? His loyalty. His integrity. But what of his loyalty to me?

I spat on the deck to rid myself of the bitter taste of angry grief. "Damn you, Henry."

"Miss, er, Captain?" Ben stood beside me with a stack of parchment in his hands. I hadn't even noticed him. "Are you well?"

"Yes."

He gave me a reassuring smile. "I miss him, too."

Then he turned and walked away, hollering an order to recount the chickens to one of the sailors. Ben had settled well into his role as boatswain already. Henry would have been proud, and the bubbling returned to my stomach.

Quetzalli nuzzled my face and hopped off my shoulder to explore. Even she could not abide this grief. I wondered if she missed him, too.

"Hell," a low voice behind me said.

I turned my head to see Wheatley. He looked odd in plain sailor's clothes, brown breeches and a loose white shirt. Younger, less stiff. He had donned his uniform for too long.

"The pirate attire suits you, John."

He gave me a half-smile that didn't reach his eyes. "No need for a lieutenant's coat here."

"No, I suppose not."

He glanced up at the sky. "Clear skies as far as we can see. Wind is good. If we keep this pace up, we'll reach Madeira in ten days."

"That's not likely."

"No. But unless we meet a nasty storm, I expect us to arrive in a fortnight."

I nodded. Wheatley gave me a sidelong glance but said nothing about my reticence. I appreciated him for it.

"I'll gather the women for sword training after I discuss the state of the bulwark with Theodore. Do you want to be there, Captain?"

"Aye. I'll hand off the helm to Ben." I sighed and looked up at the azure expanse, unblemished even by a stray cloud. "It begins."

"It begins," Wheatley agreed, with a hint of anticipation mingled in his stoic voice. He went off for his duties, leaving me alone with my thoughts.

The morning passed quickly and without incident. At the noon hour, we gathered our new recruits on the main deck to assess their skills. Most of the men were passable with a sword, and I sent them with Wheatley to spar. A few women were handy with a dagger, as they had taught themselves for defensive purposes. Men were a brutal lot, after all, but I would make certain these women were far more brutal.

We worked on stances and basic maneuvers before I paired them off to practice, correcting as I went. Across the deck, Wheatley barked commands. I kept my voice gentle, the way Henry had all those years ago.

We broke after two hours, and I sent the women down to find bread and cheese to replenish their energy. They had made good progress. I smiled to myself, then called to Quetzalli. The rat bounded across the deck and scampered into my arms. Together, we descended the ladder that led to my captain's cabin.

Quetzalli nuzzled my cheek before leaping onto the hanging bunk, eager for her midday nap. I poured myself a glass of rum and sat at the small table I now used as my desk. The room was much smaller than the captain's cabin on a ship-of-the-line, but in all my years on ships, I had stayed in far more cramped quarters. It would do.

Memories flooded me as the amber liquid burned my throat. I closed my eyes, remembering that first day with Henry. So much time had passed. So much had changed. I recalled the day vividly, though I could not recall myself. That naïve, blushing girl had died long ago. When? I wondered. Certainly, she was gone before Henry met his fate. She was already gone when I decided to stay aboard and turn against the crown. Was she gone when Father died? I could not recall.

I thought of Deirdre. Had she grown, too, in her service as a nun? Was she happy? I hoped so. I wondered what she would think of me now, captain of a pirate ship full of rebels and whores, hell-bent on revenge against the king's navy.

The image of her disapproving stare made me laugh. I poured myself another glass of rum. My thoughts passed through the people I'd known over the years, the places I'd been. None of it quite seemed to have led me here.

The hatch opened, and Wheatley stuck his head down. "I brought you some food."

"I'm not hungry."

He lowered himself into my cabin and handed me a plate of bread, mango, and cheese. "You're going to eat, Hell."

"Am I now?"

He ran a hand through his sable hair in exasperation. "As your quartermaster, I must insist that you stay hale for our journey."

Barking out a laugh, I met his eyes. "Is that part of your duties as quartermaster?"

"As your friend, then."

He stared me down, waiting for my refusal: of the food, of his friendship. I hadn't had many friends in my life, and how strange that Wheatley was the one extending the olive branch. With a smile, I tilted my head in assent and took a bite of cheese.

Chapter 43

Ten days into our journey, our fortunes improved once more. We'd since finished off the fresh beef and fruits, and there were few chickens left to slaughter. Madeira was only about four days of dried meat away.

"Ship ho!" Thérèse called from the crow's nest of the sloop's only mast. "Starboard bow!"

I scrambled to the stern of the ship and pulled my telescope from my belt. Three-masts, likely some sort of brig, and flying a white flag with some sort of red emblem.

"Netherlands!" I called. "Merchant or passenger."

"Orders, Captain?" Ben said from somewhere behind me.

"Hoist the English flag for now. Have the black at the ready."

"Aye." He hurried off the find the flags.

I turned around to find Wheatley. He stood near the mast at attention, awaiting my commands. I beckoned for him to join me then handed him the telescope.

"'Tis a beauty," he observed.

"Aye. Fast."

"Not a galleon."

I nodded. "We do not need a large booty. But a second ship. . ."

"Captain." His voice was skeptical but not reproachful. "The women have been wielding arms for less than a fortnight."

"But they've been dealing with stupid men their whole lives." A smile spread across my face. "I have a plan."

"Good morrow!" Wheatley called to the ship that had pulled alongside our starboard. "I'm Captain Wheatley of the *Salvation*. I have goods you might be interested in procuring."

He gestured to the other women and me, where we stood huddled near the mast. I wore naught but two petticoats and a bodice pulled low to highlight my bosom. The others wore much the same. But petticoats and bodices could conceal almost anything, especially when sailors only stared at our chests.

Someone translated to the captain of the merchant ship and responded, "An intriguing proposition indeed. Where are you headed?"

Wheatley's hand flexed at his side, his tell for nerves. "We sail for the African coast. A new colony has need of. . . entertainment."

When the interpreter relayed this, the entire Dutch crew burst into raucous laughter. Rage filled my stomach like hot coals.

"Come aboard, man, and bring the lasses. We shall discuss payment for an hour or two of your time."

Ben lowered the gangplank, and the women of my crew filed across to the other ship. I brought up the rear and gave a slight nod to Wheatley for playing his part well.

He sniffed. "Look alive, girls!"

We straightened at his faux order. I pushed my bosom outward and slapped a smirk on my face. The other women sauntered around the men, who whistled and licked their lips. I swallowed the acid in my throat. This was familiar territory to most of the women, but not to me.

Wheatley addressed the captain and his interpreter. "I have a special one for you."

The captain jerked his head at the interpreter, sending him away, then asked if Wheatley spoke French. He must have sensed the noble-born air about Wheatley.

"*Oui.*"

They continued in the lingua franca, while I played ignorant.

"This one is special. Best of the best."

"Oh? You've had her then?"

Wheatley covered his uncomfortable laugh with a cough. "Nightly. I don't usually let other men have her."

Sinking my teeth into my lower lip, I looked down to keep from laughing myself.

"And you offer her to me?" the captain said.

"Well, she is worth good money to me. We had to repair sooner than expected, and I need the coin. For the right price for all these girls, you can have her."

I raised my chin as the Dutchman eyed me up and down. "She is quite exotic."

I hated that word.

They negotiated a price amidst the sounds of catcalling from the Dutch and disingenuous flirtations from my crew. Two hours' time for a sizeable sum of gold.

Business as usual.

The captain shouted the terms to his men, and they descended on my scantily clad crew like vultures. A wave of nerves threatened to make me lose my balance as the captain held out his hand to me. What if this did not work before I was taken advantage of? Or my crew that I had sworn to protect?

"Get on, lass," Wheatley said in a sharp voice that I knew hid his understanding. "I'll be here if there's trouble."

I took the captain's hand and allowed him to lead me toward his cabin. As we reached the gilded door, I paused and turned to look back at Wheatley. I nodded, and he let out a loud bird call.

What happened next was a blur. We drew the daggers hidden in our skirts and bodices. The men on my crew readied the cannons and a few, including Ben, hopped over swords and pistols drawn.

I had my dagger at the Dutch captain's throat as I surveyed the scene. With sharp implements pointed at throats and cocks, no one dared move against my women.

"What is this?" the captain panted in panicked Dutch.

"Cooperate and no one will be hurt," I answered in his own tongue. I glanced over at Ben and ordered him to bring the rope to the mainmast in English.

"Now, order your men to bind themselves 'round the mast. Anyone who fights back will be dealt with swiftly."

"Bitch," he spat. But he called to his crew, who reluctantly obeyed, swords and daggers at their backs. My crew tied rope around the circle of bodies, and I handed the captain off for Wheatley to deal with.

"I am Captain Hell Spencer of the *Salvation*." I addressed the captives in Dutch, to their surprise. Murmurs of "Captain?" echoed in the sea breeze.

"My crew and I sail for Madagascar and beyond, in search of Moghul fortunes. We keep no flag save our own. And we are in need of a second ship."

I paused and met the eyes of several of the Dutchmen. "We will also need a crew. I invite you to join us, masters of your own fortunes and fate. Sign our oath and seek riches beyond what you have ever dreamed. You will be treated as an equal partner in this endeavor.

"Those who do not wish to join us will be kept below and released in Madeira to find your own way home. Those who attempt to betray our hospitality will be dealt with accordingly."

I paused, assessing the reactions from the Dutch, although they were mostly quiet. A few whispers here and there. "Wheatley, Thérèse, find out what's below deck. Take the captain so he cannot sway his men. The rest of you, keep your eyes on the crew."

I made my way to the captain's cabin. As I expected, it was much larger and nicer than the hovel on the sloop. The bed was large and suspended from the ceiling. An oak desk sat in front of the glass window, positioned to overlook the sea. A small table and two chairs for dining were in front of a large wardrobe. And there were bookshelves. I smiled. It would suit me nicely.

An hour later, we had twenty-five new crew members and ten men in the hold of the *Salvation*. I noted to Ben that we needed to build a cell for future captives. I set a rotation of my most trusted men and women to keep watch on those in the hold, lest their newly rogue brethren attempt to release them.

Then we began to divide the crew between the two ships. A handsome, tall, blond man who had not shown any interest in the women spoke in low whispers to Wheatley about the names and abilities of our new crew members. A blush crept into Wheatley's cheeks as they discussed.

Wheatley would man the *Salvation* while I took the captain's cabin on the new barque. Thérèse and Ben came with me, along with half the women, a handful of the Dutch, and a few crew members from the *Integrity*. The barque, which we christened *Absolution*, was far sturdier and swifter than the one we sold to Every. She was nearly as fast as the *Salvation*, so we were only a quick boat's row at any time.

The booty from the Dutch allowed us to divide it between old and new crew alike for a happy salary while also giving us plenty to trade with in Madeira. In just a few days' time, we would reach the Portuguese-controlled islands and prepare for our journey south.

And somehow I had already found myself in command of a fleet.

Chapter 44

As we docked in Madeira Bay; the sun shone bright from beyond the Mediterranean. I shielded my eyes against the glint on the water as we dropped anchor to catch a glimpse of a land I had not seen in many years. Madeira port was the gateway of the world, a stopping point from the spices and silks of Arabia, the resources from Africa and beyond, the sugarcane from the Caribbean, and the colonialism of Europe.

As a child, it was my fairytale. I was never one to dream of castles and dragons. But an island at the edge of the Atlantic filled with vibrant colors I'd never imagined, scents I could only read about, and the sounds of every language of the world? That was my utopia.

We were to be docked for three days to resupply and allow the crew to enjoy time on land. Madagascar was a far journey, and any ports we might reach along the way were far poorer and less exciting. I had decided we would release our captives on a nearby island with a boat as we sailed away. Thus, Ben had established a strict schedule for guarding them, lest they try to escape.

Thérèse, who now bound her breasts and went by Thierry, walked the market with me and some of the other women. Many found treasures from their homelands from whence they'd been taken. They ran their hands over acacia wood and spun silks with tears in their eyes. Others stuffed food from their cultures in my mouth, eager to convince me that they were far superior to English fare. I did not need much convincing.

But unlike most sailors, they kept their gold close at hand, making only frugal purchases of something they could not resist. Usually, these were practical items, and they haggled over every named price. Between the lot of us, someone could speak a tongue that the merchants spoke.

"Sailors go through their coin like a sieve," I observed. "But not you."

Thierry smiled. "Most sailors are men. They do not think further than their stomachs or cocks can think."

Amara agreed. "The madams taught us well to manage our money. 'Twas all we had to our names."

One of the ladies whose name I could not remember spoke with bitter scorn. "When they didn't take more than their share."

"I kept the books for Madam Liza," Thierry said. "She hated it, preferring to be out amongst the rogues and ruffians."

Liza's was the most well-run brothel in Nassau. Money flowed healthily through. The food was coveted for its quality. Even the ale tasted less like piss than other taverns. And the girls were always dressed in finery.

"Thierry. Do you enjoy keeping books?"

"Oui, Captain."

I grinned. "Then you are the new ship's purser."

Her—his, I corrected myself mentally—face lit up. "Aye. Cheers, Captain."

The day was bright with fair winds. We had filled the cargo holds of both ships with plenty of food, rigging, shot, and, of course, copious amounts of Madeira wine. We'd gathered a few new crew members: wenches and freed African women eager to spread their wings under my captainship and find their own fortunes and revenge. The men had grown accustomed to all the women on board, for the most part, even accepting Thierry as one of them. But we kept a watchful eye on them in case.

We were ready to set sail. The last of the crew who had shore leave had made it back in the early light of dawn, bellies full of ale and bodies full of pleasure.

The crews buzzed with excited chatter about our journey to the southern edge of the world. Everyone was eager to set sail, with one glaring exception.

"Where in God's name is Ben?" I asked. I stood at the edge of the pier next to Wheatley. Quetzalli chirped in my ear her annoyance at Ben's absence as well. He always returned with a fresh treat for her.

"I haven't seen him since last night," Wheatley said. "Old Pete says he disappeared with a lass around midnight."

"Oh for Christ's sake." I gestured to two of the men nearby. "See if you can find the boy and remind him that my patience only goes so far."

They hurried off to find my trusted boatswain. If it were anyone else, I'd leave them behind. But Ben. . . he was the closest thing I had to family other than Wheatley. And Henry would never have left his protégé.

Twenty minutes passed, and the two men returned with no sign of Ben. I glanced at the sun overhead. We were nearing the noon hour, losing valuable daylight to get into safer, open waters away from the French and English navies.

I sighed and shifted Quetzalli to my other shoulder. Wheatley placed his hand on my back. "I can go look for him. But Hell, you have a new crew who may question your—"

"My leadership. Yes, I know." I rubbed my temples. "A half-hour. We give him a half-hour until we. . ."

"Captain!"

I jerked my head up at the sound of Ben's voice to see my normally trustworthy boatswain running down the pier, clad in naught but a small pillow that he held clumsily over his manhood.

Behind me, the crew burst into laughter. Even Wheatley snorted at the sight of Ben in his god-given clothing. I just gaped.

"Boatswain," I said, my shock turning to giggles, "I hope you have a good explanation."

"She stole it, Captain! She stole everything!"

His wide, panicked eyes set me roaring along with the others. "Some whore stole your clothes?"

"You're not known for being particularly well-dressed, lad," Wheatley said, his voice cracking.

Tears of mirth welled in my eyes at his comment, but I was determined to find out what had happened.

"Who stole your clothes?"

"Not just me clothes, Cap'n. Me boots, me dagger, me purse." In his frantic desperation, he had lost the grammar Henry had forced him to acquire.

"Who, Ben?"

"She bewitched me! I know she's a witch! It took me hours to wake up, and I didn't know where I was."

"Ben!" I yelled sharply. "Calm down, boy. Who stole your belongings? Where can I find her?"

He turned and pointed, revealing his bare ass to the crew, which resulted in more raucous jeers. It was better than showing all of Madeira, I supposed.

I closed my eyes and counted to ten. "Someone bring him some trousers, please."

A few minutes later, Ben had dropped his pillow and laced up a pair of trousers far too big for his small waist.

"That's more of Ben than I ever cared to see," I whispered to Wheatley. He let out a most unmasculine giggle.

"Aye. I agree."

With one hand holding up the faded green pants, Ben led me past the main part of the town, rambling apologies and stories of a witch's brew and a lovely brown-skinned woman who had made him feel special.

"I really thought she loved me, Cap'n."

"After ten minutes of meeting you outside a tavern?"

His face fell, and guilt twinged in my gut.

"You're a lovable boy, Ben. But no one falls in love in a matter of minutes."

He cocked his head. "Even you and Captain Martin?"

My breath caught, and memories came flooding back. I swallowed the lump in my throat. "Even Captain Martin and me."

Ben gave me a half-smile. "I want that one day. What you and he had."

And look where that had gotten me, I thought bitterly. I forced a warm face. "You will, Ben. You're young yet."

We stopped in front of a hut. I smelled it before I could see it. Herbs and spices weaved through the smoke from the small chimney, wafting blends of smells that were pleasant and foul in waves. I could see how one might think a witch lived here.

The hut was ramshackle in construction, but clean. Vibrant flowers bloomed along the outside, and any lingering scents of chamber pots had been washed away by the herbaceous smoke.

"Were you robbed by a grandmother, Ben?" I said as I rapped my knuckles against the sloppily shingled door.

But it was no grandmother who answered the door. Instead, a goddess greeted me, and I pinched myself to make sure I had not died.

Before me stood a tall, slender woman with large, brown eyes and a wild crown of ebony curls that framed her artisan-sculpted face. Her skin was the color of fresh, wet sand on an isolated beach, and I wondered if it felt as silken as wet sand, too. I resisted the urge to reach out. A blush the color of rosy seashells spread from her cheeks and down to the swell of her breasts, which peaked out over a sky-blue silk gown.

"Yes? Can I help you with something?"

Her melodic contralto in perfect Portuguese pulled me from my haze, and I remembered why I was there.

I cleared my throat. "I'm Captain Spencer. You've robbed my boatswain of all his effects."

She peered out the door, craning her long neck to see Ben, where he stood several feet away. "Ah, yes," she said, in English this time. A fellow polyglot. I smiled in spite of myself.

"So you admit it."

"I stole nothing. He gifted them to me."

My eyes darted over toward Ben. He put his hands up in defense. "I did not!"

"He did. One moment." She disappeared inside the low-lit hut and then reappeared with a piece of paper. I glanced over the list of items she had scrawled on the parchment. On a line below, next to an X, was an illegible scribble that might have started with a B.

"That's not his signature."

She shrugged, and my eyes trailed up her bare shoulders. She followed my gaze with her own amber eyes, then met mine with a sultry grin.

"Ben," I said without turning toward him. "Go back to the ship. Tell Wheatley I'll return after I take care of the. . . thief."

"But Cap—"

"I don't want you witness to anything I may have to do."

"Oh. Be safe, Captain."

Then his footsteps sounded on the dirt path, fading as he walked away. Let him think I'd kill her if necessary. And if it came to it, I would.

I hoped it wouldn't.

"Do you wish to come inside to discuss the matter?" She flashed a half-smile that sent heat straight into my depths.

"Aye."

Inside the hut, a small fire burned in a hastily built hearth. Candles lined every surface, casting a warm, eerie glow. In various bowls and jars and even hanging from the thatch ceiling were bundles of herbs, the likes of some I had never seen.

I understood why Ben had called her a witch.

"You're an herbalist?" I asked without looking at her. I needed to keep my wits.

"Yes. A healer."

I scoffed. "A healer who drugs and defiles men and steals their belongings?"

"I do not defile them."

Now I turned to meet her eyes with my eyebrow raised. "That's not what Ben said."

She shook her head. "They do not remember anything. What they infer happened is not always what did."

"You expect me to believe you're not a whore and a thief?"

"I don't fuck men." Her honey voice turned harsh. "Conscious or not."

I put my hands in front of me in acquiescence. "Forgive the assumption."

Her stony face softened once again. "'Twas a reasonable one, I suppose."

"Another question, if you'll allow it." She nodded, and I continued. "Why, if you are a healer, do you moonlight as a rogue?"

She shrugged. "Everyone wants the brown-skinned girl's skills, but no one wants to pay her what she is worth."

That I understood. I switched subjects. "Your English is good, but I cannot place your accent."

"My mother was Oromo from Abyssinia."

Eastern Africa, I recalled from my studies. Studies that seemed so long ago. "And your father?"

She shrugged. "Some rapist or another."

I nodded. A common story, unfortunately.

"When one is from Madeira, one is from everywhere. My accent is the result of growing up in a port city."

She was no threat, I decided. Not to me. Oh, for certain, she could be a threat in her way if she wanted. I had assessed that much from her sheer spirit and was aware that more than one of these herbs hanging from her ceiling could fell a large man with a sip of tea.

It was her turn to interrogate me, apparently. "And you are. . . a ship's captain?"

"Yes." I rolled my shoulders back and inclined my head.

The woman smirked and stepped two steps closer to me. "How does a proper English lady find herself in command of a ship?"

The thick air began to affect my head. I shook myself. "An opportunity arose, and I took it. Like you, I have skills that are underappreciated due to my sex. I decided to make my own fate."

Another step closer. Perhaps it wasn't the herbs or the air in the hut. "Skills, mm?"

I swallowed. A bead of sweat rolled down her temple to her chin, and I willed myself to answer her.

"I'm a trained naturalist and linguist," I managed to choke out.

"And now a pirate?"

I paused. Officially, here in port, we were merchants. Piracy was met with a quick slip of the rope, though ships with a king's seal could commit the same crimes with no consequence. But she operated outside the law as well as me, no matter what contracts of sale she drew up.

"Takes a thief to recognize another." I gave her my best close-lipped smile. This time, I stepped forward to close the distance between us. We now stood half an arm's length apart. I could hear shallow breaths.

She licked her lips. "There are types of people who can recognize themselves in others. Or rather, their shared interests."

Her voice was lower, thicker. My heart thudded in my chest. Not knowing what else to do, I nodded again, feeling foolish and helpless.

She reached her brown hand out and wiped a bead of sweat from my neck. Her touch sent sparks through my body. I released a low moan, one I could not have held in had I wanted to.

And then her lips met mine, and I was lost to her intoxicating touch.

Kissing her was unlike any other experience. It was not soft and comforting, like kissing Deirdre. It was not warm and passionate, seeped in history and destiny, like Henry's kiss. Though her lips were smooth, her kiss was raw and burning. A means to an end.

She pulled my shirt over my head and tore at the laces of my stay. My hands frantically tried to figure out the ties of her dress, a style I had never seen. She laughed into my mouth as she lifted her hands to cover mine and guide them to undress her.

Her dress fell to the floor in a pile, leaving her exposed in her velvet skin. She was thinner than the women I normally lusted after. Her breasts were small but full and pert. Eager to find out if she felt as soft as the glistening beaches she resembled, I ran my hands over her sides and abdomen.

"Stunning," I murmured.

I kissed the crook of her neck and moved my mouth lower and lower, finally taking one dark nipple in my mouth. She arched her back and whimpered.

"What is your name?" I whispered against her smooth skin.

She laughed. "Maggie."

"Maggie?" I raised my head up and lifted an eyebrow. "That's an English name."

She rolled her eyes and pushed my head back to her breasts. "I was born Makeda."

"Mmm." I nuzzled against her chest, breathing in her earthy scent. "The Queen of Sheba."

"You know your history," she panted.

"That's not all I know."

She tugged me down to the ground then, pulling at my shoulders until I lay over her. Her wild black hair splayed behind her like a crown. I nipped and licked my way over her slender stomach. Maggie arched her hips up, inviting me to take her, to quench my parched desire. She tasted of salt and spice, and I quickly found the frantic pace that had her clawing at my shoulders.

She swore in a language I did not know as her legs quaked around my head. I climbed the length of her body to kiss her again.

Maggie was not Deirdre, who needed tenderness in every act. She was not Thierry, who had made pleasure his business. She was a queen who knew what she wanted and took it. Pushing me to my stomach, she straddled one of my legs and put her hand between my thighs. She found pleasure for herself as she fucked me with her nimble, healer's fingers.

I groaned and arched backward as she stroked. She was not gentle, but I was not fragile. She sank her teeth into my shoulder as we found our climax together, her wetness spreading over the back of my thigh, me pulsing around her fingers. It was quick and messy and freeing.

After, we lay side by side, panting and laughing. I glanced over at her. "I need a healer on my crew."

"No butcher-surgeons on board?"

"Barber-surgeons?" I corrected.

She shook her head, her mane of hair brushing against my arm. "I said what I said."

"Come with me. I have other women in my crew. You could be rich. Rich as the Queen of Sheba."

She rolled her eyes again, but this time they were alight. "And what? I warm your bed?"

"If you'd like."

She propped herself on an elbow and looked at me, lips straight and brow furrowed. "I will not fall in love with you."

Heat flushed my cheeks. "I didn't ask you to."

"You misunderstand." She shook her head, her brow furrowed as she searched for the words. "I like fucking. I like friendship. I don't like romance."

"I'll settle for fucking and friendship." My lips twitched, hiding a smile. "And a healer."

Her gaze deepened, and I felt more exposed than just my nudity. I folded my arms, but how does one hide their soul when it's on display?

"Whatever loss you grieve, I am not that type of healer."

She was astute. Knowing. Briefly, I wondered if she was a sorceress of some sort. Or maybe empathy and understanding was a sort of magic. "I don't seek healing from him. I seek revenge."

Maggie studied my face, looking for signs of falsehood. Satisfied with whatever she saw, she said, "Then give me an hour to pack."

Chapter 45

Two weeks into our journey, Thierry and I had our heads bent over his ledger as he explained where our accounts stood after our recent prize—a merchant ship that had left Accra. Maggie had encouraged me to offer a place on our crew to the two dozen slaves but leave the merchants dead in the water. "If it had been an entire slaver, I would have killed the Europeans myself and given the ship to the slaves," she said with the most emotion I had seen on her stoic face. "My mother was sold in Accra. Along with millions like her."

I worried about the extra mouths to feed, as we had no plans to make landfall until we reached Madagascar, but we managed to secure a few barrels of water and dried meat from the merchant ship.

Maggie sat in the corner reading, and Quetzalli yawned from her napping place on my desk. A knock sounded, and the door opened without waiting for my permission to enter. Wheatley entered and my rat scampered over to sniff him. I glanced up at him. "I did not know you were taking a boat over today."

We had decided to meet twice a week unless there was an urgent need, and he was not scheduled to leave the *Salvation* until two days' hence.

"Everything is well," he assured me. "And good day to you, too."

I chuckled. "Ledgers never put me in a cheery mood. Nor does a demanding healer."

"Lies," Maggie said as she exited.

"That is why you have me, Captain Hell," Thierry grinned. "But that is all I need from you. I will leave you to discuss whatever has brought Mr. Wheatley over."

Thierry closed the door as he left, and I poured Wheatley and myself each a dram of wine.

"Eager to finish off the good Madeira wine so soon?" he asked as he took the chalice from my hand and sat opposite me.

"I will have you know I still have many more bottles." He raised an eyebrow, and I rolled my eyes. "Two bottles. What brings you to my door besides passing judgment on my drinking habits and bedding habits?"

He put his hands up to placate me. "No judgment. But I have a favor to ask you."

I waited for him to continue, but he was quiet. With a wave of my hand, I said, "Go on. Do not leave me in suspense."

Wheatley took a deep breath. "I need you to teach me to speak Dutch."

I blinked. He had acted as if he were asking for my permission to flog Ben for sport, but this was hardly a reason for nerves. "I see. And what brings about this shocking request?"

He flexed his right fist that rested in his lap, then took a sip of wine from his other. "It would make communicating with the Dutch crew members easier."

I leaned back in my chair and put my booted feet on my desk to study him. Quetzalli climbed up on my shoulders and stared at Wheatley as if she, too, were assessing him. I wouldn't have put it past her, the clever rat.

"Any particular crew members? Tall, blond, and handsome ones?" I asked. But he simply sipped his wine and studied his fingernails. "Who is he, John?"

His shoulders dropped, and he lifted his head with a small smile. "Joost."

Joost had been elected boatswain on the other ship. He was a cheerful man with piercing green eyes and a broad smile.

"Joost speaks some English, yes? And some French?"

"Yes, but. . . I thought that. . . He'd appreciate the gesture of me learning his native tongue."

"And does he reciprocate these feelings?"

"I'm quite certain. At least, he did last night." He grinned. "He's an artist. He sketched me and truly captured my likeness."

I swallowed the lump in my throat at a distant memory. "John. It does not seem practical for me to teach you Dutch when you are on another ship."

"Well, yes. Perhaps we could add lessons to our meetings."

A smile spread over my face at the eagerness in his voice. "Or you could ask him to teach you."

His eyes widened. "Do you think he would?"

"Do you know how Henry learned Spanish? He asked me to teach him when he taught me to fight." Wheatley's smile faltered as I spoke. "Those lessons are some of my fondest memories."

The air hung heavy between us as we remembered Henry. How much he had meant to both of us. Deep in my soul, I knew I would never find another love. But if Wheatley had a chance at happiness, I was glad. I laughed a little.

"What?" Wheatley asked.

"I was thinking how much I despised you when we first met."

He grinned. "And I you. Things have changed."

"Indeed."

He rose from his chair and set the chalice on my desk. "I'll join you for dinner. Your cook is better than mine. But I'm off to find Ben."

When he left, I crossed the room to dig through my trunk. Quetzalli climbed down my back as I bent over, chittering in protest at her lost perch upon my shoulder. I flipped through several old journals until I found the one I wanted. At the bottom of the trunk was a brown leather, weather-worn journal. The edges of the pages were yellowing, and the binding crackled as I opened it.

Carefully, I turned each page, smiling at my old drawings of plants and animals. Perhaps I would find the journal with my first sketches of Quetzalli later.

My heart stopped when I landed on the page I was looking for. I inhaled with a sob. Henry. The only likeness I had of his face. I ran my fingertip along his strong jawline, smudging the graphite as I reached his chin. A tear ran down my cheek. I couldn't even touch a sketch of him without ruining it.

Despite the open windows, the air in my cabin was suddenly stifling. With one last longing glance, I closed the journal. Quetzalli licked my tear away as I prepared to return the journal to the trunk. I paused then placed it under my pillow. I wiped my face and rolled back my shoulders.

It was time for dinner, and a crying captain would not do.

The crew were in good spirits after our successful bounty. Below deck, they laughed and talked over one another, recounting their exploits with great exaggeration. I noticed the women and men still sat apart, but there had been no issues between them to date.

I sat at the end of a long wooden table with Maggie, Wheatley, Thierry, and Ben. Ben still eyed Maggie with suspicion, but at least he would speak to her. Dinner was a large spread of salmagundi, the cook having collected chicken, eggs, and a few fresh fruits from the prize ship. The briny, salty assortment and variety of textures from the tough turtle meat to the soft mango was a welcome change from hard tack and salted beef.

We drank and feasted and drank some more, losing track of the hours. Some of the old sailors began spinning stories about their adventures at sea. Several claimed to have faced sirens and krakens and whales the size of Port Royal. I sipped my ale and laughed along with my crewmates, picking up bits of conversations here and there.

I paid no heed until, "Captain Martin was as brave a man as there ever be. Honorable, he was. To the very end."

I stared into my mug of ale, wishing it would refill itself ad infinitum or until I forgot my own name, whichever came first.

"Bloody English. They never cared for none of us! The fact that any of us survived is luck." The man, a grizzled fellow by the name of Brooks with a scar across his cheek, held up a talisman bound in leather. "Won me this in a game dice, me did. Made by a real witch in Jamaica."

Maggie snorted next to me. "Men."

"Seamen," Wheatley corrected. "The most superstitious lot on earth."

Brooks continued. He was a captivating storyteller, emphatic with his gestures and inflection. With polished speech, he would have thrived at theatre. I closed my eyes to listen to his fond memories of Henry.

"The ship burned like hellfire, it did! We landed little more'n a scratch on one of the navy ships. I shan't say I shit myself but. . ."

Laughter filled the lamp-lit deck. Too loud. Too loud. I clenched my eyes and jaw. This was not a story I wanted to hear.

"An' Captain Martin, he looked straight at ol' Gresham and said he weren't loyal to the king nor the ship nor the sea no more. Only one lady for 'im. Loyal only to our pretty Captain Hell, he was."

My head jerked up. This was not a part of the story I knew. Dozens of eyes turned to stare at me, and I was grateful the low-lit cabin hid the color that warmed my cheeks.

Brooks leaned forward and lowered his voice. His rapt audience let out nary a breath, and I squeezed my eyes shut once more. "He yelled, 'Abandon ship!' And we did. I was one of the last off the ship before it exploded to hell and back. So was Cap'n. He looked

up and down the ship and said, 'It isn't worth it.' Then he dove off the portside, and I
dove starboard and BOOM!—"

My eyes popped open. "What did you say?"

Everyone turned back toward at me, but my glare focused on Brooks.

"Er, boom?"

"No, you imbecile! About Henry!" I rose to my feet. "What did you say?"

Brooks chuckled nervously and fiddled with his filthy shirt. "He dove portside?"

"He abandoned the ship?" My voice was low, threatening. Wheatley placed a hand on
my arm but I shook him off. "Is that what you are saying?"

"Aye, Captain. But no one can blame him, they can't, after those bastards—"

"The last time you saw him, he was alive?"

Brooks swallowed. "Aye. He was off before the ship blew, though others weren't so
lucky."

"But he was alive when he entered the water?"

"Aye, Captain, but the explosion, it. . . many men drowned. Those who had jumped,
that is."

The symphony of gunpowder exploding. The wall of thick, black smoke obscuring
every English ship. Some of the men had floated toward the island. But others would have
been pushed upon the waves toward the naval vessels. How had I not thought of this
before? How had I not heard the story?

"This story is true?" I asked. "This is no sailor's fable?"

Brooks shook his head. "On me honor, Captain, every word is true. The last I laid eyes
on Captain Martin, he was alive."

Chapter 46

MAY 1697

We rounded the Cape of Good Hope three weeks later, delayed only slightly from a small storm and two days in the doldrums. The sun was bright, and the weather fair and temperate. We'd been weeks at sea with no prize ships and no ports. Rations were running low and spirits even lower. But on the day we reached the southernmost tip of Africa, there was a buzz of excitement in the air, and the crew decided to celebrate.

I sat on the steps of the main deck that evening, twirling the dagger Henry had gifted me years before in my fingers. The crew sang and danced, happy that we were mere days from Madagascar. Someone played the squeezebox and another the fiddle, but the noise would not drown out the ache in my heart. Thierry and several others showed off their modified stays that allowed them to bind their breasts without harm. They'd spent countless hours of the last weeks experimenting with needle, thread, and scissors. But even Thierry's bright-eyed smile could not pull me from my own mind.

The last I laid eyes on Captain Martin, he was alive.

The plan was unchanged for now. Wheatley had convinced me not to turn around to find out if Henry was still alive or if he had been at some point after the attack. We needed more money, more crew, more ships. I wanted a fleet to go after the English, and the Pirate Round was still my best chance.

But every waking moment, questions swirled in my mind. Was he alive? Was he rotting in some prison cell? Had he been captured and put to death as a pirate? Had he escaped and looked for me?

I needed information. But we were still months away from returning to the Caribbean. Doubts crept into the corners of my mind in the late hours I spent alone in my cabin. Maggie and Thierry both fretted over me. I turned Maggie away from my bed more often than not. Ben reported to Wheatley that I wasn't eating, which earned me a lengthy lecture and Thierry glaring at me until I ate every meal.

If Henry were alive, how would I reach him? What if we failed in the East and returned poor and defeated?

"What if you drink and forget your worries for a time?"

I glanced up to see Maggie holding out a bottle of gin. "What?"

"I can see the 'what if' questions on your face. But it is an auspicious day, a cause for celebration."

I forced a smile but reached for the bottle. "Thank you."

"Mm. Perhaps I have selfish reasons for pulling you from your thoughts." She gave me a lecherous grin, and I laughed.

"Selfish or not, I do need an escape." I gulped down several mouthfuls of the gin in one swig before handing it back to her.

She sipped it herself. "You certainly drink like a pirate."

I shrugged and scooted over to make room for her on the steps. "There are few pleasures in life, but a strong spirit is one of them."

"Do you truly believe that?"

"That liquor is one of life's pleasures? Yes."

She elbowed me. "No. That there are few pleasures in life."

I took the bottle from her hand and took a long drink as I thought about her question. "Once, I did not believe it. Life was joy with a few storms. But now. . ." I shook my head. "I was naïve."

"You were in love."

"I still am, though with no object of my affections. It's worse, somehow, knowing there is a chance that he survived."

I handed the bottle back to her and watched her take a dainty drink. The gin had begun to loosen my thoughts, and I found myself mesmerized by her throat as it swallowed.

"'Tis the unknown," she said. "The unknown is always worse."

"Yes."

"Ben said that you were parted from him once before."

I shivered at the memory of cold, gray Manchester. "And I believed him dead for a long while then, too. I should have known. . . should have believed that—"

Maggie shook her head, her tight black curls flapping like the sails. "No. You saw the ship explode and sink. And he might be at the bottom of that bay, Hell. Don't do that to yourself."

"If I don't believe it, now that I know there's a chance, I'll go mad."

She laughed. "You're a woman who captains a pirate crew. You intend to avenge the death of your lover. You set out on your own as a naturalist. Hell, I do believe you have gone mad long before I met you."

"Perhaps." I chuckled. "Perhaps you are correct. I know many would have me sent to Bedlam for my behaviors and beliefs."

"The same for me. Maybe it is better for the world to see us as a little mad. To underestimate us. Or even fear us."

I grinned. "'Tis much more satisfying when they realize they were wrong." I stood, swaying from intoxication, and reached my hand out to Maggie. "The night is young, and I can think of one more of life's pleasures that would make it better."

She took my hand, and I led her to my cabin, two madwomen and their secrets behind locked doors.

The lush treeline and sparkling sand of Île Sainte Marie greeted us like expected guests. A whale swam off our port side where the white-foamed waves ushered us into the bay. The bay of the colony was a large inlet bounded on the west by tiny barrier islands. Behind, the landmass of Île Sainte Marie loomed. In the center of the bay lay a smaller island, the length of some five or six ships-of-the-line. Several ships were anchored in the turquoise shallows, all bearing black flags.

My heart raced in anticipation. We had sailed directly into a den of pirates. It was wild here, less civilized than even Nassau, which still operated under the guise of the crown. There was no loyalty here. Despite our rejection of God and kings, I could not help the fear in my blood at approaching a colony of thieves, murderers, and rogues.

Despite being one of them.

I glanced astern to ensure our own black flag flew. It flapped in the cool breeze, and I could see another dark flag behind the other ship. At least our ships looked the part. Perhaps we wouldn't be murdered on sight. I studied at my crew, mostly young women. Murdered or worse, I thought.

We dropped anchor alongside our sister ship and lowered our boat betwixt us. I climbed down the side of the hull with Quetzalli on my shoulder. If things turned against us and the ships were sunk, at least she could run off to the thicket of jungle trees. Brooks climbed in after me, a strong fighter who now felt compelled by God to protect me, to assuage his guilt for not telling me of Henry. We waited for Wheatley and Joost to join us from their ship before rowing across the bay.

None of us spoke. We felt the stares from other pirates as we rowed past more ships. A memory of Deirdre reciting scripture appeared unbidden in my mind.

Yea, though I walk through the valley of the shadow of Death, I shall fear no evil.

But the shadow of Death was a jungle, not a valley. And there was no God here. No laws of man. I swallowed and wiped my sweaty palms on my skirts.

A half dozen pirates with pistols greeted us on the beach of the small island, gazes hard and fingers stroking the trigger of their firelocks. I hopped out of the boat into the shallows and helped Brooks pull it ashore, glancing behind me every few seconds to ensure the pirates stayed stoic twenty yards away.

When the boats and oars were on the sand, the four of us turned and faced our welcomers with jaws set and eyes wary.

One of the pirates stepped forward, a tall man with sun-dyed blond hair and ruddy skin.

"What business have ye here?"

An Englishman, then. I straightened my posture. "I am looking for Captain Baldridge," dropping the name Captain Every had given me in Nassau. He was a friend and former compatriot of Every's and was said to run the pirate colony at Île Sainte Marie.

"Baldridge is gone."

I swallowed my panic. "Oh?"

"Decided to sell some o' the natives here on the island. Tribe found out. Bloody messy business. They killed many of the pirates here, but Baldridge escaped."

What was the appropriate response, I wondered? I debated my words until the man released me from my conflict.

"What's a lass in men's breeches and a bodice doin' in St. Mary's? Baldridge plant a bastard in ye?"

I made a face of disgust. "No. Captain Every told us St. Mary's was a good base for seeking a fortune."

"A lady pirate, eh?"

"Aye."

"What's yer name, lass?"

"Captain Hell Spencer."

He smiled. "Captain? I see. Hell is an interesting name."

I inclined my head. "Yes."

"You've a rat on yer shoulder." It was a statement, not a question, as if he had seen thing stranger things. Perhaps he had.

"Yes."

The man laughed, and behind him the others relaxed their grips on their guns. "Very good, very good," the man said. "Me name is Robert Culliford. Captain of the *Mocha*. Come hither, m'lady Captain. We've ale and meat, and we can talk business."

"My thanks, sir."

I followed him from the small beach to a path in a break in the trees, Wheatley close behind me. The trees stretched high, the canopy hard to see from where I walked. Bird calls I'd never heard before rang in a symphony around us. And a collection of small monkey-like creatures with long arms and legs studied us from afar. A few moved by hopping upright toward trees to get a better look at us. My hands itched for my long-neglected sketchbooks.

Culliford spoke about the settlement here as he led us deeper into the jungle. I kept my hand on the hilt of my sword, though it did not feel like a trap.

"We no loot other pirate ships here. What ye do out in the blue is no matter. But here, we offer respite from the plunderin'."

Honor amongst thieves, I mused. "I understand."

"If ye find yerself with a surplus of drink or supplies—lumber, rope, food, and the like—'tis always nice to help keep St. Mary's up. No set tax, just a charity to the cause."

"The cause?" Wheatley asked behind me.

Culliford glanced back. "Yer men do speak, eh? Aye, the cause. A haven for the brethren from the Crowns of the world. From those who seek to take our freedom and choose our fates for us."

A smile spread across my face, but it quickly turned to a gape as we entered a large clearing. Hastily constructed buildings of lumber and thatch, a dozen at least, centered around pens of livestock, more than I'd seen since leaving England. Hundreds of pirates milled about, drinking and laughing and tossing dice. Whores fanned themselves outside one of the structures, bored with the antics of the pirates.

A pirate haven, indeed.

Culliford led us to an open-air structure of strong tree trunks and thatch near the center of the small village. A bar stood at the back, constructed from ship planks set upon barrels. Culliford gestured to a woman who wiped out mugs and then sat at a table. He waved his hands toward two open seats.

I sat, and Wheatley sat next to me. Joost and Brooks stood at our backs. Another man took a chair next to Culliford. He was not tall, but his shoulders were broad, and wore his dark hair tied back with a leather. His amber eyes looked at Culliford with something like admiration but not quite.

"Captain John Swann," Culliford said, clapping the other man on the shoulder. "Meet Captain Hell Spencer."

Swann nodded at me, his face unreadable. I nodded back.

"John is my husband."

Wheatley leaned forward. "Husband?"

Swann growled. "Is that a problem?"

Wheatley froze, and I placed a hand on him, urging him to sit back. "Not a problem at all. We've no issue with buggery and the like," I said. "We have just never heard of marriage between two men."

"*Matelotage*," Culliford explained. "Though we'd hang for it elsewhere—"

"We'd hang for quite a lot more, love," Swann chuckled.

"Indeed, yet 'tis quite common 'mongst sea rovers and rogues. Share our loot, have someone to take our property when we die."

I arched a brow. "A strictly economic relationship?"

Culliford winked at me. "There are no rules to *matelotage*. Law has no place in affairs of the heart."

Wheatley inhaled deeply, and I glanced behind me at Joost, who looked down at Wheatley with wide eyes and a small smile.

The woman from the bar brought over mugs of whiskey, and Culliford continued to ramble about *matelotage* and other pirate oddities. He told of some men who fell in love with a whore and brought them into their partnership. A marriage of more than two. How far I had ventured from the gentry mores of Northern England. Swann asked how we had found ourselves under the black, and I enthralled them with my tale.

"Now, what brings ye to run the Pirate Round, Lady Captain?" Culliford lit a pipe and leaned his chair back.

"I seek fortune. Capital for a fleet. And I wish to purchase another ship before we hunt. Fast and heavily gunned."

Swann nodded. "There's a good many who would sell, though the ships might want for repairs."

"A non-issue." I waved my hand. "We can pay."

Culliford grinned. "I like ye, Lady Captain. Captain Hell. But ye need to convince the others. Stay for a time. A fortnight or so. Let yer crew enjoy the pleasures of wine and flesh. Meet the other captains."

And so we did. We whored and drank and smoked interesting plants that made the world spin. I found time to sketch the new flora and fauna. For a time, for a time, I was able to pretend I was happy.

I purchased a large, three-masted brigantine. There was a sloop that I had my eye on, as well. But the figurehead of the brigantine caught my eye. Carved in mahogany, she was a winged woman, her elegant features drawn into a vicious scream. And atop her head, there was no halo.

There were horns.

Chapter 47

"She still needs a name," I said as I peered through the telescope at our mark.

"Then give her a name," Wheatley said dryly. He peered through his own scope at the large treasure vessel sailing our way, bearing thousands of pounds of gold and spices and other finery from the East.

My small fleet was obscured for now in the shallows of a small island, but soon we would be spotted. I wanted to time our approach with as little opportunity for the vessel to prepare for battle as possible. Our fate would change today, with luck and courage. I did not want to sail an unnamed ship into battle.

"She cannot have any name. It has to be the right name."

Ben sighed from behind me. "Perhaps name it 'Right Name' then."

I snapped my head around and glared at him.

"Sorry, Cap'n. But it's been nigh on a fortnight, and you've come up with naught."

"Well, if my bumbling crew had any decent ideas. The best you've thought up is the 'Big Rat.'"

Wheatley snorted. "You did say you wanted it representative of you."

"A pox on you both. Incidentally, Ben, have you secured my big rat?"

"Aye, Cap'n. She's gnawing on a hunk of cheese rind and is none the wiser that she is locked in the cage."

I smiled. "She's the wiser. She just cares more about cheese." At least I had bought her a larger cage from the blacksmith on St. Mary's, with enough room for a small bed of cloths and parchment. "And the hold?"

"Enough shot to blow Versailles to the moon."

"Good." I looked back at the treasure ship. Still not close enough to raise sails. "Now all we need is a name."

Wheatley groaned as Maggie joined us. "Surgery is prepared with plenty of water and cloth, Captain. What's wrong with him?"

"She is still prattling on about needing a name for the ship before battle," Wheatley explained.

It was Maggie's turn to groan. Traitor.

"Why must you name it before battle?" she asked.

"*She* needs a name because when my crew tells the tale of the day we became rich beyond all imagining, they cannot say they sailed under Captain Hell of a ship with no name. It kills the story."

"Ah. Something to stroke your ego, then?" she teased.

"Her ego is big enough." Wheatley placed his telescope in its pouch upon his belt. "A few more minutes yet."

I nodded.

"True enough. Why do you sail, Hell?" Maggie asked.

"I've told you."

"Tell me again."

I sighed, exasperated. "I sail to get rich to buy a fleet to destroy the English Navy."

"And why do you want to destroy the English Navy?"

"For Henry." She smiled and nodded at me. "To make them pay for what they took from me. For rev—" My jaw dropped. It was so obvious now. "Revenge."

Maggie looked surprised and then grinned. "I expected you to go with *Henry*. But yes, I think it fits you."

Wheatley and Ben smiled in agreement.

"The *Revenge*," I whispered. A name fit for a legend. A name to strike fear in the hearts of men. I cleared my throat and shouted to the crew to be heard, my team of cast-off sailors, and whores, and freed people, and some that fit in two of those categories. "Listen!"

Their attention turned to me, pausing in their work preparing us for battle. I had their attention. Their loyalty.

"Today, our fates change. Today, we take back what has been taken from us. From what we are owed. We sail to avenge our friends, our homes, our freedom, our honor. The powerful men of the world have deemed us unworthy, and so we sail for revenge."

A cheer, loud as cannon fire.

A wicked smile spread across my face. "Today, you sail into battle under my command, but you fight for yourselves. For your due. Today, you sail aboard the *Revenge*."

I gestured at the ship we stood on. No one would ever accuse me of lacking for drama. "We shall christen her first with blood. And tonight, with rum!"

"Three cheers for Captain Hell," one of the men who sailed on the *Integrity* cried. "Hip hip!"

"Huzzah!" the crew answered in thunderous celebration.

"Hip hip!"

"Huzzah!" I heard Wheatley and Ben cheering behind me. Maggie simply smiled and nodded to me.

"Hip hip!"

"Huzzah!" The cheer had spread to the other ships. I wondered if the sound had made it to the treasure vessel.

"Sails up! Anchors away!" I yelled.

The order echoed across the deck, and the crew scattered to their posts for sailing.

"Raise the black!"

The merchant vessel was English.

A pit grew on the inside of my stomach when we saw their flag. Ben looked at me nervously. I licked my lips, unsure what else to do. We needed this and yet. . . they were countrymen.

"What's wrong?" Maggie asked in her amalgam of accents.

"They're English," I replied.

"And?"

I darted my eyes over at her. "In case you had not noticed, I am English."

Her brown eyes studied me with skepticism. My skin burned under her intense gaze. I shifted uncomfortably. She had a way of seeing more than anyone. Far more than I intended.

"Are you?"

"Am I what?"

She rolled her eyes. "English. Are you truly?"

I opened my mouth like a fish and closed it. I wanted to say of course. My father was English. The Spencer family went back centuries. But my mother was Nahuatl and Spanish. I knew nothing of her family or her culture and had never claimed it. Was I English?

I had lived on English soil, had loved and lost there. But I had no loyalty to England, I realized. No connection to her. Most of the time I spent there, I had loathed every minute. And yet, I was not Nahuatl nor Spanish. I did not remember my mother or her people. I'd never lived among them that I recalled.

Cannon fire exploded, jolting me from my crisis of identity. A piece of the bowsprit broke with a resounding crack.

"Return fire!" I yelled and turned toward the enemy. "They damaged my new ship, the bastards."

"Countries were created by small men playing at gods." Maggie nudged me. "You are of the sea."

I smirked and lost myself in the sound of battle. Wheatley was at the helm, steering the newly christened *Revenge* with skill. My other ships sailed to surround the merchant ship. Their cannons fired randomly. Their frenzied shots did not land on our ships at all. I could almost feel their frantic cries as they struggled to maintain a strategy.

They were surrounded.

Slowly, the cannons quieted. We sailed ever closer through the smoke and ash. My throat burned. I swallowed against it, letting the calm settle over me. It fueled the flame like a gentle breeze. I focused on the ship in front of me, losing myself to only the battle drums of my heartbeat.

We were within fifty yards, and still they had not flown a white flag. They would try their hand at combat then.

They would lose.

"Prepare for battle!" I cried. My crew readied themselves with whoops and hollers. The sounds of swords unsheathing reminded me of gnashing teeth. A group of women began lifting the gangplanks, while the others prepared to cross over.

I made eye contact with whom I deduced was their captain. He was a broad man, and his square jaw was set in anger. His eyes widened in confusion, no doubt at the amount of women with blades drawn, some in full skirts, others in men's clothing, and most in some combination. Wheatley pulled the *Revenge* along the merchant ship's port side.

And then it began.

I stepped back and let my eager pirates board their enemy's ship. Some of them leapt while others rushed the planks.

Maggie smiled at me before heading below deck to wait for the injured. "Good luck."

I nodded, raised my sword, and threw myself into the fray.

Blood rained over the deck. I squinted through the clouds of dust and gunpowder to find my enemy. The faces blurred together as I strained to ensure I was not fighting my own crew.

The second ship had arrived and swarmed the upper deck as the crew from the *Revenge* descended to the lower decks. The third ship, the sloop, waited fifty yards away for a signal if we needed their support.

My cutlass seemed to move outside of me. The thrill of battle lies in the silence. The fight is loud. There are screams and clashes and gunshots. There are moans of pain and swearing. But the rest of the world falls silent. There is nothing to think about but the reach of your sword arm, of moving to avoid an attack from behind. There is no hunger or thirst. It's a dance of survival, with only the basest awareness in your mind.

The merchants put up a good fight, but the battle was short. Their captain called for surrender. Weapons clattered to the ground, and the sailors put their hands up. I panted and blinked away the sweat from my eyes to survey the scene.

There were some two dozen bodies on the deck. Most appeared to move. Some did not. Most were the merchant sailors. Some were not. Damn.

Ben had already begun organizing the captives and giving orders to the crew. I spared a smile at him. He made me proud. How far he'd come. How far we all had come.

Thierry ran up to me, patch over one eye. "Captain, you'll want to see this."

My heart raced. I could not read his voice. What horrors awaited me below deck? I steeled myself before climbing the ladder to the lower deck.

He led me down one deck further. My eyes struggled to adjust to the darkness. But as we reached a door, Thierry struck a match and lit a lantern. He stepped back, handed me the lantern, and gestured toward the slightly ajar wooden door.

It creaked as I pulled. I lifted the light above my head and stepped inside. The glow filled the darkness of a massive room, glinting off of something.

I blinked. Crates and barrels had been opened to reveal piles of gold and rubies and sapphires. I walked in awe to see more of the treasures. Spices and fine silks and stones the like of which I had never seen. And those were just a few of the hundreds of containers that had yet to be opened.

No wonder the merchants had fought so hard. Today, my ragtag crew of former whores and slaves and Navy men, my brave pirates, today, we became rich.

Chapter 48

The rum burned as it went down. I sat in the open-air tavern on St. Mary's island, a lovely woman in naught but a shift and a stay on my lap. She licked the dribble of rum that ran down my chin and giggled. I grinned, or at least I thought I did. It was getting hard to be aware of my own movements.

"Another!" I slurred, holding the cup above my head.

A new cup slammed down on the table in front of me. I took a long drink and grimaced. "That's water."

"Very good." Maggie's voice was dry and humorless. She shooed the girl away.

"Oi! I paid her!" I sipped from the cup again. Still water.

Maggie sat down next to me. "And I'm certain she is grateful. Perhaps she'll honor her end of the purchase later. But for now, Captain," she said sarcastically, "you need to do something besides whoring and drinking yourself into oblivion."

I leaned forward, bracing myself on the table as the tavern spun. "But I'm rich. I don't have to."

She rolled her eyes. "Is that what we are to do, then? Piss away our money on this sorry excuse for an island."

"'S great is—'" I hiccuped—"island."

"And I'm certain this is the best way to honor Henry. In fact, if he is alive, perhaps he'll magically show up here."

I drew my dagger from its sheath and pointed it at her. "Don't. Don't mention him."

Maggie took the dagger from my hand easily. "Hell, what is wrong with you?"

I shrugged and stared into the cup that still hadn't turned into rum. We were silent a long time as I muddled through my swirling thoughts. Thoughts I had pushed away for a week.

"'Twas a lot of death," I said.

"Is this about the English merchants again?" She shook her head. "Hell, those men were no innocents. Do you think their wares were freely given by the Mughals? And they were merchants. Merchants trade in human lives."

I thought for a moment. She had a fair point. It was no different than capturing a prize ship from a country England was at war with. Battles were inevitable. But it wasn't just them.

"But we lost a dozen of our crew. Women and men I had sworn to protect."

My voice was thick with stifled emotion. I closed my eyes. The haze of the spirits had begun to ease, bringing with it a headache and heavy grief.

Maggie placed a soft, brown hand on top of mine. "You can grieve them. You should. But you cannot waste away blaming yourself. They knew the risks. No one becomes a pirate expecting to live a long life. They wanted a taste of freedom for however long they could have it."

"It feels like my fault. I put them in danger."

"Hell, look at me." Reluctantly, I raised my head to meet her shining brown eyes. She gazed deep into my soul, always seeing so much more than I wanted anyone to. "You chose this life. If this is the life you want, you must accept that death will happen frequently."

"I—"

She put her hand up to silence me. "No. If this is what you want—freedom, vengeance, power—then you must accept it. No one can raid ships and seek retribution from the English Navy without loss. No one can save everyone from death. Even you."

"And why not? Why shouldn't I try?"

"You're human, Hell. You are not God. Try, but give your crew the dignity of taking what they want despite the risks, in the same way you do." She paused and chewed her lip as she thought. "You can only control your destiny, Hell. Not anyone else's."

My head cleared at her words as if she'd dunked me in a bucket of water. A memory rushed to the forefront of my thoughts. I stared at my dagger, the dagger from Henry, that Maggie had set on the table. I remembered choosing my own destiny years before when I'd been stripped away from my happiness. That dagger had grounded me in my intent.

No one would steer my destiny except for me. Isn't that what this was all about? I deserved choice and power in a world that never wanted to give me either.

I stood, wobbling a bit from the copious libations. "You are correct. Tomorrow, we will see about purchasing more ships. We'll do repairs, then sail for the Caribbean."

Maggie grinned. "Good. And today? The sun is still high in the sky."

"Today, my destiny is buxom redhead named. . . well, I don't remember her name." I shrugged. "Thank you, Maggie. You are a true friend."

She laughed. "Go, find your fire-haired lover. Tomorrow, you're back to being Captain."

And I was. By week's end, my fleet had grown to five ships, the fastest sloops and brigantines money could buy. We recruited new pirates, some who had sailed under other captains and some, mostly women, who wanted more than a life on this island.

I offered a command to Captain Culliford, but he declined. "I've enough of this life. I want to live with my husband in peace. I can enjoy the sea from the shore."

I commissioned one of my crew members, who had a talent as a seamstress to sew me dresses from some of the silks included with the booty. There were yards of an exquisite sapphire blue with elaborate gold embroidery shimmering throughout. The beauty nearly brought tears to my eyes. I imagined Evelyn's face if she could see me in it. Nothing so lovely had ever graced the shores of England, I was certain. A pirate I may be, but I could still appreciate a pretty frock.

We cleared the ships of barnacles and repaired them for a long sail. Ben and Thierry oversaw the gathering of supplies. And Wheatley announced over dinner one evening that he and Joost planned to marry in the *matelotage* fashion before we left Madagascar. He asked me to officiate since priests were in short supply in a pirate colony.

And so, the day before we set sail, I donned my fine new mantua. I even wore a fontange in my hair and dark velvet mouches, spots on my face to mimic beauty marks. The whole colony gathered on the beach as I gave Wheatley and Joost their vows. With a quick kiss, the ceremony ended, and we drank and feasted in their honor.

I gazed up at the midnight sky. The stars were so different here in Madagascar. I thought of Henry and wondered if he was alive. In my heart, I knew he was. I would find him. If my destiny was my choosing, then I would choose a happy life with Henry.

Chapter 49

A FEW MONTHS LATER

"Stop with your hand, John," Ben said. I laughed.

Wheatley looked at him. "What?"

"You flex your hand when you're nervous," I said. "Dead giveaway."

"I do not!"

Joost patted him on the back. "Darling, you do. Not good for spy."

Wheatley folded his arms across his chest. "Very well. But if anyone recognizes me and knows I am supposed to be dead. . ."

"Then you'll tell them the story we rehearsed. Captain Martin dropped you in Barbados and released you from your service because you refused to commit treason."

Wheatley nodded. "Yes. Believable. It feels wrong to speak of Henry like that."

I smiled sadly. We were approaching Barbados, and Wheatley was about to enter the lion's den. He and a small crew of Englishmen would enter the port of Bridgetown with our smallest vessel. They were disguised as a small fishing vessel and flew an English flag at the stern. Wheatley said there was a tavern where the naval officers frequented. He hoped to gather intelligence about Henry's fate.

And we would wait a dozen leagues away.

Joost and Wheatley shared a moment before my quartermaster descended into the tender boat to reach the other ship.

"We should storm the town now. Burn it down."

I turned to find Thierry glaring northward toward Barbados. "What?"

"'Tis one of the largest slave ports," he explained. "And where my mother was sold."

"And me," one of my newest crew members from Madagascar added. They were not the only ones. Several of my crew had dark ties to Barbados. It was easy to forget, with my English blood and lighter skin, the atrocities that my kinsmen committed day after day.

Maggie stood quietly, eyes glazed with haunted memories. It had not been Barbados for her and her family, but it was no different.

Rage filled me. I would never understand, but these were my friends. My family. And how many countless others like them did not get the freedom to sail and raid for riches? Millions.

I realized, then, what they chose when they chose this pirate's life. I wanted power that I could have in no other way: the power to choose my own destiny. I sought the power to choose freedom and vengeance. My crew chose the same, though their wounds went far deeper than lost love.

"We will raid them," I promised. "But we must first know what we will encounter. If there are a dozen man-o'-wars in the harbor, we stand no chance of approaching by sea. I'll not increase the risk to your lives with foolhardy plans."

And so we waited.

I did not handle the waiting well. I tried to read and sketch and check over the ledger that Thierry had left on my desk to no avail. Instead, I alternated between pacing my cabin and staring blankly out the window. For the first while, Quetzalli thought we were playing a game, and she chased me as I paced. Then she grew annoyed with me and curled up on top of the ledger to nap.

Ben knocked on the door later that evening. "Supper's ready, Captain. Do you want it in here or with the crew?"

"I. . ."

"You should take it with the crew. He won't be back till tomorrow at the earliest."

I smiled. "You are right, Ben. I will join the crew."

"Good." He turned to go.

"Ben?"

He paused at the door and glanced back. "Yes, Captain?"

"Are you. . . happy? With this life?"

He cocked his head. For the first time, I noticed how much older he looked. The sea aged men quickly, but Ben had seen far too much for his young years. He had only turned nineteen two months prior. But then, I wasn't yet four-and-twenty myself.

"I dunno if I know what happy is, Captain. But I'm a lot closer to it now than I ever have been before."

My heart ached at his words. "You have never been happy?"

He shrugged. "'Appiness is for the rich folk, innit?" His voice slipped back into his unpolished accent. "S'not for orphan bastards covered in Covent Garden grime."

"Oh, Ben."

"I donnut need no pity. But I like the pirate's life mor'n the Navy."

"Why?"

He grinned. How had I never noticed what that grin masked? "'Tis no station 'igher than another, innit? I never stood a chance to be respected in that life. But here. . . there's no class."

"You're a smart lad, Ben. You deserve to be truly happy."

"I dunno 'bout all that, Cap'n. But I think perhaps I'm lucky never knowin' it, see. You've known it and lost it and that sounds much worse." He gave me a sad smile. "Turtle stew tonight. Cook don't care much 'bout your preferences."

"Well, with the spices she collected in Madagascar, I'm certain it will be delicious."

As I ate my supper, which was delicious enough to change my mind about turtle, I thought of what Ben had said and watched the crew eat. Whores sat among career pirates and former sailors. Some had been enslaved; others might as well have been. And they laughed and whooped and shared horrid, bawdy verses and even worse jokes. Women and men and those that didn't seem to be either. We all dined together, fought together, bled, and died together.

And though they trusted me as their captain, we followed pirate code. They could vote me out of my command at any time. I did not bear their trust lightly. It was a social contract based not on tradition or hierarchy, but mutual trust and respect.

For this, we were declared *hostis humani generis*: enemies of humankind. We, the outcasts and outliers who valued equity and justice agency. My crew was not composed of Enlightenment scholars, musing on democracy and free enterprise from their posh parlors with the privilege they had as wealthy men, and yet we lived their theories. Proved them as possible.

We had found freedom through authenticity and choice. Too often, I was powerless. Not now, and not ever again.

If I could never find the happiness I had lost again, then that power would be enough.

Wheatley returned the next day with a black eye and a grin. I dropped the end of the sail I was mending and handed the awl to one of my newest recruits.

"I want to hear the story that led to this." I gestured to my eye. "But first, what news?"

"Let a man catch his breath, Hell." He laughed. "Where's Joost?"

I rolled my eyes. "Below deck. But do not take the man to bed until after you give me news."

"Pour the good rum you're hiding, and that can be arranged."

Wheatley joined me in my cabin a few minutes later, and I handed him a mug of rum. Then I sat, put my feet on my desk, and stared at him expectantly as he shooed Quetzalli from the chair and sat.

"Well?"

He sipped his rum. "He was captured alive. But there was no trial for piracy. I suspect officers did not want anyone to hear tell about their true alliances and believe it, no matter how they painted Henry."

"No execution?" I winced as I forced out the question.

He shook his head. "Not a public one, at least. He was confirmed captured, according to the rumor mill at least, and no one heard anything since."

"Who would know his fate?"

"Besides the admiralty?" Wheatley shrugged. "I can think of a few who might be privy, but I need to find out who was present when they attacked us that day. I never discovered which ships besides the *HMS Charles* were there. There was no time."

We fell into silence, remembering those last few frantic moments as Wheatley and Ben forced me away on their captain's orders. I stared into my mug, looking for answers or healing. I didn't know. The rum held no truths for me.

"Cayman," Wheatley said, shattering the heavy silence. "I think we should go there next. It will be riskier. More naval presence, and more chance someone will recognize me."

"I'll chart the course. What is the presence in port? The crew wants to raid."

He set his mug down and raised an eyebrow. "Raid the town?"

"Yes."

"Send some by land and raid at night, then. I think we could stand against the ships, but we would take too much damage. And we need to keep a degree of anonymity. Too much notoriety too soon will harm our chances of finding Henry."

I nodded. "I'll task Amara with a raiding party." I set my glass down and smirked at him. "Now, about your black eye."

He shrugged. "Nothing too exciting. Tavern brawl broke out. I took the opportunity to land a few good punches on a captain who insulted Henry. . . and his 'dark-haired whore.'"

I laughed. "Thank you for defending my honor."

"It was not yours I was defending," he said, but he smirked.

"Of course. Your husband won't be happy with you getting yourself injured like that."

Wheatley rose and set his mug down on my desk. "I know. I'm certain I'll find a way to make it up to him."

"If you would take care to remember that your cabin is adjacent to mine when you do," I called after him.

He snorted. "We are far from even on that front, Captain."

"I don't plan on barging into your tent!"

"It was broad daylight!"

We laughed, and he shut my cabin door and whistled on his way to presumably find Joost. Quetzalli climbed on my shoulder when I stood and crossed to look out the window. The sea was calm today, and the late afternoon sunbeams refracted off the water, casting a fiery glow.

The rat nuzzled my ear and chirped. She was happy and I. . . I was something akin to it. An old emotion settled in my chest, strange. . . yet familiar. It took me a long time to realize that it was hope.

Chapter 50

And so we began a pattern of spying and raiding through the autumn and winter. Wheatley's knowledge of various naval officers and customs allowed him to steer conversations in subtle ways. No one would put together that just prior to a pirate raid, a sailor showed up in taverns curious about the fate of Captain Martin and his crew.

We did, however, gain notoriety as a fearsome pirate crew, unrelenting and indefatigable in our destruction, yet never killing and raping innocents. When I went ashore before an attack, I savored the gossip. Women pirates! Women dressed like men! Skin tones of all shades fighting together! They could not decide which was more scandalous.

I did not attend every raid, but when I did, Quetzalli began to accompany me. A giant rat perched on my shoulder struck more fear in the colonists' hearts than a woman with a cutlass. Quetzalli, for her part, enjoyed the sounds and smells of battle, chittering with excitement in my ear every time.

We docked in Nassau to resupply. Nassau had further established itself as a Republic of Pirates, though in name it still belonged under English control. For a price, the appointed leadership became blind to everything the rogues were wont to do. Captain Every had retired in the last year to some unknown paradise with his fortune, leaving his days as a rogue behind.

On one such day, Quetzalli and I moseyed down the dirt road to the beach after leaving our offering with the governor's man. The grey clouds filtered the sun as if through a window, leaving the day cool and pleasant. Rain would come later, but no signs of a large storm threatened the day.

"Angelica? Angelica Spencer?"

I spun on my heel at the gritting English accent using my given name, the harshness of the g filling me with painful memories. No one called me that, and I had all but dropped my surname in my roving ways.

A blonde woman dressed in faded finery shrieked a bit. "Is that a rat on your shoulder?"

"Evelyn Campbell." The words were sand in my mouth. Quetzalli puffed up in her best attempt at menacing.

Evelyn shifted from foot to foot. "Well, it's Evelyn Davy these days."

"Oh, yes. How is dear old Laurence?"

Her face fell the most imperceptible amount. "Oh. Well. He's. . . well. He was gifted a tract of land on a nearby island and. . . it's been. . ." She shook her head, her towered coiffe bobbing with instability. "We came to give our salutations to the governor and purchase some furnishings for the house."

I snorted. "Furnishings? In Nassau?"

"Yes. It is the capital of the Bahamas, you know. I didn't expect it to be so. . . uncivilized." She wrung her hands and glanced around. "And how nice to see a friendly face so far from home! What brings you here, Miss Spencer? Is it still Miss Spencer?"

A friendly face. I rolled my eyes. "No."

When I didn't elaborate, she said, "I see. My felicitations then, I suppose. You know, I don't think your rat likes me."

"She must have spotted a snake," I deadpanned. The insult was not lost on Evelyn. Her eyes widened and her lower lip quivered.

"Oh, perhaps we can put all that behind us? Moving to the ends of the earth has a way of putting things in perspective." Her voice was shaky. "I know I was never quite warm to you, but. . . Well, it's good to see someone from home."

"Never quite warm?" I scoffed.

She raised her head. I could see her attempt at regaining composure and status. "Well, you weren't the nicest either. After all, you did, you know. . ."

"Fuck your fiancé?"

"Angelica! Must you be so crass?" She blushed. "But, yes."

I pulled my hat from head and swept into a low bow. "Apologies, m'lady. We are, as you said, 'uncivilized' in these parts."

I do not know what I expected from her in response, but it was not tears. Nay, sobs. The last semblance of her frayed control broke and Evelyn Campbell Davy stood in the grimy street of Nassau, crying the ugliest, loudest of cries.

We began to get strange looks and jeers, which just made Evelyn cry harder. "Shh. Evelyn. It's all right," I said as I stepped closer to her. This was not how I wanted to spend my afternoon, but I also did not want someone from my past drawing attention to me here in port. I sighed and reached out a reluctant hand to pat her on the shoulder.

A mistake. She turned and threw her head against my shoulder, the one opposite Quetzalli who squeaked in protest and climbed atop my hat.

"There, there." I patted her gently on the back and tried to ease her off my person.

"It's just that—"she sniffled and wiped her nose with the back of her hand—"I never wanted to come here and be so far from Papa. But Laurence insisted. I thought perhaps. . . Well, that we would be held in high esteem, and he'd forgive me. I could host other ladies from England in my grand home and throw dinner parties, but. . ."

She looked at the ground.

"But you found it's not like that here?"

She shook her head. Her eyes were puffy and red, and despite my best attempts, I felt sorry for her. "Our house is tiny and filthy. The servants hate me. No one cares to visit and become friends. Laurence drinks all the time. He hates me because I haven't given him a child yet. And I try! I do!"

"Evelyn," I said, a thought occurring to me. Nassau was a dangerous place. "Where is Laurence? Do you have a manservant with you?"

"No." She began to cry again. "He's off in some pub, probably gambling away his inheritance. I'm alone. And I'm terrified. The men. . . they leer at me and. . . I just want to go home."

I turned my head to the sky and huffed out a sardonic laugh. If there was a God up there, He was laughing at me. "Come with me."

She swallowed and nodded. I led her back up the road toward the Governor's house. She followed along behind me, though not quite without question.

"I say! You're armed!" she said. She had only just noted my cutlass and pistol hanging from my belt.

"Yes."

I picked up the pace, and she hurried along until she reached my side. "That's quite a lovely dress. Wherever did you get it?"

"I stole it from a merchant ship off the coast of Africa."

She laughed a high-pitched laugh until I darted my eyes over at her. "Oh."

"Evelyn, do you know which pub Laurence is in?"

She nodded. "Near the state houses. Something about a horse."

Black Horse Tavern. What in Christ's name was he doing there? I grabbed her arm and took a left past the blacksmith to reach the pub that had become a favorite among the captains, merchants, and rogues alike. It was a dangerous place for a fancy toff like Laurence Davy.

The smell of sweat and spice rum accosted my nose as we entered. The landlord nodded at me in greeting. "Cap'n."

"Bill. Looking for a man who doesn't belong here. He belongs with this one." I nodded at Evelyn, who had pressed herself against me in fear.

Bill pointed a finger. "Losin' 'is coin like a bride's virginity, he is. Not givin' 'im any more drink."

"Good." I tossed him a coin. "For your troubles."

"Cheers, Cap'n. Fancy a pint?"

I shook my head. "Later perhaps."

Not trusting the men in the room with Evelyn, I pushed her ahead of me toward the table where Laurence played dice with two pirate captains and a French merchant. Playing and, from the looks of it, losing. His aquiline face was red and blotchy. He was slumped forward with his cheek in his hand.

"Laurence Davy!" I slapped the back of his head.

He looked up in confusion, then surprise when he saw me next to his wife. "An-an-gel—?"

I cut him off before he could finish my name. "Are you bloody mad? Leaving your wife to wander the streets of Nassau alone?"

He had the decency to look sheepish. "I—well, she didn't want to come here."

"Can you blame her? She's the daughter of a baron." I gestured around. "This is a den of pirates!"

Evelyn gasped. "Pirates?"

I pinched the bridge of my nose. "Yes, you dolt. If the smell of piss and the sight of street brawls didn't clue you in, the harbor full of black-flagged ships surely did?"

She gaped like a fish.

I turned my head back to Laurence, who was also gaping. "You've a rat on your shoulder!"

I snapped my fingers in his face. "If you would return to the matter at hand, sir. You drag your wife across the ocean far away from her family, then let her wander the streets of the most dangerous town in the New World whilst you what? Drown your miserable life's choices in a pint of ale and take your chances shooting dice with pirates and sailors?"

"You don't even like Evelyn!" He threw his hands up in protest, spilling his drink all over the table and his tablemates.

"Oi!" one of the captains shouted. He rose and began to draw his sword until I put a hand up to stay him.

"How much does he owe the lot of you?" I asked. I shook my head at the sums they each gave me. "Go to my purser, Thierry. Tell him I've sent you to square the debts of a pathetic Englishman from my past." They gave me their thanks and stood to leave. "And don't exaggerate the sum. I know where you sleep."

"Aye, Captain Hell."

"Wouldna' dream of it."

When they left, I pushed Evelyn onto a stool and sat next to her. Quetzalli hopped off my shoulder and began to chew on the crumbs left behind by the others. I leaned forward on my elbows and held Laurence's eyes with a glare.

"Here is what will happen. Evelyn is returning to England. She can concoct whatever horseshit story she wishes about why. I don't properly care." I waved my hand. "You can right the course your life is taking or continue to piss away your inheritance, get syphilis, and die. Still don't care. But you will not force her to remain in the colonies."

Laurence opened his mouth to protest.

"I'm not finished. Who do you think the baron would side with, hm? An impulsive rake or his darling daughter?" I stood and held my hand out to my rat, and she obediently scampered back up my arm. "Come, Evelyn."

She stood without a word, sparing the smallest sad glance to her husband.

Laurence wobbled to his feet. "You can't do this! You have no right! I'll—"

"You'll what?"

"I'll call you out!"

Evelyn chirped in dismay. "Laurence! She's a woman, silly!"

"I don't care." He ran a hand through his thinning hair. "I'll do it! I demand satisfaction!"

The tavern erupted in raucous laughter. I drew my pistol, cocked it, and pointed it at his face. "Are you certain?"

"Ponce wants to challenge the Pirate Queen!" someone whooped.

Next to me, Evelyn let out a breath and whispered, "Pirate Queen?"

Laurence put his hands up and sat back down. He buried his head in his hands as I led Evelyn out of the dimly lit pub. It was nearly dark. "No one lays a hand on her!" I yelled as we left.

She hurried to keep stride with me as I led her further uphill. "You're a pirate?"

"Yes."

"A captain?"

"Yes."

She panted as we walked. "How, uh, how did that happen?"

"Long story."

"Where are we going?"

I stopped in front of a large pink house. "Governor's mansion."

The butler merely raised a brow when he answered the door and led us to the sitting room. Evelyn was blessedly silent as she stood in the corner waiting. I made myself comfortable in a plush chair and put my feet up on a stool.

"Captain Hell. To what do I owe this pleasure?" The governor's gravelly voice suggested it was anything but. I glared at the squat man. He had hastily thrown his wig on, and tufts of gray poked out.

"Governor." I flashed a faux smile. "This is Evelyn Davy."

"Ah, yes. Mrs. Davy, a pleasure to see you again. Where is your husband?"

Evelyn looked at me.

"Her husband won't be joining her. Evelyn finds herself needing to return to England post-haste. Would you be so kind as to host her until you can find a reputable vessel to take her as a passenger?"

The governor shot his eyes between us several times. His brow wrinkled in confusion, but he did not question. "Of course, Captain. My wife will be most happy to have a lady in the house for a few days."

"Excellent!" I stood and clapped my hands. "Please ensure her safety. It is important to me that she return unharmed."

"Of course."

I paused as I passed him on my way out of the room and whispered, "Not a naval vessel. I would hate for something to befall her."

He nodded. "Understood."

"Would you give us a moment to say our goodbyes, Governor?" He paused, shifting his weight. "Yes, Governor?"

"Yes, Captain. It's only that. . . perhaps you know that booking a fare is expensive these days and. . ."

"I'll send my boatswain tomorrow with a fee." Shaking my head, I scoffed. "You're greedier than a bloody pirate, guv, and far less honorable."

"That's why I'm in politics, my dear."

He swept from the room, striped banyan flapping behind him. I leaned against the doorframe and met Evelyn's eye.

"Angelica, thank you."

"Listen to me. You do not know my real name. When you get home, you never saw me. Do you understand?"

"Yes."

I drew my purse from inside my skirts and placed it in her hands. "Keep this on your person at all times. Inside your stay is safest." She nodded, and I bent down to pull one of my many spare daggers from my boot. "This, too, though, keep it easier to access."

Her eyes widened as I placed the cold metal weapon in her hand. "Why are you being so kind to me?"

"I'm not. But you don't deserve misery just because some louse of a man decided your fate. No woman does." I tipped my tricorn at her. "Goodbye, Evelyn."

Chapter 51

S t. Martin's. I'd hoped I would never see that dreaded colony again. Everywhere I looked, I saw the scars of a life that could have been—the life Henry had deserved. But it was inevitable that I had to return here, where everything changed.

We had sailed through the Caribbean, leaving a trail of smoke and vengeance in our wake. We anchored far from established harbors while Wheatley went ashore, listening, questioning, learning. My fleet, now consisting of seven vessels, had become the most fearsome sight in the New World. Whispers of an army of women and pirates echoed in the breeze. And yet, the official wanted posters refused to acknowledge that there were women aboard. Refused to acknowledge my sex, only naming me as Captain Hell.

The pattern of attack on English colonies did not escape the notice of the governors and admiralty, but Wheatley's espionage remained a secret. Drunken sailors did not care about a sailor-turned-fisherman or merchant or whatever his cover was that day, asking questions about the infamous Captain Martin and his treason. To avoid suspicion and recognition, we replaced our smallest vessel before each new target, either through capture or purchase, and Wheatley, along with a few men, would take the new ship ashore.

In Saint Kitt's, he learned that Henry had not been executed but taken to a prison camp somewhere in the American colonies. A public trial had not been held, and the admiralty could not hang him for piracy without at least a farce of a trial.

They were scared that someone would believe his stories of Jacobite rebellion in the navy, no matter how they tried to discredit him.

And so, there were two men who would know for certain where Henry was imprisoned. One had returned to England. The other, Admiral Ronald Wells, was now the highest-ranking naval authority in the New World.

He was docked in Saint Martin, and he had a taste for lovely women.

Which is why I found myself subjected to the torture of Thierry twisting my hair into the highest coiffe possible.

"I have not missed this." I pouted my lip, which Maggie took as an opportunity to smear red dye on it.

"The hair or the face paint?" Thierry asked. "Stop twitching."

I closed my eyes as Maggie applied rouge over my powdered face. We had no arsenic powder, so we stole flour from Cook. "The hair. I do not mind the paint, as I look incredible with a bit of red on my face."

"Says the pirate," Maggie murmured. "We should have used blood instead of dye."

I laughed, which earned me a sharp swat from Thierry. I swore he pulled harder on the next intricate curl. Once he set my fontange in place, adding several more inches to my already towering hair, he stepped back and studied his work with satisfaction.

"Bon. Très belle."

I reached for my mirror, but Maggie stopped me. "We still must do the mouches." She stared at the black paint in consternation. "I can do a. . . square. Mayhap a diamond."

"Let me," Thierry said. He set to work on my face, using a tiny paintbrush to create small beauty spots on my cheeks and eyes. He had decorated many faces and crafted many coiffes as Madam Liza's main prostitute, and he had the skill to prove it.

The hair of the brush tickled. I tried to guess the image from the motions, but Thierry's movements were so small, I could not. His breath was warm on my face. I shivered.

"Non. I know what you are thinking, Captain." He put one final touch on my cheek. "Perhaps when you return."

I winked. "I'll bring you more gold to count."

Thierry and Maggie laughed. Maggie handed me the mirror so I could finally admire at their work. I smiled. I once again looked like Angelica Spencer of Manchester, and yet, somehow, so much more. The black mouches Thierry had drawn included a small flower by my right eyes, a swirl pattern on my left cheek. And there, on my left temple, was the tiniest skull and crossbones, partially curtained by a strand of hair. One would have to be quite close to decipher the image.

"It is time," Maggie said. "You are the picture of English perfection."

I unfolded my silk fan, one I had taken from the Mughal horde. I wore my finest frock, the sapphire and gold mantua with matching petticoat.

Tittering, I fanned myself. "Oh, I do hope the admiral finds me pretty."

We left my cabin in laughter, and I walked carefully across the plank to our new vessel. My fiercest fighters acted as the crew, the women amongst them in trousers with their chests bound and their hair hidden beneath scarves and hats. Wheatley grinned at me from the helm.

"My lady," he bowed.

I secured my dagger in my skirts and adjusted the lace fontange in my hair. "I suppose I shouldn't steer her in."

"Best not, lest someone see."

Sighing, I crossed the deck and disappeared into the tiny captain's cabin. "Then I will wait here so as not to muss my hair."

Admiral Wells' ship was set to leave St. Martin before sunset, per our intelligence. His ship was blessedly still in harbor when we arrived. We docked along the pier. Amara played my maid, as a highborn woman would not walk about unaccompanied—unless they were Evelyn apparently. She fanned me with a large silk fan that hid a dagger. One of many weapons that I'm certain was on her person.

The crew began to unload crates and barrels of fake cargo so that our ship did not draw suspicion. Inside the cargo were pounds upon pounds of gunpowder. While I attempted to gather information on Henry's whereabouts, they were to "deliver" the cargo to various points around the harbor, the Admiral's house, and the tavern frequented by officers near the fort.

I made my way to the Admiral's house, hoping he had not yet left. He was walking down the path as I arrived. The desperation in my voice was not faked, though my reasoning was a lie.

"Admiral Wells!"

He glanced up. "Do I know you?"

I stopped in front of him, panting from my rush, and curtsied. "No, my lord. Forgive me. I have the most need of your assistance."

The man studied me with his unsettling green eyes. They were the same shade as Deirdre's, I noticed, with none of the kindness or goodness. A lecherous grin spread across his face. "How can I be of assistance, madam? It is madam?"

"Lady Helen Wheatley, at your service, Admiral." I worried my lip to look like a proper worried wife.

"Apologies, my lady." He glanced down at his timepiece and back at his house. "I am on a schedule, Lady Helen. Would you accompany me down to the harbor and share your concerns on the way?"

He held out his elbow, and I stifled a shudder. "Cheers, Admiral." I took his arm. Amara rolled her eyes at me as I turned around

"Now tell me, Lady Helen. What has a beautiful woman like you running around St. Martin in such a frenzy?"

"I am searching for information about my husband, Lieutenant John Wheatley. I expected him home more than half a year ago."

I glanced at his face. He showed no sign of recognizing the name. He encountered many lower-level officers, and a man like Wells couldn't be bothered to pay attention to his lessers. Even though outside of the Navy, Wheatley and he were of equal rank in the peerage.

"A missing husband, you say? How utterly tragic. I am sorry." He didn't sound sorry at all. "He was here, in the New World?"

I nodded. "We live in Barbados. I've traveled here to see if you knew if he had perhaps been reassigned or. . . worse."

Wells gave his best impression of a man who cared, although his gaze settled on my decolletage. "Of course. On what vessel was he assigned?"

"The *HMS Integrity*." I watched as his face darkened. "Do you know it, Admiral?"

He stopped on the road and turned to face me; eyes narrow. From the corner of my eye, I saw Amara tense. I schooled my features into innocent, ignorant worry until his expression eased. "Lady Helen, I regret to inform you that the *Integrity* was sunk some months back. I am surprised news did not reach you."

"Sunk? In battle?"

"Er, yes." He extended his arm again, and we resumed walking.

"Please, sir. Tell me what you know. Is there any chance my husband could have survived? I must know what fate he met." I held my handkerchief against my mouth to stifle a fake sob.

"Well, it seems his captain was a traitor to the crown."

My jaw quivered in anger. I turned away as if I were overcome with emotion. I was, though not with the emotion the admiral would expect. How dare he besmirch the name of the most honorable man in the king's navy. "Captain Martin? Surely not! He seemed to be so noble."

"Yes, he had us all fooled, the lad."

"And they were all hanged? I cannot believe that my husband would be part of treason. John was such a good Catholic man."

"Catholic, you say?"

I nodded. "'Tis why he bought his commission years ago, sir. His father did not approve of his religion," I lied. "We felt it was best to leave. But please do not think my husband a rebel, sir. His loyalty was to God first and the navy second."

He smiled. "And his loyalty to you?"

I stared down at my feet. "We loved each other, but he loved the sea."

"Ah, she is a cruel mistress indeed."

"And my husband is dead? You're certain?"

He looked around then leaned in. "I cannot be certain. We did take a dozen or so to a labor prison in the American colonies. The captain and a few others."

"A labor prison? So there is a chance he's alive?"

It wasn't Lady Helen who spoke, but me. Hearing it from the Admiral himself, the one who gave the orders, kindled the flame of hope I tried to keep tempered.

"Yes, the Carolina shipyard." He studied me and licked his lips. "Perhaps we could come to an arrangement. I could try to find out if your husband survived, perhaps even give you a letter to free him. I am a Catholic myself, you see."

"Of course, sir. I would be most thankful."

"But I would need something in return, you see. Quid pro quo." He raised an eyebrow, then made a show of staring me up and down.

"I understand. I would do anything." *If I could just get him alone on board his ship,* I thought. I could show this man exactly what I would do for his crimes.

"Good, good. I return in a week's time, my lady. I look forward to our business."

Shit.

"A week, sir?"

"Yes, just a quick jaunt to Saint Kitts. I really must be off. Call on me when I return." He tipped his admiral's hat and bowed. "A pleasure, Lady Helen."

And he was gone.

"Fuck. Change of plans, Amara."

We found a member of our small crew in place near the blacksmith. "Change of plans. As soon as his ship clears the horizon, carry out the plan. We'll meet you at the rendezvous point."

"Aye, Captain."

Amara and I rushed back to the small ship. Five of our crew remained behind to set fire to the planted gunpowder. We would pick them up off the shore two miles east with the fleet. The admiral's first-rate ship was already headed out of the bay when we hoisted the sails and raised anchor.

"Like the wind, Wheatley." I nodded as I pulled my fontange from my hair and began to remove my stomacher from my dress on the deck. "We are moving to our second plan."

"Aye aye, Captain."

It did not take long to reach our fleet. Wheatley and I climbed back on board the *Revenge*, and the crews reassembled themselves on their proper ships. We saw the smoke from the first explosions soon after and made haste to pick up the crew members we left behind.

They were waiting in the longboat when we sailed up and climbed on board a sloop at the rear of the fleet as the *Revenge* sailed forward. Once changed out of the impractical frippery and into my usual attire of stays, shortened mantua, trousers, and boots, I steered her southward. It would not take us long to gain on Wells's ship. We were easily twice as fast, even heavily laden.

The sun set off the starboard side as we sailed past St. Martin's, leaving a trail of smoke and vengeance in our wake. As the sun lowered beyond the horizon, it cast a reddish glow over the sea. I shouted the order to extinguish all lights. When our lanterns went dark, the other ships quickly followed. In the final moments of light, I slipped an eyepatch over my left eye to make it easier to adjust to the dark.

Soon, only starlight illuminated the water, ghostly reflections lapping against the sides of the ships. My crews prepared for battle in near-silence. Quetzalli rode on my shoulder, eager for an adventure in the night. With my rat and my eyepatch, my cutlass on one hip and my pistol on the other, I felt every bit the pirate queen they called me.

"Ship ahoy!" the woman at the crow's nest called down.

"Raise the black, hoist the topsails!" I yelled.

The naval vessel was so heavily lit with lanterns that it shone like a beacon on the open sea. But we would be invisible under night's cover until it was too late.

The *Revenge* sped ahead of the other ships, racing to catch up with Wells. He sailed with no accompanying vessels, although he likely had at least 300 men on board. But I had five ships and two hundred of the most feared pirates in the world under my command. They were outgunned, and though their numbers of sailors were higher, we easily outmanned them by sheer ferocity.

We were already close enough to the ship to hear their bell ring when they spotted us. "PIRATES! Prepare for battle! PIRATES!"

Their ports opened, but we stayed to their stern to avoid the range of most of their guns. The *Revenge* and the *Absolution* would get close enough for us to climb on deck. If more were needed, they would cross from their ships across the front two to get to the ship of the line.

Cannon shot whizzed past us, hitting the front mast of my rearmost ship. Other shots landed in the water, sending waves crashing up the sides of the hull.

"Attack!" I screamed. "NO QUARTER!"

The smell of fear mixed with the smell of burning wood and gunpowder as the first wave of pirates leapt onto Wells' ship. From the stern side of his ship, I could see Wells pacing in the well-lit cabin. Coward.

"Shoot out his window there," I said to Wheatley and Ben, pointing.

"Always with the theatrics," Wheatley laughed, but he told the gunner to rotate the cannon.

The glass shattered, and I saw Wells ducking for cover under his desk before I raced ahead and leapt onto the man-o-war. When I boarded the ship, the battle was well underway. My crew did not hold back. The sailors were caught unaware and were not well-armed or prepared. I stepped over dead bodies and found my way to the admiral's cabin.

Wells was crouched in a corner holding a pistol. I saw no bag of shot, which meant he had one chance to hit me.

"I just didn't think I could wait a week, Admiral," I said in my most simpering voice. I felt Quetzalli puff into defense mode on my shoulder. "Good girl."

"Lady Helen?"

"Not exactly. Helen is my middle name." I leaned down and put my hands on my knees as if I were talking to a child. "You might know me as the Pirate Queen, but you can call me Captain Hell."

His hands shook as he pulled the trigger. I leaned toward the side, easily avoiding his careless aim. The bullet lodged itself in the wall.

"I never leave my crew to fight battles alone. I've more blood on my hands than all of them combined." I shrugged. "So the stories go."

"What do you want with me?" His voice was barely a squeak. "Money? I have money."

"I have more money than the king and queen." That much was possibly true. "No, I don't want money."

"What then? This is no prize ship."

I shook my head. "No. Too slow. And it smells like cowardice. Once that stench is in the planks, she must be burned."

"Please. Tell me what you want. I'll give you anything."

"Anything?" He nodded. "Admit you framed Captain Martin."

"I. . ." He hung his head. "That's what this is about? A pirate who defends the Dutch king?"

"No. That is what you forced Henry to become." My voice was shrill. I barely recognized it. I thought I had felt rage, but any anger I felt before paled in comparison to what I felt now, facing the man responsible for Henry's death. "After you forced us all to commit treason."

"Us? Who are you?"

I smiled. "Stand up like a man." He straightened, and I smiled. "I'm the naturalist and interpreter of the *HMS Integrity*."

"Martin's whore!"

"Martin's avenger," I corrected. "I've already gotten the information I sought from you today."

"His location."

I tapped my temple with one hand then scratched Quetzalli. He eyed her with fear. "You're catching up, Admiral. Very good. Now, can you deduce why I'm here?"

He trembled. Nodded. "Ye-yes."

"Yes, *captain*." I circled around him.

"Yes, c-c-captain."

Leaning forward, I whispered in his ear, "If I had the time, I would drag this out until you begged for death. Keelhaul you, and I'm quite overdue for a careening. Those barnacles would do a number on your flesh. Perhaps I'd tie you to the top of the mast for a time."

He shivered.

"I could sharpen my dagger, a gift from Henry, and peel your skin from your bones. See what pure evil looks like on the inside. I'm a scientist, you know."

"Please."

I cocked my head. "Please, what? Are you begging for your life or your death?"

"I don't know." He sobbed, tears streaming down his face. A familiar smell accosted my nose.

"You shit yourself!" I slapped my knee and laughed. "However did you become admiral if you shit yourself when facing a lady pirate?"

The door banged open. "Captain, the ship is sinking. We need to hurry."

"I'll be along momentarily, Wheatley, thank you." He disappeared into the battle beyond. I looked at the confusion on Wells's tear-soaked face. "Oh, yes. Wheatley. Not my husband. He was one of the thirty or so that survived when you sunk one of the king's vessels."

"It was a mistake! Please!"

I pulled my dagger from my belt. It was familiar in my hand, like an old friend. An old lover. I walked behind the admiral. "Unfortunately, I don't have time to give you the death you deserve. I'm only not killing you face to face, so you don't get blood on my gown."

"Pl—"

His words died on his lips as I slid the blade over his throat then leapt back. Blood rained everywhere except my dress.

I wiped the blade with my silk handkerchief and left him grasping at his throat as he crumbled to the floor on his sinking ship.

Chapter 52

FEBRUARY 1698

The Carolina shipyard and labor prison lay just past the barrier islands of North Carolina. A small village and a poor excuse for a fort sat nearby. No ships, completed and armed ships anyway, waited in the harbor. Any guns the timber-guarded fort had would not reach us. They were a deer laying in wait for a wolf.

Seven wolves, as it were. A fleet of them.

"No quarter for the guards. Any prisoners that want to come aboard can, or they can find their own freedom on land." I laid out our plan to the crew.

"Is there any booty?" one of the women piped up.

I shrugged. "Take what you want. I doubt there's much. We'll take a prize once Henry and the others are safe."

"Wot iffee's dead?" a toothless pirate we'd picked up in Madagascar asked.

"Then have fun killing soldiers, burn the place straight to Hell, and get back on the ship."

That answer seemed to suffice. The crew were getting restless with battles that resulted in little treasure. We needed to capture some merchant vessels before they began to question my leadership. Luckily, we were near major ports. Booty should be easy to come by.

We anchored off the bay, a quick row ashore. Some of the crew decided to swim ashore instead, though I took a boat with Wheatley, Ben, and Joost.

"I hope those idiots don't have pistols," Wheatley said as we watched a few dozen men dive into the water.

"If they do, they're not getting new ones," Ben replied. "I'm tired of replacing weapons lost due to stupidity."

"No women." Joost pointed, and I laughed. "You are the superior sex."

"Smarter for certain," I agreed.

My knee bounced as we rowed. Wheatley placed a reassuring hand on my shoulder. Henry was here. If he weren't. . . I couldn't think on it.

A small contingent of guards met us with rifles and bayonets. They were easy to overtake. A quick shot to the knee and a slice of the cutlass to the neck, and we moved into the shipyard. The next guard I killed had a ring of keys tied to his belt. I took them. Wheatley did the same to the next officer we encountered.

Beyond the shipyard, we heard cheers and shouted insults hurled at Redcoats as they rushed to defend the prison. But these were soldiers with comfortable jobs, defending prisoners who were unarmed. They were no match for pirates, many of whom had cut their teeth on violence.

A bell rang overhead. "Hurry!" I shouted. "They will have reinforcements soon! Find as many keys as you can!"

We rushed the prison cells, unlocking gates and removing shackles from the ankles of press-ganged workers. Soon, we had strong, angry prisoners fighting the Redcoats. They were unarmed but unafraid. What did they have to lose after losing everything? What brutality had they suffered?

Shots were fired. Swords clashed. I looked everywhere as I fought my way into the prison. I saw no familiar faces from the *Integrity*.

No Henry.

Screaming, I launched myself at another soldier. The Pirate Queen turned berserker. What had these men done to Henry? "WHERE IS HE?" I screamed. "WHERE IS HE?"

Blood splattered my face and boots as I swung my sword, mingling with the sweat running down my face. Or tears. I couldn't be sure. I was not within myself.

The dust and smoke from flintlocks swirled my vision in a dreamlike haze. A nightmare. My feet floated along, my weapons defending a body my mind had fled.

Where was he? Where was Henry?

The world was silent, though I knew battle raged around me. With a hiccup and a blink, I felt my feet return to the earth, felt my sword in my hand. I stood between half a dozen corpses, all dressed in fine English red. My knees began to buckle. He couldn't be dead. He had to be here. I couldn't bear it if I was too late. If I'd lost him again, and for good.

"Where is he?" I sobbed.

"Hell?"

A voice I hadn't heard spoken aloud in so long, but a voice that called to me in my dreams. I turned, squinting through the smoke and dust.

"Henry!"

Chapter 53

"It's you. It's truly you."

Henry squinted hard at me. A vicious, raised scar ran across his right cheek and nose. His blue eyes stared in surprise. His cheeks were gaunt, and his eyes were tired. New lines had worn themselves on his face like canyons.

But it was Henry.

A shot sounded near us, and Henry startled at the boom. But then he smiled, and I saw in him the man I had fallen in love with so many years ago.

"It's me."

I stepped closer and reached out to touch his weather-worn and scarred face. Smoke and shouts circled us, but all I could see was him. I ran my fingers over the lines of his face. Old, familiar ones. New, angry ones.

He closed his eyes and leaned into my touch, pressing his cheek against my hand. I swallowed the lump in my throat that threatened to explode in a storm of tears.

"Captain!" Thierry yelled, pulling me from my entrancement. "We've taken it. We must go."

Henry's eyes widened. "Captain?"

"I shall explain when you are safely aboard. Come, Henry."

I squeezed his hand and turned to make my way to the ship. The burning clouds of smoke began to settle, leaving a bitter taste of gunpowder in the air. Henry coughed, a deep, hacking noise, but the scent of battle no longer phased me.

I turned back and saw that he was more than a few paces behind. "Make haste, Henry. The explosions will have drawn more soldiers from the fort."

He tried to speed up, but his left leg dragged stiffly.

"Are you injured?" my voice raised an octave. Had he been hurt in our attack?

He shook his head. "No. Well, yes. An old injury."

I pressed my lips together and looked around the remnants of the shipyard, thinking, searching. He needed to move faster, but he towered over me, and I was unsure that my support would give us the speed we needed.

Twenty yards away, I spotted our solution.

"Wheatley! Joost!"

When Wheatley saw Henry, he sprinted toward us. He appeared unharmed.

"John?"

"Hello, Captain." Wheatley grinned and embraced Henry.

Henry patted him on the back. "I do not think I am your captain anymore."

"True. Your protégée has surpassed you in skill."

I shook my head. "There will be time for this later when we're safely aboard the *Revenge*. He cannot keep up. I need you to help him."

Wheatley nodded and offered his shoulder to Henry. Joost took the other.

"Who are you?" Henry asked as they helped him hobble. I brought up the rear, pistol drawn in case we encountered an obstacle.

Joost smiled. "I am Joost."

"My husband," Wheatley added.

Henry paused, forcing them to stop. "It would seem I have missed much."

A pained cry sounded around the corner. "Move. Get him into my cabin. I will meet you there."

"Aye, Captain," Joost said.

"Hell?" Henry's voice sounded pained. Frightened in a way I had never heard him speak.

"I shall return, Henry. I promise."

With that promise hanging in the air between us, I ran off to the source of the commotion, gun in one hand and cutlass in the other.

One of my crew, a Dutchman whose name escaped me, was cornered against the stone wall of the prison by two injured but armed Redcoats. I fired a shot at the back of one's head. As he crumpled to the ground, the other turned in surprise. Before he could react, I thrust my sword through his chest.

He died with a scream on his lips.

"My thanks, Captain," the pirate said in Dutch.

I nodded. "Where is your weapon?"

"Lost in the frenzy."

I handed him my pistol and bag of shot. "Back to the ships. Make haste."

"But your gun, Captain."

I pulled another revolver from my boot and a small bag of shot and a string from between my breasts. "I'll be fine. Go."

He ran off. I made a quick survey of the shipyard and prison cells before running after the last of my crew. A longboat awaited me at the docks, and I rowed as fast as I could with Thierry and two others.

Once aboard, I made contact with Maggie, who tended the wounded to see if all was well on her end. She waved me off. I ordered anchors away and pulled on the ropes to the mainsail.

"You're delaying, Captain," Ben said from behind me.

I fought the urge to brandish my dagger in his face for his insolence and closed my eyes. He was right. I was delaying the inevitable.

What does one say when there were thousands of miles and moments between us? Emotions crashed over me in tempestuous waves. Guilt at my parting words to him. Anger at what had occurred. Shame. I had turned to piracy to avenge him. This was no noble cause. This was not about loyalty to king and country. I had no country. I claimed no heritage save the sea.

The sea had molded me in her image, calm at times, raging at others, but always beautiful and always dangerous. In my quest to avenge him, I was no longer Henry's naturalist. Henry's paramour. Henry's. . . everything.

I was my own.

At some point, I realized my reign as the so-called Pirate Queen had moved beyond my quest to save Henry. Though revenge was at my core, I wanted justice for so much more. For the roles propriety had forced upon me. For the judgments of gentry and lower nobility. For the death of my father and my legal disinheritance.

I wanted vengeance for the men who had been press-ganged into the service of a navy who cared naught for them. For the women whose only chance at any independence was prostitution. For the people torn from their homelands and forced into the cruelest of enslavements. The ones abandoned by men whose honor only extended to those with titles. But more importantly, I realized with a heavy sense of shame, that I enjoyed piracy. My crew looked upon me for inspiration. My name struck fear in the hearts of officers. The surprise in the eyes of those I felled when they saw me, a woman, wield a sword or aim a pistol with more skill than the highest-trained soldier.

Yes, the sea had molded me. She had formed me into a powerful force of nature. Long ago, I had sworn that I was a tempest, but I had not known the sweet taste of power. I had chosen, then, Henry as my fate. But when he was lost, and I thought him dead, I had to choose another course.

I chose me.

All this now laid between us, an ocean of change. How would he see me? What if this ocean was the one we could not cross?

A hand rested on my shoulder. Ben.

"Captain. Go to him."

I nodded and let go of the rope. In my distraction, I had stopped heaving, resulting in rope burn. My palms were as raw as my soul, I thought. I ignored the pain of both and crossed the deck to my cabin.

With one final moment of hesitation, I inhaled deeply and turned the cold, metal doorknob.

I let out a breath when I saw Henry. He sat on a chair, washing himself with a cloth and a bowl of water. Quetzalli sat atop the table and nudged his hand, and he pet her with soft strokes. Even after a year, the little rat remembered him. He had removed his ragged, filthy shirt. I bit my lip to keep away a gasp. He was so thin, every rib visible. His shoulder blades protruded like knives. And yet, he maintained so much muscle, a testament to the grueling, back-breaking labor of his imprisonment. The contrast was stark. Blinding.

Scars and bruises decorated his back and torso. A painting not of oil colors, but suffering. Pain.

Whatever other emotions I had felt washed away, leaving only a burning rage.

"Captain," Wheatley said. He leaned against my desk, arms folded and eyes alight. He glanced at Henry and back at me. "That feels strange to say."

I tried to smile but couldn't. "Yes."

Henry looked at me, eyebrow raised. Behind the light, there was something haunted in his gaze. Unfocused.

No, I realized. Only his right eye was unfocused. The left stared at me intently. It was unnerving. I glanced away.

"John, do we have numbers yet?"

"Five that I know of. Joost went to collect final counts."

I closed my eyes. Five more of my crew dead. Sometimes, the weight of lost lives threatened to suffocate me, stacking on me like the metal weights the courts used on their prisoners. But Henry was safe here. I sighed and banished the ghosts.

"And the vault?"

Wheatley smiled. "Far too easy. Not a large sum, but the crew will have enough for a few pints when we return to Nassau according to Thierry." He stood upright and clapped his hands. "Very well. I must be off. Duties and the like. Henry, rest well, my friend. I shall visit you later."

"John. I am glad to see you are well. And happy."

My quartermaster smiled as he left. Before he reached the door, he paused next to me. "Patience, Hell," he murmured. "It may take time."

"Patience has never been a strength of mine." I nudged him with my shoulder.

He chuckled. "Well, there is a first time for everything." He squeezed my arm, then left me alone with Henry.

I stood, frozen. I had faced many foes, had run headlong into battle. But faced with my oldest friend, my captain, my lover. . . I had never known so much fear or uncertainty.

Henry spoke first, bless him. "You and John are friends."

"Aye."

"That might be the biggest shock of the day," he said with a smirk.

I huffed a small laugh. "It shocks me every day."

A pregnant pause.

"Hell—"

"Henry—"

We both let out an uncomfortable laugh that time. Henry and I had always been at ease in each other's presence. These were uncharted waters. I waved a hand to encourage him to speak. It was not politeness but cowardice, as I knew not what to say to him.

He placed the cloth in the basin, which now was slurry of dirt and blood. He scooped up Quetzalli in one hand and scratched her behind her ears. His movements were stiff; he lacked the grace he'd had before. But he was still beautiful.

"You saved me, Hell. You came for me. I don't. . . I can't. . ." He shook his head. "You found your way back to me. Again."

"Always, Henry. I will always find my way back to you. In this life or the next, I will search for you and find you." I stifled a sob. "We thought you dead for a long while. So many. . . so many died. Some washed ashore, but the rest were claimed by the sea."

"They took thirty of us. Only half a dozen survived to the prison. It was. . . a horrific journey." His eyes darkened, and for a second he seemed to shrink. "The shipyard, the labor, was a respite."

"Henry. . . what did they do?"

He swallowed hard before stumbling over his travails. The goal of the traitorous officers had been utter humiliation, it seemed. Weeks of torture aboard the ship. Every crew member had an opportunity to do as they pleased. The punishments the officers bestowed upon them, well, I did not know a single pirate who would ever tolerate such acts.

The rage I had felt earlier grew hotter and hotter. It threatened to boil me from the inside out. I shook as he listed one atrocity after another. Even poor Mr. Gresham had been subjected to the inhumanity. Henry had lost sight in his right eye. His leg was broken at the shipyard and healed improperly.

Any punishment meted out by an officer of His Majesty's Navy was legal. And they say that pirates are *hostis humani generis*.

I went to him in two strides and knelt at his feet. "They shall pay."

He placed his calloused hand on my cheek, and tears welled in my eyes. A warmth spread through me. Not a boiling fever of fury, but a comfort. A well-loved blanket on a chilly night.

"Look at you, Angélica."

A tear rolled down my cheek, breaking my control. No one had called me that, in its proper form, in too long. "Henry," I whispered.

"I have heard rumors in recent months. A pirate queen terrorizing the seas. Fearless, the bastard daughter of Lucifer himself. And I wondered. . ."

"I am so sorry, Henry."

"Sorry? For what?"

"For—" I paused. Was I apologizing for piracy? I did not feel sorry. I had claimed everything I wanted and collected the resources to rescue Henry. For not coming sooner? I came once I knew for certain where he was. "For what you must think of me. A pirate."

"What I think of you? Hell, I think you are incredible. Incomparable. I think you are my savior, my compass. You are my destiny."

I closed my wet eyes and kissed the palm of his hand. "Let's get you to bed, Henry. You can rest now. Truly rest."

I stood and dusted the knees of my skirts. Henry stood with a grimace, but as he took a step, he collapsed.

"Henry! Are you quite well?"

He held a hand up. "Need my sealegs, that's all. Give me a moment."

It was a lie. He groaned and his face contorted in pain. He rubbed his ruined leg before attempting to pull himself to his knees.

Attempting with no success.

I watched, frozen, as the man I once knew gave up. He lay crumpled and broken on the floor of my cabin, labored, heavy breaths punctured by small groans. He bit his lip and furrowed his brows in consternation.

Henry, the war hero. Henry, the man for whom hundreds had betrayed their country. Henry, my virile, vibrant companion. A paragon of strength and courage.

Defeated.

I knelt once more, wordlessly this time, and heaved him into a sitting position. He placed his arm around my shoulders, and together we rose. Slowly, I led him to the bed.

His face the moment he relaxed into the cushioned mattress and soft fur blankets nearly broke me. It had been too long since he had known basic comforts, the feeling of safety and security. But no more. Now, he would rest. I would protect him.

And I was not done avenging him.

"I will send my healer to see you," I murmured as I stroked his hair from his sweaty brow.

He shook his head. "No opium."

"But you're in pain."

"If I cannot have my healthy body, I want my healthy mind." He grabbed my hand. "Please, Hell. Being back with you is the only balm I need."

I nodded. "I shall send her along to assess you otherwise. She is an herbalist, a traditional healer, and may have something which will not addle your mind."

Henry smiled weakly at me. "Very well."

"Get some rest, my love."

He was asleep before I finished my sentence. I gazed at him for a few moments. He had aged, and he had a scar that marred his perfect face, but he was still lovely. He would want for nothing with me, I promised silently. What were my riches worth if not to bring him to health and happiness?

But while he might have needed no other balm, the only thing that would soothe my soul was vengeance. With an excited Quetzalli on my shoulder, I slipped out of the cabin and took command of the helm. The deck was bathed in red from the setting sun.

"Heave her round! Prepare shot for the cannons!"

Wheatley and Ben rushed over.

"Captain? What is happening?" Ben asked, wide-eyed in the quickly fading light.

"The things they did to him. To the others. They must pay."

Wheatley nodded. "I've seen the cruelty of naval officers. For Henry, it must have been. . ."

"Unfathomable," I said.

I caught Maggie's eye and waved her over. "He's resting. Will you see to him soon?"

"Of course." She squeezed my upper arm. "And you?"

I glared straight ahead. "I will be fine."

The sun had set by the time we reached the colony once more. The fort cast a looming shadow in the moonlight, blanketing the village in a ghostly hue. It would be alight soon enough. Visible from the heavens. If the royals sat with God, then let Lucifer's bastard daughter light fire beneath them.

I laughed to myself like a madwoman. Lucifer's bastard daughter, indeed. I do not think my father would take so kindly to the implication. But then, he probably would not take kindly to his daughter at all now. The thought sobered me.

"We are in range," Wheatley said. "Are we raiding?"

"No." I shook my head. "Set her aflame. Take out the ships first."

My orders passed through the still night. I knew the crew was confused, but they would not be harmed. They trusted me. I closed my eyes and breathed in the salty night air. Quetzalli turned eager circles on my shoulder.

"Ready, Captain!"

"Fire!"

The cannons rang through the darkness like thunder. We were close enough that shouts of surprise echoed through the ringing and crashing. And soon, the night brightened with orange and red flames. I smiled.

Explosions roared as the fires reached barrels of gunpowder. Stones crashed, an avalanche of hasty masonry as the fort began to fall. A cannon whizzed past the mizzenmast. They had begun to return fire. I turned the wheel in haste as the thrill of battle flowed through my veins. I licked my lips. The taste of vengeance was smoke and shot and sweat, and it satisfied my deepest cravings.

"Hard to starboard!"

"Hard to starboard!" my crew echoed. We sailed with great speed out of the bay, firing our guns until we were out of range. The fires of Hell raged astern. Wheatley and I grinned at each other as we sailed into the abyss of the night.

"Hell?"

I turned at the sound of Henry's voice, smaller than I'd ever heard it. He stood leaning against the frame of my cabin door. In the lantern light, his face was painted with exertion.

"Henry."

"What have you done?"

Chapter 54

When Henry and I had reunited in Liverpool, we fell back into our liaison with ease. It was as if we had never been apart. I had naively thought this time would be the same.

It was not.

He had been angry after our attack on the colony, asking about the innocents. I maintained that none of them were innocent.

He slept often, gaining the rest he had not had in so long. In his waking hours, I was often busy elsewhere on the ship. I took my meetings and charted our course in Wheatley and Joost's room so as not to disturb Henry. We took some meals together in my cabin, but sometimes I ate with the crew, and he could not descend the ladder to the lower decks.

Our conversations were stilted, awkward. We made small talk about the weather and the state of the ships. I asked how he was healing. He asked where we were headed next. We shared a bed, but there was no intimacy. We kissed quickly goodnight and good morning, but our lips did not linger.

Maggie's salves and tinctures had lowered Henry's pain drastically. They had not, however, improved his nightmares. He woke several times a night screaming. Every time, he was drenched in sweat, no matter how cool the night breeze was. Sometimes, he grabbed me or tried to shield me from some invisible threat. Each time, I held him in my arms and stroked his hair, speaking softly in his ear until he woke from his terrors. Then he sobbed until he fell back to sleep. Sometimes it was minutes and sometimes hours. Quetzalli had taken to curling up on his chest whenever the initial screams subsided.

We did not speak of it during the day. But his pain fueled my fury. We continued our attacks along the eastern shore of the American colonies, sending English strongholds into a frenzy and then raiding forts and treasuries.

After one such attack, I entered my cabin buzzing with excited energy. We had secured enough shot and oil for the lamps for all the ships.

Henry sat in the chair next to my desk and watched without a word as I wiped the blood and soot from my face. He was normally asleep by the time I returned after a battle and counting the booty.

"You should have seen it, Henry," I said as I unbraided my hair and combed my fingers through the black locks. "We left them without so much as a round for a musket!"

I unhooked my stomacher from my shortened mantua and placed the dress over the back of a chair. "And oil for the lamps! Do you know how expensive oil is these days? Ridiculous. Of course, we can afford it, but it's always better to not have to pay coin for it."

I laughed as I unlaced my stay. "They'll have to burn lard for light."

"Were there any deaths?" Henry spoke for the first time. His voice was low and steady.

I turned toward him, wearing only my shift tucked into my trousers. "Just two."

"And from their side?"

I shrugged. "I didn't stay to count a bunch of dead Redcoats."

He nodded, then looked away.

I sighed and plopped on the bed to remove my boots. "Say what you wish to say."

Henry didn't speak for a long time. He stared out the window at the blue expanse. When he did speak, it was barely above a whisper. "Are lost lives not a high cost for oil?"

I cocked my head. "It's not a quid pro quo."

"No, it's far too unbalanced for that."

Heat flooded my neck. "We don't raid for oil and shot and gold. We raid for what they did to you."

"Do you?"

"Of course!"

He shook his head. "All three hundred pirates under your command sail because of me?"

"They have their own reasons. The English military has never treated any of them with kindness."

Henry looked at me now with a sad smile. "Hell, I am here. You've saved me. You've won. There is no more vengeance to be had."

I rose to my feet. "No more vengeance? They've tormented you. The chains you wore 'round your wrists may be gone, but they've chained your mind. You cannot even rest properly!"

I paced the floor and raised my voice. "They broke your body and your spirit. And what they did to Mr. Gresham and the others!"

"They're gone, Hell. And the men you're killing at each town and fort had nothing to do with that."

"But didn't they? They're all part of the institution that thrives on subjugation and humiliation. How many others like you have there been? How many slaves have they beaten and whores have they raped? How many of them have taken rightful inheritances of women or cast out bastard children?" I clenched my fists. "No, Henry. There is still need for vengeance. So much more than I am capable of."

Henry nodded and rubbed his weary eyes with his palms. "What's next then? Destroy every English fort, pillage every fort? Will you turn to the Spanish next? The French?"

I froze at his words, my back toward him as I stared out the windows. The distant future was not a luxury a pirate thought she was entitled to. "I don't know. . ."

"What will you burn when you've turned everything to ash?"

Tears threatened to fall, and I swore, angry at my reaction. "What they did to you. . ."

"But it's not about me anymore, is it, Hell?"

Heated fury flooded my body, and I trembled from holding back the waves of emotions. "It's always about you, Henry!"

He shook his head. "All right then."

I spun on my heel and glared at him. "All right then? That's all you have to say after you criticize my captaincy? My *Integrity*?"

"What do you want me to say?" he asked in a tired voice.

"Fight back, Henry! Once, you would have fought back!"

"I'm tired, Angélica. I'm tired of death and pain and the smell of gunpowder." He shook his head. "You are an incredible captain. Anyone can see that. Fiercely loyal to your crew."

"I'm loyal to you," I whispered, lowering my gaze to the floor. It hurt to look at him.

"What was the last new book you read?"

The abrupt subject change jolted me, and I raised my head. "I don't—"

"The last philosopher you studied?"

I shrugged. "I'm not certain. But that doesn't. . ."

"The last new plant you sketched or animal you trapped to study?"

My lip quivered as his words pierced through me. "That's not the point."

"Isn't it? If this life brings you the joy you felt as you crafted an argument about ethics or mapped the sentence structure of a new language, then I will never speak of it again. If raiding and plundering fill your soul the way tromping through the jungle to make a new discovery does, then so be it."

His chest raised and lowered as he took a deep breath. "If it does, then I will not stop you. I want no part of it myself, but I will stay with you."

He closed his eyes, and it dawned on me. "You would, wouldn't you? Confine yourself to a different sort of prison to stay with me?"

With a wry smile, he looked at me. His eyes glistened with unshed tears, a mirror of my own. "Does it bring you joy, Angélica?"

I let out a ragged breath. "Joy. I know it no longer."

Tears burned in my eyes, and I didn't know why. "I learned from the best." I squeezed my eyes shut until the urge to cry passed. "I have to go. I need to check in with Thierry and Ben."

Henry said nothing. I pulled a linen shirt from my wardrobe and pulled it over my head. As I reached the door, Henry spoke.

"I will never question that your heart is in the right place."

#

His words circled in my mind that night. He slept restlessly, and I gave up on sleeping all together. I watched the reflection of the moonlight on the sea from the windows of my cabin. Silver gleamed, reflecting off the surface, but it still was not bright enough to illuminate what lay below the dark waters.

"What will you burn when you've turned everything to ash?"

Captaincy suited me, that much was true. But I could no longer lie to myself about why I continued my path of destruction. I had wanted nothing more in my life than power and freedom. Freedom to be me, to find joy where I wanted it. I had found both of those things, and what was left?

Many of my crew sailed for freedom, too. And that was how it should be—sailing without agenda besides adventure and wealth. Not whatever plot I had wrapped them up in.

Joy. I had forgotten about that emotion until Henry spoke it. Pushed it down and locked it away. And I had pushed it so far down that I had not even felt it when I reunited with Henry. Relief, yes. Satisfaction. But not joy.

At some point, blood had stopped healing my heart and started breaking it apart instead. And I had not been too blind to see it. Nay, not blind but angry. Grief-stricken. Joyless.

I had sought to redeem each loss with more loss. But nothing would bring back my lost crew members. It would not bring back my father or change the way Deirdre and I had parted. It would never change what had happened to Henry or to me. Blood lust had become my doldrums, but I needed to sail on.

I turned around and looked at the bed. Henry lay on his side, one arm extended over my empty place, as if he reached for me even in sleep. He would stay by my side, no matter what. And I owed him the same.

Gently, I slipped under his arm. He grabbed me tight, though he never stirred from his slumber. I studied his scarred face in the silvery moonlight. Despite everything that had happened, everything from the moment he extended his hand to me before our first sword fighting lesson all those years ago, one thing had never changed:

I loved Henry Martin to the depths of my soul.

Chapter 55

SPRING 1698

T hings changed after our confrontation. We knocked down the first bricks of the wall between us. Henry began to walk around the main deck, using the rigging to steady himself. He used his charm to win over my crew. He joked with Ben and dined with Wheatley and Joost on occasion. Soon, he was a fixture on the deck like the capstan; everyone expected him there and appreciated his company.

We sailed south into open water toward Nassau. It had been a long few weeks full of battle, but at Henry's words, I began to pull away from attacking colonies. We only took one easy prize, a small merchant vessel from the Netherlands that we crossed paths with. No blood was shed as they surrendered the moment they saw our fleet. With full holds and full bellies, the crew enjoyed leisure and made plans for how they would spend their money in port. Their plans mostly involved rum.

One morning, I watched Henry dress. The rays of the sun made his tanned skin glow as if he were from heaven itself. I smiled dreamily from the bed.

"What?" he asked with a grin.

"You're so handsome."

He laughed. "You're too kind, madam. But I think your eyes deceive you."

"No, they don't." I sat up. "Your scars, they don't make you less beautiful, Henry. They bear your strength. Your resilience. Your will to live."

Henry stared at me, mouth agape. "You truly believe that?"

"Yes, Henry. I love every inch of you. That has never changed and never will."

He shook his head. "To me, they are reminders of my failures. I wonder where I went wrong."

"The Jacobites—"

"No. What took me to that path? I didn't fight. I created an image of myself as a captain who would say yes. I was a bastard-born boy in their eyes and. . . I should have done more. I should have been stronger."

I sat up. "Henry, you are the strongest man I know."

"Then you must not know many strong men. I know where I went wrong, Angélica. I should have fought for you."

My eyes widened. "What do you mean?"

"I should have married you after taking your honor."

With a glare, I folded my arms. "My honor has never lain betwixt my legs. And we were young, Henry! We were powerless. And I've never desired marriage, despite Father's best attempts."

"I should have come for you, then. I should have followed you. Or once I was a captain of some repute, told you I was alive and brought you to me then. Married you."

"I wouldn't have married you. I still wouldn't." My jaw twitched. Old feelings of anger and grief that I had thought long buried bubbled up from my gut. "You should have told me you were alive, yes. But you would never have made an honest woman of me."

He sighed and ran a hand through his hair. "You are the most honest woman I have ever known, Hell. That is what I love about you. You live authentically, society be damned." He rubbed his leg. He'd been standing in one spot too long. I wondered if he even noticed the ache at that moment; it had become such a part of him.

"I have never been worthy of you, Angélica Spencer. But I wish, God how I wish, I had had your courage. I wish I could have insisted on being with you despite my unworthiness. And then I did it again. I chose the navy over you when. . ."

"That is a lie." Now I was on my feet, the hem of my shift catching on the edge of the bed. I yanked at it in anger. "You jumped. Your men saw you jump."

"But too late!" He yelled, the first time he had raised his voice since his rescue. "I am a coward who has never deserved you and now. . ."

He gestured at his bare chest, his bad leg. "Look at me. I finally look the part."

"Stop it! You're being absurd! You have more integrity and goodness in your heart than I could ever hope to have." I pulled at my hair. "Argh! I'm not going to argue back and forth about who doesn't deserve whom. Do you know what I wish? In that moment, watching the lashes hit you, I was powerless. You did not deserve that pain, and I had no power to stop it. I had no power to insist to stay with you."

I broke into a sob and tried to catch my breath before I continued. "I didn't deserve that powerlessness. No one does. But I was born with tits instead of a cock." I spat and balled my hands into fists. "And I have fought every day to never feel that way again."

He moved toward me, but I backed away. I was shaking. It hurt. Damn, it hurt. All I wanted was power over my own fate, and I didn't even have power over my emotions. I pressed my fists against my eyes as if it would quell the flow of tears.

"Angélica." Henry's voice was gentle. His hand touched my shoulder. I tensed, but he did not move. "Hell."

His hand was warm through the thin material of my chemise. I relaxed and let the warmth spread. It steadied me. Slowly, I dropped my hands from my wet eyes. When I did, his ocean-blue eyes sparkled at me. I stepped forward into his embrace. We stood like that for a long time, his arms wrapped around me. The world slipped away, and I knew I was where I wanted to be. I would let nothing tear us apart again. No man, no storm, no act of God could keep me away from the only person I had ever truly loved.

I raised my head to look into his eyes once more, but I only got a moment's glance before his lips captured my own. Sighing into his kiss, I parted my lips to deepen his touch. He smiled before his tongue slipped inside, eager to reclaim what he'd lost.

His hands slid down my sides to my hips, and he pulled me closer to him against the hardness between us. I gasped as he nipped my bottom lip.

"Henry," I moaned.

He smiled against my mouth. "I love it when you say my name like that."

His hands grabbed my buttocks, and he groaned. I pulled at the laces of his trousers and pushed them over his hips. He wobbled as he removed them, but I steadied him.

"Bed," I commanded.

He shuffled backward toward the unmade bed, tugging my shift over my head as I followed. We collapsed into the mattress, laughing and gasping, our lips never staying apart for long.

He laid on his side as he traced his fingers over my breasts and stomach. "You are exquisite."

"Mm. Tell me more."

I closed my eyes as his fingers slipped lower into the thatch of dark hair between my legs. "You have the body of an angel."

"Just the body, though."

"True. My Hell." He chuckled as he lowered his head to take my nipple between his teeth. I bucked at the jolt of beautiful pain, and his tongue replaced his teeth. I arched my back and raised my hips, allowing his fingers to easily slip into the slick heat.

He groaned as I cried out. "Hell, I'm afraid it will be quick. It's been a long time since. . ."

"Quick is fine. We have all the time in the world to regain your stamina." I smiled at him. "Now, resume what you were doing."

"Aye, Captain."

His fingers stroked the small bud, sending lightning through my veins. "Fuck!"

He didn't stop, just replaced his fingers with his thumb, giving him the freedom to curl two fingers inside me. He bit and licked my earlobe and neck as he guided toward my release. I came with his name on my lips.

"I want you," I whimpered.

"Say no more." He shifted to pull himself over me.

And cried out in pain.

I sat up abruptly. "What's wrong?"

He rubbed his right leg and rolled onto his back with a grimace. "I. . . don't think that will work. I'm sorry."

I waved my hand. "Stop. 'Tis nothing to me. What do you need? What will work?"

Henry took a deep breath and looked away. Red tinged his cheeks. "I. . . this is all right."

"Don't be embarrassed." I kissed him gently and straddled him, taking care not to hurt his leg. "You know I enjoy being in control anyway."

He chuckled. "Power."

"Yes. Power."

He laced his fingers through mine. I slid down, allowing him to sheath inside me. We both moaned as he filled me. I stilled, savoring the sensation that I had missed so much. It was better when you loved the person beneath you. My heart was full again with him inside me. For the first time in too long, I felt whole.

"Good?" I asked as he caught his breath.

"A moment more. I want it to last as long as possible." His voice was husky, his eyes half-lidded in pleasure. He released my hands and ran his along my thighs to my hips. My skin tingled under his touch. His strong grip emboldened me, and I wiggled, but he held me in place. It did not matter how we laid in bed or stood in the world. Henry and I were equals, and that was a greater power than any amount of piracy could give me.

He nodded when he was ready. I lifted my hips and began to move. He tried to maintain control, but I felt him succumb to the pleasure when I grazed my fingertips over his scarred chest.

It did not last long; he had been right about that. But as he rolled his head back with his release, I found my own again. We came together, falling deeper into our love, past the pain and loss and grief that had shaped us.

After, we lay intertwined in the blankets and with each other. The world had righted itself again.

It was Henry who broke the silence. "Hell? Now that you have power—an immense amount of it, I might add—what do you want to do with it? What would you choose?"

I thought for several long breaths before I answered. "You."

"You have me. But what else?"

Propping myself on my elbow, I looked him straight in the eyes. "Do you remember what we used to dream about? Before the world went to shit?"

He smiled. "Running away together, sailing the world on a small boat. Answering to no one but ourselves. You studying exotic flora and fauna. Me, studying you."

"Yes." I laughed. I thought of Culliford and Swan. Culliford had said he could enjoy the sea from the shore. "Perhaps we don't need a boat. We could find some place on a beach, perhaps near a jungle with plenty to discover."

"That sounds nice." He glanced at me then stared down at the floor. "I'm a broken man, Angélica. Why would you give this up for me?"

"Because it's always been my destiny to find the power to choose you."

"Why me?"

I guided his head to gaze into my eyes. "Because. . . in all my life, you have never tried to change me. You've never set out to shape me into your own image of who I should be. Of all those who've claimed to love me, you're the only one who accepts me as I am. And when I have changed, as is inevitable for any human, you've stood by my side. Questioned me, yes, but never demanded of me. You may walk with a gimp leg and need tinctures for the pain. You may wake screaming in the night. But the one thing that hasn't changed in all these years, through all these trials and tribulations, is your heart."

I sat up on my knees and placed my hand over his heart. "I choose you, Henry Martin. I always have, and I always will."

He laughed a laugh full of mirth and pulled me down on top of him. "You said we had all the time in the world."

"I did." He nuzzled my chin with his stubble, and I giggled.

"Then let us commence."

EPILOGUE

A YEAR LATER. . .

"Quetzalli! Time to go home!" The rat looked up from her papaya with curious eyes, then back down at her fruit. I laughed. "You act as if I don't feed you." She tucked extra fruit in her pouches and then scampered ahead of me down the worn path through the tall grasses at the edge of the jungle. I tucked my journal and pencils into my bag and followed her back to the village. When we reached our modest, ramshackle cottage built of ship planks, we found Henry outside hammering something into the wall near the window.

"Fixed that leak, finally?" I asked. Quetzalli made her way inside through the open doorway.

Henry turned and grinned. "If the rain ruined one more of your books. . ."

"I'd steal a ship and keelhaul you." I leaned up on my tiptoes and kissed him. "Thank you."

"A productive day?" he asked. He limped inside, his gait stiffer than usual. A storm must be coming in soon, though the skies were clear. I made a note to visit Maggie later to get some salve. I followed him and removed my muddy boots by the door.

"Three new insects!" I exclaimed. The rainforest on this island would keep me occupied in my studies for decades. "And Quetzalli feasted on papaya."

"Then she won't want salted pork for dinner." He stretched out on a chaise we had traded for in Curacao. The rat jumped onto his lap and went promptly to sleep, as if she had worked hard all day.

I laughed. "You know that's not true." I glanced at the book on the small table, Henry's first furniture project. It still wobbled. "Spinoza again?"

"A favorite." He waved a hand. "Ben and Thierry arrived today. Thierry's brought a dozen freed slaves."

"Do they all have a bed for the night?"

He nodded. "All taken care of."

"I should go see Ben, get the news from the sea." Ben and Thierry returned to our little island haven regularly with supplies, news, and more people for the village looking for freedom. We had found a small, uninhabited island near Curacao to serve as a sanctuary for those of my crew who wanted to leave the sea behind for a quieter life. Some chose to start new lives elsewhere. Some chose to stay at sea. Thierry and Ben had remained pirates and often sailed their ships together. Thierry had a crew entirely of African-descended men and women, most of whom had been slaves. Some chose to live here, though most preferred to go on and build villages of their own.

As for Henry and me, we ran a haven for whomever needed it. I had time for research and reading. Henry regained his strength and vigor day by day. And together, we found joy again. The nightmares still plagued him; the grief still struck us when we least expected. But together, we began to heal. It was not lost on me that Henry and I had a life not unlike what Deirdre had wanted for us, a quiet life in a quaint cottage. But while I had known much love in my life, of all types, none of them quelled the storm in my soul like Henry.

He was my forever, my destiny, the fate I chose. But more than that, I had found a family and a purpose. For so long, it had been Father and me, and I believed I only needed one person. But Wheatley and Ben, Maggie and Thierry, and so many others were an intrinsic part of my life. It wasn't a quiet life that had invoked such a strong reaction when Deirdre had suggested it; it was a life with someone who did not accept me as I was.

"You can see Ben tomorrow," Henry said, pulling me from my musings.

I raised an eyebrow at what sounded like an order. He smirked. There were too many captains in this house at times. When Maggie was around, it was even worse.

"Hell, do you know what today is?"

I stared blankly. I easily lost track of time here. If I didn't check the calendar that Henry diligently marked each day, I wouldn't even know the month.

"Tomorrow's your birthday," he said. He laughed at the surprised look on my face.

"I forgot," I mumbled. My cheeks were hot. "That's why both Ben and Thierry are here?"

"Yes, my little devil. But before I have to share your attentions with everyone tomorrow, I have plans for us tonight."

He winked at me, and the heat from my cheeks moved to my core. "I like the sound of that. Can we begin?"

"After you eat. Then we'll go for a swim." He licked his lips. "You are wearing far too many layers for my taste, so I had to think of a reason for you to remove your clothes."

"I do enjoy a swim." It was good for Henry's leg, too. Helped with the pain. And it always ended with a languorous lovemaking session.

"And if you're very well-behaved, I shall give you your gift tonight."

"I'm never well-behaved."

"That's true." He shrugged. "But I promised Maggie she could have you tomorrow evening. She claims I am keeping you from her."

"She's dramatic. But she has her reasons."

He laughed. "Well, it's my bed you'll warm tonight and tomorrow night, whenever we stumble in from the festivities."

"It's our bed," I corrected him. I stood and held my hand out to him. He took it and rose, stiffly from the lounge with a grimace that he quickly replaced with an adoring smile. "And I will warm it every night, Captain Martin."

He winked. "Aye aye, my queen."

Acknowledgements

I can't take full credit for this book, not when I nearly gave up so many times. This book took over five years, and in that time, we had a pandemic, I had a baby, and I changed careers.

My deepest and inexpressible gratitude goes to my writing and critique group. From texts about plot points and sensitivity concerns, to constructive feedback on my chapters, Michelle Monárrez, Rosalind Wulf (who also served as an alpha reader), Sam Richards, and Casey Rafael deserve the thanks of everyone who enjoys this book. It would not have happened without them.

Thank you to my editor, Salt & Sage Books, for thoughtful, invaluable polishing. Thank you to Emeph Alvarado for her emotional labor in sensitivity reading, and Bailey Van Den Heuvel for beta reading. I'd also like to express my gratitude for my cover artist, Holly Perret at The Swoonies.

Thank you to my baby dragon for sharing your mama with these characters so I could finish this thing. You're still the greatest thing I'll ever create.

And finally, the hero of my own romance, Michael. Thanks for listening to me ramble and letting me zone out in writing land. Thank you for always faithfully supporting me and for being my biggest fan. Your support means more than you'll ever know.

Yours,

Krystal

AUTHOR'S NOTE

Hell's Revenge: Memoir of a Pirate Queen is a work of historical fiction. As such, I took some liberties with historical fact, although much of the story is highly accurate.

For example, the Jacobite assassination plot mentioned before Hell leaves with Henry from Liverpool actually occurred. However, there was no grand Jacobite scheme amongst the Royal Navy admiralty. With many people loyal to King James, and many small plots, this was a perfect opportunity for my story.

Most ships during these years would have used rudders to steer instead of wheels, but that didn't match my aesthetic.

The Pirate Round and the pirates mentioned—Henry Every, Robert Culliford, and John Swann—were very real. There is also ample evidence that Culliford and Swann were lovers. Matelotage, or ship marriage, was a common practice. Queer history matters.

I was also careful to calculate accurate average speeds across the distances that the ships sailed. Ships were not fast in this time. This is why there are large time jumps and why the novel spans several years.

Any other historical inaccuracies were either made by choice or by oversight.

About the Author

Krystal N. Craiker is the Writing Pirate, an indie romance author and content manager. She sails the seven internet seas, breaking tropes and bending genres. She has a background in anthropology and education, which brings fresh perspectives to her romance novels. When she's not daydreaming about her next book or article, you can find her cooking gourmet gluten-free cuisine, laughing at memes, and playing board games. Krystal lives in Dallas, Texas with her husband, child, and dog. Check out her website or follow her on Instagram.

Printed in the USA
CPSIA information can be obtained
at www.ICGtesting.com
LVHW070434100524
779587LV00016B/1059